FOR REAL

a spires story

ALEXIS HALL

sourcebooks
casablanca

Copyright © 2015, 2018, 2024 by Alexis Hall
Cover and internal design © 2024 by Sourcebooks
Cover design and illustration by Elizabeth Turner Stokes

Sourcebooks and the colophon are registered trademarks of Sourcebooks.

Published by Sourcebooks Casablanca, an imprint of Sourcebooks
P.O. Box 4410, Naperville, Illinois 60567-4410
(630) 961-3900
sourcebooks.com

Originally digitally published in 2015 by Alexis Hall. This edition issued
based on the paperback edition self-published in 2018 by Alexis Hall.

Cataloging-in-Publication Data is on file with the Library of Congress.

Printed and bound in Canada.
MBP 10 9 8 7 6 5 4 3 2 1

FOREWORD

Gosh, it's this time again.

When I wrote the foreword for the re-release of *Glitterland* back in 2022—and *oh my* isn't it refreshing to write down a date that feels recent and have it actually *be* relatively recent at time of writing instead of somehow contriving to be six years ago?—I said that I'd always wanted to write a foreword to one of my books. Now I'm doing it for the third time and, well, it still feels strange and gratifying and terrifying, just with an added dose of "I should really be better at this by now."

Coming back to *For Real* is especially unusual because prior to *Boyfriend Material*, it was by far my most successful book. And it's... Well, it's *really rather different*. Not, perhaps, as different as they appear on the surface; I don't like analysing my work for the reader but, well, I do have themes I keep coming back to and while *For Real* sets them against a backdrop of kink rather than jokes, long-time readers will, I think, still see all of my core stories here. Although the obligatory Alexis Hall food-focused scene is, umm, *quite distinctive.*

Looking back, one of the things that stands out about *For Real* more than most of my other books is how strongly it was shaped by the context it was released into. I didn't write it quite at the *height* of *Fifty*-mania, but there was definitely a very strong demand for BDSM fiction at the time, especially within erotic romance. So I suppose another parallel between *For Real* and *Boyfriend Material* is that in a lot of ways they're both my attempt to provide my own spin on the Thing That Was Big At The Time. For BM that was romcom, and for FR that was, well, kinky sex. The specific spin I wanted to give Alexis-Hall-Does-BDSM was to interrogate some of the assumptions that I, at the time, felt were baked into a lot of the way kink was portrayed within the genre. Assumptions about power (in its various forms), status, and sexuality and how they all fit together in life and in love. Or to put it in a more hopefully TikTokable soundbite, "it's a kinky relationship but...the sub is the experienced one!"

It was also very important to me that while kink was a massive part of how Laurie and Toby interact that it not be the heart of the conflict in the book. A common feature of post-*Fifty* BDSM fiction was for there to be a very strong emphasis on questions like "but is it *okay* to like *spanking*?!?" and I really wanted to start from "yes, obviously" and build from there. I like my books—as in the books I write and for that matter the books I read—to be specific, and what I wanted more than anything with the use of kink in *For Real* was for it to feel specific; something that manifests in a particular way in a particular context between particular people, rather than as a symbol for things sexy and forbidden.

Hopefully that worked.

Whether you found me through *Boyfriend Material*, or through the original *For Real*, or through any one of my now far too many other books, I'm so glad you're here, and I hope that whether you're encountering Toby and Laurie's story for the first time or the fortieth that you...umm...like it?

Alexis Hall
July 2023

P.S. Laurie's surname is pronounced DEE-ELL not DAL-ZEEL. This is in the first chapter but people still miss it.

Content Guidance

This content guidance is not intended to be exhaustive and may include spoilers.

For Real contains sexual content, heavy kink, grandparent in a hospice, death of a grandparent (happens off page), grief, talk about the London 7/7 terror attack, and parental neglect.

Take me to you, imprison me, for I,
Except you enthrall me, never shall be free,
Nor ever chaste, except you ravish me.

☆

John Donne, "Holy Sonnet XIV"

1

LAURIE

"Look, I've come straight from work, and I've had a really long day, and I simply haven't had time to slip into a spiky collar or a mesh shirt or whatever else you deem necessary to get into your haven of safe, sane, and consensual depravity."

That was me, making an arse of myself on the door of Pervocracy, the club that was supposed to be different, and inevitably wouldn't be.

But everything I'd said was true. It had been a really long day. And I'd always hated the requirement to dress up. It was almost as if the Scene ran on fairy-tale logic: A pauper in a ball gown was a princess. A wolf in a nightcap, a grandma. A wanker in a pair of leather trousers, a dom.

The alternative-lifestyle pixie (otherwise known as community volunteer) didn't look very impressed with me. I couldn't really blame her. Even putting aside my lack of interest in communicating my sexual inclinations by wearing a silly hat, I'd been unnecessarily rude.

I tried for a more conciliatory tone. "I'm on the list. Dalziel."

She fingered her iPad. "D-e-e-l—what?"

"D-a-l-z—"

She gave me an *Are you fucking kidding?* look.

I could have said "Like *Dalziel and Pascoe*," but there was such a frighteningly high possibility she was barely alive in 1996 that I decided to give up instead. The universe clearly didn't want me to go to a BDSM club. Which was absolutely fine with me because I agreed.

"Forget it."

☆ I turned to make my escape, when the door to the gender-neutral toilets behind her burst open, and the two—for want of a better term—friends who had insisted I come out tonight tumbled into the corridor. Sam seemed to be dressed as a steampunk pirate. Grace was wearing a rainbow-patterned corset and extremely frilly knickers. They had no problem at all communicating their sexual inclinations by wearing silly hats.

"He's with us, he's with us! Laurie, come back."

I came back.

The pixie hesitated. "He's with you?"

"Yeah, I vouched for him. Look." Grace leaned over in a squish of breasts and lace and tapped the screen.

"But"—the pixie pouted—"costume is mandatory. It's important to the culture of the club."

"I am in costume," I snapped. "I'm in costume as a really tired and pissed off trauma doctor trying to get into a BDSM club in the vain hope of meeting a not-too-cack-handed stranger who'll whip him into some semblance of satisfaction before he goes home again."

"It's a good effort," said Sam, deadpan. "Very convincing."

"Fine. Fine." The ALP gave a despairing wave, green-painted fingernails gleaming. "Go on in."

We went on in. And as I squeezed by, I heard her mutter, "Can't believe he's a sub."

That made two of us.

It had been the best part of a year since I'd bothered with the Scene. About six months ago, Sam had asked me why, but I had no answer for him. No story to tell. No abuse, no drama, no great epiphany. Just glancing round at a party, and realising it could have been any other night. The same people looking for the same things. So I went home and looked up a half-remembered paragraph of Anthony Powell that Robert had once quoted at me: "The image of Time brought thoughts of mortality: of human beings...moving hand in hand in intricate measure...while partners disappear only to reappear again, once more giving pattern to the spectacle: unable to control the melody, unable, perhaps, to control the steps of the dance."

And thought: *Yes, that*. Nothing but a dance to the music of time. As meaningless as it was ultimately unchanging.

Besides, with the internet being what it was, you could get degrading sex with people you didn't like delivered right to your doorstep. Unfortunately, Grace and Sam didn't agree. They insisted I needed to get out more. Actually meet people. As if that was ever going to happen at a BDSM club.

But there I was. Not so much out of hope for myself, but in the hope it would make my friends shut up.

Pervocracy fostered a self-consciously carnival atmosphere. And cupcakes. It was like they were saying, *See what multidimensional humans we are. We're not just kinky, we're hipsters too.* But it was the same faces. Just like always.

Grace went to try and get us drinks, so I stayed with Sam as per the rules. They had a cutesy little acronym for it on the charter, but essentially we were meant to be policing each other. Ensuring nobody got hurt. Or rather, that nobody got hurt in a way that they hadn't explicitly consented to be hurt. All very sensible. All very nice.

So terribly nice.

I was also supposed to have brought a shtick of some kind—like gifts or a Hula-Hoop—to help me be charming and easy to interact with. Except I had about as much interest in being charming and easy to interact with as I did in being nice. Nice had no power over me. It couldn't make me scream or beg or come or feel whole.

Sam knew nearly everyone. Some of them even remembered me. But I brushed through the conversations. The topics were mainly restricted to art, sex, and ourselves, three things I really didn't see the point in talking about.

Eventually—because it was that sort of club—we were obliged to watch cabaret.

"It's at times like this," I told Grace, looking dismally into my glass of warm lemonade as someone subjected us to erotic performance poetry, "I really wish I drank."

"And I thought you were supposed to be a masochist." She put an arm around me and pulled me briefly into her side. I hated how good it felt just to be held.

I scanned the gathered revellers. And, of course, among all the half-familiar strangers, there was Robert, who time will never make a stranger, no matter how much I wish it could. Whatever magnet drew us once was broken now. It had left me simply spinning, a compass without a lodestone, while he didn't see me at all.

He was with his new...boy, lover, sub. Who wasn't new anymore.

When the ordeal with the performance poetry was over and the music began again, I broke the rules and slipped away from Grace and Sam. Wandered.

The organisers had tried hard to transform this piece of nowhere East London into a *space*. There were lots of intricate little corners, apparently designed to encourage play in the purest sense of the word.

The last thing in the world I wanted to do was play. In any sense of the word.

Voices—talking, laughing, screaming, coming—washed over me like the sea. The dungeons and the make-out rooms were less an orgy than a queue. In my experience, one of the less well-advertised secrets of group sex was how often it came down to logistics.

Karmic spite sent me stumbling by the playrooms in time to see Robert and his...his other.

We'd never been public, Robert and I. What we'd had, what we'd done, had been too private and too precious. We wouldn't have displayed it before the world any more than we would have let someone watch us in bed on a Sunday morning, where he would bring me toast and tea and the *Times*, and lazily suck me off. It'd been ours.

Now his and this other man's.

This other man who suffered for him and begged and wept and carried Robert's marks and kisses on his skin. The secrets that used to be mine.

I stumbled away before I was spotted—staring like a man through a window at something he would never have—and went in search of Grace and Sam. I found them sprawled on a tatty velveteen sofa. They shifted apart to make room.

"I'm sick of seeing Robert everywhere."

"Oh, baby." Grace gave my arm a little squeeze.

"I feel like I'm stuck in a reverse Alanis. Every time he scratches his nails down someone else's back, I feel it."

Sam blinked. "Wow, man, that's a seriously dated reference." ☆

After six years, they'd pretty much run out of sympathy

on this one, and I didn't blame them. There were only so many times you could wipe up someone's tears and tell them there were more fish in the sea.

I used to think there were too, but I was tired of swimming. And either Robert was a merman, or I was just a really weird fish with a particularly obscure mating ritual. Even to other weird fish.

"Nice crowd, though," tried Sam. "Friendly. Safety conscious."

"Kink crowds are the same the world over. The good ones are already taken"—I gestured to them both—"the hot ones only talk to each other, and everyone else is desperate."

Grace rolled her eyes. "You do know you're one of the hot ones, right? You could have any dom in this room if you looked marginally more approachable than an underfed piranha having a bad day."

"I've had all the doms in this room."

"You're extra specially hot when you're slutty," purred Sam, stroking the inside of my thigh, which, even through my trousers, made me shiver. Which he knew it would. He went on in a very different voice, "Even if you're blatantly lying."

Literally the case or not, it still felt true.

"Oh my God." Grace sat up abruptly. "Look at the foetus."

We looked at the foetus.

He was on the edge of a conversation, not quite part of the crowd, thin and wary and absurdly young. There wasn't much of him from this angle, just a curly flop of dark hair and the pale gleam of his wrist as he pushed it out of his face.

"How does he even know about this place?" Sam sounded fifty percent shocked, fifty percent admiring. "At his age I was still sending laundry back home so my mum would do it, not coming to kinky sex parties."

"He's adorable," Grace cooed. "Like a bijou sub-ette."

"You can't have him, Gracie. No breaking Britain's youth."

"But we could get him a little kennel. Give him his own ☆ Converse to chew on. And...and an iPod for listening to Panic! At the Disco."

I'd only half been paying attention. "Listening to what?"

"A popular beat combo," explained Sam, smirking. ☆

"Someone should talk to him, though." Grace glanced across the room again, but I could have told her he'd moved away. "He looks a bit lost."

"What are you going to do?" Sam's voice softened. "He'll be fine, honestly. They're pretty careful who they let in. Think of the trouble we had getting Grumpy Bastard here through the door. And he's probably just got a deceptive face. He could actually be forty-two or something. Uh...dude, where are you going?"

That last bit was for me. But I ignored him.

And found myself in the next room, searching for the boy. He was easy to find. Deceptive face. Bollocks to that. He couldn't have been more than eighteen.

I put a hand on his shoulder—so frail and sharp—and spun him round. He seemed surprised but not frightened. If anything, slightly irritated.

He wasn't particularly attractive. He was too unformed, ☆ all angles and irregularities, acne divots peppering the edge of his jaw.

I gazed down at him, into his oddly dark blue eyes, the sort of ☆ eyes that would always look as though they had liner round them. And I said, "You shouldn't be here. This isn't Junior Kink-Off."

He shook me off with a restless kind of ease. "Thanks for the unnecessary, unwanted advice. I think I'm good."

I should have let him go. But I didn't. "Is this your first time?"

"First time at a kinky party? Or first time having a dickhead acting like he knows what's better for me than I do?" He didn't give me time to get out a comeback, which was probably a good thing because I didn't have one. "Yes to the first. No to the second."

Don't laugh. Not something I often had to struggle against. But he was a little bit magnificent in his defiance. A little bit magnificent, and a little bit absurd. "I think I probably deserved that."

His eyes widened, flashing all their blues at me. In a handful of years, I thought he might be stunning. Not pretty, not handsome. But people would look at him.

There was a silence, just long enough to be awkward.

"Wow. Um." He pushed the hair back from his forehead. "I don't know what to say. I wasn't expecting that."

I shrugged. And now I was awkward too. Damn him. "Well, I know I can be kind of a dick. But I try not to actively persist in it."

"Wow," he said again. "Most people just do, y'know?"

I thought about it for a moment. "I suppose you're right. They do."

And now he smiled at me. All teeth. The way only people who hadn't learned self-consciousness knew how to smile.

"I know it sounds patronising but you should be careful."

"Dude, I'm nineteen."

I choked on air.

His hair had flopped again—*Get it cut*, I thought—and he shoved it impatiently out of the way. "Yeah, yeah, I know what you're thinking. How can a nineteen-year-old possibly know what he wants. Well, I do. I...feel it like...here." He tapped a closed fist in the incorrect location for his heart. "I feel it, okay? Like being gay. It's just there."

I stared at him. At this too-thin, too-sincere boy. This person.

Because I knew what he meant. I understood exactly. And

I'd felt it too, that interior certainty. But over the years, I'd let all the fervour fade. I'd stopped believing in it, somehow. I'd let it become something I did, not something I was.

And then I was suddenly deeply, uncontrollably sad. For this boy who might become me.

His still-clenched fist swung into the air, not quite a full Scarlett O'Hara but nearly. His whole body was practically vibrating with frustration. "I know what I want. I really know what I want. I just don't know how to get it."

That sounded all too familiar as well.

"You've never...?" I asked, with a futile attempt at delicacy.

"Well, there's the internet. And I've messed around with boyfriends or randoms or whatever. But"—his words came too quickly now, their honesty its own challenge—"it's not right, or enough, or *something*. Basically, it's not what I want. It's not even a little bit like what I want."

I needed to walk away. Leave the young knight to chase the questing beast on his own. Maybe he would even find it. Plenty of people apparently did. "What do you want?"

His head came up. God, his eyes. In a few years...in a few years I didn't like to think what someone with eyes like that might do to me. Or make me do.

"What I *don't* want," he said, "is someone like me. Like, what's the point of that, y'know?"

He was silent a moment, chewing at his lip, hands shoved into his pockets. I had no idea what he was thinking, but it seemed to be quite a big deal to him.

So I waited. I waited for him. As I hadn't for anyone in years.

I didn't know what I was expecting. Some kind of blurted confessional. Not what he gave me, which was his unwavering gaze and his utter conviction. "I want someone like you."

It felt as though he'd pulled the entire universe out from under my feet, shaking me loose and into a terrifying free fall. So I tried to make light of it. "Someone far too old for you?"

"Someone who knows who he is, and acts like he owns the whole fucking world."

Ah. "Look, I..." I blushed. I actually fucking blushed. "Look, um, I don't...really switch. At all. It's not...my thing. Not that you aren't—"

"God, no." It was almost a relief when he cut over me. Almost. "Not like that. I'm not interested in that. I'm a dom."

It should have been ridiculous. It *was* ridiculous. A skinny nineteen-year-old with his adolescence still written on his skin. I nearly said, *You're not a dom, you're a child.*

His expression grew sheepish, and I was glad I'd held my tongue. "Well, thanks for not laughing. It's the best reaction I've ever got." He sighed. "I'm so confused. I don't know what to do."

This was officially beyond me. Telling him to go home, I could deal. Being sort of bluntly hit on, maybe. Giving him a spontaneous personal, social, and health education class in the middle of a BDSM club, absolutely not.

☆ "It's like," he went on tormentedly, "you're not allowed to be a dom until you're forty and six feet tall and own your bespoke bondage dungeon. But I'm probably not going to get any taller, and forty is forever away, so what the hell am I supposed to do *now*?"

"I have absolutely no idea." I'd been with Robert, and we'd somehow figured it out together.

"I just want to know what it feels like, y'know?"

"What?"

"Anything. Any of it. Something really basic. Like"—he drew
☆ in a deep, surprisingly steady breath—"I want to know how it

feels to have some guy on his knees for me. And not a kid. I want a man, a strong, hot, powerful man, doing it because he wants to and because I want him to."

When I'd thought he'd be stunning in a few years, I was wrong. He was stunning now.

He twisted both hands into his hair until he was all edges and angles, fingers and wrists and elbows. "I think about it all the fucking time. When I jerk off at night. But I'm so bored of the fantasy. I want something *real*. I fucking need it. I need to know how it really feels."

I didn't know why I did it.

Maybe because he was beautiful then, so earnest and vulnerable and unafraid.

I couldn't believe that lack of fear. It gave me vertigo, as though he was the edge of a cliff and I couldn't bear the view.

Or maybe it was because Robert was there, Robert and his lover, and I'd never done this for anyone but him. I'd been with others, yes, but I hadn't given them what I'd given Robert.

And maybe, at last, I was going to take it back.

So I did it. In the middle of some East London party, beneath the eyes of untold strangers, for a nineteen-year-old boy whose name I hadn't even bothered to ask, I mustered what little grace I could remember, and went to my knees.

Clasped my hands behind my back.

Some doms, maybe even most doms, might have wanted me to bow my head, but I still wasn't sure who I was doing this for, and I wanted—*I* wanted—to look at him.

There was a stillness in the room. Because nobody had ever seen me on my knees before. I'd bled and screamed but never knelt.

And in the silence, my boy just gasped. It felt like his mouth on my cock. His eyes were wide, as hazy as stained glass on the brightest imaginable day. He swayed a little and put a hand against the wall to steady himself.

"How does it feel?" I asked.

He swallowed. "Perfect. It's...perfect. Can I touch you?"

Oh God. Too complicated. Don't. Yes. "Not if you ask me."

He stepped into the space between my legs, and I had to crane my head right back to hold his gaze. My height counted for nothing now. Here, at his feet.

He ran a finger down the exposed line of my throat. How did he know to do that? I made a sound for him, rough and low and helpless. Then he collared me, his palm warm against my neck, and it was all I could do not to push forward into the safety and the threat of that simple, instinctive touch.

What had I done?

"How does it feel?" he asked.

Perfect. I swallowed under his hand. "Like I'm indulging you."

☆ But he only grinned and tightened his grip just a little, not enough to hinder my breath but enough that I felt my every inhalation. As though it was his choice to give them to me. The racing of my pulse filled my head like the beating of a thousand wings.

"Liar." His foot nudged my cock.

☆ Oh God. I was so hard for him. For this.

"Fuck." He gave a soft and lovely little moan. "Fuck. I could come from this."

I had no answers for him.

Except, suddenly, I did, my voice hoarse beneath his hand. "Come home with me, and you can."

2
TOBY

Oh my fucking God, I've pulled the shark. Well, not pulled. Whatever it is when some guy goes to his knees for you in the middle of a club and then offers to take you home.

And it's like nothing and everything I've imagined.

My hand on his throat. My foot against his cock.

I don't know where I found the courage to do this. But I think it's because of how he's looking at me while he kneels there. ☆

He makes me feel like I could do anything.

I hold out my hand to help him to his feet, because it only seems polite somehow, but he ignores it, and he's up, *whoosh*, so graceful, and all I can think is how badly I want to strip it from him. Make him give that to me too.

I'm not graceful, and I'm never going to be. Mum says it's something you grow into, but she's been saying that for about ten years now. It kind of sucks: the moment you look in the mirror and you realise that there isn't going to be any more growing out of or growing into or growing full stop. That this is it. What you're stuck with.

I mean, it's fine, don't get me wrong. I'm not Quasimodo. But in my head I'm about six foot two, and I'm hot and dangerous and definitely not fucking cute.

☆ If I got to choose, I'd want to look like he does, and that's a weird thought. Like there's a confused zone of lust-envy where wanting to do someone spills over into wanting to be them. Or the other way round.

I don't even know how to describe him. I'm not even sure there's a word for it. Not one I've ever heard before anyway. I run through them in my head like I'm helping him try them on, but none of them stick. He's not handsome. He's not pretty. And beautiful isn't right either, because he just isn't. I think he might be a bit ugly actually, but somehow looking at him makes my stomach fizz like paracetamol in Pepsi.

He's sort of stern and wolfish and chiselled and kind of too much, like his nose is too long and his mouth is too wide and his chin is too sharp. There's a bit of grey in his hair, and when he's in profile he looks really crazy harsh, all lines and angles, full of locked-up secrets.

And there's this weird distance to him. He's not cold—not exactly—but there's this sense of wildness almost, like when you're watching a nature documentary and you see a tiger and you're all like, *God, that's gorgeous* and *God, that could totally rip my face off* at the same time. It's not something you can put your finger on, like height (though he's taller than me) or strength (though he's stronger than me), but there's something there. This power. Like being ordinary is just a mask he wears.

I've been watching him all night. Like literally unable to stop staring.

Wanting. Imagining this constant depraved porno of all the messed-up shit I want to do to him.

Never for a moment dreaming he might let me.

Certainly not when his first impulse appeared to be reading me a lecture.

But. Oh. My. Fucking. God.

My cock is dying of joy. Birthday, Christmas, Easter, Boxing Day, May Day, even, like, Pancake Day all come at once. I really shouldn't have worn my pulling jeans. Because right now they're my strangling-my-knob-off jeans.

I hobble after him, trying not to care that people are staring. Though, actually, not caring isn't so difficult. Because nobody in that club mattered a damn the moment he came in, looking so passionate and uptight and angry and sad all at the same time. And so perfect, so fucking perfect. Like he belongs on his knees, waiting for me to hurt him.

My gaydar is genuinely defective—I didn't even notice the ☆ gay one in Union J. But I've got this other thing. I don't think there's a word for it—subdar sounds crap—but sometimes it gets pinged so hard, usually by the sort of people you wouldn't think would ping that way. Except they do, and I'm usually too chickenshit to do anything about it.

He's waiting for me by the front desk, calling for a taxi. On ☆ account. It'll tell you what sort of a fucking ridiculously sheltered life I lead because that's just about the classiest thing that's ever happened to me. Last date I was on, we had to ring his dad for a pickup because the Tube had stopped running, we were both shit scared of the night bus, and neither of us had any cash.

He tucks his phone away. "Get your coat."

"Didn't bring one."

Next thing I know, he's dumping his full-length, silk-lined, ☆ cashmere-wool blend over my shoulders. For such a big coat it weighs practically nothing at all, and it trails along the ground behind me like I'm a really short-arsed emperor. I want to tell him I don't need it, but I don't know how to do that without sounding like a petulant kid. And I really, really don't want him to think that about me. At least, not until he's knelt for me again. It's silly, but before he did that I just sort of fancied him, and I didn't really care what he thought.

But now I do. I care really hard.

I had no idea it would be like this. That having someone on their knees for you would make you so vulnerable.

I guess it's because there's nowhere left to hide from what you're into. And that's a pretty naked feeling, standing there with a boner and all this hot, tight need inside you, desperate for somebody to understand.

Also, his coat is really nice, and it turns out I'm a bit cold. So fuck my principles.

"And phone someone. You're going to Addison Avenue."

Wow, it's really hard to believe he ever smiled at me.

Knelt for me. Looked at me the way he did.

"Okay." I go outside obediently and pretend to make a call.

Come on, who am I actually going to tell? *Hi, Mum, went to a kinky sex club, and now I'm off to the house of a complete stranger so he can get on the floor and I can jerk off over him, because that totally turns me on.*

She thinks I'm staying over at a friend's. Except I don't actually have any friends anymore because they're all at university, growing as people.

Truthfully, I probably could have told her. I've yet to find something she isn't cool with, which should be good, right? But there's still stuff you seriously don't want to tell your mother about your sex life. *Wants to shag boys*, I can cope with her knowing. *Wants to shag boys while they're tied up and crying*, just no.

So maybe I'm about to do an incredibly stupid thing. And tomorrow morning I'm going to be a headline. *Achingly Priapic*

Gay Teenager Found Floating in Thames. But if this guy was dangerous, he wouldn't be doing all the safety stuff, right?

Right?

The taxi comes and we get in, and we sit there in silence because I can't think of a single fucking thing to say. He's looking out the window with his face turned away, so all I'm getting is this glossy mess of shadow and light over his profile. Makes me feel miles away. Like I don't know him at all.

Which I don't.

Shit.

We stop outside one of those white fairy tale houses. They're reasonably common in the posh bits of London, but they're so pretty and costume drama-ish that it's hard to believe they're real and that people really live in them. I honestly half expect a rosy-cheeked, honey-blond woman to come round the corner wanting to know who will buy her sweet red roses.

He unhooks the little iron gate and I follow him up the steps to the front door. It's so weird. Stairs on a street-level house. But there's a sort of basement-type thing underneath, I guess for the servants you'd have had if you lived here in 1812 or whatever.

In the hallway, I give him his coat back, and he hangs it up in a cupboard before leading me into what I guess would be a sitting room in an ordinary house, but is probably a reception room in a place like this.

Even knowing precisely fuck-all about interior design, I can tell it's super nice. Clean and cream, and during the day I guess it'd be so full of light from those big arched windows. I wonder if this is where he'd sit in summer, all sleek and golden like a lion pretending to be tame.

God, I really want to see him naked.

But we're not even talking, just standing a polite distance

from each other in the middle of this gorgeous room, and I have absolutely no idea what he's thinking.

At last he breaks the silence, because I sure as hell can't. "We can do this wherever you like." He sounds so perfectly collected. Like this is normal. Maybe it *is*. For him. "Only not in my bedroom or the locked room on the top floor."

"That's really Bluebeard of you."

"Sorry. I don't use it anymore."

I'm not going to ask about the bedroom. Don't need to. No getting ideas above your station, Toby. And I'm honestly not sure if I'm meant to be prowling about the house, seeking an appropriate wanking zone. It'd totally serve him right if I went for something weird like the closet, or the loo, or the pantry. Instead, what comes out of me is, "But what about your carpet?"

Argh.

Don't laugh at me, don't laugh at me.

But he meets my eyes steadily, and I suddenly remember why I liked him so much. "I don't care about the carpet."

"How about here, then?"

In your living room. God. Fuck. Fuck.

He nods, crosses to the windows, and pulls the curtains. Bedroom or not, that seems intimate, like we're closed into our own little world. There are dimmer switches, so the artificial light is mellow somehow, not harsh. Magical, as he goes to his knees again. And this time it's for me, just for me, and it's even better than before.

Better, and still nothing like enough.

"I want to see you naked."

Holy shit, was that me? That *was* me. Shit, I've gone too far. I always go too far.

He doesn't move for a moment, like he's thinking about it or struggling with it, and I can't tell if he wants to do it or he doesn't want to do it, and I don't know what I'm doing, and I'm clearly a bit bobbins at this, but I want it so badly that I kind of don't care.

Then he's on his feet again. And he's doing it. He's actually doing it. He's taking his clothes off. His hands aren't quite steady, and that makes me feel good, so fucking good.

And, wow, his body. He's not a gym bunny, but that always looks kind of pretend to me anyway, and I want to be like, *Stop trying so hard. Eat a muffin.* But he's strong and lean without ☆ being intimidatingly ripped, and the light catches the hair on his chest and stomach and forearms so he sort of glows a bit. I love that, and I know I'm staring at him, but what would be the point of asking him to take off his clothes if I didn't look? Oh, and he's hard as well, just from this, and I love that too.

It's kind of embarrassing to tell the guy who's way hotter than you how hot he is, but I have to. I can't not. And it's totally the right thing to do because he gets this gorgeous dark slash over his cheekbones—which isn't quite a blush—and I get to see his throat work as he swallows. And I can suddenly remember how it felt under my hand.

At last, he's kneeling again. Same as before: hands behind his back, knees slightly parted, as though he's just waiting for me to nudge them wider.

Except this time he's looking down.

Because it worked at the club, I try, "I want you to look at me."

I wonder if I should mind that he hesitates when I tell him to do something. If this was porn, I'd probably be all, *Do it now, bitch,* or something. But I can't say that to him. Jesus. Why would I want to?

And—is it weird?—I like the way he hesitates.

Everything I say, a choice he makes, a step he takes.

☆   Which is how I know it's real for him. And that makes it real
for me.

He lifts his head.

Wow.

It had been too dark at the club, but he's got these...what do
you call it...heterochromatic eyes. They're winter-day grey all
the way to the inside edge of his irises and then, *bam*, there's this
ring of gold.

And I love his mouth. It's got secrets, just like the rest of him.
Carefully severe when he's not reacting or speaking, but right
now it's so soft I want to kiss it.

I don't.

Instead I sort of fish out my cock, which is totally ready to go,
and try not to feel too silly, standing there holding it.

Then I remember something. "Shouldn't we have a
safeword?"

Maybe this isn't the right thing to say because, at last, he
replies, "I'm kneeling at your feet while you wank. If I don't like
it, I can stand up and walk away."

Well. I guess he's got a point. But I kind of wish he hadn't
said that. And my cock isn't madly keen on it either because it
actually sort of shrinks a bit, like it's trying to tuck itself back into
the foreskin where nobody can make it feel awkward.

Then I wonder if *he's* feeling awkward—even though he's
so amazing down there, naked and golden and supplicant and
mine—and maybe he's trying to protect himself. By making it
less. A game we're playing.

When it's more than that.

Which is how I remember that what felt realest of all was
when I was talking to him. That's what brought him to his knees,
really. Whatever I said. Or some part of it because I said loads.

So I talk. I stand over him, and I talk. It's stupid, but I tell him everything.

"You know...I...kind of...like, I wanted you from the first moment I saw you in that boring-arse club." Something happens to his mouth. Something...light, not quite a smile, but its own little yielding.

And, weirdly, everything gets easier. The more I say, the more I find to say, my hand stroking my cock on a kind of lust-fuelled autopilot. "It was like this short circuit in my brain, and all I could think about was you and getting you like this. All these crazy, impossible fantasies. Like maybe if I could sort of...kidnap you, or something, and you'd find yourself cuffed and naked and at my feet in some dark room."

Oh fuck. Now he probably thinks I'm psycho. But he doesn't flinch away or jerk to his feet, and whatever I see reflected in his eyes isn't shock. I'd been about to blurt out that I wouldn't really, but suddenly I know I don't have to say that. Not to him. So, instead, I just plough right on with the dirty talk.

"So...there you are...all helpless in front of me...but I don't think you're scared...or maybe you are, but mainly you look angry. Like you'd fucking kill me if you could get loose, except you can't, so you've got no choice but to...like, submit, I guess, to whatever it is I decide I want to do to you."

He makes this sound, deep at the back of his throat, like it's a different sound he's swallowed.

I'm insanely hard again. Like, *do you want any pictures hanging* hard.

Exactly like him.

And he...well...wow... My cock is just, y'know, my cock. It's ☆ fine. Does the job. Feels good when I rub it against things. But his I could be kind of obsessed with. It's really...*beautiful*, all strong and straining, needy and aggressive at the same time, and sheathed in gleaming skin, with these drops of moisture crowning the tip, like tiny perfect opals. I think they'd taste of heat and salt and tears and him. If I got a hand round the base, he'd be so exposed, all the tender places, vulnerable and at my mercy. I could run my tongue up those blood-bright, writhing veins. Get under the ridge. Into the slit. Make him scream with the softest of my kisses.

Oh God. Oh Fuck. Oh Godfuckyes.

I work myself ferociously, almost painfully, but it's amazing, this harsh pleasure zinging all through my cock and from there to my whole body. Best wank ever. The room fills up with the sound of skin moving against skin, as I tell him, "There's part of me still worries sometimes that it's kind of messed up. Like a wire got crossed somewhere or a gear is bent, because I see someone like you and this is what I think about, this and other stuff like it. Bad stuff, I guess. Like hurting you. Making you cry. And beg. Except it doesn't feel bad to me. Or it does, but in a good way. Does that make sense? Like it lights me up inside."

Another one of those sounds. Stifled and naked at the same time, making me wonder what it's like when he really screams.

"Fuck." That's what I say next. The only thought I can get out. "Oh fuck." Because I'm wet with looking at him, pre-come sliding between my fingers as I stroke myself up and down, up and down, rough, then rougher, like I'd touch him.

 Breathing sort of hurts, and the sound of me trying fills the air, ragged and raspy. And, underneath, there's the echo of his, and that's so hot, our bodies not touching, but our breaths all tangled up together. It's nothing, it's *air*, but it seems so visceral, and so there, like our mouths are fucking.

The world has gone all shiny-sharp at the edges, like I'm an envelope coming open, and I feel so good, I feel so fucking good, that I kind of lose control of my mouth. And words are falling out of it that hardly sound like words at all anymore, just these jaggedy, groany things that I'm dropping everywhere.

"I'm going to remember this for, like, my whole fucking life. It's going to be on me forever. God." My hand tightens and so does the pleasure, twisting into corkscrews inside me...nearly nearly nearly. "Fuck."

His eyes, his gorgeous fucking magical eyes, never waver. Because I've told him to look at me. Even though he's shaking, and I mean really shaking, like it's his cock I'm holding, and there's sweat glistening on him, gathered on the tips of his hair, sliding down his skin, like he's jewelled in all the tears I want to make him cry.

"And it'll be on you as well. Because...because...you want it too."

I'm not expecting anything, but after a moment he nods, blushing again, and that blush is the sweetest fucking thing I've ever seen. It makes me feel like I'm a million feet tall. Like I'm a king.

Because it makes this more than the physical. More than simply the act of kneeling down. And suddenly I know what I felt in the club was right: he's raw in this wanting and in the rightness of it. We're the same.

And just like that, in these frantic jerks like my cock's been electrocuted, I come all over him. I try to control it—and where I'm aiming—but it's all I can do to stop my knees folding up like deck chairs. I'm all over his chest, across his throat and jaw and cheek. I'd be kind of impressed at myself for the porno load if I wasn't out of my head, fucking delirious and in that kind of weird pre-embarrassment stage. Where you're still floaty, lost in the sparkly, amazing time-out moment of *ohhhhhfuckingyeahhhhh*, but you're starting to get that vague sense that it's going to be weird and awkward when you blink the stars out of your eyes, and you're sticky and limp and drippy, and standing over a naked, kneeling stranger who you've basically covered in come.

Except that next bit is a long time coming because it's basically been the best fucking orgasm of my tiny rubbish life. Like recognisably, definitively, memorably good. Like *I'd better start a list so it can be at the top* good. And all I can do is be stunned and happy and grateful, and at the same time, totally and completely wrung out. I'd probably be crying if I hadn't spurted, like, literally all my body fluids everywhere.

When my heart stops exploding and I remember breathing is a thing I can do, I open my eyes. He's kneeling. Still hard as anything. Still looking at me. And suddenly I get really stressed out about what he's seen: me all goofy and babbling and helpless, coming everywhere.

Very slowly, he lifts a hand to his cheek. Runs one finger through the mess I've made.

Then he closes his eyes and sucks the finger clean.

The way he looks when he's doing it... Fuck... I can't... And I swear to God, my cock nearly comes back from the dead.

Afterwards, he opens his eyes again and climbs gracefully—always so damn graceful—to his feet. Which has to be some kind of weird little act because if I'd been kneeling that long on carpet, I'd have felt it.

I've sort of half forgotten how tall he is. And how remote, locked up again behind his wolf eyes.

"We're done here."

That's what he says to me. "*We're done here.*" And we really are. Because that's all it takes to turn me back into a pumpkin.

Not a dom, not a king, not anything special at all. Just some clue-less kid who's somehow got lucky. "Yeah...but...like...what..."

"There's a taxi number and an account code on the board in the hall. See yourself out when you're ready."

He's still stark bollock naked, but he leaves...he fucking leaves. Sweeps out of there with all the dignity I've never had. Leaving me alone in his beautiful living room, limp dick in hand, staring at the spot where he'd been kneeling.

3

LAURIE

Thirty-seven years old, and I was hiding in my own bathroom from the teenager I'd brought home with me. The teenager at whose feet I'd just been kneeling. Whose pleasure I wore like a garland, and whose taste still lingered in my mouth, salty, sharp, and sweet. And, oh God, I knew nothing about him and I'd taken that risk. Mild though it was, I should have known better.

I thought I heard my front door open, then close.

Thank God. Thank God. He could have looted the place for all I cared, as long as he left.

Sinking to the floor, I tried to still my shaking and told myself that what I felt was relief. To a degree, it was. I feared what I might have done if he'd stayed. Crawled back to his feet, possibly, and begged him to touch me, hurt me, use me, whatever he willed. Let myself be utterly undone by a boy who had barely laid a finger on me.

My throat warmed beneath the memory of his hand.

He had left me so full of aches and empty spaces, my skin too tight to contain it all, and I hadn't even asked his name. I had meant to keep him just another stranger, someone I could allow to wring from my body something of what I craved in return for a shadow play of submission. But what we'd almost given each other was something else.

No wonder I'd fled. What could there possibly be between that fierce, fragile creature and me? Had I ever been that earnest or that helplessly young, so much raw skin and burning need? Making me burn, too, with its strange power.

Against the protests of my knees, I made it to my feet and into the shower, turning the dial until the water beat down like hail. If I had thought I could silence in a clamour of sensation whatever it was he had woken in me, I was wrong. I rested my ☆ forehead against the tiles and shuddered and wanted and felt eerily weightless amidst the steam, until I found myself again in the dull familiarity of my own hand. Such a hollow thing, my own pleasure, without something—someone—to give it meaning.

After everything I'd done, or not done, I didn't deserve to think of him, and I had that much self-discipline, at least. At least, not until after. And then I caught myself imagining that small, slim figure disappearing into the dark.

He would be fine. There was absolutely no reason he wouldn't be.

Close to twelve thousand car-occupant casualties in London this year. Five thousand pedestrians, four and a half thousand cyclists. About twenty-three percent of our trauma calls were knife- or gun-related. Last week alone, I responded to six stabbings, one requiring a prehospital thoracotomy, and two shootings, though the first had been a hoax.

But he would be fine. And even if he wasn't, I would have no way of knowing. We were strangers.

I turned off the shower, dried myself, and pulled on a dressing gown. I was tired, but restlessly so, like a bell tossed upon the wind, and I wandered my own house like a stranger.

He had left no trace at all. Not even where I'd knelt and watched him touch himself, and broken on the edge of his words. I crossed to the bookshelf and took down a random volume of Dance from amongst all the medical textbooks and journals, flipping through it as though seeking my future in the family Bible: this relic, this talisman that Robert had forgotten to take with him.

I made myself a cup of tea and didn't drink it.

Then I climbed to the top floor room. (*"That's very Bluebeard of you."*) Stood for a while at the centre of its emptiness, waiting for it to mean something and listening to the rain. I lost all track of time. And, finally, I cried. Because, the truth was, the room no longer meant anything at all. It was simply a space between four walls, and I was lonely and alone. Tired and sad and sick with yearning. And I'd treated someone badly, for no reason other than selfishness and fear, which was never who I'd meant to be. So much shame and loss and frustrated lust. Bitter indeed.

———

I was crawling into bed when my doorbell rang. At first I thought it was a mistake and shoved my head under the pillow in order to most effectively ignore the buzzing, but it didn't stop. So I reclaimed my dressing gown and—reluctantly—went to answer.

On the doorstep was an exceptionally bedraggled nineteen-year-old. Every line of his thin body was pulled so tight he almost seemed to be vibrating, but his wet-lashed gaze was fixed on the ground. "Look, I'm going to need that account number, okay?"

"My God, what happened?"

"I didn't want to take your fucking whore taxi, okay?" His furious eyes met mine. "But there's no Tube, and the buses are shite, and then it started to rain, and then my phone ran out of battery so I couldn't use Google Maps anymore, so I had to come back."

"Where were you trying to go?"

"Tabernacle Street."

"Shoreditch? That's miles away."

His shoulders jerked into a frustrated little shrug. "Six, according to Google."

"I never meant—"

"You never meant what? Seriously? What didn't you mean?"

I had no answer for him. He was right. "I'm sorry."

"Save it...just like...save it." He sounded flat and tired and sparkless. My handiwork. "And get me a fucking taxi. I want to go home."

I hated myself, and the part of me that was cowardly wished for a simple solution: an exchange of pain for forgiveness. But life didn't work that way, and fucking up was forever. "I really am..." And then I stopped. Selfish again, keeping him there in the rain while I protested my sincerity. He had no reason to believe me, no reason to care. I'd given him none. "Of course. Do you want to wait inside?"

"Doesn't matter. I'm not getting any wetter."

"Please come in. I don't want you to catch cold."

He jammed his hands deep into his pockets and glared up at me. "Yeah. Right."

At that moment, he sounded very much the teenager, and I wished I hadn't pushed him to it by treating him so carelessly. I stepped away from the doorway, and—after a moment—he came inside, bringing with him a rush of cold, damp air.

"Shit," he muttered, shuffling his feet in their saturated Converses. "Your carpet."

"I really don't care about the carpet." The echo of my own words hurt.

I closed the door, flicked on the hall light, and reached for the phone.

☆ "Oh my God." Whatever was in his voice—the warmth, I think—took me utterly by surprise. And the next thing I knew, his wet body was shoved up against mine, his freezing hands cupping my jaw as he dragged my face down to his. "Fuck. I knew aftercare was a thing."

I blinked at him helplessly, not even thinking to pull away. "W-what?"

"You've been crying."

"I..."

"Dude, I can tell. Your eyes are all red."

His were the colour of damp irises. Glorious. And I was mortified.

"It was me, wasn't it? Shit."

I managed something that might have been a smile. "Don't flatter yourself, Junior."

"What's the matter, then?"

What could I tell him? That I missed so profoundly something I might never even have had. And that the things he wanted were the things I wanted, and I couldn't find them either. Horrifyingly, my eyes prickled with fresh tears.

He threw his arms around me and hugged me so tightly. That silly, too-earnest, too-beautiful boy. After a moment, I bent down and pressed my face into the damp skin of his neck, breathed in rain and mist and a touch of sweat, and hugged him back. Until he was shaking slightly against me, and the cold had saturated us both.

"I fucking hated you," he muttered.

"I'm sorry."

"Like who the fuck does that? Explodes your brain and then chucks you out."

"I'm so sorry."

He pulled back and touched the corner of my eye with the tip of one icy finger. "It *was* me a little bit, wasn't it?"

"Yes," I told him. "It was you. A little bit."

"Good. I mean not...*good* good. But I kind of needed to know it mattered."

"I'm sorry I tried to pretend it didn't."

He peered at me as though he was trying to see through frosted glass. "You're kind of sorry a lot."

I nodded. "When I'm a dick, yes." I didn't want to get into the complexities of apologising. The terrible powerlessness of being unable to do anything except wait for mercy you couldn't earn and didn't deserve. I hated being forgiven almost as much as I feared rejection. It felt too much like a debt you couldn't pay. Instead, I said, "You shouldn't be standing around in wet clothes."

"Why?" He gave me a sullen look. "What are you going to do? Get me out of them?"

The words were more challenge than flirtation but, oh God. A child should not have been able to make me blush. Except he wasn't a child. Which was why I was blushing.

"Mate," he went on, "it's fine. We're not in the eighteenth century. I'm not going to, like, catch a chill and die on a chaise longue."

"I could put them through the tumble dryer, if you want?"

He scowled. "Look, I didn't want your whore taxi, and I don't want your pity tumble drying, either."

"Actually, it's a guilt tumble drying."

"Wow, you're really selling it."

Whether you were on your knees or not, people still had their ways to flay you. I drew in a breath, and it shuddered in the space between us, like my skin to his command. "If I hadn't made you leave, I would have waited there, at your feet, and begged for anything you wanted to do to me. And, afterwards, I don't know, maybe you would have stayed the night, and maybe we'd have washed your clothes. It's nothing I wouldn't have done before."

He shoved his hands squelchily into his pockets. "I seriously prefer that version. Especially the begging bit."

"Well, I'm not begging to dry your clothes. Just offering."

After a silence that contained the rise and fall of at least six or seven civilisations, he nodded. While he was working off his shoes—without stooping to untie the laces—I went to get him a towel.

When I came back, he was still standing in my hall, his socks balled up and stuffed into one hand. He seemed very small in his dampness, somehow, and his knobbly, naked toes were oddly beautiful.

I imagined his hand in my hair, pushing me down. How it would feel, that moment of instinctive outrage, and then the long, dark slide, the shame and the pleasure of being not-quite-forced to do the things I wanted. I would lick the gleam of rainwater from the arch of his foot.

I led him down into the kitchen.

"Raised ground floors do my head in." His footfalls landed softly on the wooden floor. "It's like this is a basement, but it's not a basement, and you're not on the same level as the street, but you are on the same level as the garden. How the fuck does that even work?"

"Space-time dilation," I told him gravely.

I was gratified, so ridiculously gratified, to hear him laugh.

He hovered by the staircase as I opened the door that hid my washer-dryer and fiddled with the programme wheel. "Uh, this is a really nice room." He sounded painfully uncertain.

"Thank you."

"And you've kind of got your pans on a...hangy thing."

I nodded.

There was about a fraction of a second of silence, even more uncomfortable, if possible, than the conversation. Then he gasped. "Holy shit. Is that an AGA?"

"Hmm?" I glanced at the warmly slumbering behemoth, which was absurd because it made it look as if I didn't know the contents of my own kitchen. "Oh. Yes."

Wooed, perhaps by "iconic design, exceptional quality," he padded into the room wary as a wild colt and, with a lingering look at the cooking range, finally made his way over to the washing machine. His fingers curled under the hem of his T-shirt and tugged. Then he froze. "You're not going to watch, right?"

"God. Sorry. No."

I spun away, a strip of pale skin seared across my vision like I'd stared straight into a camera flash. Then came the swoosh of fabric, the scrape of a zip, and finally the slam of the washing machine door and its slowly gathering hum. Turning back, I found him robed waist to ankle in towel and waist to neck in goose bumps, hugging his own elbows and shaking.

"F-fuck, it's c-cold." He made a dash for the AGA, one lean, lightly muscled thigh briefly exposed at the join of his makeshift garment.

Traces of rain glistened still on his chest, throat, and upper arms. There was a barbell in the shape of an arrow through his left nipple and a rash of fading acne marks across his collarbones. He looked unbelievably fragile just then, all bones and youth and awkward angles. But there was something else as well, a deep steady flame—conviction perhaps, or courage, an instinct of valour that too much living could so easily strip away. I wanted to be on my knees again. I wanted to let him burn, as free and wild as our hearts could bear.

"Can you stop staring? I know it's not much to write home about, but it's what I've got to work with, okay?"

"Sorry." What else could I say? *You're beautiful. Please let me... please...* When he was half-naked and trapped in some stranger's house? "I think the spin cycle is about an hour. Would you like something? A warm drink? Another towel? Some clothes." Good God, why hadn't I thought of that earlier? "I'll lend you some clothes."

"Yeah, that'd help. Just need to get dry and warm up."

A drop of water, silver-edged in the half-light, slid slowly from the tip of a clump of hair, hung suspended for a moment, and then landed on the side of his neck. He flinched, and it burst into infinite, infinitesimal tributaries, rushing this way and that across his skin.

"You could have a hot bath?" I offered. "If you wanted."

He shuffled. "You don't have to. I mean, I know you feel guilty and shit, but this is too much. You could just go to bed or whatever, and I'll get my stuff when it's ready and call that taxi."

I propped my hips against the farmhouse table in the middle of the room. "I don't think so."

"Why? Do you think I'm going to nick your AGA if you leave me alone?"

He made me smile, and it felt so strange, standing there in my kitchen, talking to an angry boy in a towel, and wanting to smile. "If you managed to steal it, you'd deserve to have it."

He huddled in closer, still shivering. It would have been so easy to fold him in my arms, and warm him with myself, but also utterly impossible. Wrong, even. And I couldn't help internally cringing from whatever it was—my own hypocrisy, perhaps—that made kneeling naked at his feet acceptable, when a simple gesture of comfort was not. The truth was, it was easy to deny the intimacy of the first (though, in fleeing from him, I had failed to do so). Much less the second.

"So. Look." His hands curled into fists. "This bath, right? Is there bubbles?"

It had been a long time since I'd taken a bath—I usually preferred, or perhaps defaulted to, showering—but I recalled some bottles tucked into a corner. "Probably."

He gave me a haughty look. I had no idea how he managed it, my little, towel-draped prince, but he did. "Well. All right, then."

So we trooped upstairs, and I ran him a bath and poured half ☆ a bottle of Radox Nourish into the water.

"Dude."

"What's the matter?"

"Like a capful is the recommended human average."

He was right. By the time I thought it prudent to turn off the taps, the bath was mostly a pile of bubbles.

"I'll, err, leave you to it," I said. "Take as long as you like."

"Aren't I keeping you up? Isn't it really late?"

"It's probably about three in the morning, but I have tomorrow off." I could see him on the brink of asking a million personal questions. "So," I added quickly, "it's fine."

His drying hair was curling again at the ends, and he twisted a longer piece absently round a finger. "You don't want to keep me company?"

"I'd really better not." I was actually slightly proud at how calm I sounded.

"Don't flatter yourself. I meant talk to me, not soap all my dirty places."

Rather than lose myself in imagining the way his water-slick skin would ripple beneath my hands, I gave him a sharp glance. "Yes, you did."

"Yeah, all right, I did." He held my gaze for a moment, and then glanced away, the corners of his lips twitching cheekily upwards. "But what are you going to do, throw me out? Oh wait."

I shouldn't have laughed. It would only encourage him. "There's no mercy in you at all, is there?"

That brought him straight back, his eyes like arrows, cobalt-tipped and deadly sharp. "There is. There's lots and lots." His voice had taken on a husky edge. "When I'm properly motivated."

"Well, I'm not motivating you anymore." I, on the other hand, sounded like an exasperated schoolteacher. "So get in the damn bath."

"You'll stay though, won't you?"

God. How could he turn so quickly from wicked to vulnerable? It made me dizzy and sweetly helpless, these bonds of silk and mischief. "What's next, a bedtime story?"

"Do you have Winnie-the-Pooh?"

"If you don't get in the bath, I'll drown you in it."

He gestured imperiously. "Turn round, then."

I sighed and did as directed.

I heard the towel fall. Then there was a splash, followed by a yip. "Shit. It's hot."

"Traditionally, baths are." I risked a glance over my shoulder, and when it inspired no squeal of outraged modesty, tucked my dressing gown into place, and sat down on the marble step that led to the sunken bath. It was less undignified than the toilet lid, but I still felt strangely like the...attendant, consort, plaything of some capricious, adolescent god-king.

And some part of me thrilled to the notion.

I imagined the unforgiving chill of the marble beneath my knees. The tug of chains at wrists and ankles. Perhaps the pinching weight of clamps...perhaps...perhaps other violations. He would want his toys adorned.

Oh God. What was I thinking?

The steam in the room was suddenly unbearable, and I twisted, trying to get comfortable in a cocoon of clinging heat.

My guest, my shame, my fantasy princeling, was tucked at one end of the tub, legs drawn up to his chest, so all I could see were the pale humps of his knees and shoulders rising from the bubbles. He grinned at me. "I wouldn't really make you read Winnie-the-Pooh."

I sensed some kind of trap, but I had no idea what form it might take. "I'm glad to hear it."

There was a brief pause. He trailed a finger idly through the foam, making ribbons. "I'd make you read something else."

I was determined not to ask him what. That would have been entirely foolish.

"How about..." His eyes gleamed at me. "How about... 'Thou ☆ shalt blind his bright eyes though he wrestle, Thou shalt chain his light limbs though he strive; In his lips all thy serpents shall nestle, In his hands all thy cruelties thrive.'"

I curled an arm over the edge of the bath and hid my face in the crook of my elbow. I couldn't bear him to see me right then, stripped tenderly to the bone by the blade of his voice.

"'In the daytime thy voice shall go through him, In his dreams he shall feel thee and ache; Thou shalt kindle by night and subdue him. Asleep and awake.'"

The sound I made, muffled though it was, echoed off the tiles until it seemed infinitely loud, infinitely helpless. I had no idea what he was reciting, but the words hooked into me like thorns.

And, yes, for his wishing and for his pleasure, I would have recited them. For my merciless, smiling prince.

"What's your name?" he asked.

And, in that moment, I was his, so I answered, "Laurence Dalziel. Most people just call me D."

"At the club they called you Laurie."

"My friends call me Laurie," I corrected him sharply.

"I'm going to call you Laurie."

I lifted my head. "You call me what I say you call me."

"It was aspirational."

"We're not going to be friends."

☆   He blinked at me through a coal-dark fringe of water-heavy lashes, and I felt like a prick. "Please." His eyes got very big. "Please can I call you Laurie? I like it better."

The kid was dangerous. But I'd known that all along. "Oh all right." It wasn't a graceful surrender but, then, they never were.

☆   He splashed me. Playful conqueror. "I'm Toby. Toby Finch."

I didn't know what to say—it seemed a little late for *pleased to meet you*—so I just nodded. Toby. His name was Toby. It seemed as though I'd always known it.

He uncurled without warning and disappeared under the bubbles in a flurry of skinny limbs and gleaming skin. He surfaced again, a second or two later, shaking the water from his hair, and lay back with a sound of absolute sensual abandon. "Being warm after you've been cold is totally the best feeling ever."

Like pleasure after pain. And I was as hard as a horny teenager, just watching him enjoy himself.

He stretched out, straining a toe towards the taps and not quite reaching them. "This bath is epic. I can't remember the last time I had one. I mean—" He flailed into a sitting position, this time shifting enough of the bubbles that I caught sly glimpses of him beneath them, the shadow of his pelvis, the curve of his calf, the ridge of his ribs. "I do wash and stuff. We've got a shower at the loft."

I wasn't supposed to be encouraging him. "You live in a loft?"

"Yeah, at the top of this tobacco factory conversion thing. This guy gave it to my mum."

"Someone gave your mother a loft?"

"Yeah." He lifted an arm out of the water and peered at it. "Look, I'm going all pruney."

I suspected him of none-too-subtly changing the subject, but I let him. As I'd said, we were never going to be friends. "Time to get out then."

He did the now familiar *turn around* gesture.

I rose, then sighed. This was getting ridiculous. "Toby"—his head jerked up at his name on my lips, and indeed, it was sweet to say it—"Toby, do you really think I'm going to be so overwhelmed with lust at the sight of your naked body I won't be able to control myself?"

To my horror, he went bright red and curled into a tight ball at the bottom of the bath. "God. No. I'm just...I'm just shy, okay? Jesus."

"You're...what?" I repeated stupidly. The boy who had called bullshit on me at a BDSM club, brought me to my knees, told me all the things he wanted to do to me, shown me need and want and naked ecstasy, and come back to me through a rainstorm because, while he was proud, he wasn't stupid...he was shy?

He pressed his forehead against his knees and said nothing. So I took a fresh towel from the heated rack and opened it out, holding it between my outstretched arms. "I'll close my eyes."

"Okay. But no peeking."

"I promise."

More splashing. Behind my eyelids, I tried not to imagine the shimmering rush of water droplets down his body. Then I felt him—not so much the shape of him, but the heat of him—and I closed the towel around him, realising only at the last moment that I was now effectively hugging him.

He made another of his unabashedly happy noises. "That's so nice."

"Are you a virgin?"

I opened my eyes. Startled at myself, more than anything. Why the hell had I asked that? And so bluntly. It was absolutely the opposite of my business.

He went rigid in my arms and yanked the towel away, spinning round to glare at me. "I said I was shy, not sexually stunted."

God, what had I started? "You're still very young. It's actually perfectly normal—"

"Jesus, I'm not a virgin. The first time I had sex I was fourteen."

Something flared inside me, as hot and sharp and sick as acid. "Toby, I—"

"It's not what you think. It was my best mate at school. We said we'd take turns, so I let him do me, but then he wussed out and never spoke to me again." He shrugged. "But I've got laid since. A bunch of times, actually."

He sounded so proud of it. As though he was still keeping count. "I'm sorry I...doubted your promiscuity. It's just, well, you've seen me."

"Yeah." He stared up at me, still holding the towel tight around his neck. "Yeah, I have."

"So, what's there to be shy of?"

He sighed heavily and rather patronisingly. "Maybe the fact you look like you, and I look like me?"

For a moment, I had no idea what he was getting at. I half

thought he might have meant old. And then I remembered the praise he'd lavished on me. At the time, I'd attributed it to a kind of power-intoxication and the heat of the moment, but I had, once again, misjudged my boy. He'd meant everything. Every word. Of course he had.

"Oh Toby." I hardly recognised my own voice. "You do know you're beautiful, don't you?"

He was red again. "I'm okay. Not like you. Not like I'm supposed to look."

"How are you supposed to look?"

"I don't know...taller, stronger, more muscular. Less acne."

"Toby, Toby." It was like some terrible enchantment. The more I said his name, the more I wanted to. "Please. Let me..." I had no idea how I was going to finish that sentence. But it didn't seem to matter.

My hands had covered his, and the tightness of his hold, almost imperceptibly at first, began to relax. I saw, felt, sensed the tension leave his body.

"Yeah," he whispered, sounding almost drugged. "Yeah."

The towel slipped, exposing one shoulder, a little of his upper arm, and the sweep of his clavicle with its dark-red rosettes. His eyes, pupil-dark and hazy, did not waver from mine.

God help me. For whatever reason, he trusted me.

I could probably have stripped him and seduced him, and he would have let me, but I was powerless with tenderness. I dried him, uncovering him piece by piece, blotting up water with the towel, my fingertips, occasionally my lips. I stroked his slender muscles, his fragile bones. I kissed the inflamed places of his skin.

He quivered. "Fucking hate it."

"It's not severe. Are you using a benzoyl peroxide cream or gel?"

"Tea tree oil. My mum doesn't believe in chemicals."

"Just as effective."

He didn't reply.

☆ "They're not ugly, Toby." I ran my fingertips very gently over a rash of spots just above his nipple. "They're just there."

"Yeah, well." He shifted his weight from one foot to the other. "Given the choice, I'll take not there, thanks."

"They'll fade with time."

"And if they don't?"

"Well, then it'll just be you and the other eighty percent of the country."

He growled, clearly unsatisfied by this answer. His mouth was so close to mine. Kissing close. To distract myself—and him—I draped the towel about his hips and knelt down on the carpet. He made a rough little noise, his eyes growing even darker. I slid my hands about one of his ankles and lifted his foot onto my thigh. With the trailing ends of the towel, I collected and banished the water that clung to him. Each and every drop, one by one. I did the same to his other foot, then began working my way up his legs, through the crisply curling hair on his calves, over his knees, to the smooth planes of his thighs, their silky-soft interiors.

"Fuck." Toby was shuddering against my hands, and his erection had become undeniable. "Fuckfuckfuckfuckfuck."

"Are you...all right?"

"Yeah. It's just, like, this is the sexiest night of my life."

And because it was what I had wanted to do before, and perhaps what I should have done, I slid a hand around his leg and let my head rest a moment against his knee. I closed my eyes. His fingers moving lightly through my hair, and everything was still and dark and silent. And good, so very good.

Time curled around us both and held us tight.

"Y'know," he said at last, "my clothes are probably done."

It was a long journey back to my feet, and I was suddenly exhausted. I drew the towel up and tucked it round his shoulders. "Would you like me to call you a taxi?"

He turned his face briefly towards the window, where greyish light seeped beneath the blind. "I reckon the Tube will be running again soon."

"I don't want you wandering around on your own in the early hours of the morning."

"For fuck's sake, I'm not a kid. I wander around on my own all the time. Nothing's going to happen."

About a hundred and seventy homicides committed in London per year on average. About seventy thousand assault-with-injury offences. Approximately four thousand incidents of gun-enabled crime, approximately twelve thousand incidents of knife-enabled crime. "I know, but I'd still rather you took a taxi. Or..." The word was out before I could stop it.

"Or?"

"Or...stay the night. What's left of it."

His eyes narrowed, and I realised I had once again made myself vulnerable to his unsubtle machinations. Worst still, there was no hiding the fact that I'd done it quite deliberately.

"Stay where? On your sofa?"

"I have a spare room."

"Thanks, but I think I'll take my chances with the Tube."

I made my voice as stern as I could manage. "Don't manipulate me, Toby."

He grinned at me, utterly unabashed. "I'm not manipulating, I'm negotiating. You don't want me to get the Tube home. I want to stay with you. *With* you."

Oh, but losing to him was its own terrible pleasure. "If you stay with me, nothing is going to happen."

I'd expected (hoped?) that he might protest, but he just nodded, and so eagerly I wondered if I'd folded to an opponent with a handful of nothing. The idea troubled me less than perhaps it should have done. "All right. This way."

And so I took him into the bedroom I had once shared with Robert.

Toby let out a low whistle. "God, man, your house."

The time I had lavished on it seemed entirely lost. The hobby of another man. I gave him a little push towards the bed.

He dropped the towel and dived into the sheets, but not before I caught the pale flash of his haunches, the dimples at the base of his spine.

I flicked off the light so I didn't have to watch the shapes his body made beneath the covers as he wriggled himself into a comfortable position, then I stripped off my dressing gown and climbed in gingerly beside him.

He was still wriggling, making odd little purring noises at the back of his throat and tucking himself so firmly into the duvet I wondered how I was ever supposed to get him out of it again.

I didn't usually sleep on my back, but I thought it prudent to lie that way.

"G'night, Laurie."

"Do you need an alarm?"

"No, s'fine."

God. When he was tired, his voice had that husky edge it took on when he was aroused. It had been quite a while since I'd shared my bed with someone. I'd forgotten what it was like to have that awareness of another body. I almost thought I could hear the flicker of his eyelashes. Feel his heart beating.

Which was impossible because he had settled on his side,

facing away from me, his whole body compressed into a tight little ball.

I listened to him breathe, until it grew slow and deep and even, and then risked rolling over myself. I didn't even feel him move, but there he was pressed right up against me, his back to my chest, his arse snuggled against my thighs. He made a sleepy, contented noise that could only have been entirely calculated.

I wondered if he was smiling.

I put an arm over him and pulled him to me, my hand closing almost instinctively over his wrist to keep him there.

In for a penny... When in Rome...etc., etc.

A soft pulse of desire went through me, not for sex or pain or humiliation or some other release, but for this, this quiet closeness. Someone to hold in the dark.

He must have felt it. The way I stirred against him, the way my breath caught. I waited, helplessly and half-afraid, for his response, for him to turn and cover me, kiss me and take me. I wouldn't have resisted. I would have welcomed him, in all his sincerity and obstinacy and his youthful ardour for forbidden things. But he hadn't lied when he'd promised me mercy. His fingers twisted back to brush my hand, and he settled his body into the curve of mine, giving me this instead.

4

TOBY

I wake at fuck knows what time in a strange bed, in the arms of a man I hardly know, and it's *perfect*. I've never been held like this before. Kind of so...absolutely. His fingers are slack against my wrist, but they're still there. This comforting weight, like he can't bear to let me go. I don't think he's moved all night long.

I'm super careful because I don't want to wake him, but I wriggle myself round in his arms until we're face-to-face.

Laurie.

His breath's morningy, but so's mine. I just like looking at him like this. He's both more and less like himself somehow, stern and soft at the same time. And, lying there in this warm haze with him, I can't believe all the things he's given me in a single night: power and submission and kindness. And now this as well. His peace.

He's also the first person who's ever taken me seriously. The first person to really make me feel beautiful. I can't help wondering what the fuck I'm supposed to be able to give him back.

Very, very lightly, I touch his eyelashes. The corner of his lips. He doesn't stir. And I'm a little bit worried this is what stalkers do.

I know we're not lovers or boyfriends or friends, and I know that he's going to wake up and call a taxi to drive me out of his life. I hope he doesn't regret me—this stupid kid he took home one night—but I'm going to remember him forever.

I'm not sure I'm the same person who snuck into that stupid club. The only thing I was right about was him. I kind of half wish I'd met him later. When I'm older, and I'm all cool and sophisticated. However that happens. I can't really imagine it properly, though. The best I can come up with is us both wearing tuxedos. And we're in this sort of...bar, I guess, which is all oak and honey and candlelight, and I'm all like, *From the top shelf, please*, to the bartender. And Laurie looks exactly the same, but I'm kind of hazy, and my brain wants to substitute Daniel Craig, and what the fuck kind of fantasy is this, where I'm played—in my own head—by somebody else?

Besides, if I had met him some other time, I wouldn't be here now. And he wouldn't be my first. And I wouldn't lose that for anything.

I hope he hasn't totally ruined me.

I've no idea what time it is. Late, I think, from the light, which is kind of bright and sharp and sparkly, like you sometimes get after seriously hardcore rain. And it's such a ridiculously gorgeous room to wake up in, a little bit fairy tale, especially since he's got this massive four-poster bed. Or some kind of posh modern take on one, anyway, since there's no curtains or canopy, just the base and the posts, which are heavily carved with arches and spirals and have that inside gleam of really good wood, so deep and rich you think it'd be warm if you touched it. It's fancy without being fussy, and honestly, it gives me a bunch of filthy ideas.

He'd look fucking amazing spread-eagled on a bed like this.

And *that's* a fantasy I can definitely imagine properly.

I'm not sure about the technicalities, but I reckon you could get somebody into some pretty interesting positions. And by "somebody" I mean Laurie. Legs up and wide, arms above his head. Exposed, vulnerable, and a little bit degraded. And so, so hot. And I know exactly how he'd look: frowning and desperate and embarrassed and turned on. And mine. Just like I'd be his for letting me do that to him.

God. What would it be like to have someone trust you and want you that much? To put aside fear and pride and shame and inhibition. All the stuff that's supposed to be so important. Parts of ourselves we're supposed to protect and care about.

I sometimes wonder what it means that I want someone to do that for me. But then I think it doesn't matter, and that it's just a thing I want. And either everything we want is weird, or nothing is. Unless it's like...avocado. I seriously don't get that. The texture makes me gag, and it tastes like you're chewing the inside of somebody else's scrotum. Who the fuck would want that?

After a bit, I slide carefully from his arms and crawl off the edge of the bed. Poor bastard must be beyond knackered, because he doesn't stir. Just makes this fucking adorable noise, nearly a whimper. It's probably nothing, but I pretend it's for me. For the loss of me.

It's kind of weird to be wandering around his house with my knob flapping in the breeze, so I wrap myself in yesterday's towel and go down to the kitchen. My clothes have gone a bit fluffy in the dryer, but they're basically fine, and I pull them on. And then I find myself doing all this weird shit.

I pad around and open all the curtains for him. Pick up the *Times* from the doormat. There's no post because it's Sunday. Then I find myself back in his kitchen, peering into the fridge. It's well stocked, actually, in this slightly anonymous *I get food deliveries* way.

I'm probably supposed to be going away. Slipping off discreetly so he doesn't have to wake up and freak out about having brought me home and let me stay.

But then I think of him upstairs, so utterly asleep, and the way he held me all night. The way he dried me, so gently and carefully, looking at me like I was precious, and going on about benzy-whatever-it-was. Making me feel all cared for. Well, that and horny. And now I want to do something back.

There's not much in this world I know for definite I'm awesome at, but breakfast I can do. I think I must've had natural skills in that direction, but half a year at Greasy Joe's has honed me into a bacon-and-eggs samurai.

I know, right? It's the sort of shit parents dream for their kids. Little Tabitha's going to be a doctor. Rory's going to run for government. Crispin is deworming orphans in Somalia. And Toby, well, Toby's not so bad with a griddle pan.

But, hey, at least I'm good at *something*. For a while there I genuinely thought I wasn't. And, anyway, I've always wanted to play with an AGA.

I want to show off and do him a full English, but with the stuff he's got lying around it would be more like three-quarters, and I don't like doing things half-arsed. So scramblies it is.

I spend a little while like a contestant on *Deal or No Deal*, opening all the doors of the AGA and peering inside, trying to figure out what the shit is going on in there until I work out which one is probably the roasting oven. I find a grill rack insert, line up some pieces of bacon, and stuff it in there, near the top. Then I find a kind of metal badminton racket that opens and closes, and I guess it's either for kinky shit beyond my wildest dreams or making toast, so I stick it on the boiling plate to heat.

And then I get performance anxiety because scrambled eggs ☆

are like this...art form. They're the wax-on, wax-off of cooking. Simple on the surface but infinitely complex and diverse. Totally magical.

It's got to the point that all the regulars at Joe's will say, "You know how I like them, Toby," and the truth is, I do. I'm literally walking around with twenty different variations of scrambled eggs in my head. Bit of a comedown for somebody who was supposed to be a lawyer, but beggars can't be choosers. And egg maker is way better than beggar, isn't it?

But the thing is, I don't know how Laurie would like them. And that's kind of a problem because I want to make him the best fucking scrambled eggs he's ever had or even imagined possible. Is he traditional or American style? Big curds or small? Pre-seasoned or post-seasoned? Creamy or buttery?

Jesus. It's carnage in my brain.

So I go for what I like best. Well, usually when I cook for myself, I just go for quick and dirty, but I make for him what I'd make for me if I wanted to show myself a good time. If that makes sense.

I break the eggs into the frying pan, add some butter and seasoning—he's got proper sea salt and everything—and give them ten seconds in the roasting oven. Basically, there's two ways to go from here: stir like crazy or hold off, fingers twitching.

I let my fingers twitch and distract myself by putting the kettle onto the boiling plate. Then I grab the pan and gently fold the eggs in. It's a bit weird, not having them on a hob where I can keep an eye on them, and I'm nervy it's all going to go horribly wrong. But then I settle into it. I know it's just scrambled eggs, not like cordon bleu, but there's something that feels right to me about cooking. It's calm and focus at the same time. And you get something real at the end of it, something that can make someone happy.

Next time I check the AGA, the eggs are pretty much done, all gold and velvety. I stir in some crème fraîche and some freshly chopped oregano and pile them onto a plate on top of the crisscross-patterned AGA toast, along with lots of butter and the grilled bacon. And, of course, I steal a little of the leftovers, just to make sure I'm not about to serve him a pile of ming. But, no, it's fine. It's good. Creamy, but not too creamy, fluffy and indulgent. See, this is the other thing I like about cooking: you always know when you've got it right.

I can't find anything like a tray, but I manage to make it back upstairs, balancing the paper, the plate, and a cup of tea. He's still fast asleep, curled around the space where I'd been lying, in the warmth that maybe I'd left. I put everything down on the bedside table and perch next to him. I've never tried to wake someone up, like, romantically before. I've no idea how.

"Uh...good morning... Hi."

Yeah, that probably wouldn't have woken a napping mouse.

I lean in to shake his shoulder, and it feels like a ridiculously intimate way to touch someone when they're kind of helpless and out of it and you're awake. "Laurie?"

If I was going for gentle, I fail hard. He jerks from oblivious to frantic in about a nanosecond. And his face is like this magic mirror of responses: surprise, confusion, loss, awareness. There's even this moment in the middle when he looks happy to see me, but it's gone as quickly as the rest. Eventually, he's Laurence Dalziel again, and saying in this dry, resigned way, "Good morning, Toby."

"Hey." I grin at him because I'm an idiot. "I made you breakfast."

First, he's all bewildered again and then unflatteringly worried. "You didn't have to do that."

"It doesn't suck."

"I'm sorry, I didn't mean—" He's still trying to shake off sleep.

"Yeah, you did, but it's okay. Come on, sit up. There's tea as well."

That gets his attention, and he uncurls. The covers fall away a bit, and suddenly I remember he's naked under there. And holy shit. I mean, I know I've seen him already, but the novelty is nowhere near wearing off.

I want all the naked, all the time.

In this light, I see different things, different shadows. Sun dapple on his shoulders. Sparks of gold at the tips of the hair on his arms. Though it's harsher too, picking up grey sometimes and imperfections on his skin, the places where his body is rough and lived in, its muscles earned.

He was gorgeous yesterday, kneeling and burnished and kind of a fantasy. And he's still gorgeous this morning, rumpled and tired and real.

Shit. I'm meant to be doing stuff. Not just staring at him lustily, thinking of all the things I want to do to him. And, for the record, some of those things are perfectly normal. Like kiss him.

I pass him the plate, wafting it a bit so the scent of butter and herbs fills the air. He's still slightly dazed, so I forgive him for the grateful *OMG, it doesn't look awful* expression that crosses his face.

"You really didn't have to."

I shrug. "I wanted to."

"What about you?"

Oh yeah. Me. "Wow, I totally forgot."

For some reason, my stupid makes him smile. God, I'll be sitting around doing *he loves me, he loves me not* with a daisy before long, but he's got such a good smile. Makes the gold in his eyes shine. "We'll share," he tells me.

So we sit there in his bed, probably in the middle of the afternoon, and he feeds me morsels of toast and egg, and I feel kind of cherished and turned on and so fucking happy. And I wish I didn't have to go and get on with my messed-up life.

I wish *this* was my life instead.

Just great eggs and a hot guy and no worries at all.

And they *are* great eggs, by the way. I can tell he likes them.

That's the other beautiful thing about food: watching somebody enjoy it. Admittedly, it doesn't normally get me horny, but Laurie's a special case.

"Where did you learn to cook like this?" he asks. I'm both surprised and chuffed he cares. Or maybe he's just making conversation with his slightly-more-than-one-night stand. Either way, I like this glimpse of him. Relaxed and sleepy-eyed and looked-after. A little unprotected piece of who he is.

"Nowhere," is what I tell him. But then his head tilts inquisitively, and I can see that he's not going to let me get away with that. "I kind of cooked for myself a lot when I was a kid."

"Why?" Now he sounds sharp. "Does your mother not believe in food either?"

Whoops. I guess I've accidentally painted myself as some kind of abused, underfed guttersnipe. Which isn't true at all. When I was younger, Mum and I had some rough patches, but I've kind of got over it now. She's my mum, y'know? What can you do? "No, she does. It's just she doesn't believe in time."

"I beg your pardon?"

I have to laugh at the expression on his face. "She's not a ☆ martyred slave of time." He's still blank. I get this a lot when I have to explain my mother. "Baudelaire?"

Nothing.

I sigh and crunch the last piece of bacon. It's so good. Salty and rich, with just the faintest hint of charcoal to give it depth. "She believes you should do things when you feel moved to do them, or else you become nothing but a mechanism of chronology or something. But, me, I'm totally a martyred slave. I want to eat three times a day, and I want the savoury bit to come first and the sweet bit to come second, and I want to sleep through the night and wake up in the morning."

He sits up a bit straighter, which makes the duvet slip down, and I'm briefly distracted by...oh God...everything. Nipples and hair and hard ridges of muscle. He's all rough and delicious and—

Fuck, he's talking.

"So she just left you to fend for yourself?"

"What? No. There was always food. But I got sick of Cup-a-Soups and Super Noodles, so I started experimenting." He had that *social services* look I'm pretty familiar with. "Laurie, we do okay."

"I'm sorry, but your mother sounds like a nutcase."

"Oi!" Nobody gets to call my mum a nutcase except me. "She's a genius." Then he gets the other look I'm familiar with. "And I'm aware they probably seem pretty similar from a distance."

That's why I don't like talking about this stuff. People always get the wrong idea. It's not the Super Noodles that grind you down, it's spending your whole life being second. Like, don't get me wrong, Mum loves me. She loves me more than she loves anyone else in the world. I've never doubted that for a moment. But there's something else: the ever-fading flame of inspiration, or whatever.

That's where my mother dances.

Not for the ordinary shit like scrambled eggs or school reports or anybody else's dreams. And I get it. And it's okay. But she's never going to understand what it's like to...*not* have that. She'll always support me in whatever I do, whether I'm studying law or working for £5.03 an hour as a kitchen porter at a greasy spoon, but that's kind of the whole fucking problem.

Laurie breaks the silence with, "That was delicious. Thank you."

"'S'okay." I go kind of squirmy inside with pleasure. I like it so much when people enjoy my cooking, and that makes me embarrassed and self-conscious. Because it's kind of pathetically needy, when you get right down to it. Like wanting to be first.

There's butter glistening on his fingers from the last piece of toast. He's got good hands. Because, frankly, he's got good everything. They're strong and blunt and very, very steady. Except, sometimes, when they're really not. And that's a wild thrill all by itself.

I know so little about this man, but I know he unravels hands ☆ first.

I swoop in and clean him up, my tongue getting right down in the tender little V between his fingers, where he tastes so very much like him.

It makes him groan.

And my cock perks up like a Labrador at walkies.

"Toby." There's warning in his voice.

I look up at him, the tip of his finger caught between my teeth and cushioned by my lips, and I make my eyes as big as they can go.

"Please stop that." There's something else in his voice this time.

And, uh, I'm so confused. *Please stop that* should in no way press the *Go* button in your brain. And, honestly, it doesn't in a real way. I know what the rules are and how to take no for an answer.

But the way he says it.

Right now, it's ambiguous in the wrong way. But I can so easily imagine it being ambiguous in the right way.

I want him to say that to me and mean it and not mean it, knowing I might not stop. I want him to say it in pleasure, and I want him to say it in pain. And I want the power to deny him. Just because I can. Just because his suffering makes me hot.

I let go of his finger with one last kiss.

And then we stare at each other because it's suddenly awkward as fuck. I'm supposed to be leaving but I'm not, and he's not asking me to.

"Won't your mother," he says finally, "be wondering where you are?"

She probably hasn't noticed yet. Wait. That sounds bad. She would notice. She definitely would. It's just her maternal panic sensor is kept on the lowest setting.

I shake my head. "But I should be going, right?"

"Yes, you should."

"Yeah." I chase a crumb round and round the empty plate with my finger. "Or we could—"

"No."

Shit, I've gone too far. I always do that. There was reluctance before, but now certainty's come down like a wall. I keep trying though. Probably because I'm an idiot. But what have I got to lose? "You don't even know what I was going to ask."

"I don't have to."

Whoa. Talk about quelling. I sigh. "Well, it doesn't have to be wall-to-wall kinky shenanigans. We could...fuck or talk or go for a walk. Anything."

Shit, could I sound any more desperate? But I kind of am. Also: go for a walk? What the fuck. Who does that?

"Toby." Wow, I hate it when he's this gentle. "We can't do any of those things."

I really, really don't want to sound petulant, but I know I will anyway. "Why not?"

"Because I'm thirty-seven, for one thing."

"And people who are thirty-seven don't fuck or talk or go for walks? That must totally suck."

"Not with nineteen-year-olds."

"You know, if this was ancient Greece, you'd be buggering me senseless by now."

"Yes, well, we no longer live in a world of socially mandated pederasty."

I nearly go, *And you say that like it's a good thing*, but for fuck's sake, it's not funny. I'm nineteen and I'm not a kid. I know what I want, and he wants it too, so why is it suddenly not okay? "Your main objection is some vague perception of social stigma? Not, like, not fancying me or not wanting to fuck me?"

"It wouldn't be right." He pulls the duvet up to his chin, like he's trying to hide under it. It's kind of cute, or would be if he wasn't trying to hide from me and a bunch of true stuff. And that's when I catch it—the faintest tremor in his hands. Fuck yeah.

"And what we did last night was?"

He goes all red. "It was...different."

I'm kind of hovering on the edge of cross now. I mean, it's nice he doesn't want to exploit me or whatever, but fuck it, I'm so ready to be exploited. I lean a little closer to him. I'm being way too intense, but I can't help it. "Are you telling me what we did before wasn't sex? Wasn't intimate?"

He stares at me, all rainy eyes and wildness. Lost, just like me. Then he shakes his head because he's not a liar. I knew that about him from the first.

"So, what's the big deal?"

I guess he's trying to figure it out because he's quiet for ages. I want to smooth the frown lines from his face. Then he says, "In five, ten years, when you're closer to my age, you're going to look back on this and think, 'What the hell was I doing?'"

"Whatever age I'm at, I'm going to look back on this and think, 'Fuck, yeah.'"

"No, you're not. Someday, you'll be me, and then you won't think, 'Wow, intriguing older man.' You'll think, 'God, what a sad, lonely bastard, sleeping with teenagers.'"

"So you'd sleep with me if I was twenty? That seems pretty fucking arbitrary."

He gets that look I'm starting to recognise, amused and exasperated at the same time. I reckon I'm in with a chance as long as amused nudges ahead of exasperated. "You know it's not that simple."

"Maybe not, but it doesn't have to be unspeakably complicated either. Can't you just see yourself as...I don't know, the gay male equivalent to a cougar or something?"

He blinks at me. "What, an ageing queen?"

That idea's so impossibly crazy I actually laugh. And, after a moment, he laughs with me. "And anyway," I press, "it's not like you habitually go around banging younger guys, right?"

"The room I told you not to go into? It's full of twinks."

"Aww, I thought I was special."

"You know you are." He sounds like he did last night, wrapping me in a towel and telling me I'm beautiful.

It's not like it's true or anything. But I believe he believes it.

And that's...that *is* special.

So there's no way on fucking earth I'm letting this guy out

of my life without knowing what he feels like inside me. It's that simple.

"Okay." I hold up my fingers and begin ticking them. "Way I see it, your main objections are social stuff, when nobody will ever know, and worrying what I'll think about you in however many years' time when you'll totally have forgotten I exist anyway."

"Toby..."

His stern voice ripples all the way down my spine, and I kind of want to arch into it, purring and wriggling, until he turns smoky-rough and sweet instead. "Don't 'Toby' me. I'm serious. If you don't want me, then that's one thing, and it's okay. But saying no because you're worried about what people will think, that's another, and it's not okay."

He reaches out suddenly, hand brushing my cheek. And I press into his touch, wanting it, wanting it so much. "I can't believe you're trying to talk me into bed."

"You're already in bed."

He smiles his odd, shy smile at me.

"So come on." I don't so much put my cards on the table as throw the whole deck out the window. "Tell me you don't want me."

I'm waiting for him to do it. Expecting it. Braced for it. And I kind of realise a second too late that even if he doesn't mean it and he just says it to make me go away, it's still going to take a rock hammer to my stupid little heart. And then I'm thinking that maybe he's right. Maybe I'm too nineteen for this. Because this shit is big and real, and I'm probably going to dash myself to pieces on the realness of it.

"I can't decide," he murmurs, "whether I'm being seduced or bludgeoned."

"Maybe a bit of both?"

That makes him blush again, and I get to watch it sort of slide all the way down his naked throat. It makes me brave, the way only he can. I crawl fully onto the bed and straddle him. It's not exactly something I've had much practice at. In my head, it's all graceful and natural and I sort of swing myself over like a cowboy into the saddle. But, basically, I kind of scrabble and then plop but, hey, it gets the job done. And shame about my clothes, and shame about the duvet, but I can just about feel the shape of him under there.

And his cock, which seems pretty seduced.

He lets out this...not quite a gasp, more this sort of an uncontrolled breath, that tells me how much he's struggling.

All that control. And he's letting me undo him like a bow.

God. He's perfect. He's fucking perfect.

"It's kind of a classic," I tell him.

I'm kneeling over him, so he has to tip his head back to look at me. His eyes have that hungry, stormy look. "What is?"

"The rhetorical approach."

He tries to laugh, and it comes out all shaky. "I don't think people usually surrender their virtue to the power of rational argument."

"Oh man, they did all the time in the seventeenth century. There's this whole branch of, well, not love poetry, but shag poetry I guess, which is about convincing chicks to bone you because Reasons. It ranges from like, 'Hey, you'll be dead one day so why not?' to 'We both got bitten by the same flea so we've pretty much done it already.'"

He's kind of silent, but his body is all noise under me. Thunderous.

I smile at him. "That's my favourite. 'This flea is you and I, and this our marriage bed, and marriage temple is.' Isn't that way, way hotter than 'eyes like suns, lips like cherries'?"

His hands come up and frame my face.

Kiss me, is what I think.

Forever limps by.

"What do you want, Toby?"

Dangerous question to ask me when the answer is *everything*. ☆
But that probably isn't what he means. So I go for the obvious: "I
want you to fuck me."

And then he's on me like a breaking storm, and it's fucking
terrifying and fucking wonderful and actually fucking happening. I'm on my back, and he's on top of me, and wow he's strong,
and he's tearing at my clothes—like, literally, tearing because I
hear something pretty serious happen to a seam even through
the heart-pounding, blood-rushing tumult of our moving and
breathing and coming together. He slides a hand up my chest,
the touch more protective than sexy, and for a moment I'm bewildered at what it's doing there, but then he's dragging my T-shirt
over my head and I realise he was making sure the fabric didn't
snag on my nipple ring.

I catch onto his shoulders and stare into his face, which is all
flushed and wild. And, holy shit, there's some kind of...I don't
know... It's just so fucking precious to me that he could be so far
gone and still remember something that trivial.

And it's exactly the thing I need to hold on to right then,
because, God. Unleashed is what he is. And I'm kind of pinned by
him and overwhelmed by him, but I know, more than anything
else I know, he's never ever going to hurt me, not even in the
teeniest, tiniest, most accidental way. And the truth is I like him
and I want him—far too much to be scared. Even though he's
right between my legs, pressing me wide in this rough, really...
definite way. No hesitation at all, like his whole body is saying,
I'm going to fuck you, I'm going to fuck you.

And I love it.

Because this is mine too.

I did this to him.

Me. Too skinny, too weird, too intense, nobody me.

And this is something I can have. Something I can really have.

He flings my T-shirt...somewhere, and then his mouth sort of opens over my nipple, and, oh my God, heat, hot, hot wet heat. And then his tongue, holy shit, his tongue flicks the end of the arrow, tugging at the skin very lightly, and it's fucking electric. This thin-bright, not-pleasure-not-pain feeling that ripples outwards like a Catherine wheel. My spine arches helplessly off the bed, turning me into a goddamn croquet hoop, and I make the sort of noise nobody should make from only getting their nipple licked.

That's when I know I'm outclassed.

I wasn't lying when I told him I was *sexually active*, as they say at the clinic. Yeah, sexually active and responsible, that's me. But sometimes I wonder if my relationship with sex is this sort of unhealthy mixture of insecurity and hormones. Because I like it when people want to shag me—that's undeniably good for the ego—and I have this low-level, pretty much permanent desire to be having sex at all times. But sex itself... Well that's kind of meh, isn't it? Not awful, or anything, but nothing to really beat a good hard wank.

There's no pressure when you're wanking. When you're with someone else, it seems a bit rude to, y'know, be somewhere else in your head. But when I'm flying solo, I can fill my brain with as many hot guys in chains as my imagination can fashion.

Maybe it's because of the kinky thing.

Or maybe I'm a bad lay. But mainly it's kind of wet and

awkward, and you're both kind of touching each other like you aren't really sure what you're doing.

Probably because you aren't.

But, fuck, I want to be touched the way Laurie touches me. Like he knows where my pleasure lives, even if I don't, and he's going to drag it out of me screaming.

And I want to learn how to touch him that way. Because I really, really like the idea of him screaming. Kidding. Well, not kidding, not really, but it's not only about the power. It's this sheer crazy gratitude and wanting to pay it forward. Backwards. Pay it somewhere.

Make him feel this good. This completely touched.

He lifts his head before I die. And I just lie there, incandescent, taut, and panting. His fingertips brush my throat.

And I spill another stupid sound. Beneath his hands, my skin is so light and tight I half imagine I'm transparent. I'm glass for him, all the way to my blood-red, shining heart.

Then his hands are at my waist. I lift up for him, and he peels me out of my jeans. Not exactly a classy moment—I'm like a giraffe, all bulging knees and kicking legs—but I forget about it the second he comes down on top of me, naked. So warm and strong and still a little bit rough. Not in an aggressive way, but in a sure way, which makes me believe I'm strong too, like my body is designed for this. To take his. Encompass all his power for my pleasure.

I wrap myself around him, tight as I can, and I fucking *glory* in it.

I love how solid and heavy he is against me. The way his back shifts under my hands. His cock jammed up against mine, which is kind of awkward and intimate at the same time. I swear to God I can feel the blood in it, beating hard under the skin, sort of its own little pulse. And, at the top of his groin, where the hair is thinner, individual spirals of it pressing into me like he's leaving me this message in our own private graffiti.

We hold there for a bit, in this full-body embrace. His head is tucked in the space of my shoulder, his breath pooling hot against my neck, and I can sort of sight like a sniper down the sweep of his spine, all the way to his frankly magnificent arse.

And I think of all the secrets in him. The way his throat fluttered under my hand. How he looked when he knelt for me. The tenderness in him when he wrapped me up in a towel. And fuck, I want to know more. I want to know how his mouth feels round my cock. I want to know how he tastes in places I've never wanted to know how anyone tasted before. I want to pull his legs open and scratch my nails up his inner thighs. I want to make him hurt.

I'm so fucking greedy. I want to have everything.

"Jesus, Laurie." I twist my fingers in his hair. It's shockingly soft, especially at the nape of his neck. And he looks up, straight into my eyes. He's got that desperate flush that makes my stomach turn cartwheels. "You're like fucking..." I don't actually know what I'm going to say. There isn't a word big enough for how much I want him and for the way this makes me feel.

But it turns out I don't have to say anything else.

"Turn over." His voice has gone so low he actually sort of growls at me. Which is the hottest thing ever.

Though I don't know why he says it, because he doesn't give me a chance to do it. He just flips me. So fast I'm breathless. And staring kind of helplessly at the footboard which... Look, I'm a bit sheltered, okay? Whenever I've had sex before it's usually been at somebody's house, on a single bed, very, very quietly. Not that I've really felt much urge to scream the place down. But, yeah, I guess it never occurred to me not to lie with my head at the head end in the designated bed-occupying position.

But here I am now, with a guy who wants to fuck me so badly that I'm kind of diagonally sprawled and facing totally the wrong way, and he doesn't care.

Yeah, okay, it's a small thing. It's pathetic. But it means something to me. There's something kind of romantic about this idea he's got and is sharing with me. That I've somehow become this crazy, lust-inducing version of me.

Instead of who I really am.

I reach out and curl my fingers over the beautifully carved end piece of Laurie's four-poster. The wood is smooth as skin under my palms and warms up quickly. It's weird, the sensory details you catch onto. There's a man dragging my legs open... putting his mouth on the back on my neck, oh my fucking God...grinding his cock against my arse...and the detailing on his bed is kind of burned into my eyes like I'm never going to forget it.

I guess it's my brain's way of making sure I don't explode of bliss.

Because, Jesus, nobody told me the back of my neck was directly connected to my cock. When he kisses me there, it's hot and cold and sort of bright all at once, as if my veins are full of light. He's everywhere, inside and out, and I melt under him into this puddle of wriggling, groaning *yes*. And I'm glad I've got something to hold on to because I could fall through the cracks in the universe on feeling this good.

I let my head flop between my outstretched arms.

Do it again. Do it again.

He pulls away instead, but before I have a chance to be seriously disappointed, his tongue paints this wet streak of ecstasy from the crease of my arse and up my spine. At first it's mainly surprising, then it's kind of nice, and then it's fucking incredible as all the nerves in my back sit up and take notice, tingling with anticipation and then fizzing with response as he ignites them one by fucking one. I'm so alive, so intoxicated with it that I have no idea where his tongue is even supposed to be. It feels like my whole back is touched, all at the same time. And I lose everything in sensation. Everything but him.

Suddenly, I notice I'm kind of...making this noise. Like *hnn-nnnnnn* except my breath is all shaky so it's more like *hn-nuh-nuh-nuhhhhhh*, like I'm a lawn mower that won't start. And I try to stop it, but I can't. I can't.

Apparently that's what happens when you lick my back.

Who knew?

His open mouth is at my nape again, hot and damp, and the scrape of his teeth, and oh God I nearly come. Pure panic is just enough to hold back, well, most of it, but I lie there twitching, in a pool of wet, and want to die in a bad way.

"Toby?" His voice at my ear.

Nope. I'm too embarrassed for actual words.

"What's the matter? Too much?"

If I don't say anything, he'll forget I exist. *La-la-la-la-lah.* Toby Finch has left the building.

"Toby? Please, what did I do?"

God, he sounds genuinely scared. I hide my face in my upper arm. "Dude. I just nearly came."

"Pardon?"

I turn my mouth a bit to the side. "I. Nearly. Came."

His lips follow the top curve of my ear, which makes me go all tingly again. "Isn't that rather the point?"

"Err, no." It's hard to think when he's touching me... I'd say *like this*, but it's really *at all*. "The point is to come at the right time. Otherwise it's premature ejaculation."

"The right time to come, darling, is when you want to come." ☆

He called me "darling." Turns out, my cock likes that too, and I whimper a little bit as it drips. He tugs at my lobe, and that's it. Undone. I start lawn-mowering again.

"I want"—there's a catch in his voice—"to please you, Toby."

Arrrgh. That's not helping. I squeeze the rail. Twelve times one is twelve. Twelve times two is twenty-four. Twelve times three is— He nuzzles into the side of my neck, rubbing me with the roughness of his unshaven jaw. I don't have a fucking clue what three twelves are.

"Please let me."

His hotness blows my tiny mind once more. I can't believe he's...actually begging to make me feel amazing. Life just doesn't get better than this.

And there's more. I can tell he's shaking. So hard.

"You have no idea," he whispers, "what you do to me."

He's right. I don't. I have no idea how I can possibly do anything to anyone really. But, God, it's a fucking awesome notion that I could.

"You seriously have to fuck me," I tell him. "Like right the fuck now. Because you might not think so, but as far as I'm concerned, if I come without your cock in me, it's really bloody premature."

"Oh, Toby." He's heading back down my spine, pressing my own name into me like gemstones. "Toby. Toby."

He sounds so wrecked. It's beautiful. I have no fucking idea what I've done in my life to deserve something this wonderful, but I swear, I'm about to get religion.

He leaves me all gloopy and shivery, and I hear the *szvvvt* of a condom wrapper tearing. And suddenly I get this really strong sense of how I must look to him, kind of spread out on his bed, sweaty with lust and shiny-wet from his mouth, legs splayed open, and hands clinging to the foot rail.

Talk about a fuck-me pose.

And it's so good. So fucking raunchy. I'm going to carry this image of me—the Toby that Laurie sees—with me from now on. Forever. My own secret.

The bed shifts under his weight. There's a click and a squirt and then there's a finger inside me. And...*whoosh*...the breath goes out of me because it's like...hello. I'm expecting it, obviously, but maybe I'm kind of not.

Because what it's like right now is a finger inside me.

And it doesn't hurt or anything—there's a controlled stretch—but that's kind of it.

I mean, I know this feeling. The slightly alien, *Hey, there's a thing up there* feeling. It's fine.

But I guess I thought it might be different with him. I grit my teeth and wait for it to get better. Which it probably will when he gets round to hitting my prostate.

Okay. Two now.

I stare at the wall, kind of ordinary again. Well, as ordinary as you can be when somebody's sticking their fingers up your arse.

It's weird how much I'm up for this considering how little I'm into it when it happens. What's with that? It's like my body forgets how banal it is, and I start...craving it. Or, maybe, when I think about it, I imagine other stuff and convince myself it's there.

My cock has gone from sixty to zero in what seems like less than a second, though it probably wasn't.

It'll be okay once he's in. I'll get that kind of closeness you get, and the fullness, and that deep, dark inside pleasure that builds and builds but never really goes anywhere. I like that. I do really like that. And later I'll touch myself and dream of his lips and his fingers on my body. Actually, even if this bit is a bust, it's still probably the best sex I've ever had. And just the idea of it is enough, really: me and him. Laurie fucking me, his body in my body, the sounds he'll make when he comes.

Yeah.

I guess I'm ready because he's out again.

I hope I'm ready.

He was pretty diligent back there in his not-very-seductive *got a job to do* way.

The thought drifts across my mind that this might be how grown-ups have sex. And I can't tell if it's worse or better than the fumbling, insecure, faintly desperate way I'm used to.

I try not to get too sad about it. It's just... It had started off so promising. I should have let him lick me to orgasm.

Next thing I know, he's hoisting me up by the hips so my knees slide under me and I'm sort of teetering there, top half squashed flat to the bed, bottom half waving like a flag on the breeze.

I'm honestly not sure I'm mad keen on it.

It's kind of a shock, how helpless it makes me. And I can't quite forget how absolutely exposed I am. Not least because there's cold air literally wafting over my arsehole.

It's probably staring right at him.

Mirroring the slightly *oh* look I've got on my face right now.

So I'm lying there, horrified and slightly physically uncomfortable. And what's deeply weird is that, totally out of nowhere, some part of me sort of sits up and goes *huh*. Because there's something...honestly...a little bit exciting about this moment of absolutely, definitely, undeniably about to get fucked. And if I could get myself into a position to punch myself in the head I totally would, because what's it going to take to make me learn that getting fucked is not actually that great?

Then he's pressing into me. And it's this one long glide, not rough, but relentless almost, opening me up with a press and a twist, like I'm a music box and he knows the mechanism to all my hidden places. I feel him so deep inside me, it makes me breathless.

And, God, the things I like about this are better than they've ever been. No longer some distant consolation, but right there in front of me—well, technically, behind me I guess—and suddenly it doesn't matter how I'm lying because it's not ridiculous anymore. It's fucking amazing.

I try to push back, to get closer to the promise of whatever it is he's offering, because I'm sure...I'm one hundred percent sure...there's something waiting for me, some revelation just out of reach. But he tightens his hands on my hips (I hope they bruise) and won't let me move. Makes me wait there like that, with my body wrapped around his, and the possibility of all this pleasure beating the air.

When I can't bear it a moment longer, he pulls out again, comes in different, and lights me up like a fucking firework.

I think I actually scream.

The last coherent thing left in my brain is: *Oh, so this was what I was looking for.*

And then I let him fuck me into a mindless, moaning, trembling mess, and I love it. I completely love it. I can't even get a handle on when I begin to come. It's like I'm coming the whole damn time. Everything's just a blur of sweat and heat and the strength of him, pounding into me, pushing me higher and higher and deeper and deeper until I can't think, can't breathe, can't see, can only feel and feel and feel.

I'm making such a bloody racket I only half notice he's saying my name.

I say...everything.

Yes. God. Fuck. There. That. Harder. Deeper. Yes. Yes. Ohhhhhh yes.

Embarrassing porny stuff I can't even believe is coming out my mouth.

I think I maybe tell him I love him.

Because, right now, I do. I totally do.

At some point, God, it's not even like it crests, but something happens to the pleasure. It pulls in tight as a universe, and then it's everywhere like falling stars, and I'm just taken by it. By him.

Little death, my arse. It's a fucking massive death.

And I die for ages.

Next thing I know, I'm kind of limp and fucked, my lungs tight and my heart pounding, my hands aching from where I've been holding on.

My fingers uncurl and my knees give out by inches until I'm flat on my face, and he's still buried inside me, which is just on the verge of being unbearable, except I don't want to lose him or a single last second of this pleasure. Though what I'm experiencing right now is way too big for pleasure.

I think it might be rapture.

He comes down on top of me, catching himself on his elbows before he smooshes me like a grape.

"Unghh," I say.

"Toby." Wow. He can still do words. "Toby...can I..."

Well. Ish. He actually sounds about as wrecked as I do. My balls do this weird sort of spasm thing—like they're checking their pockets for anything else they can squeeze out my cock—and come up empty.

I wish I could see him. I can sense the strain in him as he

shudders against my back, but he probably looks amazing right now. Nothing but taut muscles, ferocity, and desperation.

I want to tell him to turn me over and finish that way, so I can watch him come apart in me, for me, because of me.

But all I can get out is, "Yuhhhh."

"Oh God." His voice breaks with need and gratitude.

And I made him feel that too.

A few thrusts is all it takes, and honestly, that's a relief because, yeah, it kind of hurts. But his hands reach round me and find mine and we tangle up together and that's how he gets there. Clinging to my fingers, his body pressed tight to mine, his mouth open against the back of my neck where he lavishes my skin with all his smothered groans.

He comes gasping my name.

And I'm seriously starting to love the way he says it. It doesn't sound like me anymore. It sounds like some other, different, better Toby. A Toby who can bring someone to his knees. A Toby who gets expertly fucked.

His Toby.

I don't know how he manages it—same magic as whatever makes him awesome at sex, I guess—but he eases out of me carefully and without too much mess. I hear the *schloop* of a condom coming off, and then he falls onto his back next to me.

We lie there a bit.

There's lube drying in weird places. And to say I'm in a wet spot would be to seriously underplay the enormous ocean of come he's amazingly fucked out of me.

Jouissance, is what I think.

Which annoys me because that's the name of my mum's most famous painting. The one I really hate and really, really don't want to be thinking about now. Eww.

"Are you all right?" he asks.

How could he tell? I'm still face-first in a bed.

"Yeah." I sort of nod into the sheets.

"Thank you." He gently tucks a few pieces of sweat-heavy hair out of my way, and I shiver. And then I guess I'm unconscious.

When I wake up again, I've been cleaned up, wrapped up, and I'm lying in his arms. If he'd been asleep too, he's awake now. He's not staring at me, or anything creepy like that, but his eyes are open. He's got that closed-down, faraway look he sometimes gets.

"Uh, sorry. I think I nodded off."

He smiles, and he's back with me, at least a little bit. "It's quite all right."

I don't know why, considering not so long ago my arse was sky-high, but I'm kind of awkward now. It's just not the sort of thing people usually do for you—hold you while you sleep or fuck you into oblivion first. But it's so goddamn nice of him, it makes me sad.

Another of his secrets, I guess. How incredibly kind he is ☆ behind that stern mouth and those cold eyes. I don't think anybody has been quite this kind to me my entire life. Or done so much to make me feel special.

And I suddenly realise there's other fantasies to go alongside the filthy, kinky ones. I want to cook for him. Make him smile more. Do something about the dark circles under his eyes.

I want to fucking take care of him back.

Jesus fucking Christ. Could I be any more of an idiot? I can barely live my own life competently. What the fuck could I contribute to his?

I move a bit and…I'm sticky and sore. In all sorts of places. "I should probably be going."

He nods. This time, there's no hesitation. He pulls away and— *urgh*—I already miss the way he holds me.

I think about asking if he wants to see me again. I could do it really cool and casual-like. Except, of course I can't. My dominant (no pun intended) discourse seems to be needy as fuck.

But I don't think I am needy, not really. It's just I've never come this close to getting something I wanted before. Not that he's a thing.

So it's hard to just be mature and let it—him—go.

But I get that I have to. He might enjoy kneeling for me and fucking me and maybe that could be enough for me, but considering the epic oratory required to get him to that point, I reckon it would be a hard sell to him.

I wriggle out of bed and pad gingerly around his bedroom, collecting my clothes. I don't catch him doing it, but somehow I get the sense he's looking at me. The thing is, I'm not exactly a striptease master at the best of times, so I have literally no clue how to make putting my shit back on even remotely appealing.

On the other hand, it's not the worst feeling in the world: being watched from bed by a naked man while you both think about the sex you've just had. At least, I hope that's what he's thinking about. He ought to be. It was totally three-Michelin-star sex.

Normally, I'd be dying and scrambling about, but under his gaze I sort of start making a show of myself. I pick up things and stretch probably a bit more than I need to. I even catch myself doing that bend-and-snap thing from *Legally Blonde*. I don't have much snap, but I'm hoping my bend makes up for it.

"Toby." Oh, I love his severe voice. It makes me want to sort of crack him open like a mussel. "Are you trying to make me fuck you again?"

Ooh! "Is that an option?"

He sighs, and I can't tell if it's impatience or regret. "No. No matter how much you twitch your pretty little arse at me."

I've got a pretty little arse? Awesome.

The first time I see myself in the full-length mirror, I kind of freak out a bit. I mean, after I've dealt with the pang of disappointment that we didn't think to fuck in front of it. But, God, my hair looks like an electrocuted hedgehog, and there's stubble rash all over my face, and my eyes are completely huge like I'm tripping or something. And don't even get me started on the mess of my neck and the finger-shaped bruises on my hips.

Best.

Sex.

Ever.

I grin at Laurie, and he glances away, blushing.

"I'm sorry," he starts. "I'm... I..."

But I shut that shit down hard. "Seriously. Don't. It's fucking perfect."

When I'm pretty much done getting my clothes on, he gets out of bed and wraps himself in the dressing gown he was wearing last night. Wow, it's fluffy. I hadn't realised that then. I don't think you'd go for something that soft unless your life was like substantially lacking in hugs.

Poor Laurie. If only he was mine.

I'd hug him and hurt him. And save him too.

We troop downstairs together. In the hall, he touches my cheek lightly. "You'll be all right, won't you?"

"Yeah."

"Thank you. For today. And yesterday."

I try to smile. "You really don't have to thank me. I was totally up for all of it."

His eyes go sliding away from mine. "Sorry. It's...a polite habit, I suppose."

Habit? For some reason my brain catches onto the word and won't let go. Like I'm recognising something. Something he's maybe trying to offer me or ask me for. Something that's meant to be mine.

"For breakfast," he says.

"Uh-uh."

He still won't meet my gaze, so I reach up, catch his chin, and make him. He flinches, and then, well, it's not quite a sigh, but the rhythm of his breathing changes. Slows. His eyes soften slightly, and I realise it's how he looks when he's at my feet.

He swallows. Then whispers, "Thank you, Toby, for letting me kneel for you."

And, holy shit, if I hadn't just come all the come in the universe, I'd probably be coming right now. My cock actually sort of staggers like a punch-drunk boxer who doesn't know when to stay down.

My touch has become a caress. And, somehow, we're leaning into each other. So close. If I angle my face just right, I know he'll kiss me. I know he will.

But if I let him, I'll be lost. My heart can't take it.

The kiss he's about to give me, I need it from someone who's not about to chuck me out of his house and never see me again.

So I pull away.

I don't know what to say. So I open my mouth and, "Uh, well, byeee," plops out.

And that's how I leave.

On *byeee*.

Just...fuck my life.

5

LAURIE

I couldn't tell if it was a sort of irony that my life had been not once but twice bisected. First into Robert and After Robert. And then into Before Toby and After Toby. It seemed a rather harsh fate, to live always in aftermath. That Robert, who had shared my life for over a decade, should have affected me seemed right. Even fair. But Toby Finch, who had burned like a comet for half a night and half a day? That was simply maddeningly cruel.

Over time, of course, I had come to terms with Robert and everything that had happened. I had passed through anger, hurt, and betrayal until only loss remained. And gradually, all there was left to miss was the life we had built and shared. The same life he had destroyed and remade so easily with another. Someone in whose eyes Robert still saw reflected his most idealised self. Whereas at the end I had shown him, what? Too much truth? A single memory he could not bear, one that drove him so far from me he would only find himself again in some other man's arms. Some other man's submission.

Yes, I missed Robert. The boys we had been. The men we had grown into. I missed being known, in the simplest of ways and the most sweetly shameful. In our hubris, for I could only call it that, we had actually pitied those who lacked our good fortune. We had found love first and then, almost by accident—though it felt inevitable—this unfolding enchantment: the correspondences of our natures. It had been so easy then, a slow seduction of trust and pain, submission and service. How limiting it had seemed to us, to go the other way—to wring love from correspondence, instead of finding correspondence in love.

In truth, I still believed it was.

But it was nevertheless where I found myself, just some other empty-hearted fool, waiting for hope beneath the falls of a stranger's flogger.

After Robert, I had tried, at first, to be—for lack of a better word—normal. As if everything we had done together was some expression of *us* rather than some facet of *me*. It didn't work. I met men who might have loved me, and I ached for them to hurt me.

Besides, I was busy. Work had its own demands, and looking for a future was a time-consuming business. I could not consciously recall having given up on love. It was never quite so dramatic. I went to the munches and the clubs. I joined the websites. I had the conversations. I learned the jokes. I gave my body to doms in leather to do with as they willed within carefully negotiated limitations. And it was release. If nothing else, it was release, and it was enough.

And then came Toby Finch. Too young, too thin, too earnest, too everything. With his sharp elbows and his knobbly knees. Hair that wouldn't stay out of his eyes. Acne on his collarbones. His sulky, kiss-bruisable mouth and the grin he had not yet learned to temper.

Nineteen years old—*nineteen*.

I had barely known him, but—as the days slipped into weeks—I realised I missed him too. My cruel and tender god-king, still so lost between all the contradictions of adolescence and adulthood.

And suddenly enough was not enough.

When Grace and Sam asked—as they inevitably did—I told them I'd just made sure he got home safely. Which was true, if you ignored the part where I threw him out of my house in the middle of the night, then let him in again, and then fucked him into insensibility.

God.

Toby.

————

In December, twenty-something days AT, we made our monthly pilgrimage to Torture Garden, which required wriggling into my only pair of leather trousers, an indignity no nearly-forty-year-old should have to endure to get laid in the way he wanted to get laid. As ever, it was fifty percent fashion show, forty percent club, ten percent sex party, and one hundred percent annoying. But I would have neither chosen nor wanted to go back to Pervocracy, and while I didn't want to go to Torture Garden either, I was very unlikely to run into Toby, and more than likely to run into someone who would hurt me and fuck me and not leave me missing them.

Over the last year or so, I had preferred to set up my...trysts... online, but with every encounter that had not gone horribly wrong, I was conscious of the mounting statistical likelihood that the next one might. Anonymity and physical helplessness did not seem a fortuitous combination, but even that unhealthy thrill was scant consolation for the inevitable rituals of power and powerlessness, as abstract and arbitrary as dancing for rain or the appeasement of nonexistent gods.

So the music played, and the dancers danced, and we all came round again.

I left my friends grinding slickly at the centre of a sea of rainbow latex and found somewhere, not too dark, not too out of the way, and not too close to the dungeon, where I could wait to be recognised. Inevitably, I was. I'd been around for a long time, but so had everyone else.

Thom? Jon? Tim?

He had a good reputation. And I was relatively sure we'd played (I so hated that word) together before.

So I let him take me home, where we exchanged the usual codes: no unprotected sex, no scat, no piss, no blood play, no breath play, no gags, no blindfolds, no permanent marks or modifications, no kneeling unless I was sucking cock, yellow to slow, red to stop, et cetera, et cetera, et cetera. No depth. No truth. No meaning.

He made me strip. Call him master. Display myself to him in ways that might once have left me raw.

And all I felt was a certain social embarrassment. A soft, squirmy self-consciousness, devoid of shame's sweet-sharp sting or the self-annihilating rush of humiliation. It had been like this before, but I'd always managed to subvert it. I'd even found it slightly piquant—a private scourging of my self-respect—to be so utterly controlled by my physical needs that I would not only allow this, but seek it, and cede mastership of my body to a man who needed a title to claim it. Far better to find ways to enjoy such a truth, than face it.

He made me suck his cock awhile, condom-sheathed, of course, so it tasted of latex and chemicals and nothing. As he fucked my throat, he pulled my hair, and the gesture seemed familiar. I wondered if it was him I was remembering, or simply someone like him.

Everyone was like him.

I tried to lose myself in my own skin, but the anchor points he had given me were not enough, and I was stretched between them, as thin and tight as a grass whistle.

Toby had also curled his fingers in my hair, his spring-cricket legs hooked over my hips. Pulling me close, so close.

Toby.

A withdrawal left me dizzy with sudden breath, and a slap from his cock left a smear of spit and spermicide across my cheek. "Are you with me, boy?"

I hated it when they called me boy, but I couldn't remember if I'd mentioned it, and it wasn't worth ending the scene over.

"Yes"—my stomach twisted as I forced out the word—"master."

Guilt stuck almost immediately. I had wanted this. I had. I had looked for it and made it happen. And this man had brought me here on good faith.

I rested my palms on my thighs and, squinting up at him through my still tear-burning eyes, I tried to see him. I wondered if he would see me back.

Or if there was nothing but...correspondence.

"Eyes down, boy."

I obeyed without a thought, because it cost me nothing. Technically, I was kneeling to him too, but that didn't matter either. Neither of us were here.

"By the time I'm done with you, boy, you'll be begging for my cock."

There was a time a statement like that would have likely made me feel...something. Defiance, anticipation, a kind of nervous longing to be so utterly overpowered. Robert and I had loved the struggle. And, although it had always ended the same way, with his blissful victory and my equally blissful defeat, it had never felt like a foregone conclusion.

Unlike this prearranged surrender.

My own fault, but somewhere down the years I had made it a choice, the when and how of my yielding. And now I lacked the strength, the trust, to not choose.

"Yes, master," was all I said.

My lapse had not been intentional, but it was an excuse to punish me. "You like that, boy?"

I contemplated the complexity of the question. No and no and sometimes and almost. I wasn't sure "like" even came into it anymore. Dimly, I realised I was probably...in some way... annoyed. At him, at me, at this. He'd done nothing wrong, but everything was wrong. I was wrong. I had been for years.

"I said, 'Do you like that, boy?'"

"Y-yes."

"Yes, what?"

I unlocked my jaw and delivered the required answer. "Yes, master."

Satisfied, he dragged me up again—I felt leaden, hopeless, a mannequin—cuffed me, and chained me to a Saint Andrew's cross, because it was always a St. Andrew's cross. I leaned into its embrace, enjoying at least the peculiar combination of support and vulnerability it offered.

And then he flogged me. He was good at it. He warmed me up, which was more than I deserved, with something light and supple, until I was blood-flush and sensitive, suspended there on the softest edge of pain.

God. Yes. More. Deeper.

A kind of interior quiet, a sense of bodily peace, made me lean into the restraints. And a sense of waiting crept up my spine like the warmth of touch.

Touch.

If only he would touch me. In desire, as well as mastery, or from desire of mastery, or something, something. Something that would make this more than action and reaction, script and performance. Or maybe I was wrong. Maybe this was exactly what he wanted.

"Please...please will you..."

But I didn't think he heard.

He swapped to a braided cat, and, oh, that truly hurt. He had left me naked to its sharpness, its scrape and bite and sting, and the sear of my own sweat.

The air was full of noise. His breath, my breath.

Then my cries, though I did not beg for anything again.

He knew when to stop before it got too much. How to let the pain possess me but not break me. And when I was fully its creature, mindless and shuddering, he fucked me, one hand on my shoulder, the other on my hip. When his rhythm turned ragged, he reached round, twisted my nipples until I screamed, and came.

He was done. But afterwards, he kept me there, shoved up against the cross and still impaled on his wilting cock. I tugged on the chains—scene over, fucking scene over, please—but he wrapped his hand round me, forcing me through the pain and exhaustion, the loneliness and the sorrow, until I was hard for him again.

"Let go." His breath stirred the fine hairs at the back of my neck. I almost didn't recognise him because it wasn't his master voice.

The pressure of his body against mine shoved me into his hand. Made me fuck it, as though it was something I wanted. For some reason, that was what tipped me over an edge I didn't even know was there, and I came, moaning softly, the closest to surrender I'd let myself come since Toby.

He pulled up his trousers and let me down, checked my circulation, tended to my back a little. I got dressed again, feeling dazed and empty and restless.

As we left the playroom, he turned to me. "Do you want to do this again? I mean, more than once a year?"

I'd been right, then. We had been here before. "I'm not sure. I don't really do regular or long-term."

"I know you don't."

Something about the way he said it made me stop and look at him. He was probably a handful of years older than I was, handsome, in a square-jawed, iron-haired English way. It was easy enough to imagine him in a boardroom and, if his house was anything to go by, probably not far from the truth.

He shrugged. "It's no skin off my nose. You can do what you like. I'm happy for you to come home with me once in a while, to be hurt and used. That's what you want, isn't it?"

I nodded and told myself I was too old, too familiar with this dance, to blush.

We creaked upstairs in our matching leather club wear. Absurd. Utterly absurd. At the front door, he reached out a hand to stop me. It seemed I'd been having a lot of conversations in hallways recently, a reflection that inevitably made me remember Toby and his not-quite-offered mouth.

It had been for the best. I had done the right thing.

But...damn him. He had ruined me in a single night.

"You obey, D, but you don't submit. And, don't get me wrong, that's your choice too. But"—Master Whatever's eyes caught mine for a moment—"is it what you need?"

I was sure I was usually less transparent. Alarm and a touch of guilt prickled through me and made me snappish. "I don't think what I need is any of your business."

"No, but it could be." His gaze was steady on mine. There was no denying, the man had something, a presence perhaps, now that I was paying attention to him. "I'm willing to make it my business."

I gave him a sharp look. "Why?"

"Why not? I like fucking you, I like hurting you. I want you on your knees, and I think you want to be there."

Presence or not, it was too much. Too much from him, anyway. "What the fuck do you know about what I want?"

"Nothing, but that's only because you've never told me."

I tried to imagine a future with this man whose name I couldn't remember. What it would mean. What it might be like. But I couldn't. It seemed impossibly alien. Even the thought of kneeling to him, of offering him that small amount of power over my heart and mind and will, made bile burn at the back of my throat. And the darkest, most confused and desperate part of me wanted to do it precisely because I hated it, and that would—in some twisted, terrible way—be pleasurable. I dragged my dry tongue across drier lips. "And...and what if I did? Tell you."

"Well, then we'd discuss it." He made it sound obvious, as if getting what you wanted was simply a conversation you could have. He probably had a checklist we could go through together. But how could I explain that what I wanted was not to have a conversation about what I wanted? "I'd expect to push your limits, though."

"My...my private limits are very different."

He nodded. "Most people's are."

There was a long silence.

"I don't—"

"D, I know you were with Robert, and I know you were together a long time, and I think what you really want is something that's gone."

This was getting worse by the second. It was unbearable that he knew these things about me. And equally unbearable to know these things about him: that he was perceptive, that he was kind in his way, lonely perhaps, and that he too wanted more. If only one could safeword out of a conversation.

"You can never have that," he went on. "But you can have something else. If you'll let yourself."

"You?"

"Yes."

"I—"

"Don't answer. Think about it first."

In spite of myself, I swallowed. "And if...if I..."

"Then you come to me, and we'll talk about it. And then you'll get on your knees, and you'll let me give you what you need. Because I don't think I've even come close to your limits, have I?"

I shook my head, exposed in my truths, my loss, and all my lies. For a moment, I genuinely resented him for seeing me and for forcing me to see him. In some way, it made it worse that we had no greater connection than his needs, and my needs, and the barely there boundary where we could force them, inadequately, to meet.

Something must have shown on my face, because he patted my shoulder. "It's all right. Trust is earned, and you've been too long without a master."

Too long without something, certainly. "I should go."

☆ He stepped past me to open the door. Then paused. "I play the alto sax."

"Uh?"

He smiled unexpectedly. "I just wanted to remind you that I may be a dom, but I'm a person too."

I wasn't quite sure how to respond to this information, so I kept my expression carefully blank. "And you thought alto sax would be the clincher?"

"You've got to admit, it's pretty hot."

"You should have said earlier." I tried to smile back. It seemed the least I could do. "I'd be on my knees by now."

Clearly it was the wrong thing to joke about because he grew serious again. "Think about it, D. I want you, and I'd be good for you."

I pulled on my coat, fastened it so nobody could see I was dressed as a complete prick, and hurried into the night. I could have called a taxi, but even though I was tired and my body hurt, I felt like walking.

It made the pain sing a little. It made it mine.

I took the Tube back to Holland Park, standing somewhat gingerly and watching my own reflection ripple like the moon in the windows of the nearly empty carriage. It took a while before I saw a man I recognised beneath the smudges of someone else's perception.

It would have been easier if he had not, to some extent, been right about me. I obeyed. I did not submit. But how could I, to shadows and charades and strangers? He had understood better than most, and still he had thought what I needed was a firm hand, the right master, discipline.

God. Maybe he was right. Maybe it was all that was left for me to have.

But how could I like myself through his eyes? He had made me weak, as though my needs were not also my choices. The things Robert and I had done had never made me weak. Even as I had wept and screamed and bled and begged for him.

In truth, they had made me strong. Proud, too. And I'd never really separated the drive to submit, to be hurt, and sometimes to be forced, from what seemed to me the most natural impulses of love: to be touched, to be known, to be naked, to be safe.

That came After Robert.

And, suddenly, I found myself thinking of Toby again. He had not made me feel weak either. He had made me feel...beautiful, powerful.

Free.

When I got home, I found Master Whoever's business card in my pocket, and I threw it away. I tried not to think about what he had said to me. For a while, I even stopped seeking out strangers to hurt me and forget me, and be forgotten in their turn.

I'd made such commitments in the past and never held to them. But I felt the inadequacy of what I would likely find more keenly in the wake of Toby, and it seemed almost like a betrayal of him. Tarnishing the memory of his passion, his sincerity, and his fearlessness with meaningless games and empty pleasure.

So I simply worked, and slept when I could, and gave myself to the familiar routines of my job, the day-to-day hospital business of life, death, and paperwork. Christmas came and went. I spent it with my parents. New Year's with my friends.

Then came my air ambulance shift.

A multiple-car collision. A cardiac arrest. A motorcycle accident. A stabbing, most likely drug-related. A child who had run into a glass door and severed an artery.

It was a night not easily left behind.

I lay awake, long beyond exhaustion, tasting the sour remnants of adrenaline, blue lights flashing in my memory.

Somebody had said to me: *"We'll kill you if he dies."*

He had. His heart in my hand, his torso spread open like a Rorschach test.

I could still smell petrol, burning skin, and metal from the crash sites.

Marijuana smoke from the house.

Blood.

The next evening, I sat at my computer and logged into the usual places. I looked at my ticks and crosses, my lists, and after a moment I removed blindfolds, and then I removed gags. That would let somebody take my sight. Take my voice. I let the idea possess me slowly until yes, I felt something. A quiver of uncertainty. Fear, unfurling into something else entirely.

I considered breath play and then left it alone. I had no wish to become a statistic.

After a while, I fell into an exchange of instant messages. And an hour later, I was calling a taxi to take me to a stranger's address. But halfway there, I asked the driver to stop and turn back.

What was I doing?

Just...what was I doing?

I sent my apologies, but received no response.

Which left me in bed, alone, still seeing blue lights, one hand on my largely disinterested cock, the other resting against my throat, where nineteen-year-old Toby Finch had touched me once.

For the next few days, I stayed at the hospital until nine or ten, sometimes eleven, at night. There was no shortage of things to occupy me there, and anything else had become almost unbearable.

Sleep came more easily when my body conquered my mind.

One night in early January, as I crossed the road to my house, I noticed an oddly shaped pile of shadows on my doorstep—probably either somebody else's lost recycling or one of those charity collection bags. Annoying.

But then it moved.

☆   For a moment, I was alarmed. And then disbelieving: it was Toby uncurling, getting to his feet, his hands tucked into the pockets of an oversized hoodie. And then I was frantic with a joy I had absolutely no right or wish to feel.

It was too dark for me to be able to see much more than the outline of him—hunched shoulders, jutting-out elbows, weight resting a little bit defiantly on one leg—but even that was enough to stir me like a touch upon the strings of a long-silent harp.

I wanted to run to him, drag him into my arms, turn his face into the light—see the shape of his mouth, the colour of his eyes, his pointy chin. Because in that moment of recognition, all I could think was how truly and deeply I'd missed him. And while I had never expected to see him again, some unacknowledged part of me had nevertheless grieved and hoped and waited.

"What..." I managed. "What are you doing here?"

"Looking for you." That was his *duh* voice. He shifted slightly, hands digging deeper, thin body growing taut and tense.

"Yes, but—"

☆   "Look." His head came up, the moonlight catching in his eyes, making them shine. "You've totally ruined me. And...and I think you should take some fucking responsibility for it. Or...or like at least fucking apologise."

I stared at him. Some rational part of me was wondering

if I wanted to be angry or concerned about the teenage stalker waiting on my doorstep. Apparently I didn't. "God, Toby, what's wrong? What did I do?"

"What did you do?" His voice broke. "You were *perfect*. Don't you understand? Fucking perfect. And you gave me stuff I've been wanting and dreaming about my whole fucking life. And also the best sex I've ever had. And now I'm just supposed to... supposed to...what? Settle for less than that? Pretend like nothing's changed when you changed everything?"

His hands flew out of his pockets in a pale flash and covered his face. He spun away from me, and I realised he was crying.

Wordless and helpless, I watched his back shake. Then I came up the steps and put my arms around him. Toby. It was all I could think, his name gleaming in my mind like a talisman of hope. "I'm sorry."

He sniffed and gurgled, but didn't pull away from me. "Just so you know, I fucking hate you right now."

His body was so cold against mine. "How long were you waiting?"

"Since I got off work. So six or something."

"I'm sorry. I'm so sorry."

"You're always sorry, Laurie." He wiped his eyes and let out a shuddery breath. "Seriously, I was this close to building a fucking willow cabin."

"Not many willows around here."

"Jesus." He shook himself free and whirled round, furious and tearful and Toby. "Are you laughing at me? I'm broken, and you're laughing. What the fuck is wrong with you?"

"You're not broken, and I'm not laughing at you. I just..." I stumbled and had to stop.

"What? You just what?"

"I'm just so"—something inside me yielded, and it felt effortless—"happy to see you."

He folded his arms and glared. "Well, if you're that happy to see me, why the fuck did you let me leave?"

"Can we talk about this inside?"

"I don't know. It seems like every time I get into your house, you're chucking me out of it."

I sighed. "What was I supposed to do? Tie you to my bed and keep you?"

"You realise there's like a middle ground between kidnapping someone and making them feel like they're completely unimportant to you. Did you not maybe consider saying, 'Hey, Tobes, why don't we *not* never see each other again?'"

I squeezed past him and unlocked the door. "As it happened, I didn't. Now, are you coming in?"

But Toby wasn't easily distracted. "Wait? Why didn't you? Didn't it mean anything to you at all?"

"Of course it did, but you're nineteen and I'm not, and I didn't think it was appropriate."

"Well, I'm still nineteen, you're still not, so what's changed?"

I paused on the threshold. The truth was, I had nothing to lose. "What's changed is I don't care. I'm unhappy and I'm lonely, and when I was with you I wasn't. So either go away or get in my goddamn house."

Toby stood there for what seemed like a very long time, his eyes fixed on mine.

I waited for him and tried not to flinch, feeling very far from perfect just then. It was hard not to wonder what he was seeing when he looked at me. If I seemed as old and weary and lost to him as I did to me.

He crooked his finger at me. "Come here."

"Why?"

"You need a reason? Because I'm here. Come on. It's like two steps."

Now it was my turn to hesitate. It wasn't very far at all, but it seemed farther, and it was just a little like a power game, something I had always strictly avoided outside the bedroom. But Toby didn't look like he was playing games with me. He looked small and fierce and terribly, terribly earnest. What was the difference, really, between him coming inside, and me going to him? Maybe it wasn't about power at all. Maybe it was simply about choices and honesty.

I took a step forward, and he grinned his huge crescent-moon grin.

My second step brought us together. He put his hands on my shoulders and jumped into my arms. I caught him on instinct alone, my hands just about getting into the right place to support him as he locked his legs around my waist and clung to me like an overly friendly monkey.

I didn't even think about it. I kissed him. Just my closed lips against his, which were rough and chapped and salty from his tears. Perfect, exactly as he'd said. He tightened all around me, his cock rising almost immediately to press against my stomach. His mouth parted on a very soft and tender moan. And he stayed close enough that I felt the shape of his words before he whispered them. "I'm going to make you so happy."

I kissed the tip of his nose, which was red and a little bit damp. "No promises, Junior."

My arms were already aching, but I carried him inside anyway because it seemed like the romantic thing to do and something about Toby made me want to be romantic.

No fool like an old fool.

☆   Less romantic was the groan of relief I couldn't quite suppress when I dropped him heavily onto the sofa in the living room. But he didn't seem to mind, just pushed the hair out of his eyes and smiled at me again, a little shyly this time.

I took off my coat and flung it over the arm of a chair. His eyes followed me hungrily. And when I sat down next to him, he reached out, took the end of my slightly crumpled tie and tugged me forward. My gasp roared in my ears, far too loud, far too desperate, as I stared at the blue silk between his fingers, holding me leashed.

☆   "You're always so smart. Are you a lawyer or something?"

"No," I said dazedly. "I'm a doctor. Consultant, actually."

"Wow, hotshot, huh?" He twitched my tie. He hadn't even touched me, and I was hard for him. "What do you consult about?"

"Emergency and prehospital medicine... And I...I'm with London's Air Ambulance. Toby...I..."

"I work in a café." He pronounced it *caff*, a touch of East London creeping into his voice. "Just so you know. Started as a kitchen porter, then Hairy, who was the chef, broke his leg, so I got a promotion."

I gazed at him, breathless and aroused. Why was he telling me this?

"I just thought you ought to know what a classy gent you're getting, Dr. Dalziel." Clearly, he thought he sounded terribly cynical. But he just sounded hurt. "What a catch I am."

I slid my hand over his wrist, holding him there holding me. "It's Mr., and I don't want you to be anything but you."

He pressed his spare hand between my legs, stroking until I groaned for him. "I guess you do want me."

"Oh God. I do. It's madness but I do. However you'll have me."

"Then why the fuck did you let me go?"

I'd closed my eyes at some point during the sweet torment of his caresses, but now they snapped open. "Why did I...?"

"Before. You let me go. Would it have cost that much to say, 'What's your phone number?'"

I'd had reasons, and they'd seemed sound at the time, but now...now I could barely remember them. Or find the energy to care. "I'm sorry."

"Don't be sorry. Don't do that shit." He huffed out a breath, stirring the tips of his fringe. "It's been crap, you know. Trying to figure this out without you. I've been fucking miserable." He wrapped my tie around his hand and leaned in to meet me, stretching up so his lips could brush mine, my jaw, my cheek, the edge of my nose, the dark circles I knew lay beneath my eyes. "And you've been miserable too. I can tell."

I shuddered and nodded. Was that more acceptable than sorry? All my need and longing and shame, exposed for him.

"You know, I went back to that club looking for you. Twice. The second time they caught me, so I waited on the pavement. You didn't show up."

"No, I was—"

"Avoiding me. I get it. I tried to get over you too. I really did. But nobody else is right."

"I know."

He scowled, tugging on the tie, pulling me in even tighter. "You'd better not do this to me again."

Oh God. I wasn't ready to make promises. I was barely ready for whatever was happening now. Barely ready and desperate at the same time. "I...I'll try."

We were silent a moment, both of us strangely solemn.

He blinked, looking young suddenly, and confused. "So...

we're...like...boyfriends? I've never had a boyfriend before. Not a proper one."

"And you don't have one now."

His face fell. "Oh."

"This is...what it is. And, someday, probably quite soon, you'll meet someone who *can* be your boyfriend. Someone you really want to be."

"And"—his nose wrinkled sceptically—"then I just randomly bugger off with this imaginary guy, do I?"

"Yes."

"And what about you?"

I gave him my sternest look. "I've somehow survived for thirty-seven years without you, Toby. I'll contrive to go on."

"Well, you didn't do very well the last couple of months. I hardly know you and I can see you're wrecked."

"That," I said sharply, "is not the point." I made to pull away, but his fingers tightened on my tie and my cock, and the truth was, I didn't want to be let go.

"All right. All right. We'll just do"—somehow he managed to get sarcastic air quotes around the word without the use of his hands—"'this.'"

I swallowed and nodded again. The relief was almost unbearable, and I'd put up no fight at all, simply allowed a nineteen-year-old to come in from the cold and sweep me off my feet.

"But no more chucking me out of your house."

I tried to smile. "*Mi casa es su casa.* You leave when you want."

"And I have to see you at least once a week."

"My job is not forgiving."

"Nonnegotiable. I don't care when it is or what we do or if you just lie next to me completely unconscious, but I want to see you and I want to be with you."

I opened my mouth to protest and then realised it would have been ridiculous. The idea of seeing Toby every week was... delightful. The problems would come when he met someone else, lost interest, or his life took him elsewhere, but I could deal with that when it happened. And, in the meantime, I could simply...simply enjoy him, an unexpected, unasked-for gift from the universe.

And, frankly, fuck everything else.

I deserved a little happiness. A little peace.

"All right."

Toby's eyes flared like twin stars. "Then congratulations, Mr. Laurence Dalziel, consultant in emergency and prehospital medicine, on your acquisition of one slightly used, but otherwise prime condition Tobermory Finch."

"Tobermory?" I asked, trying not to laugh as he swung round ☆ and straddled me.

"Call me that and I'll seriously have to kill you."

Then he kissed me, and I forgot about anything but his hot, eager mouth and his tongue pushing clumsily against mine. If he lacked finesse, he made up for it in enthusiasm and a certain ferocity. It was wet and our teeth clashed more than a few times, but—like the tie he still held—it was undeniably a claiming. And in the midst of all that damp velvet softness, I felt something else, something smooth and warm and hard gliding against me. A tongue stud? God. A rough little secret at the heart of his kiss.

I let him have his way with me, opened for him, offered myself to him, and held him close. In time, it turned a little wild, the sort of urgent, grinding kiss that I hadn't shared with anyone since Robert and I were Toby's age and hornier than we were competent. I'd forgotten how pleasurable it could be, this particular cocktail of lust and uncertainty, how liberating and intoxicating.

Heat gathered between us, between our mouths and at the places where our bodies met, where my hands touched him. Our breaths turned ragged together. And when I dragged him closer so I could drive my cloth-trapped cock between his thighs, he arched into me, moaning and frantic. It was maddening and wonderful in almost equal measure, these rough collisions of mouths and cocks and selves.

I threw him off me, and he landed on his back on the sofa, legs parting instinctively to allow me between them. I came down on top of him, catching his spare hand and pinning it against one of the cushions. His fingers curled into mine and still we kissed and writhed and clung to each other.

At last, Toby tore his mouth away from mine. "Hey. Like... hey..."

I jerked back, releasing his wrist. "Oh. Oh. God. Sorry."

"It's fine." He seized my face and pulled me into another kiss, teeth scraping my lower lip, making me groan again. "It's just...I'm still kind of ticked off at you."

I gazed down at him. He didn't sound ticked off or look it really. What he looked was thoroughly debauched, his mouth swollen, his cheeks flushed, and the blue of his eyes almost entirely lost to pupil. But then I understood, and my cock, impossibly, grew harder still. "I'm sorry." God, I was no better at being sorry than he was at being angry. My voice was thick with longing.

He folded his hands behind his head and stretched somewhat theatrically. His hoodie rode up, showing a gleam of pale skin. "That's just talk, Laurie. If you're really sorry, I think you should show me."

The words sent a dark thrill through me. I straightened. "What do you want me to do?"

He patted my hip. "Up."

It was hard not to remember our previous encounter as I got myself off the sofa and moved into the centre of the room. "All right?"

He nodded his approval—and God help me—that thrilled me too. "Yeah. Now, strip."

I glanced towards the floor-to-ceiling windows, through which the moonlight and streetlight streamed in bands of alternating orange and silver. "Can I...um...close the curtains?"

"God. Fuck. Yeah." Toby flushed and squirmed a little, which was not what I had wanted at all. "Totally."

"Thank you."

He smiled at that, still a little awkward. I crossed the room and saw to the curtains, and on the way back, he gestured me over.

I wasn't quite sure what he wanted, so I went to one knee by the sofa. "Yes, Toby?"

He sat up, crossing his legs, and for a moment, he was silent, just looking down at me. Then he leaned in and kissed me chastely. "No, seriously, thank you. You've got this... You kind of... You make me feel like a fucking prince, you know that?"

Heat rushed over me, gratitude and pleasure and a touch of embarrassment. "I-I sometimes imagine you are one."

"Oh yeah?"

I nodded.

"Like when?"

"When you were in the bath. I imagined you were...a prince and I was"—I suddenly couldn't look at him—"your slave, I suppose."

"Oh my God, really? That's so hot. What kind of a prince was I?"

"Capricious. Spoiled. A little...cruel."

"That's totally the sort of prince I would be." He sounded rather taken with the idea. "Would you mind?"

I looked up again, trying my best to keep the laughter from my voice. "Terribly."

He made a helpless little noise and pressed a hand against his cock. "Yeah?"

"Yes. I'm proud. You'd make me suffer."

"Jesus, Laurie. Don't say that shit. I nearly came."

I rested my head against his knee to hide my smile, and his fingers moved gently through my hair. "One thing at a time, hmm?"

"Yeah, but I've filed it away for later. You should beware of what you wish for."

Oh God. "I already do, darling."

He tugged on my hair, sending prickles of pleasure-pain all the way down my spine. "I hope you don't think you can sweet-talk your way out of this. You're meant to be taking your clothes off, remember?"

I gave him a look of...something. Mock disappointment maybe, but I was feeling too much that was real to manage a pretence of anything else. Then I stood on slightly shaky legs and did as he commanded. I'd stripped for Toby before, but it was different this time. Perhaps because I could no longer claim it was anonymous, or that I was merely indulging him. I wanted this, and I'd chosen it. Him.

When I was naked, trying to not shiver even though I wasn't cold, Toby peeled off his shoes and socks and rose to his feet. I half expected an inspection of some sort—it was probably what anyone else would have done—but he just spanned his hands across my chest and muttered, "Fuck, you're hot." And somehow, that flayed me so utterly that it was nearly a relief when he added, "Now, on your knees."

I went down gratefully.

"And pass me your tie and your belt."

For a moment, I was frozen, caught between instinctive surface resistance and the deeper-set, more powerful desire to do whatever he asked. Bend my will to another's pleasure.

As always, desire won, leaving me filled with a strange energy and an even stranger peace.

I'd left my clothes in a pile nearby, something only a nineteen-year-old dom would likely have let me get away with. I leaned over to pick up my tie and—

"Uh, Laurie, did I say you could use your hands?"

I shuddered, freshly aroused and freshly shamed, and bent down to lift my belt between my teeth. Toby made another of his breathless, excited noises, which gave me just enough strength to go through with it. A handful of seconds later, he was taking it from me, his thumb stroking over my lips in praise and reassurance, soothing the sting of mortification.

"Now your tie."

I struggled again, but he didn't push me or rush me, and so—somehow—I did it. The repetition didn't make it any easier, but it took me a little deeper, drew me away from myself, towards Toby and the submission I wanted to give him.

He draped my tie over a shoulder and stood for a moment, turning my belt between his fingers, sliding the end through the buckle and twisting it this way and that. "Right." He frowned. "Okay."

He didn't seem to be talking to me, but he'd given me his patience, so I gave him mine. In truth, I would have been content to wait at his feet as long as he wanted. Even the rub of the carpet was fading into the experience—the pleasure of pleasing and the sharp edge of anticipation.

"Right," he said, more decidedly this time. Then he stepped behind me, still holding my belt, and crouched down.

☆   The heat of his clothed body rushed over my naked one, and heedlessly, I leaned back, seeking him. I expected a rebuke—I surely deserved one—but his arm went round me, steadying me, holding me tight. I trembled against him, as helpless in the face of kindness as command. I turned my head a little, his name spilling from my lips before I could stop it.

His mouth grazed the corner of mine. "I'm here. Can I have your hands?"

I gave them without a thought. Just then, I would have given him anything.

I had no idea what he'd managed to do with my belt, but the cool glide of leather encircled one wrist, then the other. He pulled somewhere, and both loops tightened, cuffing me, trapping me. I drew in a short, sharp breath that seemed to bring no air to my lungs.

God. Naked and helpless. The fear went straight to my cock.

Toby kissed my neck. "This okay?"

No. No. No. But all I uttered was a breathy, lust-soaked groan. And when Toby reached around to drag his hand up the straining, dripping length of me, what I said was, "Oh yes."

He released me, and I whimpered, rocking my hips in pursuit of his touch.

"Fuck." Toby's breath was hot against the skin of my shoulder. "You're fucking amazing when you're desperate. But you don't get to come, okay? Not until you've shown me you're sorry."

Perfect. Yet again. I nodded miserably, my cock already aching.

His nails scraped lightly over a nipple, and it was all I could do not to beg. I had no idea what for, but it would have been a release, of a kind, to unravel mindlessly all over him.

Then he slipped the tie over my eyes, and I lost everything in silk and darkness. "T-Toby...I–I don't want—"

"I know." His voice shook like mine, the same mixture of excitement and trepidation.

He didn't move, holding the tie rather than knotting it, leaving me a moment to accept the powerlessness he was giving me. "I don't... I'm..." *Afraid.* But I couldn't say it. In case he stopped.

I wanted to be afraid for him.

"I know," he said again. "But I want this, so you'll let me."

I closed my eyes behind the blindfold. Darkness within darkness. "Yes."

He pulled the silk tight and tied it into place, kissed me again, and stood. I tugged at the belt wrapped around my wrists, testing. It held. That comforted and frightened me in almost equal measure, swirling into the gathering maelstrom of desire and submission.

"Laurie. I can totally see what you're doing."

What was wrong with me? I never fought, never pushed. At least not for years. Not with the strangers to whom I had given, in retrospect, so little. I had with Robert, but that had been different, part of the rhythms of what we did together. And now it was different again. Not some hollow performance or the shadow or something I'd shared with someone else.

With an effort of will, I settled. The stillness brought with it an almost unbearable awareness of myself: blind, restrained, hopelessly excited. And how good it felt, how right, to be that way.

Usually it was pain that brought me deep into my body, but tonight all it took was Toby.

"I'm sorry."

"Don't be. It totally turns me on when you struggle, but I'm not sure it'll hold. I got an F for my Design & Tech GCSE."

"They should have let you make bondage gear. You'd have got an A." I moved my wrists again but more carefully this time. "It's secure."

I heard the scrape of a zip and the drag of fabric against skin. "Yeah?"

"Yes." Of course, I couldn't see him, but I turned my face to where I thought he might be. "I'm at your mercy."

"Good. That's where I want you." The air stirred as he stepped closer. "Now show me."

Show me.

The command flared hotly across my skin, and I felt him everywhere, like a kiss or a hand on my cock, in the silk across my eyes and the leather round my wrists. And I groaned in eagerness and shame, knowing how sweet it would be to obey him, abase myself for his pleasure and deny my own.

I leaned forward, seeking him, clumsy and uncertain, desperate to please, and terribly, terribly vulnerable. He did nothing to help me, but that was right too. At last, I brushed his thigh with my cheek, and I couldn't hold back a soft sound of relief and connection. His fingers curled gently into my hair, and my heart filled with gratitude. And, suddenly, I wasn't helpless or afraid. Or rather, I was, but tucked inside all that, cocooned in my private darkness, I felt infinitely tender, warm, and safe. I felt like I was his.

I could have nuzzled my way to his cock. It was what I had intended and probably what he expected, but the impulse of the moment took me down, not up. It was awkward without my hands and perilously like falling but it seemed as foolish to cling to grace as it did to cling to pride, and I trusted he would catch me if I needed it.

As my mouth touched the arch of his foot, a shudder ran through him, and I heard him gasp.

"I'm sorry," I whispered. "I'm so very sorry."

"Holy fuck."

Beneath my lips, I could feel the individual ridges of his metatarsal bones, sleek beneath the skin. Feet had never particularly been one of my preoccupations, but these were Toby's feet, and when I touched them, he responded so very sweetly, lavishing me with murmurs and sighs, and at one point, "Oh my God, that has no right to be this good," followed by "Don't stop" because I'd had to smother my laughing against his toes, consumed by the sudden joy of simply being where I was.

I licked the taut spaces between all those fragile bones and kissed my way across his toes and up again—intermediate cuneiform, navicular, talus—until what had started off as little more than whim and humility became something more. Something I had long believed lost and forgotten.

At last, I levered myself back onto my heels and rested a moment against his thigh. The muscles of my back and upper arms were burning faintly, and the edge of the belt was pressing into my wrists, but these small aches filled me as brightly as fireflies. Because I was aching for Toby. I turned my head and kissed the side of his leg.

His hand returned, his fingers stroking me gently, sliding on the sweat that had gathered beneath the tie.

"Will you turn round?" I asked.

He stilled a moment. "Uh...yeah. I guess so."

He did it carefully, shuffling close so I didn't have to find him again, and I brushed my lips over the backs of his thighs, kisses that were not quite kisses. I learned the textures of his skin—the cool, smooth places behind his knees, the rougher, hair-stippled ones above, and then the smoothest of all, right at the tops of his thighs, where the curve of his arse began.

And I realised I didn't need my eyes to know he was beautiful. Or, from the noises he was making, to know I was pleasing him.

I dragged my tongue up the seam between his thighs, and he jumped. "Jesus. That feels obscene. Do it again."

I did, nuzzling as much as my position allowed into the supple, tender places of his flesh, making them slick and hot. He spread his legs, moaning, and thrust himself against me.

God. The things I could have done to him if I'd only had my hands.

"Toby?"

"Yeah?" It was little more than a gasp.

"Can... Will...you help me?"

"What do you want me to do?"

"Will...you hold yourself open for me? So I can... So I can—"

He actually yelped. "Fuck. No. I can't do that."

I pushed my tongue into the crease of his arse, and the sound he made this time was definitely not a yelp. He wriggled helplessly against me, his body practically begging for more, and for one terrible moment, I thought I was going to disgrace myself and come.

I pulled away, trembling, and so did he.

"God," he muttered. "I can't. I've never... I just can't."

I adjusted my position, still a little shaken, and far too conscious of the moisture that gathered at the tip of my cock and then slid tauntingly down its length. I'd been with some people who liked to give me orders I couldn't obey, simply for the excuse to shame and punish me, and I hadn't particularly objected to such games. But it had been a long time since I'd come so close to losing control.

"You don't have to do anything with me you don't want," I told him.

"Oh, I want to. It just...feels weird. Embarrassing."

"I'll never embarrass you, Toby. It's always up to you."

"But what if I'm hairy? Or I taste icky?"

"You're not hairy. I've seen you, remember. And...the thought of tasting you just nearly made me come, so I don't think you have to worry."

"Seriously?"

I kissed him rather playfully on one delicious little cheek. "Seriously."

"So like, while that's flattering, if you come, I'll be super cross."

"I know. I won't. I won't let you down." I leaned into him, ragged and needy and blissfully unashamed to be that way. "But please let me...please you. However you want."

He moaned in answer and trembled under my mouth. I kissed him again and teased him with my tongue, seducing, inch by slow inch, the reluctant line of flesh at the centre of his arse, until he was leaning forward and arching his hips to allow me deeper.

"Fuck it," he wailed. "I'm doing it."

I felt his hesitation as his hands came round, but suddenly he was open to me, and I pushed forward into all that soft, hidden heat.

Toby's whole body was rigid with anxiety. "This better feel fucking amazing."

Before he had a chance to protest or change his mind, I pressed my tongue inside him, breaching that tight ring of muscle in a single damp and ruthless thrust.

He howled and spasmed wildly, some frantic movement rippling all the way down his spine. "Omigod-it-does-feel-amazing."

From that moment, everything became blissfully impossible. Toby couldn't keep still and couldn't stay silent, and—bound as

I was—I couldn't do anything to settle him. Not that I wanted to. It was pleasure enough to kneel there and let Toby writhe and grind and fuck himself against me, moaning and babbling like he was losing his mind.

I wished I could have seen him, tousled and sweaty, twisting wildly upon my tongue.

But I could feel him, hear him, taste him.

And he tasted deeply and simply of himself, sour-sweet, and intimate.

He was panting barely coherent obscenities, but they fell upon me like kisses. I hurt—my wrists, my jaw, my knees, my balls, my cock—I hurt for him, I hurt with desire for him. But it was how he touched me, this pain he gave. How he touched me without touching, turning absence into caresses.

"I seriously wish I had another hand... My cock is going to... Oh fuck...Laurie..."

Suddenly there was nothing but his silence and his stillness. Then he shuddered uncontrollably, uttered the softest, most broken cry I'd ever heard, and...and...I wasn't entirely sure what happened next, but he was limp, sweaty, and mostly naked in my lap, his arms around me and his face pressed into my shoulder.

Oh God. Too much. Too much skin. Too much Toby.

I bucked frantically against him. Terrified I was going to fail him at the last possible second. Not sure if I was coming or coming apart. "I can't. Don't." I hardly knew what I was saying, only that I was clawing at a cliff of need, and I was going to fall. He pushed the tie away from my eyes, and I flinched, light-blinded. "Please. I can't."

"It's okay." Toby's voice was smoky from yelling, but so gentle, so very gentle. "You can."

I couldn't. I couldn't. The pleasure was tearing me to shreds.

I struggled to breathe.

To not disappoint him.

Couldn't stop the tears. Or maybe that was just the light.

Toby's eyes were a blur of blue forever.

But I did it. I held back, though it felt like dying.

Because he'd said I could, and—right then—I believed him, and it was all I needed. And he held me while I gasped and sobbed and didn't come.

Afterwards came a deep silence, nothing but our skin and slowly steadying breath. A paradox of fulfilment and frustration, and I never wanted it to end.

He did at last untangle us, though when he undid the belt and released my wrists, I groaned, for freedom just then was perilously close to loss. He tucked himself around me, and rubbed my arms until some of the stiffness eased.

"Laurie?"

"Yes?"

"Uh, do you really like those books over there? Like, are they valuable?"

I blinked through moisture-heavy lashes. "Well, sentimentally, perhaps. Why?"

"I kind of..." He picked at a bit of fluff on the carpet. "I kind of...projectile ejaculated all over them."

Sore or not, I pulled him into a hug and laughed myself breathless against the side of his neck.

"It's not funny. Have you got a tissue or something?"

"Oh, don't worry about it. Let's go to bed."

———

It was strange, after what we'd just done, to gather ourselves and go about the very ordinary business of getting ready to sleep.

Toby got me a glass of water—which I had no idea I needed, but drank almost in one go—and I got him a spare toothbrush. He watched me see to my laundry. I watched him futilely attempt to comb the tangles from his hair.

It was banal.

It was intimate.

And while I was turning off the hall light, Toby—still naked and minty-fresh—flew past me, dived into bed, and snugged himself up in the duvet until there was only his head poking out. He gave his happy little purr. "I missed your bed."

"I knew you were after something." I yanked a corner of the duvet free and climbed in next to him. My shoulders throbbed. I was going to pay for tonight, but I wouldn't regret it.

"I missed you." He rolled over and curled into a tight little ball. "Hold me like you did last time."

"Whatever your highness desires."

He laughed and wriggled into my arms, curving himself into the space of my body that seemed designed to accommodate his.

My poor cock twitched pathetically, and I stifled a whimper of thwarted longing.

"Wow, you're...really hard. And hot."

"No shit, Junior."

"And grumpy."

"See previous."

He stretched languidly, rubbing himself against me, his arse parting as sweetly as a peach around my shaft.

"God. You're cruel."

"You like it."

Tormented, entranced, I kissed the nape of his neck. "Yes." He shivered in response, goose bumps gathering instantly under my lips, and I...I broke. "Oh, Toby, please. When will you let me come?".

He didn't even hesitate. "Tomorrow. In me."

I opened my mouth to answer, and only a groan came out.

"Cruel," he murmured, "and also merciful."

"Perfect," I told him, catching his wrist and holding him tight.

"Only to you." His drowsy, husky voice. "But it's fucking amazing."

I wasn't sure if I would manage to sleep, my cock heavy with promises of tomorrow, but somehow I did, lulled to it by Toby's warmth, his steady heart, and his every long, slow exhalation.

But something roused me a few hours later. Nothing I could have identified, but somehow I knew Toby was awake beside me, his body sticky-hot and tense, his breathing not quite steady.

"Toby? Are you all right?"

He turned, burying his face against me. "Kind of... Yes... No... I don't know."

Dear God. He regretted me. I'd grovelled on my knees and sobbed in his arms, and now he despised me. I pushed away sleep and panic and my own ugly fears. "What's wrong, darling?"

He was quiet for a long time. Then, so softly I barely caught it, "I'm scared."

I wasn't sure if I should be touching him—if that was what he wanted—but I dragged my fingertips down his spine and he relaxed, just a little. "Because of what we did?"

"Yeah. Kind of."

"It wasn't what you'd imagined?" Somehow I managed to say it without cringing. What had he imagined? Some pretty fantasy, far removed from the messy reality of me in pieces at his feet.

"Oh, it was way better than I imagined." He lifted his head and repositioned himself more comfortably against my shoulder, arching into my touch. "It's just massively different to want something, and have it, y'know?"

Relief, such relief. "Yes. I do know."

"And I was just thinking that maybe wanting it means something different now."

I kept stroking him, my hands drifting over his skin like leaves on water, soothing myself as much as him. "How?"

"Because...because I really like you, Laurie."

Once again, his fearless honesty left me defenceless, and I found myself blurting out, "I really like you too," as if we were children exchanging vows in the playground.

I wasn't sure he heard me, though, because he didn't reply. He just nuzzled into me, pleasure-soft noises falling from his lips. Contentment crept through me in return. I was tired and not precisely aroused, but he had left me with a quiet awareness—of him, of my body, the needs he had fulfilled and the ones he had left to throb and burn and build inside me.

It felt strangely indulgent to be awake. Nights were for sex, sometimes, and sleeping. Blue lights and urgent skies. Death. And sudden, unlikely life. I couldn't remember the last time I'd stayed up simply to talk. Perhaps with Robert, at university, when we were young and in love and time had meant nothing.

"It's just," he said, after a while, "how will I know it's okay? Like when I put the tie round your eyes, you said you didn't want it, and"—an odd, hesitant note crept into his voice—"I did it anyway, and it turned me on. It turned me on a lot." His cock stirred between us, and he gasped and tried to shove it out of the way. "God. I'm sick."

It had been a very long time since I'd thought my sexual preferences worth questioning. And, while I understood his concerns—and, to an extent, I was glad he had them, as the alternative would have been worse—I was also faintly exasperated. Excavating one's navel for lint struck me as a futile and uniquely adolescent pastime. I didn't want him to feel guilty about what he did with me, but I didn't particularly want to analyse it either. "You know that's not true."

"I *think* it's not true. But sometimes I...forget." He sighed. "Don't you ever worry about it?"

"One of the few advantages of getting old is that you come ☆ to realise some things just aren't worth worrying about. I'm gay. Submissive, if you want to call it that. Masochistic, in my way. Some people like clay pigeon shooting or *Coronation Street*. What the fuck does it matter?"

"So, what we did tonight...what I did to you...that was really, honestly, completely okay?"

Toby Finch and the Infinite Tenacity. I steeled myself for honesty, a blunt knife for a complicated knot. "More than okay. I wanted you to blindfold me. Or rather, I didn't want you to blindfold me, but I wanted you to do it anyway. I wanted you to do whatever you wanted. That was what I wanted."

He was quiet for a while, his fingers tracing idle patterns down one of my arms, making the blood dance under my skin. "I don't know how I'd live with myself if I actually really hurt you."

I should have been expecting that. Yet somehow I wasn't. A badly healed crack in my heart split a little but did not bleed. There was only dust. "I hope," I said softly, "it would be with me, rather than without me."

"But would you still want me? Trust me?"

Would you believe I did? A shadow of the past. I closed my lips on that answer and chose another. I chose hope. "Oh yes, Toby, yes." I tightened my arms about him. "There's risk inherent in most things that matter."

"Yeah, but most people aren't tying each other up and stuff."

"Physicals risks. Emotional risks. Who's to say where the lines are?"

For a little while we said nothing. It was enough simply to touch and be touched, to feel the heat of him beneath my hands, the roughened patches on his skin and the smoothness of the rest, and softly ache.

☆   "You really get it, don't you?" he whispered. "Get me."

I should have told him I didn't know him. That this was simply sexual compatibility. But instead: "I've had a long time to think about these things, and believe me, there are many ways of thinking, but the way you spoke to me at the club? You didn't give me much choice."

He gave a muffled little groan. "Urgh, don't remind me. I was such an idiot."

"You were irresistible." The words were out before I could stop them. Utterly sentimental, none the less so for being true. I'd forgotten the aftermath of submission sometimes had the power to do this to me.

In answer, he slid a knee gently between my thighs and increased the pressure until I swallowed a groan. "How do I know you're not just *indulging* me?"

I should have known he wouldn't let me escape my earliest transgression. My first lie. I couldn't have repeated it now, even if I'd wanted to. "I shouldn't have said that. It was cowardly. And wrong. And...not true." The merciless little bastard had got me hard again. And with no hope of release until morning. Unless I begged? God.

I caught the gleam of his grin in the darkness. "You'll just have to prove it to me."

His leg nudged at me tauntingly until resistance crumbled, and I began to move with him, desire mingling sweetly with despair. "Anything. I'll do anything." And just then, I meant it.

"I'll hold you to that."

"God...Toby..."

"Something you want?"

"Getting to come might be nice," I muttered.

He laughed and tucked himself in even tighter. "You're extra tormentable when you're grumpy."

I gritted my teeth and lay there, anguished with wanting. His fingers skated lightly over my chest. Found a nipple to circle like vultures. I teetered, desperate to be touched, desperate to stop him. "Oh fuck. Fine. Please. Is that what you want to hear?"

"Please what?"

"Please let me come. I don't care...how. Just...please. I really need to—"

"Nope." Such awful, beautiful glee. "I just wanted to hear you beg. Wanted to know what it sounded like."

"Did it live up to your expectations?"

"Well, it was kind of grudging. So I'd give it maybe two out of ten."

I wasn't sure whether or not to be insulted. I caught his wicked hand and brought his fingers to my lips to kiss them. "Then you'll have to try harder."

"Or you will."

"You know"—God, what was I saying?—"there's a box in the spare room. I think... I think there's something in there you could use to...to..."

"To what?"

"Make sure I didn't—" I felt hot and awkward in the darkness. This was certainly a new level of something. Asking for a chastity device. "It would ensure my obedience."

"God, no. I'm not *helping* you." Toby's hand slid between ☆ us, enclosed me blissfully, and the sound I gave him was pure, heedless gratitude. "And I like being able to touch you when I feel like it."

"What if I come by accident?" I might have actually whined.

"Well, we'll figure that out when you do. Either way, it's going to be fun." He was quiet a moment, still holding my cock with maddening tenderness. "Um, this is kind of a whole lot more than you kneeling on the floor while I wank. Are you absolutely sure we don't need a safeword?"

It was getting increasingly difficult for me to think at all, let alone keep up with him as he jumped from topic to topic, from instinctive control to confessed uncertainty. "Yes, I'm sure."

"But aren't we supposed to?" He let me go, and while my body regretted him, my mind cleared a little.

"They don't come round and check, Toby. Confiscate our sex licences." His silence suggested he wasn't amused, and I realised I was being too glib. Taking too much for granted. "If it would make you feel safe, then of course, we can have a safeword."

"Fuck *my* safety." He whacked a hand against my shoulder. "You're the one who comes off worst if something goes bum end up over a barrel."

"And you think," I asked as patiently as I could, "a magic word is going to protect me?"

He sat up abruptly, dragging away the duvet and much of our shared warmth with him. "I don't think you're taking this seriously."

"I take your comfort very seriously indeed."

"And I feel the same way about yours. The fact you think I don't is, like, fucking insulting, Laurie."

It should have been absurd—a nineteen-year-old worrying about my safety. But all I felt was helplessly touched by it. "Oh, darling." I caught his face between my hands and pulled him into a kiss, our bodies falling together once more. "Safewords are useful—necessary even—when you play with strangers, but the rest of the time, I–I don't know."

Light was beginning to creep into the room. Toby was a pale punctuation mark on my dark sheets. I swept my hand from his shoulder to his thigh, learning his curves and angles, his harmonies and awkwardnesses. Beautiful. And, in this moment, mine. He shivered sweetly under my touch. "Wouldn't it stop you getting hurt, though?"

"Believe me, the things that have hurt me in my life have had nothing to do with whips or chains."

His hand groped beneath the duvet and found mine, his fingers curling protectively round me. "I just don't want to...do anything bad to you. Like ever."

What could I do with a boy who had brought me to my knees twice, yet still held my hand in the dark? What could I give in return for such kindness? Such faith? I would so gladly bear all the pain he gave me, intended and incidental, and the loss of him when his inclinations took him elsewhere. "You might, but I trust you, Toby."

He was silent for a very long moment. And then, very solemnly, "I trust in your trust," leaving me naked and breathless, bound and on my knees all over again.

Unable to find a sensible answer, or at least one that wasn't too much, too revealing, I babbled. "It's my responsibility to communicate to you what I'm feeling and what's too much, and it's your responsibility to be receptive to that communication. I don't necessarily believe the best way for that to happen is me saying 'banoffee pie.'"

"That's your safeword, is it?" asked Toby, when he had finished laughing at me.

It had been largely an accident, but the lighter mood came as something of a relief. My wary heart and my sense of self-preservation could only countenance so many truths and confessions. "Yes. 'Lemon meringue pie' to slow down, 'banoffee pie' to stop. I'm not particularly keen on lemons—though I can tolerate them—but I really hate bananas."

"Oh man, you just haven't had the right lemon meringue pie."

I was smiling foolishly, even though he couldn't see it. "I'd eat lemon meringue pie for you, darling. Any day."

"If you tasted my lemon meringue pie, you'd get down on your knees and thank me for it. People do, you know. Well, not the knees part. But they tell me it's the best they've ever had."

"That's a low bar."

He gave an outraged little squeak. "You are so going to regret that."

"I look forward to...regretting it."

"God, Laurie, you fucking kill me." He arched into me, moaning, his suddenly very hard cock sliding against the groove of my hip.

I swallowed a gasp. "Oh, to be nineteen again."

"It's not funny. You think I like being perma-horny? How am I supposed to sleep now?"

"You don't have to sleep. Use me." Invitation. Command. Plea. "Let me help you."

He stopped squirming for a moment. "You mean I get to come twice, and you not at all?"

"Revel in your power, princeling."

"And you don't mind?"

"I mind not coming. I mind a lot."

"Ha-ha, not that. You're stuck with that. Like you don't...mind me...all the time?"

God. He really had no idea. "It would be my delight and my

privilege to get you off whenever you want in whatever manner you want." I'd been going for dryly humorous. It didn't last. "It'll drive me insane...but God...yes, please. Take your pleasure from me."

There was a power too at the heart of powerlessness, and he had never once withheld it or denied me. If anything, he had lavished me, drowned me, seduced me utterly with it—my power to affect him, arouse him, satisfy him.

"Yes." The word was little more than a rough sigh.

I wrapped a hand around him, his cock jerking at my touch. "Do you want my palm? My mouth? My body?"

"Oh fuck. Wow." He scrambled off me, and this time, there was more than enough heat between us to leave me full of warmth and wanting. "Grab the headboard."

I reached up and closed my hands around one of the crossbars. The carvings were intricate but smooth. It was partly why I'd chosen the bed and something I'd almost forgotten until now.

"I love the way you look when you're all stretched out."

I shivered, taut and—in some very small way—vulnerable. Toby knelt over me, his thighs enclosing me, and dragged his cock over my lips. It was a sensation I'd always found compelling in its contradictions, soft skin and blunt pressure, at once tender and intrusive. I was eager to taste him, to please him, but I let him force me to it.

"Open. Oh...shit...wait... Do I need a condom?"

"Fuck the condom." Knowing better, apparently, did not preclude actually giving a damn. I wanted him, and I wanted him bare.

"I haven't... I'm like totally—"

"Please, Toby, just let me suck your fucking cock."

And then he was inside, with a groan. He didn't give me much chance to adjust, but I let him take everything: my mouth, my breath, control. He didn't brutalise me, but his eagerness was its own roughness and claimed me just as surely. He came in less than a minute in a crescendo of breath, babbling wildly, his cock nudging the back of my throat and his body shuddering above me, all skin and shadows, making me wish I'd thought to turn a light on so I could see him properly.

He collapsed next to me, leaving me gasping and full of the taste of him. Then he rolled into his usual ball and tucked himself in tightly, nestling against my once again painfully desperate cock.

"That was awesome. Like...best ever. Wish I'd been able to make it last more than a nanosecond."

I pressed my tongue against the corners of my mouth, gathering up the last traces of him. "My pleasure. Always. And...thank you."

He twisted round to look at me. "For what?"

"For"—I kissed him lightly, my lips still throbbing a little—"letting me suffer for you."

He said something that sounded like *ngh*, cuddled, if possible, even closer, and once again, we slept.

I woke close to midday with a strange, jittery, Christmas-morning feeling. And then remembered why. Toby was stretched out on his front, legs and arms spread like a wanton starfish. Very quietly, I groped around in the top drawer of the bedside table until I found a tube of lube and a condom. When I was ready, I covered him with my body and slid a slick finger into him.

"Good morning, darling. You owe me, and I intend to collect."

"Oh fuck, yeah." His voice was hoarse from sleep and burgeoning excitement, and he spread his legs even wider, bucking up against me. "Yeah."

The muscle was a little tense, but I eased him and aroused him and got two fingers into him while he twisted and gasped and pressed himself into my touch. He was bed-warm and supple, a sprawl of floppy hair and languid limbs, and he smelled of sleep and sex and a little bit of me.

I kissed the tops of his shoulders—he had some acne there as well, small constellations of bright stars—and the back of his neck through the fall of his hair, fucking him with my fingers until he was writhing, breathless, and incoherent.

"Fuck. Yeah. That's good. That's so good." Though when I nudged him with the head of my cock, he cried out sharply. "Wait, wait, want to see you. Let me see you."

"Any way you want me."

I rose to my knees and dragged him onto his back. He flung his legs around me as I thrust into him, without finesse, without control, my breath falling harsh and ragged against his skin. I'd prepared him, but his groan had an edge of pain, and through the haze of desperation, I flinched for him and at myself. I hesitated, deep in his body, trying to be more careful, but then he threw back his head and arched his body, offering himself to me.

"Yeah, yeah, like that, just like that." His voice caught in the impossible space between command and supplication. "Come on, Laurie, fuck me. Fuck me. Really want it."

Undone again, I obeyed.

I seized his wrists in one hand and pinned them over his head, stretching his body into a line of heat and urgency, and fucked him, hard and fast and frantic, holding him there against me, under me, so I could somehow bear it, all the pleasure, relief, and sheer extraordinary joy. Not a reward for last night's submission and humility and denial, but a part of it, an extension. A culmination.

"Touch me," panted Toby, twisting beneath me. "Want your hand on me."

And of course, I did. I would have done anything he told me. Anything he wanted. His every delirious command was a spark beneath my skin. And I was going to ignite like a phoenix.

His cock was hot and damp, straining between our bodies, and he came with a ragged cry the moment my knuckles clumsily brushed him there. I fucked him through it, my responses lost in his and his in mine, along with all the boundaries of give and take, dominance and submission, conquest and surrender. Leaving only us and this, our bodies locked in ecstasy.

He gave a final, shuddery groan and went utterly pliant, his eyes opening after a moment to focus hazily on me. "Your turn. Want to watch you come apart."

So I gave him that as well. Those last ragged moments of clinging to control, to self, to anything, and then the helpless fall. The pleasure was starless, annihilating and terrifying, the deepest surrender of all.

Soft touches—Toby's hands on my shoulders, his mouth at my brow, the warmth of his breath—brought me slowly back. He held me through my silence and my shaking, murmuring things I shouldn't have needed to hear, until I felt at least a little like myself again.

And while I lay in bed—my mind and body temporarily soothed to still water—he made me eggs and brought me tea. Showed me the bruises I'd left upon his wrists and, grinning, made me kiss them.

He left not long after. I didn't think to ask him to stay, but everything was quiet without him. I wandered around the house in my dressing gown, a stranger of the moment, lost and almost at peace.

I thought about catching up with my reading, except Toby had left his mark even there, albeit accidentally. Not over my journals, thank God, but in a wild splash across *The Acceptance World*, *Books Do Furnish a Room*, and *Temporary Kings*. For some reason—though it shouldn't have—it made me smile.

I carried the books into the kitchen—left contrastingly spotless by Toby—with the vague intention of cleaning them. They'd been Robert's favourites all the time we'd been together, and I'd failed repeatedly to get into them, even taking *A Question of Upbringing* to Iraq in the hope I would be desperate enough to care. But I had loved that he loved them. I liked listening to him quote them and talk about them, leaning close to me, a laughing fanatic, trying to share his passion.

He could have only have left them to forget. And I could only have kept them to remember. Bundling up the whole twelve-volume set, I took them to a charity shop, returning from a grey afternoon to a house that seemed to be full of new spaces waiting for Toby to fill them.

At least on Monday the realities of life and death would take over, and I would not have to think about him until he was here again.

6
TOBY

Oh my God, I can't stop thinking about him. My days go by in this blur of not-Laurie, his finger marks fading on my wrist. I feel stupidly fairy tale about everything, but at least this time he hasn't dumped me on the cold hill side and buggered off. I can get back to his magic kingdom where I'm a prince and I'm happy and so very, very seriously, expertly fucked.

Swoony sigh.

I'm totally crap at work. I burn things, I under-cook things, I forget how everybody likes their eggs, as if Laurie is now the only egg-eater in my universe. I try to make a carrot cake without any carrots. I refill all the sugar shakers with salt and don't notice until a cabbie spits up a mouthful of tea.

I get a bollocking from Joe, but he doesn't fire me. Just threatens me with it a bunch of times, which is, y'know, pretty usual. He probably actually won't because Hairy's still in this insane boot thing that makes him look like a robot, and I'm probably just as good at cooking as he is. Cheaper too, since I've got no qualifications and no experience, so I'm still on the minimum wage. Which wouldn't keep a frugal monkey in Tesco-value peanuts.

Not that it matters because I'm still living with Mum anyway. Like the loser I am.

I've thought about saying something to Joe, but I'm kind of afraid it'll backfire. Currently I'm doing everything, which is hard, but it's still way better than someone else doing all the cooking and me doing all the shitwork. So if I push too hard, I might lose what I've got. And I'm not sure I could stand it because it's already so fucking little.

I'm just...

I don't know. I don't know what I'm supposed to be. Or how I find out.

And it'll be Easter soon, so I'll have to see all my mates from school again. I say *all* as if there's loads, but there's some, and they're kind of totally different now, totally changed. Like life is really happening for them and taking them places, while I'm still here, still the same. Maybe even going backwards, because they'll all do the university thing and have careers, and I'll be...I'll be what? Washing dishes.

I used to be exactly where they are. Except it wasn't what I thought it was going to be.

Sometimes I kind of fantasise about walking out right in the middle of one of Joe's rants. It makes me feel awesome for about five seconds, and then I get terrified because I have no fucking clue what comes next. I mean, *couldn't be a lawyer* is one thing. *Couldn't keep a shitty job in a shitty caff* is epic suck.

So I just get on with things. Every day, I wake up and get on with things, and time ticks on. It's easier now Laurie's in the picture. The week lasts forever, but it has this structure now. This reward waiting for me that makes it all worthwhile. Of course, Joe's regulars take the piss out of me because I'm so starry and ditzy. But I don't care because it means I get to hang out the serving hatch and talk about my boyfriend.

My boyfriend.

My amazing, sexy boyfriend who is a doctor—no, a *consultant* actually.

(Who gets on his knees for me, fucks me into a pile of wet tissue, and doesn't come until I say he can. Though of course I don't talk about that stuff. Not because I'm ashamed, but because, first off, it's ours, and second, some of the regulars are pretty old and it might literally kill them.)

I know Laurie gave me all this bullshit about how he wasn't my boyfriend, but the way I see it: we've had sex a bunch of times, talked about deep shit, he actually seems to like me for some weird reason of his own, I've cooked him food, stayed over at his place, and I have a standing invitation to go back there. If it walks, talks, and quacks like a boyfriend, it's a boyfriend, right? And it's not like he's ever going to find out what I call him to a bunch of East Enders.

The best times are the afternoons when Joe isn't breathing down my neck about how worthless I am, the caff is quiet, and I'm doing the next day's baking. It gives me time to daydream, which probably explains the Great Carrot Cake That Wasn't, but honestly I just really like baking. It's a welcome relief to know I'm definitely good at something. I don't have any hearth-and-home-type memories of it. I think I'm supposed to have been lovingly taught by a doting old person, but I've just kind of picked it up as I've gone along, and that's good memories too. Also, there's Mary Berry who is like the best person ever. I mean, I don't know her personally or anything, but she's on TV all the time so it's like I do.

I have to make simple stuff, otherwise there's rioting. I tried mille-feuille once, and they came out really well, just like they're supposed to, but everyone was like, "What the fuck is this French shit?" So it's cupcakes and Victoria sponge and carrot cake and coffee cake. And the occasional lemon meringue pie. But I've promised myself that the next one of those I make will be for Laurie. Oh man, the thoughts I have. Filthy and delicious and probably not compliant with food hygiene standards. I know I'm supposed to be converting him to Team LMP, but God, I'd love to lick lemon curd from his skin while he shakes and gasps and fights and tries not to come.

Ngh. Ridiculously fucking gorgeous man. How did I get so lucky?

If this is my consolation prize for totally ruining my life, I'm pretty fucking consoled.

The other big advantage of Joe's is that nobody really cares ☆ what I'm doing as long as things are clean, there's food happening, and it tastes good, so I whip up a random batch of red velvet cupcakes. I'm going to take them to the hospice for Granddad and his friends. He's actually my great-granddad, but since I don't have any others and it's kind of a mouthful, I've always just called him Granddad. He's *really* my favourite person in the world. No offence to Mary Berry.

And, well, he's kind of dying. He's got cancer. All the cancer. But he's ninety-four. So, if you're going to get cancer, we reckon that's probably about the best time to get it. And I know it probably sounds a bit weird to be taking a bunch of bad-for-completely-healthy-people cupcakes to a hospice full of the fragile and terminally ill, but that's kind of the point. The worst has already happened. They might as well have whatever they like. There's this whole thing over there about dying as, like, a person, with dignity and love and, y'know, cupcakes.

I remember when we first took Granddad in, I was shit scared it was going to be this hospital place, smelling of disinfectant and dead people. But we'd just got him settled in his room—number nine—when a nurse came in and asked him if he'd like a drink.

Just like he was in a hotel or a guest in her house or something. It was kind of the last thing we were expecting, so he wanted to know what they had, and she told him he could have anything.

"I'll have a sherry, then," said Granddad, just for a joke.

And they totally got him one. Not his usual type, but they made sure they had that in for him the very next day.

And that was the moment I knew it was going be okay. I mean, no, it's not going be okay. My granddad is going to die, and that's going to be really, really sad. And when he's gone, I'll be a bit more alone in the world. But it's going to be okay for him. Because the horrible stuff, the tests, the treatments, the hospitals, the long words and the lack of information, the too-busy doctors and the people who can't remember his name... that's over.

And all that's left for him to do is live. Until he stops.

And eat my cupcakes.

He's frail these days, really frail. But he seems all right. Sad and in pain sometimes, but all right. They make sure most of his days are good days. And I think his mind isn't quite... I don't know. Like he's still there, he's still my granddad, but I think he's losing time a bit. Recent stuff confuses him. Which is probably for the best, because it means I don't have to explain to him about me and university and all the rest of it.

It means the last things he remembers about me won't be the ways I've failed him.

I'm totally going to tell him about my boyfriend, though. I know he'll remember that.

He was the first person I came out to. Not the first person who knew I was gay—I guess my mum knew all along—but the first person where the telling mattered. I was kind of accidentally out at school, after the business with my best mate, and some of the kids were shitty to me about it and some of them weren't and some of them were shitty to me for totally different reasons, because, let's face it, school is kind of an institutionalised shittiness generator. Like the Stanford prison experiment.

The way I see it, and this is what I tell myself all the time, if you're bothered, like actually really bothered, that I fall for men, not women, then we're not going to be friends anyway. So fuck you.

But it's different when you love someone and their love is the best thing you have.

Also, it's a generational thing. Like they were raising them racist and sexist and homophobic back in the 1920s or whatever. I mean, they still are, but there's at least a certain amount of social understanding that it's supposed to be a bad thing. Like if somebody is randomly homophobic at me, they'll at least look sheepish and then give me this speech about how they're not actually a homophobe because Reasons. But my great-grandmother genuinely used to call black people the word you're never ever supposed to say if you're white. She didn't think she was being racist. She just thought that was what black people were called. Yeah. Awkward.

Probably a good thing she's dead. I'm kidding. Well, she is dead. But I was quite young at the time so it wasn't a big deal. Like, for me. It probably was for her. And Granddad. But since they didn't seem to like each other very much, who knows? Grown-up relationships are a complete mystery to me. I don't know at what point you go from being in love and bonking to not really talking about anything and being mildly annoyed with each other all the time. But at no point remembering that you chose to be with that person in the first place. Although actually I have a pretty small sample size. The Finch family can't keep men.

It's our curse or something. And I hope to fuck I haven't got it, or it doesn't count if you're gay, because now I've got a man of my own, I bloody well want to hang on to him.

But, anyway, once Great-Grandma snuffed it, Granddad started going dancing again.

That was how you got laid back in the day, and he used to totally rock at it but then the war happened, and then he was married and stuff, so it was like this amazing thing for him to suddenly have dancing again. Like a bit of lostness coming back to him after all these years. And he taught me. Really patiently because I'm a bit of a klutz. He didn't actually say it was for getting laid (though I'm telling you the implication was there). He said it was how a gentleman wins a lady's heart. An important life skill.

And so I told him. I said, "Does it still work if a gentleman wants to win a gentleman's heart?"

He was quiet a moment.

And my own heart was like *thudump-thudump-thudump*. To the rhythm of *ohfuck-ohfuck-ohfuck*.

And then Granddad said, "Definitely."

So I was a regular twinkle toes after that. Commitment. ☆ Quickstep is my favourite. It's so good, so light and elegant, like you're both flying.

I'd love to dance with Laurie. Anything. But especially that.

After I clean up and we close up, I stick the cakes in a box and head for Saint Anthony's. It's out in North London, so out of my way, but seriously, he's my granddad, who's counting? I go to see him pretty much every other day. That's another great thing about the hospice. It's not like hospital where they hate you turning up and getting in the way, and only let you in for like two minutes and sixteen seconds when Mercury is in retrograde.

You're always welcome at the hospice. It's so full of people being together. You can even stay over if you want to, or need to, or if you're scared.

It's the closest thing I know to what family means.

As I sit on the emptying, darkening Tube, I suddenly realise that if I hadn't come unstuck, I probably wouldn't have been able to do this at all. I'm honestly pretty messed up about university—and this black hole of a future I've made—but maybe what I did was to gift myself this: these last few days with Granddad.

It's dark when I get to the hospice, but that's okay because it's light inside. And I can hear music playing, people talking. Everybody knows my name. Not just the staff, but the volunteers and the families. I sort of miss some of the people who used to come here, which is weird, I guess, but you get close quickly. And you don't tell when you catch each other crying.

Soon I've given away nearly all of my cakes, and I take the rest up to Granddad because he's up in his room.

He's been in his room a lot lately.

It's not one of his best days, but that's okay.

That's okay.

The nurses helped me make the place really nice. So maybe it wouldn't look, y'know, temporary. There's always flowers in the window. And it's full of photographs and his favourite things, small stuff that's just always been around him, but I don't really know much about or why he has it. Like this battered wooden box he's got that somebody carved for him. And these medals he likes to have near but never looks at. And a lot of crap I made him when I was a kid, like this mug in pottery class and this deformed pom-pom parrot from having to do needlework because I was too sissy for woodworking.

They used to rip the piss out of me at school because when

you had to draw your family, it was always me and Granddad. And sometimes Mum. But apparently this was weird and wrong and not the way it's supposed to be.

Looking back, I just think they can go fuck themselves. I mean, I wouldn't actually say that to them. They were like six. But if I ever have a kid of my own, and maybe someday I will—I hope so—I'm not going to raise them like that. Believing the shape of their world is the only shape for the world to be. Well, I guess the poor bastard won't have much choice. They'll be starting life with two dads after all.

But Granddad's still got all those pictures. There's like a whole series of us on Primrose Hill, one for every season, stick figures in scarves and sun hats. And there's the first poem I ever wrote. It's lovingly hand illustrated, and cut out with the special scissors that do crinkly edges, and it's called "Frogs." It goes like this:

☆
Frogs
Leaping in and out of the pond.
Hop hop hop hop HOP.

That's some deep shit right there, man. Everybody acted like I was a total genius when I wrote it. It's probably the single most successful thing I've ever done. I mean, yeah, it's crap, but I was what? Five? I think I was the only one there who got that a poem was a different sort of way of writing. For ages, I actually thought I was going to be a poet when I grew up. The same way Mum's an artist.

But then I noticed the fundamental flaw in the plan, which was basically that I sucked.

☆
The weird thing is, I do kind of get poetry. A bit. Maybe in an

idiot-savant way, since I probably osmoted it in the womb and early childhood, because the only books Mum owns are art books and poetry books. But that's how I was able to recognise my own suck before anybody had to sit down and tell me.

Without Granddad, I wonder what's going to happen to all this nonsense. All this stuff only he cares about.

God, way to make it all about me. But it doesn't mean anything to anyone except him. And if it doesn't mean anything, it's nothing. Which means...so am I.

I take my shoes and socks off and sit on the end of his bed. Granddad's resting at the moment. He sounds all wheezy, but not like he's in pain, and I find myself sort of breathing along with him, like I'm helping or something.

Of course, the moment he wakes up, which doesn't take long because he doesn't sleep that deeply, just kind of a lot, he says I shouldn't have let him nap through my visit. And then I'm all like, "Yeah, you've made me late for my dinner with the Queen," and we go on from there.

He tells me he's feeling good, which is probably a lie.

I tell him the snowdrops will be out soon. We used to pretend we'd see them again together some day, but we don't anymore.

I tell him that Mum's doing this exhibition in a disused railway arch.

I tell him I've added cider vinegar to the cream cheese frosting on my red velvet cupcakes.

He tells me he'll let me know what he thinks. I don't think he's got the energy to eat one right now.

But that's okay.

That's okay.

I ask if he wants anything, but he doesn't. I get him some ☆ fresh water anyway. Because you always need water, right?

We talk a bit about some of the people we know here. You don't really call them friends. They're kind of something else, more and less than that.

It's really weird the way you can have everything in the world to say, and fuck-all. And I can see he's starting to drift again.

"Granddad?"

He blinks at me a bit. He's all in his eyes right now. That's where he lives. Not in his body anymore, which is just hollow skin. "Toby?"

"I've kind of met someone."

He lights up for me, and I smile right back at him.

"Who?" he asks. "Where? Not on the whatsit...the interweb."

Great. My granddad's a meme. "No, at a..." Oh shit. Shit. Kinky sex club? "Uhh...party. His name's Laurence. Laurence Dalziel."

"Like *Dalziel and Pascoe*?"

"Huh?" He breathes in a particular sort of way that I know is what's left of his laugh, so I let it go. It's probably some old person reference I'm never going to get. "Anyway, I call him Laurie." Casually ignoring the fact that I had to beg and whine for the privilege. It was totally worth it. "He's...really nice. Clever and funny and kind and handsome."

I'm simplifying of course. I'm starry-eyed, not completely mind-controlled. I mean, Laurie is all those things (well, not so much on the handsome, but you don't say "hot" to your grand-dad), but he's also...other things, as well. More complicated things. And weirdly, that just makes me like him more. Or want to, anyway. If he'd let me. If he'd give me enough so I could.

"He's a doctor. And you know those fairy tale houses round Primrose Hill? He lives in one. I mean, not at Primrose Hill. But one of those type of houses. The white ones. Isn't that totally weird?"

It was my favourite game when I was a kid. We'd walk past these sugar-cake houses on the way to the park, and I'd tug on his hand and go, "Who do you think lives there?" And he'd say, "A sailor who met a mermaid who gave him a pearl the size of a cantaloupe." And then we'd go on a bit further, and he'd point at one and say, "But who lives there, Toby?" and I'd say, "The prince of a kingdom trapped in a marble."

The truth is way better than any of it. Even though it's just a man called Laurence Dalziel.

"But how's his dancing?" asks Granddad.

He makes me grin, the cheeky old bugger. "Steady on. I haven't asked. Can't have him thinking I'm only after one thing. But honestly, I'd still like him if he had all the left feet in the universe. When I'm with him...it's like..." I have no idea how to explain this. Partly because it's sort of connected to kinky sex and partly because it sort of isn't. "*Zing*, you know?"

"Strings of your heart, eh?"

I nod, feeling a bit of a dork. I'd really liked that song when I was little. It sounded how I thought being in love ought to be: all bright and brassy and full of joy. ☆

In any case, Granddad seems pleased. "That's...good to hear."

I think he wants to say more, but he can't quite get the words out. I give him some water. And I know what he's probably going to tell me anyway. The truth is, my granddad's a pretty biased man. He thinks I'm this astonishing, talented, wonderful person, in spite of all available evidence to the contrary. But that's sort of what love is, I guess. A perpetual state of semideranged partiality. And I think he's sort of worrying that, without him, I'll have nobody to feel like that about me.

So I say, "Laurie gets me, Granddad. He really does." I mean, okay, he's not going to keep my frog poetry. But the least understandable bit of me—the part that wants to make him suffer and cry and beg because I like him—he understands. And that's not nothing. Hell, it's practically something. "I think you'd like him."

"Well. We've definitely got something in common."

"Huh?"

"You...you plonker."

I laugh. It's a good day when you're being called a plonker by your granddad.

But that's also when I realise Laurie is never going to meet my granddad.

Because my granddad is going to die, and Laurie isn't really my boyfriend. I can tell him to get on his knees for me, I can tell him to fuck me, but I can't bring him here. I can't introduce him to the person I love most in the world. And I can't expect him to be there when I lose that person for good.

Granddad's looking pretty tired, so we don't talk much after that. When he first got ill, I used to read to him a lot, but when we kind of realised he wasn't going to get better, we quietly gave up on novels. He likes whodunits but imagine how rubbish it would be if he died...like...in the middle, never ever knowing whodunit. Now I read him poetry. Just so he has some words to take with him, and my voice to keep him company in the dark.

I read him *Rapture*. Or bits of it anyway, which you probably shouldn't do because it's meant to be a cycle, but I want him to have only the love and not the loss, which is wrong again because you have to have both. Except I can do this for him now because he's dying. Because the loss is already happening.

I like the poems at the beginning best. The poems at the end scare me a bit. But I guess if you want "You," there has to be an "Over." And for every "Hour," there's "Grief."

I think of Laurie while I'm reading.

I wonder what it's like to be in love and—zing aside—how I'll know. If this could be love. Or if it's just sex and infatuation. And if it matters.

I know I've only been with him twice. That I hardly know the guy.

But I also don't know how you fall in love, except by wanting to. So maybe that'll do. For now, anyway.

I see Laurie on Sunday this week because I had to work the weekend, but the moment I get through his door, he pins me against the wall, and we end up fucking in the hallway.

Because that's just how we roll.

It's so good, the way he touches me, like he's been waiting for me all week, and everything comes spilling out of me, how happy I am to see him, how much I've missed him, and how much I want him, along with about eighty gallons of come. Which means my clothes end up in the washer, and me in the bath, him with me this time, and I float hazily in the water and under his hands. It's only when I'm standing on his doorstep at half past five the next morning, because he has to go to work, that I realise that the time is gone. And Laurie too, back to the rest of his life. Leaving me sore and happy and empty all at once.

And next week: rinse and repeat, with, y'know, a few variations, which are mainly how and where we fuck.

And it's not that I don't want what we're doing. Because I do. I want it so much I can hardly think straight. And it's not like we don't talk. Because we do. And it's not that he's not nice to me. Because he is. He's nicer to me than basically anyone who doesn't have to be because family and shit.

But it's like there's a line in his head or something. And I can have everything up to the line. But nothing after it. I've seen glimpses over it. The night we met. The night he scraped me off his doorstep. Sometimes after sex when he lets me hold him. Enough, basically, to make me want to live there, on the other side of him.

Except I don't know how to get there. And I'm afraid of pushing—again—in case I lose what I've got.

This is turning out to be the theme of my fucking life. The thing is, there's nothing I can put my finger on. There's nothing for me to complain about. No way for me to challenge him. The best I can do is hope for those moments when he forgets the line is there, and make him feel so safe, so perfect, so fucking cherished that he'll never want to cross back. So he'll see that this is where it's real.

But the only way I have of getting there is sex.

Which, y'know, is okay. If I've learned anything, it's how to work with what I've got. And, let's face it, the sex is *a-maz-ing*.

I like it all the ways we can imagine—and he can imagine a lot—but I like it best when I'm on my back, so I can look up at him and touch him, and we can kiss, softly or savagely or however we like. Sometimes I kind of hold his lower lip between my teeth so I hurt him while he makes me come. It makes him go fucking feral and then helpless, utterly helpless, his body enslaved to the simplest touch of mine.

Once, when we were going at it sort of slowly, for the togetherness of it, our bodies becoming one in slick, deep strokes, I reached up and put my hand against his throat, not pressing or anything, just resting there, and the sound he made. Jesus. It came into me like his cock. And all he said was, "Oh, Toby," but it was the way he said it. His voice breaking as if I'd finally touched his heart. Except afterwards, it was sealed up tight again. Out of my reach. As usual.

So, in another week or so, I wait until after, when he's quiet and lax and soft-eyed, and ask him straight: "Laurie, are you doing this with anyone else?"

He rolls over with a groan. "No, darling, I'd probably be in hospital."

Well. So far, so good. "Do you want to?"

"Why? Plans to share me?"

He says it in this totally laconic way—as if it's a perfectly reasonable fucking suggestion—but even the idea of it makes my heart clench like a fist. *Mine.* "No!"

He laughs.

And now I feel ridiculous. Gauche and on the wrong side of the line. As if I've been set up somehow. I nearly abandon the whole conversation. I hate it when he does this. When he pretends the things that matter to me—the things he gives me—are small.

"So, uh..." Fuck, how do you say this stuff? "Um...if we're like exclusive, does that mean we...can ditch the condoms?"

"I don't see why not," he says. In this bored way.

I'd somehow imagined that this might have been romantic. More of that husky-voiced *I trust you, Toby* stuff I'd got when I'd been scared of hurting him. I tried to match his tone. "Uh, cool."

What now? Do we lovingly exchange STI tests?

I lie there, awkward and uncertain until finally Laurie offers, "I was tested after Christmas, and I haven't slept with anyone but you since then."

Well. We're definitely exchanging *something*. It feels embarrassing, though. Dirty, in some way I can't quite understand and definitely don't like. Not so much the sex, or the implication of sexual history, but the fact there's a fucking health-and-safety checklist. This is about intimacy. It's not...pulling out of a parking space into single-lane traffic.

Mirror.

Indicators.

Condom.

Also, I'm going to have to 'fess up to my lack of sexual shenanigans. "I–I've been with three people, not counting you. We
always, y'know, used stuff."

"For all forms of intercourse?"

Omg. Now I never want to have sex again. Mortified, I
mumble, "Yeah."

"Then I'm sure it's fine."

"You're sure it's fine?" I sit up, kind of startled, and he makes
a noise of protest as I accidentally disturb the duvet, leaving his
back exposed...and the marks I've left there. "You're supposed to
be a doctor. Is that what you tell your patients? 'Hmm, there's a
weird blob on this MRI scan, but *I'm sure it's fine.*'"

"I am a doctor—" His voice is different now. Not apathetic at
all. Which makes me slightly pissed at him for the earlier nonsense. "But I've still had your cock down my throat and my tongue
up your arse. So it appears my desire to fuck you and please you
has consistently overwhelmed any politically correct concerns."

Okay, I'm not pissed anymore. Now I'm just worried. "Laurie."
I slide a hand over the curve of his shoulder. "Aren't we supposed
to be careful?"

He turns onto his back, and he's laughing. But it's a nice
laugh. Not the sort that makes me feel silly. "Come here, you
ridiculous, wonderful boy."

He cups a hand around the back of my neck and pulls me
down into a kiss. He doesn't kiss me so much when we're not
doing it, so it's unexpected. And good. So fucking good. It lasts
for a long time, just this slow dance of mouths, rocking together
to hidden music.

When he lets me go and I can breathe, I try again. "Seriously, though. I could be riddled with the pox like the Earl of Rochester. He was debauched at the age of fourteen too."

"Darling, you're about as debauched as a Lladró shepherdess. If you're at all concerned, I'll get tested again, but if you're not... please let me fuck you. Let me be inside you. I want to feel you come like that. I-I haven't for a long time."

"You made me come like half an hour ago."

He gives this exasperated sound. "You know what I mean."

"I do, but I like to hear you say this stuff."

His arms are still round me, holding me tight, his body growing taut and eager and subtly yielding under mine. I'm over the line, I know I am. "It's been a long time since I've been this close with anyone. Or wanted to be."

I probably should be grown-up and insist on being absolutely certain—not just *fine*—but having Laurie like this is too special to waste.

And I want this. With him.

It's not...it's not how I expect it to be. Even though we've fucked six ways to Sunday the past few weeks, I'm suddenly kind of shy again. Like I haven't been since the first time, upended and upside down on this very bed.

It's just this is a proper first time. Nobody has ever been with me like this. Touched me like this. With nothing between us.

It makes me trembly and self-conscious and *thrilled*. Even though we're back on that slight edge of awkward and Laurie ends up using nearly a gallon of lube because it's like my arse has turned into Sleeping Beauty's castle and grown briars.

This is the reality of skin: rougher than you'd think.

But, oh God. Oh *God*.

I love that extra friction, that edge of pain, the stretch and drag and burn, because it's the way Laurie feels. It's the way Laurie feels as he eases into my body.

It's not so very different in the physical sense. But it *is* different. It's totally different. I'm sure it must be all in my head, but I'm so kind of...shocked by it...and all I can think as I lie there, like a concussed rabbit, watching Laurie through the V of my own legs is that...he's in me. This stranger who I'm probably in love with is *in me*.

I know the sort of stuff that gets said about boys who like to take it up the arse. I know what it's supposed to mean.

Except it isn't anything like that.

I'm greedy and powerful and closer to Laurie than I could have imagined it was possible to be. Literally joined, our bodies fitted together, and all their secrets bared without barrier.

It makes me fly.

Because this is how it's supposed to be. When you strip away the dogma and the politics and the blah blah blah.

This is what sex is. This is what love is. And this is what we are. Laurie and me. Together. Touched and touching. As deep as two people can go.

He's looking down, watching the place where we meet, watching me take him in, and for a while we're both staring at the way our bodies fit—me wrapped around him, him pressing into me, inch by inch by inch. But then I tell him to look at me instead. And when he does, even in the gloom, I can see the fear in him. The fear and the wanting. Exposed to me, given to me, like when I put the tie over his eyes.

I beckon him, and he covers me.

Kisses me. Clumsy-rough, moaning into my mouth. And I sing right back. Same song.

We're both just so naked.

And when I'm ready, I tell him, "Okay, now," and he draws back again and fucks me the way he knows I love to be fucked. His hands tight and strong and hot on my ankles, holding me spread wide for all the goddamn glorious pleasure his gorgeous cock can thrust into me. It's even better now. Raw and beautiful and nothing held back. All skin. Just us.

I lie there, his wanton prince, and let him serve me.

He's perfect like this: all strain and shadows and sweat-gleam. Harsh breath and agonised self-control. A wild stallion of a man who tames himself for me. And that's when I come, hot jerky jets all over my chest and stomach, like my cock is surprised.

I'm almost disappointed.

Not because it wasn't good, but because it's all so good. And I don't want it to stop. I don't want to lose this heat and this fullness and this closeness.

I don't want to lose Laurie.

"God. Toby. Oh Toby."

He leans over me, and for a moment, I think he's come too, but then his mouth is on me. I feel the fluttering warmth of his breath against my chest and then the soft strokes of his tongue as he licks up everything I've spilled. I'm so sensitive right now it's almost tickly, but I like it. And especially like having his still- hard cock nestled inside me while he does it. Knowing he's desperate for me.

I think about playing with him. Pretending I'm not going to let him come, to make him beg. We'd both totally get off on that.

But not this time.

No games just now.

"Laurie." I stroke his hair. "Come for me."

He makes this lovely incoherent sound and braces himself on his elbows. His face is pressed against my neck as he starts to move again. I know this is for me as well, how careful he is with his own pleasure when I'm spent. I wrap my noodly arms around him and hold him as tight as I can. I'd do my legs too—he likes that—but I'm too shagged out to be able to move them.

When he comes—though it's telegraphed in the usual sort of ways, and I'm not sure what I can really feel in my arse because it's all well fucked and lube-slick—I'm overwhelmed all over again by the realisation that Laurie is *in me*.

Is coming *in me*.

I think, for all his casual-casual nonsense earlier, he gets it too. Because he's almost sobbing. And for a while we just cling to each other like that.

It stings a bit when he pulls out. I'm definitely kind of...warm and wet. Very aware of still having some part of Laurie up there. Though I guess it's going to...come out again at some point.

I don't really know why I do what I do next.

It's not something I'd ever have planned. But when I'm with Laurie and Laurie's like this—when I'm over his line—I have this courage I don't have any other time.

He makes me believe I can do anything.

So while he's kneeling there between my splayed legs, I roll onto my stomach. Push myself onto my knees and my elbows.

I don't need to tell him what I want. His mouth is on me, his tongue in me. Filling me with these soft shocks of renewed ☆ pleasure. Not enough to get me hard again. Although this is going to be wank bait forever: Laurie lapping his own come from my freshly—and indeed thoroughly—fucked arse. Just like he'd drunk mine from my skin.

But, God, we're definitely going to have to arrange something with light and mirrors. I need to be able to *see* this stuff sometimes.

Otherwise I could just be dreaming.

When he's done and I'm half-unconscious with...just...feeling everything...he tucks me up and kisses me gently. His lips are closed, but I shove them open with my tongue and get right into his mouth. He tastes of delicious, filthy things. Him and me and pure, unadulterated sex.

"Oh, Toby," he says. "Toby."

I grin at him. Touch his lips. "And we two...mingled be."

And I guess I must be asleep after that.

☆

I don't know what I'm expecting to happen the next morning. Something different. But he kisses me, just like usual, neatly on the forehead. And leaves me on his doorstep in the pinkening dawn.

Getting on with his life. Abandoning me to mine.

I drift through the next few days in a haze of confusion.

Like...what the shit just happened? How can he do that? Is it normal? Or am I the one being weird here? Maybe I've made up the line, and this is just what Laurie is like. What grown-ups are like. The problem is, I don't have anything to compare it to or anybody to ask, and I can't really figure out exactly what it is I want anymore. I mean, I'm getting mind-blowing, kinky sex on a regular basis with a man who is perfectly nice to me the rest of the time. And I'm...apparently...still not satisfied?

Which is when I figure it out. I want to be good enough for more than sex. I love being his fuck buddy, I love everything that we do, but I wish he could see something else in me.

But how can he? I'm nineteen. I have no talents, no future, no prospects, no clue. And he's this powerful, educated, gorgeous man. With a prestigious job and a fairy tale house and most likely real relationships against which I'm always going to fall short.

Because I'm not his equal.

I'm just...not.

It's the wet-fish slap of reality I need as I'm standing there, up to the elbows in greasy soapsuds washing up after the lunch-time rush. It's pretty fucking depressing, but...better to see things clearly, right? I promise myself, then and there, that I'm not going back. Laurie can easily find somebody else to fuck, and I'm sick of playing Russian roulette with my heart.

Except for the bit where I'm a complete fucking idiot.

Without Laurie, my life is just Greasy Joe's forever. And now that I've found what I've been looking for my whole life—now that I know what it's actually like to have a man on his knees for me—how the fuck am I supposed to go back to fumbling about with kids my own age?

Who the hell am I to get all pointlessly principle-having? To get all pissy over the hottest sex I'm ever likely to have? Granddad would say I was cutting my nose off to spite my face, and he'd be right.

Of course I'm going back. And if sex is what we have—if sex is all I'm good for—I'm going to make sure I *am* good.

Fuck school, fuck my future. Maybe this is my talent: knowing this thing about Laurie like I know it in myself. Knowing how to peel him open and take what he needs me to take. Sex, submission, pain.

Oh, I am *so* going back.

And I'm going to fuck his goddamn brains out.

So that Friday, when I'm barely over the threshold, I look straight into those wild, cold eyes of his and say, "I want to tie you up again."

He kind of flinches a bit, but I know it's not me or the idea he's flinching from. It's because he wants it too. And then he nods. "All right."

"Get me something I can use. Then meet me in your bedroom."

It's weird—and also not weird at all—that it's so easy. The truth is, I like telling him what to do, and he likes doing it, and I like the edge of uncertainty to it as well. Because it feels so wrong, wrong in a good way, to be saying the things I say with this...expectation of obedience. I mean, he could turn round at any point, and just say no, but he doesn't.

As I go upstairs, I'm kind of mulling over some stuff. Because once I got over my idiot moment, I've basically spent my week planning to fuck him.

I know this shouldn't be a big deal. Laurie's made it pretty clear that, when it comes to his body, nothing's a big deal. I can do what I like. And it's not about power, because I love how he fucks me, I really do. It's amazing, obviously, but also like I'm in control of him. Like my pleasure is chains on his wrists. A collar round his neck.

So it's not like I think sticking a bit of my body into a bit of his is going to make a blind bit of difference. But especially now there's not even latex between us, I want to know what it's like. To take him a different way.

But there's a problem. And that's... Well. I'm not very good at it. I have, a couple of times. And I know this seems a crazy-beans thing to say when I have aspirations to tie people up and hurt them, but fucking someone right is this huge responsibility. And it's hard to be responsible when the moment you get inside, your cock is all *ohyeahmanyeah*, and going for it like a beggar at the feast or whatever. Though, to be honest, before Laurie, top or bottom, most of my sexual encounters tended to include a fair bit of apologising and "Oh no, it's fine," and while that's all very polite and important, it's not...well...sexy, is it? I guess it's just experience and knowing what you want and how to get it.

The truth is, I've just never felt that way about anyone else. Putting aside the smooshy side of it, what we've got here is lust. Pure, dirty, possessive, greedy lust. The burning kind. Like a Molotov in my chest.

So basically, I know I'm probably going to explode in a fountain of stupid uncontrollable bliss the moment I stick my cock inside him. And while I know that—for whatever weird reason of his own—Laurie finds me exploding in fountains of stupid uncontrollable bliss kind of hot, it's not what I want for this. I want to make him feel the way he makes me feel. And I don't think I know how to do that. At least, not solely with the prowess of my wang.

But I can do it another way. I think.

If I can get him so desperate, so mindless, so pleasure struck, so completely mine that he's begging me to fuck him—so that just me entering him is enough to break him—then we can break together. And be whole after.

"Take your clothes off," is what I tell him in the bedroom.

And while he's doing that, I look at what he's brought me. Ropes and cuffs and chains. And a roll of what looks like duct tape, which kind of scares me for a moment, until I realise it's not sticky. I pick up a coil of rope, which is when I remember I know fuck-all about this. The rope has a slightly silky texture that feels nice between my fingers. But I got thrown out of the Scouts for smoking weed behind the community centre, and basically the only thing I tie regularly are my shoes. And even then I toe them on and off when I can.

Laurie is suddenly behind me, his now-naked body embracing mine. I lean back into his arms, into his warmth.

"It's just rope," he whispers. "You don't have to use it."

"Isn't it sort of traditional?"

He shrugs. "Some people like it, some people don't. Some people like to pretend it's a status symbol because there's a bit of skill involved."

"What do you think?"

"If you liked it, I'd like it. If the ritual was something that mattered to you." I think about it. Maybe someday. But, right now, the need to have him helpless—to *make* him helpless—is too raw. I don't have to say anything because he reads the answer, somehow, in my body. "Then I don't care how you do it. I just want you to"—one of his hesitations, so sweet they drive me fucking crazy—"tie me up. However you want."

I pull away and start faffing around with the rest of the stuff on the bed. I guess I should really have thought about the kinky side of things a bit better. I glance over my shoulder, to see if I'm fucking everything up, but Laurie's gone to his knees for me. I hadn't thought or known to ask just then, but it helps. His patience. His understanding. His acceptance. I'm still holding a wrist cuff, but I like him so much for doing that, I get down next to him and kiss him. I kiss him until it's like we can't kiss enough.

Which is when I stop.

My mouth still full of the taste of his moans.

"Get on the bed."

His eyes are all hazy like a rainy day. "How do you want me?"

"On your back, holding the rail."

He knows how hot I am for him like this. All stretched out for me. It makes his muscles line up like soldiers. Draws his body into stark relief. Shows how strong he is. To be willing to be powerless.

For me.

This is a thing he can do. He can make himself into a gift.

And what it makes me feel is humble.

Honestly, I really fucking admire him. And the more he gives me—pain, dignity, shame, tears, this weakness that isn't weakness at all—the more I admire him. The more I just totally adore him.

So much for pretending I was sophisticated enough for whatever we're doing together. But I don't give a fuck. Worrying comes later. This is now. And right now, I'm king of the world. Well, king of *his* world anyway.

I get rid of my clothes and climb onto the bed, pushing his legs apart so I can get between them.

"Toby, what are you doing?"

"I'll tell you in a minute."

Which, of course, I won't. He brings his head up and watches me in this half-excited, half-wary way. So fucking beautiful. I reach out and run my fingers across the muscles of his abdomen so I can feel the quiver in them. Turns out my beautiful man is a little bit nervous.

Good. I like him that way. It soothes me and fills me with small fires. All for him.

I pick up what I guess is an ankle cuff. It's weirdly good to touch, leather and suede and metal, this sort of weight and certainty, and it's warm and cold at the same. It's equally good to buckle it round him, and from the sound he makes, maybe it's good to have it buckled.

I wonder if it feels like my hand holding him.

I do the other leg, and he lets out a very long, slow breath, and I sit back a moment, just to look at him again. I don't know why, but somehow he seems more naked with the cuffs on. Or maybe they draw attention to the fact he *is* naked except for some bands of black leather I've put on him. There's a set of wider cuffs for his thighs. They're kind of a bit tougher. It's not like it's a fight or anything, but he kind of has to actively consent to them.

And that drives us both a bit crazy.

Heavy breathing all round. Very hard cocks. But my hands are steady with the buckles, so I'm secretly a bit proud. And when I'm done, I push against his knee, and use one of these double-ended clip things to connect the ankle cuff to the thigh cuff. He makes a startled noise at the second snap, like he's only just realised what I'm doing. It's not actually very restrictive—heh, yet—but the heel of his foot is drawn towards the back of his thigh, and he can't straighten his leg. As I do the same on the other side, he curls his knee protectively over his body. Can't say I blame him, which is why I let him get away with it. While he can.

I don't know where it comes from, but I'm suddenly having this rush of...I don't know what to call it. Joy, I guess. But it's so...so...sharp and kind of dark. And I realise this is it: I'm a card-carrying sadist. And it's okay.

As well as the clips and the rope and the cuffs, he's brought me a collection of chains. I go for a shortish one, fitted with another set of double-ended snap hooks. Clip one end to the spare ring on the thigh cuffs, and the other to this cunning little eyelet I noticed ages ago set into the bed frame itself.

I wonder if I should be bothered they're there. I mean, obviously I know I'm not the only person who's been in Laurie's life, but they're a pretty strong reminder that he's lain here for someone else. I think about it, and it turns out I'm not jealous.

Well, not really. It's becoming my new mantra: *I'm* here now. That's what matters. And the eyelets are good thinking.

So, uh, thanks, random person.

As I reach for his other knee, Laurie sort of twists away from me, the chain rattling. I think he's cottoned on to what I've got planned.

"Toby...I don't..."

"Stop wriggling." His grip tightens, which turns the sinews of his arms all knotty and delicious. *Ngh.* I pull at his leg, but he's still resisting me. "Laurie."

He shakes his head, eyes tightly closed. "I can't."

"Yeah, you can."

"Can you...can you"—his throat ripples gorgeously as he swallows—"tie my hands first? Please?"

Definitely better than two out of ten. But there's a problem. "I'm not going to tie your hands."

His eyes snap open. And now there's definitely a kind of fear there. So fucking hot. "W-what?"

"I've got things for them to do. So just...like, cling on to the rail like I've said, okay? That's your cuffs."

He throws back his head and groans. And, just like that, the muscles of his thigh yield to my pressure, and I clip the last chain into place, spreading him wide.

And holy shit, he looks amazing. Like a butterfly on a collector's tray, completely exposed. His knuckles are white, his arms shaking with the strain of not moving, and his sweat-gilded chest heaving with these deep, desperate breaths. He's got his head buried into his upper arm, like he can't bear to think about what I've done to him.

What he's letting me do.

Because he could let go of the rail, sit up, and free himself in like...a second.

But he doesn't. He just shakes and hides his face because

he can't hide anything else from me like this. I lean in and run my tongue all the way up his glistening, rock-hard cock, and he muffles a sound so gloriously needy it's practically a sob.

God. I could come right now, with the taste of him fizzing on my tongue.

"Laurie...Laurie...look at me, love."

He shakes his head.

"Come on, it's okay. Look at me."

Very, very slowly he does. There's this dark flush sweeping his cheekbones. And it's like he doesn't know if he hates me or wants me. Maybe both.

"Please," he says. "Please don't. Don't..."

"Don't what?"

I don't think he knows what. I drag my thumbs along the wide-open creases where his legs meet his groin, and his hips arch kind of compulsively into my touch, making the chains tighten and chitter a bit in their moorings.

I reckon I've judged it about right. He's not uncomfortable—except in the psychological sense—and he's got enough freedom of movement that I can still feel his reactions. But he can't close his legs or pull away from me.

"Don't what?" I ask again. "You totally want this."

"Yes, but..." His voice is so soft, so ragged, I don't know how I'm hearing him. "It's...just...it's hard to bear."

"Yeah, I know." I kiss the exposed interior of his thigh, and the powerful muscle there jumps under my mouth. "But do it for me. I like you like this. You're so fucking beautiful."

"I feel ridiculous," he mutters.

"Then you're just going to have to trust me."

For a long moment, he just stares at me, so flushed and angry and frantic and ashamed, and then his head falls back against the pillows, his body not quite relaxing, but surrendering, just a little bit, opening to me.

I press myself between his legs and drop little kisses over his stomach and hips and up, up, up, as far as I can go. He flinches under each one, greeting them with a soft *nhh* of fearful pleasure. When I fasten my mouth over one of his nipples, something like a growl catches at the back of his throat, and he pushes up into my touch, into my teeth. He tastes a little coppery. *Zing*.

By the time I'm heading south again, I think he's kind of forgotten to be bothered by the restraints, or why it matters that he's helpless and not helpless and completely vulnerable to me. There's just my lips and my fingers and the way I'm making him feel. Which, I flatter myself, is pretty fucking good.

I leave him a few souvenirs to keep him company during the week. I guess it's a bit tacky, but what else have I got? A love bite close to his heart, another on his hip, a third on his thigh. He moans really sweetly when I do them, eyes fluttering as he watches.

I settle myself between his legs again and kiss the tip of his cock kind of playfully, so that it twitches a little and weeps for me, pooling eagerly on his stomach. His balls are drawn up tight beneath, all tender and delicious and forbidden like the fruit of the goblin market. I sort of want to take them into my mouth and suck until I'm totally pleasure-cursed and can't live without them. Or, y'know, something like that.

My brain's unravelling a bit for Laurie.

Because, oh God, oh fuck, the way I've got him trussed, his arse is this unprotected valley, with a tight little knot of darkness nestled right at its heart, almost begging me to press inside and claim him.

"There's two rules." I'm totally, hopelessly dazed, but I don't care. "You have to stop when I tell you to stop. And you can only come when I'm inside you." Okay, that's ambiguous. Something I've learned recently—you can be inside someone a bunch of ways, and you don't even have to touch them. "When my cock's in your arse."

"All right."

"What's the rules?"

His lips part a moment before he speaks. The words come slowly, like I've drugged him. "Stop when you tell me. Don't come until...you fuck me."

"With my cock."

I skate my fingers over his arse to make the point, and he kind of erupts into a full-body shiver. "Until you fuck me with your cock."

"Okay. Good." I kiss the side of his knee. "Now touch yourself."

"What?"

I've startled him again. Turns out I like doing that. "I told you I had a use for your hands. Touch yourself."

"And"—I kind of see the realisation hit him—"stop when you say?"

I grin at him, nuzzling at his leg. "Yeah."

"Oh God." He unpeels a hand from the bedstead and very gingerly takes hold of his cock. Whatever he feels makes him sort of shudder and cringe at the same time. "Oh God. Oh, Toby." He gives a weird, shaky laugh. "Complicity is your master weapon."

I'm not sure what he's getting at. I honestly just like watching him. All the little responses you miss when you're distracted by involvement. Like the glide of skin over skin, how that sounds, ☆ this rough-silk whisper, the strength of his hands, with the bones all ridged up along the backs, and the way all his muscles tighten as the pleasure hits him.

And, oh my God, his face. I could watch his face forever. The flicker of his lashes. And sometimes he squeezes his eyes so tight, it's almost like he's in pain. But his mouth, his mouth has that softness to it, and it makes the softest sounds.

While he strokes himself, I crawl round to his side and slip a finger between his lips. And he just takes it in like it's my cock, like it's a fucking gift, moaning into my skin.

And I kind of come all over him. Which really wasn't the plan.

☆ But it comes out of nowhere, like an awesome sneeze. White light in my brain. *Bam*. A fucking orgasm, somehow dragged out my fucking finger.

So fuck the plan.

"Oh God." That could've been either of us, but it's Laurie. He shudders like he's been hit with a whip or something as my cock empties itself over his side and chest.

And, fuck, he looks debauched. Completely fucking debauched. Lying there, pinned open, flushed and sweating and streaked with come, one hand on his straining cock, the other still locked around the bed rail, a frantic man, half-chained and half-free, waiting for sex and covered in it.

I take my wet fingers from his mouth, and I get between his legs and circle him there so lightly. Until his arse glistens like his mouth.

"Oh God," he says again. His eyes open slowly, like they're heavy, and meet mine across his body. "Toby."

Wow. There's everything in my name just then. Hope and fear and need, and some stuff I'm probably inventing that makes me feel so warm inside. Like I want to give him everything back.

"I'm here. Right here." I rub my cheek against his inner thigh. I wish I had scent glands like a cat because then I'd own him, wherever I touched him, and all the other cats would know he was mine. Maybe I need to get a signature cologne or something. Like in that Britney Spears song. "You're so amazing right now."

He shakes his head. But his breathing has an edge to it, an urgency, and his hand is moving harder and faster on his cock, so the sound of skin on skin is a shout, not a whisper.

"Yeah, you are. Stop."

I think he's actually so close to lost he's half forgotten. I'm not sure what I'm supposed to do if he doesn't obey, or if I've misjudged it and he comes before I've said he can. But I haven't misjudged *him*. He gives this deep groan and yanks his hand away, slamming it into place on the bed rail. And I'm suddenly so fucking proud of him and so full of need because I want to hurt him and please him, make him suffer and make him happy, and all I can think is what a fucking miracle it is that just now, with him, those things aren't any sort of contradiction at all.

It's also when I know I'm definitely, undeniably, impossibly in love. With this man I know and don't know at all.

And I can't pretend anymore that this will ever be just sex for me.

It never was, and it never will be.

I love him. And I love this. And they're inextricable.

While he lies there, breathing harshly, his brow creased with the agony of denial, I scramble back over him. I'm actually trying to get lube, because I forgot earlier, but on the way I kiss him, and he opens to me, sweetly, almost hesitantly, and I slide into his mouth.

A kiss for lovers, tongues entangled like our bodies.

He arches after me, whimpering when I go to pull away, so I fall back into him, and we kiss and kiss, and kiss some more. I'm so deep in him, held by his raised knees, and I want to say it to him—the magic words I've never said to anyone who wasn't family—but I'm not sure it's fair to do that sort of thing when you've got somebody tied up and forbidden to come. Maybe after, if we can kiss like this again.

He lets me go this time, and my cock nudges up against his when I reach over him to get the stuff. I enjoy the clumsy intimacy of it, as I get back into position. "You can touch yourself again, now."

He hisses out a breath and wraps his hand around his cock, stroking himself slowly, like he's afraid of the pleasure.

I cover my fingers in lube and rub them together until it warms a bit. When I touch him, his whole body responds, his cock shuddering and leaking and his head falling back onto the pillows so that his stubble-rough throat is all ripply and vulnerable.

I press into him, and there's very little resistance.

He wants me. He wants me so bad.

"Oh...God," he sighs. "Yes."

He's hot inside, hot and tight and strong, and I can feel him all around me, wrapping my finger in this carnal embrace. Even the thought of what it's going to be like when it's my cock is enough to make me pretty urgently hard again.

I move in and out of him, just kind of teasing him and because I like the way it feels and how it looks, his body dragging my finger in, greedy and desperate. And Laurie's kind of pressing into the chains now, opening himself to me even further, moaning softly with my every thrust, and rocking his hips to meet me, his hand matching my rhythm.

I'm totally entranced. Watching him turn wild. Shameless.

At one point, I kind of slip on the lube and fall out of him, which is a complete accident but an awesome one.

He jerks gracelessly after me, arching off the bed, and bursts out with, "Oh please, God, don't stop."

So, of course, I stop. Instead, I circle him, round and round and round, with the slick pad of my finger. And I think I kind of break him just a little bit because suddenly he's begging and begging and begging, the words catching and then tumbling from his mouth like pearls on a broken string.

And I swear to God, it's the hottest fucking thing I've ever seen. The same dark, sharp joy uncurls inside me like some wicked, clawy monster thing, and it's practically purring.

"Wow, you really want me, huh?" I sound almost as breathless as he does. So much for playing it cool. But compared to him, I'm the fucking Snow Queen.

"Yes...yes, I do. Please."

He's so beautiful, and my little monster is so pleased with him that I have to reward him. I thrust two fingers inside and tear this deep, wonderful, slightly shattered groan out of him. I actually don't have a clue what I'm doing. I know I'm supposed to be sort of angling up and forward to get the high score, but maybe it's a good job I'm not sure because he's kind of going nuts as it is, fucking himself against my hand, his every breath a frantic little moan.

"God." I stare at him in a kind of blissed-out wonderment of my own. "You totally love this."

He twists and gasps. "Y-yes. I-I...love this."

"All chained up and at my command."

"Yes, yes, I'm yours."

Mine. My heart melts into blood and rubbery tube bits and wet candyfloss. "You should probably stop, by the way."

He makes another amazing sound. Pure despair. "Toby—"

"Stop."

And, somehow, he does. Both hands on the rail, chest heaving, cock throbbing, arse still swallowing my fingers. "Please...I need..." he says, so softly, so miserably. "Please."

I smile at him, completely full of love. "Please what?" There's a kind of wet gleam to his eyes. Jesus, is he crying? Is that okay? "What do you want?"

"You." He lifts his head as he says it, staring straight at me with his gold-and-silver eyes. This one moment of stark coherence he's somehow found a way to give me.

"You can touch yourself again."

"I can't. I'll—"

"Touch yourself."

He's kind of wrecked before he even touches his cock. His whole body pulled tight and held open and trembling. The sound he makes is closer to pain than pleasure, and it's gorgeous, just like he is. The truth is, I fucking love the way he suffers. It makes me feel ridiculously good, like I'm turning into caramel from the inside out.

"Show me how much you want me."

"God, Toby," he groans, "I want you. Isn't it fucking obvious?"

Technically, that's telling, not showing, but it turns out my sadism draws the line at pedantry. Nice to know. "Yeah, but I like when you go all, y'know, frantic and slutty." His breath catches on this mortified little moan. Shit. Might have gone too far. "Slutty in...like a good way. For me."

After a moment he nods. "For you."

The truth is, he *does* look kind of slutty. Impossible for him not to, really, the way I've got him, and the way he can't seem to stop twisting himself on my fingers. But it's magnificently slutty, everything about him sweaty and straining, from the sinews on his neck to his hand on his cock, and not yielding in the slightest, despite the chains, except his eyes, and his mouth, and his arse, the places he lets me in.

"Want me to fuck you, Laurie?"

"Yes. God. Yes." Now he sounds almost angry, like he's reached a new level of desperate.

I'm honestly talking it up a bit because I'm nervous. I mean, it's not rocket science, I know—locate arse, insert cock. But what if I've got him so wound up it's a letdown?

What if I've overhyped my own wang?

I'm really glad I don't have to faff with a condom. It's one more thing to mess up. I tried to put one on backwards once. It rolled about halfway, so I thought it was fine, and then it went all weird and started squeezing my dick off like a latex bear trap. And I didn't know what to do, because once you've put a condom on wrong, it's hard to keep selling the idea that sex with you is going to be fab.

"Please," he says again, somehow making my hesitation part of this whole experience, as if I'm deliberately doing it to torment him. "Fuck me. I'll be your slut. Make me yours. I'll do anything."

I totally drench myself in lube, getting it on my thighs and onto the sheets.

I really, really don't want to hurt him in a bad way. First few times I let someone do this to me, I was way less ready than I thought I was, and it's kind of hard to stop once it's started. I was fine, but I remember.

Maybe I should have stuck an extra finger in there. That's what you're supposed to do, right? One, two, three, dick. I can't remember how Laurie does me. By the time we reach that point, I'm so delirious, I probably wouldn't notice if he used a cucumber.

"Toby."

He's not pleading now, not really. But there's something in his voice—trust, maybe, and all this warmth, along with that sharp edge of need—and it gives me everything I need to stop dithering and remember I really fucking seriously want him.

So I grab myself, line up, and go for it, and I guess he's good at this too, because it goes way better than I'm used to. I don't miss, or slip, or have to apologise, and there's no kind of tense negotiation about relaxing, so I'm not hanging around like a party guest who's turned up at the wrong house.

Instead there's a bit of resistance and then it's gone. And what's really weird is it's that first moment that makes the next one—when his body yields to mine and takes me in—utterly fucking amazing.

It's nothing like the other times I've tried to do this. It's not just how insanely good he feels around me—tight, hot, silky-slick with lube, no condom in the way—it's the fact it's him. Laurie. My Laurie. So I'm just absolutely...complete. Completely held by him.

We both make slightly silly noises. I think I babble something stupid about loving him, because I do and when we're like this I can't not say it, and he just sighs out my name in that sweet, sweet way he sometimes does.

And I press into him until we're... The word that comes to me again is *joined*. Because that's how fucking ridiculously romantic I am right now, deep in his body, cradled between his thighs, my (pretty excited) balls kind of tucked against his arse, which is the weirdest, tenderest kind of intimacy, all these soft and secret places, all pressed together.

Fuck yes.

I tilt my hips a bit because it's so fucking good, though it's not like there's any more of me going in, but suddenly Laurie flings back his head and cries out, his hand tightening on his cock and his whole body tightening around me.

And God, if I wasn't about to come before, it's a fucking miracle I don't come now.

Watching him like that. Because of me.

I brace my hands on his pelvis and pull back, not fully out because I'm worried I'll screw up reentry, but enough that it's like I'm coming in again. So that there's a sense of absence and then connection, all in the deepest places of his body. And I manage to do that thing with my hips again.

He tenses, his muscles snapping into alignment, and his eyes flutter in this weirdly vulnerable way, like he's half dreaming. And then he's coming, spilling wildly between his fingers, gasping out my name again, along with an incoherent rush of *thank you thank you thank you* and tears, actual tears, all for me.

And, wow, I feel everything. I feel him come. The build and the release of it, the way it takes him, everything I've done to him.

Like this perfect apotheo-wossname.

Which obviously makes me come too. Because I can't not. Even though I'd like to stay like this forever or, y'know, a bit longer than two seconds. It's a good orgasm though, drawn out of me by his, like we're links on a chain. I let it roll through me and into Laurie, kind of vast and gentle and awesome. I don't see stars, but I see the spaces between them, and all there is...is him.

Afterwards I collapse over him, still inside, and lie there, spent and shivering, between his legs. He reaches down to undo the chains and then he folds himself round me, holding me tight in an embrace of skin and leather.

At last, I draw back, and watching my naked cock slide out of him is almost as thrilling as watching it push in. He grips me as if he doesn't want to let me go, this warm, sticky drag like the pull of a mouth. I've left him shiny and open, and I can't help slipping a finger in, wanting to feel myself inside him.

Which is probably odd of me, but he doesn't seem to mind. Just gives this surprisingly sweet little moan as I fuck gently into the wet heat of him and me together. I look up, meet his eyes. I'm sure my expression is absolutely one hundred percent goofy, but I don't care. Right then, the whole world is soft around the edges, and everything is okay. "You're the first person I've..." I don't know how to finish that sentence. But it doesn't matter.

Laurie gives me this gorgeous smile. "I'm glad it was me."

Eventually we clean up, get Laurie out of the cuffs because while they're hot, enough's enough, and then we're back in each other's arms. He's still a bit teary, which makes me feel bad and not bad at all, and anxious, and aroused. Internally aroused anyway. Externally I'm totally out of it, and probably will be for, like, maybe a whole hour.

I reach out and touch the damp corners of his eyes. "Are you all right?"

"Yes, darling. Pure physical relief."

"Okay, good. Because it's really hot."

He laughs, blinking moisture from his lashes. "You depraved little monster."

"Yeah." I wriggle in and kiss him, first on the mouth, then on his closing eyes, tasting salt. "Your depraved little monster."

We're silent a bit.

"And that was...that was okay, wasn't it?" I ask.

I guess I'd know if it wasn't. But better to check, right?

"It was... Well, 'okay' doesn't begin to cover it."

I can tell he isn't in one of his talking moods this time. I don't think he means to shut me out. But I guess it just takes him a bit of time to settle between being the man who's giving me his body, and the man he is the rest of the time. Which is obviously kind of a problem for me because I want everything.

Everyone he can be.

And I need...I need him to know I can't pretend any more. I can't play this game. I've never been playing it. All of me is his.

So I press. "Uh, what does cover it?"

"I don't know. Terrible, perhaps. Wonderful."

See, that's what I want to hear. It's like still being inside him, still having him in chains, when he says stuff like that. "So you liked it, then?"

"Yes, yes, I liked it, Toby." And now he sounds a bit impatient with me. Great.

But I'm not ready to give up yet. I push against him until he rolls onto his back, and I straddle him, not trying to turn him on or anything, but to try to get that closeness again. I lean down and kiss his chest, and he tastes awesomely of sex.

"Because I fucking loved it." I kind of *whoosh* my hands all over him. Possessive as fuck. "It was amazing. I love it when you're like that. I love having you at my mercy. I love what you let me do to you. I love watching you fall apart. And I love y—"

His hand comes up, and next thing I know, there's a finger against my lips. "Shush."

It's not exactly a ball gag. I can talk round a finger. But I'm actually too fucking stunned.

He pulls me down again and tucks me up, arms around me, mouth pressed to the back of my neck. It'd be nice except... except for...

Shush.

Seriously? *Shush?*

He kisses me super gently, all soft and wet and open-mouthed, just the way I like it. Right on that tingly spot that makes all these lovely shivers run up and down my spine.

"My beautiful boy," he whispers. "Thank you."

And I'm so fucking confused I can't even. Usually I'll say,

For what? so he has to admit how much he loves everything that I'm not really making him do at all. But this time I just lie there, curled against him, covered in his kisses, and let everything fucking die.

I feel like...

I don't know. I just don't know. I don't know what the hell I'm supposed to be doing now.

From his breathing, Laurie has actually fallen asleep. The bastard. So I'm stuck here, being held and being pissed off, which is a deeply weird feeling.

Then I just get sad. Really, really sad.

And I wonder how he can be so close to me and so far away at the same goddamn fucking time.

And what the fuck I'm supposed to do about it.

7

LAURIE

I did not feel guilty.

I absolutely did not feel guilty.

When I woke the next morning, Toby was not beside me. At first I thought he was making breakfast, but as I lay there—not quite dozing, not quite waiting—and time slipped by, I realised he wasn't coming back to bed. He'd gone. And maybe he wouldn't come back at all.

It was a painful thought, troublingly so, and I had no right to be either pained or troubled. His absence wasn't what I wanted, but what I wanted was selfish, and probably very, very wrong. If I had pushed him away, however little I had intended to, it was probably the best thing I could have done for him.

I simply couldn't give him what he thought he wanted from me. I couldn't pretend we had any sort of future. He needed someone his own age, or close to it, to share his life as it unfurled before him, as Robert had once shared mine.

I pulled the duvet up, rolled into the empty space Toby had left behind, and then turned onto my back again. But he'd left more than merely absence: aches in my muscles, marks upon my body—my skin was full of the memory of him.

The worst thing about being old enough to know better was the realisation that you weren't.

My thoughts, cycling interminably through guilt, self-recrimination, frustration, and sentimentality, were beginning to eat each other. But what did I expect? Toby and I were a closed system. I'd lost all perspective. On him, on me, on what was right and wrong. I might have told him his master weapon was complicity, but there was something else. Some way of being, or trick of living, that made me forget everything when I was with him. Everything except for the moments of our being together and some ridiculous, irresistible sense of an *us*.

Damn that impossible boy.

I couldn't use him like this. I couldn't allow myself to become more to him than a temporary...fancy? Aberration? Distraction. A story from his foolish youth he might tell some other lover.

I could have stayed in bed, pickling myself in the sweet, painful ambiguities of wanting and shame, but I knew from long experience that there was really only one response to having lost control of my life, which was to throw myself on the mercy of my friends. I couldn't imagine they'd be particularly sympathetic, but I didn't deserve sympathy. I needed common sense and my perspective back.

☆ So I got up, showered, and went to see Grace. She'd started the tradition of Pancake Sundays back at university to prevent emotional complications from whoever she'd pulled the night before. With the added bonus of being able to see her friends and eat pancakes. Sam, for whatever reason—perhaps being Australian—had not fled in awkwardness and terror like nearly all of Grace's other transitory partners. According to Robert (I'd been in Glasgow at the time), he'd wandered out of the bedroom, wearing only a towel in which he had looked stunningly good, and said, "Oh great, pancakes. And you guys must be Grace's friends."

If only all relationships could be so simple. As simple as not leaving.

After Sam, pancakes had become a kinder ritual. Lovers were invited to stay, not overwhelmed and edged out.

I hadn't dropped in for a while, for various reasons. The main one, truthfully, being Robert. When we'd broken up, we had decided we weren't going to be one of those couples who divvy up their friends like the CDs and books. It was a fine principle, but I hadn't realised how it would actually feel to meet my ex among the people who had once been part of the life we had shared.

It wasn't a matter of being over him—I was, I was used to being without him—it was simply that moving on was a kind of competition, and I'd lost. I wasn't unhappy, but he was happier. And the man all of our friends had assured me was nothing more than a fleeting, ill-fated rebound was still with him. I could be indifferently polite to both of them when I met them incidentally, but there'd been a time when Robert and I had gone to Pancake Sundays together, and memory had a way of cutting you open.

Thankfully, he wasn't there that Sunday. It turned out to be a quiet one: just Grace and Sam; Amy, who was leaving as I arrived; and one of their partners, a softly spoken, dreamy-eyed person called Angel. They were all lounging around in the living room, which meant I'd missed the initial cooking frenzy, but there were still a few lukewarm pancakes left for me to claim and dowse in maple syrup.

Grace was carding her fingers gently through Angel's hair. "Hey, who's that guy?"

"No idea." Sam lay curled up on the floor next to her, resting his head against her leg. "He's some stranger who wandered in off the street to eat our pancakes."

"Yes, yes, very funny," I muttered. "Sorry it's been a while."

"Actually, he does seem familiar. We used to know a grumpy bastard, didn't we, Sam?"

"Now you mention it, I think we did. What was his name again?"

"Lawson? Laughlin?"

I sighed. Knowing I deserved this didn't make it any less exasperating. "Do you just want me to leave?"

Grace grinned. "Don't be silly, Lawson, sit down. And have a little pancake with your syrup."

Angel, who was wearing a silk dressing gown that probably—though I wouldn't have bet on it, knowing Sam's tastes or lack thereof—belonged to Grace, moved across to make space for me on the sofa.

"I'm sorry," I said again, as I sat down and balanced my plate on my knee. "I've been busy."

Sam gave me a far too sharp look. "Busy getting laid, from the looks of you."

Don't blush, Dalziel. "That's pure supposition."

"Laurie, I can tell. You get this"—he framed me with his hands—"glow. This very lovely glow, like a fine stallion ridden hard. And occasionally put up wet."

"I don't glow," I snapped.

Grace stifled a sound that might have been a laugh but which became a cough when I glared at her. "He's just messing with you because we know."

Even though I'd come here expressly for the purpose of telling them about Toby, I flinched. I suddenly didn't really feel like eating pancakes, so I put my plate on the coffee table. "You...know?"

"Yeah"—she nodded eagerly—"Dominic said he was going to ask you out."

"Wait. What? Who the fuck is Dominic?"

They all stared at me.

"The guy you've been sleeping with on and off for the last few years?" said Grace, in her primary-school-teacher voice. "The guy who's had a crush on you for ages?"

I shook my head bemusedly. It could honestly have been any number of people.

"He...he plays the alto sax?" offered Angel.

"That's Dominic?" A fresh thought struck me. "Dominic the Dom? My God. That just sounds like an incredibly ill-conceived children's series."

Grace gave a whoop of laughter. "Dominic the Dom and Subby the Sub."

Angel and Sam immediately picked up the theme: *Dominic and Subby Go to the Sex Shop, Dominic and Subby at the Play Party, Dominic and Subby's First Orgy, Dominic and Subby and the Butt Plug of Doom.*

But when the amusement faded, Grace was frowning. "Hang on, hang on. Laurie, if you're not with Dom, who the hell are you with?"

"What makes you think I'm with anyone?" I asked, squirming and stalling unconvincingly.

Sam gave me a look. "Because you're happy, dude. Like, it's buried deep. But I know you. I can tell."

Oh God. He was right. In spite of everything—in spite of knowing how wrong it was (or should be)—Toby made me happy. Utterly, helplessly happy.

"So come on," pressed Grace, "who are you fucking? Do we know him?"

I put my head in my hands and blurted out the truth.

"Who?"

I tried again, with volume this time. "The Foetus."

There was a long, awful silence. I didn't dare look up.

At last Grace said, "Tell me he's legal."

"Of course he's fucking legal." It was briefly comforting to be outraged. It meant I didn't have to be embarrassed. "He's nineteen."

There was another long silence, probably slightly less awful than the last one. Now it was merely uncomprehending.

"But I thought," said Sam slowly, "you didn't switch."

For Toby's sake, and perhaps my own, I couldn't keep hiding. I peeled my fingers away from my face and took a deep, calming breath. As though that was actually going to help. "I don't."

"So, you're topping from the bottom?"

☆   "Less than you might think." It was the easy answer. But then I remembered how it actually felt to be at Toby's feet, in his body, or at his mercy. "Actually no. I'm not."

Sam shook his head. "I just...can't... You and...him...and... It makes my brain wibble."

"How do you think my brain feels?" I snapped. "I didn't choose this."

"Well, yeah, mate, you kind of did. You didn't just trip and fall and land dick-first into a nineteen-year-old."

"Yes, but—" But what? What the fuck was I trying to say? "I didn't think it was going to be like this."

"Like what?"

I swallowed. "I didn't think I was going to like him."

"Laurie." Sam sighed. "That's a thing that happens sometimes when you let someone do intimate things with you. You start to like to them."

This wasn't helping. "Can we dispense with the human social and sexual relations lecture?"

"Is it... Is he—" Sam paused, confused again, and tugged at his braids. "God, I sound like a perv even saying this...but, it works? I mean, it's good? You can submit to a kid?"

"He's not a kid," I answered without thinking. "He's...who he is."

"And it's not weird?"

"Not when I'm with him." I stared at my hands which were shaking, so I knotted them carefully together. "I want to give him everything, and the things I can't give, I want him to take."

He's my prince. Fierce and fragile and tender and cruel. But, of course, I couldn't say that aloud.

So I cleared my throat into yet another silence. "Come on then. Take the piss. What are you waiting for?"

Sam held up his hands. "I got nuthin'. That was beautiful."

"Oh shut up."

"I'm serious. If it works for you, then it works."

Grace had been uncharacteristically quiet, her brow wrinkling thoughtfully as the conversation bounced back and forth between Sam and me.

"Well," she said slowly, "why shouldn't it work?" It wasn't what I'd expected. And I must have looked startled because she shrugged and went on, "I mean, it's not like this stuff has anything to do with age anyway. It's about...I don't know, all these really complicated intersections: nature, preference, choice, attraction, chemistry. I think he's pretty lucky actually."

"I am?" I asked.

For some reason, that made her laugh. "Bless. You do have it bad. I meant that *he's* lucky. The Foetus. Finding you. I wish I'd had it so good back then."

"But you've always seemed so confident."

"Well, now I am. My first kiss was a complete disaster."

Angel nuzzled her shoulder. "I think most people's are."

Mine was Robert. I'd kissed a couple of girls before him, but I'd known they were nothing but lies, so I'd never counted them. University was the first place I'd felt safe enough to be who I was. For Robert, it had never been in question. Three days, thirteen hours, and twenty-two minutes after we first met, he put his arms around me, pressed our bodies together, and kissed me. It was softer than I'd expected. I'd been dreaming of a man's mouth—any man's mouth—on mine since I was eleven years old, and this was it, as tender as the moths that drifted in the hazy moonlight.

"His name was Daryl Hanlen," Grace was saying. "I was fifteen, he was eighteen, and he had his own car, so he was a major catch. He'd taken me out to Frankie & Benny's and then to see *The Matrix*—a really classy date. Back in the day. In Birmingham. On the way home, he pulled into this lay-by and he told me I was so hot I could be a Page 3 model."

Sam smiled up at her. "You do have great boobs."

"I really do. And if I get bored of teaching, I'll be sure to get them out for the lads. So, anyway, there we were, by the side of the road. He unclipped his seat belt, and I can remember thinking to myself, 'Okay, Grace, this is it. You're about to get kissed by a boy. This is going to be awesome.'" She laughed derisively. "He was really gorgeous, by the way. He had an earring. So he leaned in, and he kissed me, and it was fantastic. Just like every naughty book I'd ever smuggled home and read. Everything I'd been waiting for. All this heat gathering in all these places."

It was easy enough to imagine somehow. Fifteen-year-old Grace with her pale, bright eyes and her not-blond, not-brown hair, so full of longing. I could barely remember myself at that age: a quiet boy, I thought, who studied hard and hid all his intensities in conformity.

Grace reached down with her spare hand and idly touched

Sam's brow, his jaw, the side of his neck. He turned his body fully against hers, nestling, his cheek pressed to her thigh. "The more we did it, the more I wanted, you know? So much more. So I got into his lap, and I put my hands in his hair, and I pushed my tongue into his mouth, until everything was dark and red and hot, and he was making these sounds under me, whimpers and moans, so desperate and helpless and perfect. It seemed like we were kissing for hours. And, for the first time in my life, I felt completely and absolutely right."

When it didn't seem like she was going to continue unless someone prompted her, I said, "That doesn't exactly sound like a disaster."

She shrugged and went on in quite a different voice, "Next ☆ day, I go to school, and suddenly I've got a reputation as a crazy slut, and I never see Daryl again." Her lip curled. "Cowardly prick. I didn't let anybody kiss me again until I was at university, and I was too scared to do anything, so I just lay there with my mouth open like a dead fish." She shuddered. "But then I thought: if you can't be honest during sex, what's the point? So I went back to doing what I liked. I mean, a bunch of people still said I was a crazy slut, but by then I'd given up caring."

"That can be hard," murmured Angel.

Grace wrinkled her nose. "It's got easier as I've got older. Or maybe I've just had more practice. I mean, honestly. What's the big deal here? I like sex, and I've had a lot of it. Good sex, bad sex, kinky sex, violent sex, boring sex. But at least it's who I am, and nobody gets to take that away from me. And oh God"—she gave a self-conscious laugh—"I'm talking way too much. Somebody save me."

"All right." Sam threw himself into the silence. "Ethan Kelly. Grade 3. Behind the crooked acacia tree in the schoolyard."

Grace glanced down at him. "Huh?"

"My first kiss."

"Wait," I said. "Your first kiss was a boy?" Sam's described his sexuality as *suggestible*, but as far as I could tell his preference lay strongly with women.

He shrugged. "Carley Jones promised she'd kiss me if I kissed Ethan."

"Did she?"

"Nah. Guess I got played. Or"—he grinned—"maybe I've always liked girls telling me what to do. Your turn, Laurie."

"Angel first." *Coward.*

"Are you sure?" They sat up in a swoosh of fuchsia silk, tucking their legs under them. "It's a hard act to follow. You see, my first kiss started a riot. How many people can say that?"

Grace perked up like a meerkat. "Now this I have to hear."

"It was at The Palace, back when I was living in Bristol." They smiled, pale lips and crooked teeth, not quite shyly but something else, something close to that but different, drawing us playfully into their confidence. I didn't know Angel very well, but I was struck suddenly by how easy they could be to like, behind their wary eyes. "It used to be my favourite place because it looked a little bit like another world. One night this beautiful boy came up to me and pulled me close and kissed me. It was very light and very sweet, as if he was trying to give me something, not take it. It was lovely."

☆ They were still smiling, but their hands plucked restlessly at the ties of the dressing gown, exposing the rope burns on their wrists. "But then some people saw us, and it was all the usual fuckwittery, you know. Is it a man, is it a woman, is it a freak, what bathroom do you use, ohemgee."

"Wankers," muttered Grace.

"I know, right? My friends were seriously unimpressed. So

it quickly became an argument, which turned into a fight. I don't know who threw the first, well, slap I think—it was a gay club, after all—but then everybody got thrown out by the bouncers."

"You got thrown out?" Sam seemed rather impressed.

"Oh, I didn't. I'd slipped away with the boy while everyone was distracted with outrage. We danced and kissed all night long."

Sam glanced at me. "You see, you should trust your friends. We're looking out for your kissing interests."

"It's not that simple with Toby."

"Why not?"

I told myself it was a relief to be talking about this, rather than keeping it like a dirty secret. "Well, because he's nineteen, and I'm not, and he keeps..." It felt a little strange to admit aloud something I'd been resolutely ignoring for weeks. "He keeps saying he loves me."

"Holy shit." Sam gave a theatrical gasp. "That's terrible."

"For fuck's sake, I've only known him for a couple of months, and we basically only have sex. I've made sure of it." Well. Sex and breakfast, my new favourite part of the day.

"You mean," asked Grace, "you only want to have sex with him?"

"N-no. It's just anything more would be wrong."

"Um." She blinked. "That makes a hundred percent zero sense."

"It makes a hundred percent perfect sense. It's just about on the edge of morally acceptable to let him fuck me until he gets bored. I can't trap him in something that has no future."

"But if he's in love with you anyway—"

"*Thinks* he's in love with me."

"I'm not trying to start a debate about phenomenology," put in Sam, "but is there a difference?"

I made a frustrated noise. "Yes. It's just sex and infatuation… and…and youthful enthusiasm. That's not love."

"Well, what is?"

"What I had with Robert." The words were out before I could stop them. Before I'd even realised they were there. They crashed into the room like crockery, and suddenly none of my friends would look at me.

"That poor kid." Grace let out a long, slow breath, almost a sigh. "In love with someone so emotionally unavailable and sexually over-available."

It wasn't a particularly flattering description, but it was probably accurate, and at least it showed she finally understood the magnitude of the problem. "I really don't want to hurt him."

"Because it's morally wrong, or because you care?"

"Jesus, Gracie, both. I'm not a sociopath."

"Oh, so you do care."

"Of course I fucking care. That's not in question. But we're not in a relationship, we can't be in a relationship, and I don't want to encourage him in this…I don't know…delusion."

Sam was nodding, and I briefly thought he was on my side. "You know"—unfortunately, it was his sarcastic voice—"when I was nineteen, and I fell in love, I was delusional."

So much for that. My friends were not my allies. That was probably why they were friends.

"You don't understand." I made another desperate attempt to explain. "He's very… He's too open. He trusts me. I can't betray that."

"So instead you're pushing him away?"

I looked round at their bewildered faces. "Only because it's the right thing to do."

Grace frowned. "Laurie, I love you, but you're hurting my brain. Are you seriously saying you're feeling bad about sleeping with this kid because you like him?"

"His name is Toby," I muttered unhelpfully. "And I'm exploiting him."

"Um, I think if you were exploiting him, you'd be less concerned about exploiting him." Grace untangled herself from her lovers, leaning towards me across the coffee table and my plate of cold pancakes. "It's obvious you like him back. It's kind of cute, actually. And if you don't want to call it love, that's fine, but if he does, that's fine too."

"Is it?" I asked. "Because it seems like I'm encouraging him in something that's bad for him."

"Let me think about this." She sat back, stroking an imaginary goatee. "I'm nineteen years old, I get to have quality kinky sex with a hot older guy. A guy who seems to genuinely care about my welfare and is far kinder, far sweeter, and far better to be with than he ever gives himself credit for?" She abandoned her absurd mime. "Y'know, I think I'm good."

"The only bit of that which feels like it's true is 'older.'" And the next thing I knew, Grace had jumped into my arms and I was being ruthlessly hugged. I gave her an awkward, abashed squeeze. "Not that this isn't nice, but...uh, why?"

She pulled back so she could look at me, her expression uncharacteristically solemn. "Because we let you get so lost."

———

I pondered the conversation on my way home. It was a pleasant day, bright and on the cusp of spring, and I suddenly realised I'd seen Toby naked in every way, but I'd never seen him in daylight. I tried to imagine what it would be like to be with him now, walking together, hand in hand, coming back from my friends, or going somewhere together. A couple.

It was an idea at once compelling and absurd. How could I be his boyfriend? Presumably I had been Robert's boyfriend once, but it felt like a word—and a concept—I had left behind long ago. Surely it was better to admit that Toby and I were simply having a fling. One that, sooner or later, would seem ill-advised to both of us and come to a swift, inevitable end.

The problem was, I didn't want it to end. I wanted Toby and the way he made me feel. I even wanted the breathless declarations he surely couldn't mean and I surely didn't deserve.

But wasn't it my responsibility to be clear-eyed? To do the right thing?

Whatever it was.

A busy week at the hospital—as if there were any others—meant I didn't have time to dwell on the problem. Though sometimes, in stolen moments as I drank my coffee, walked home, showered, woke in the morning, went to sleep at night, I did. Instead of the faces and bodies and wounds of the day, I thought of Toby. His too-big, dark-rimmed eyes, his sharp face. The way he kissed, holding nothing back.

The times he had blurted out "I love you" in a babble of passion. And that final time, the time I'd stopped him, when he'd sounded so dangerously certain. He had chained me open, made me vulnerable, made me beg, then weep for him, and the shame had burned itself to nothing until there was only freedom, pleasure, joy. It had been terrible and perfect, and still he'd found a way to strip me deeper with only some words I hadn't let him say.

I missed him.

And as I waited for him that Friday, I wondered—for the first time since we'd established our weekly ritual—if he would show up. Perhaps I'd been soul-searching for nothing, and he had already moved on. I couldn't have made any clearer the limitations of what was possible between us.

Even if some terrible part of me had liked hearing the words.

Just words. An indiscretion of the moment. He couldn't have meant them. Not really. How could they have such power over me? How could he?

I was so full of good intentions—resolved, if he did come, to talk to him. Possibly to bring this impossible situation to a neat and mature ending.

But then the doorbell rang and there was Toby on the doorstep and, suddenly, everything I had thought about and worried about seemed flimsy or irrelevant. And all that was left was a vague intention of maybe talking about it next week and the purest, giddiest happiness.

Sam had been right.

I'd been living my life as if nothing had changed. But the promise of Toby had illuminated all my days, edging them with gold like the calligraphy of medieval monks.

With an ugly, frantic moan, I pulled him inside and bent my head to kiss him.

For a second or two his face was turned up to mine, as if this moment had become as instinctive and as necessary for him as it was for me, but then he wriggled away, ducking under my arm so my lips grazed clumsily over his cheek instead.

His eyes sought mine. "We have to talk."

Ah.

It should have been a relief, in a way, that he had reached the very conclusion I kept postponing, but all I felt was dread. I nodded and led him into the living room.

I suddenly realised how little time we'd spent here. I'd been on my knees for most of it, and the rest had been sex, or a prelude to sex, and now it was awkward, as though we were strangers.

Toby was standing uncertainly in the middle of the room, his hands hanging at his sides as if he wasn't sure what to do with them. He looked...young, and I wanted to hold him until his shoulders relaxed their tension and all his tight, anxious muscles unlocked.

"Do you want to sit—" I began, at the exact moment he said, "We can't go on like this."

I took a sharp breath. The fact I'd expected this didn't make it any easier to hear. And there was a part of me—the part that was neither clear-eyed nor responsible and merely ached and craved like some lonely beast—that wanted to beg. *Not now. A little longer. Please don't leave me yet.* "I know."

He shoved his hands into the pockets of his hoodie. "Okay. Right. Good."

But he sounded miserable. As miserable as I was. The least I owed him was making this easy.

"We don't have to have this conversation," I told him gently. "I always thought you'd just stop coming when you were ready. You don't owe me anything."

His head came up, and his eyes were so very blue it hurt. "Why the fuck don't I owe you anything?"

"Because...because—" For a moment, I couldn't remember the answer. "Because I'm not...anyone to you."

"But you are. And I want to be someone to you."

"I don't think that's wise."

"Fuck wise." He stepped close to me, this bundle of bones and nerves, skin and ferocity, reached up, and slid a hand round the back of my neck. It was as sure as a collar, as undeniable as steel and leather. He could so easily have brought me to my knees, but all he did was draw our mouths together. "You promised you wouldn't do this again, but you're still doing it. You're just doing it a different way. So stop pretending I could just walk away and it wouldn't mean anything to you. Stop pretending it's all about me and what I want. Stop pretending this isn't real. Just stop fucking pretending. Because you're here too." His eyes burned into mine. "You're here too."

I stared at him, held by nothing but the lightest of touches and the brush of his breath, captive, as I'd been all along. "I'm here too," I whispered.

"And I love you, okay? So you'd better get used to it."

"Toby, you can't—"

"Nonnegotiable." He curled his fingers, his nails pressing star-bright crescents into my skin. "You don't have to say it back, but it's how I feel, and I'm not going to lie about it or pretend it isn't there. I love you."

I closed my eyes for a moment. I couldn't tell if what I felt was pleasure or pain. Or if the difference mattered. Only that he wanted to say it, and that it unpeeled me. Left me naked and shuddering.

"I love you." He glared. "I love you."

If I didn't do something, he might never stop saying it. "All right, all right. You love me. Point taken. Messaged received."

I'd meant to be gentler, but to my surprise, he let me go and laughed. "Well. Okay. Better than last time. It'll do for now."

For now? Oh God. I should have been managing his expectations, but I wasn't sure how to do that anymore or why I had ever wanted to.

My legs were strangely shaky, so I sank onto the sofa. "I thought you were about to break up with me," I said pitifully, then recoiled from myself. Why had I told him that?

Toby flew across the room and practically jumped into my lap, flinging his arms around me. And I clutched him helplessly because...because I wanted him, and this brush with the reality of losing him had stripped all my justifications and consolations from me. It had left me afraid. Defenceless.

"God," he cried. "No way. Never. I love—"

"I know, you've told me. But please stop saying it."

He rested his forehead against mine. This close he was a blur of blue eyes and a grin. "It's your own fault for not listening the first time. You've built up a love debt. Like a sleep debt. You've got to pay it off."

"Can't I pay it off some other way?"

"You mean"—he drew back a little and raised eyebrows in what I was sure he believed to be a lascivious fashion—"in a sex way."

"Yes. In a sex way."

"Totally. But Laurie?"

Oh no, he was serious again. "Yes?"

"I love the sex, I really do. I spend like literally all week thinking about all the things I want to do to you. But I want other stuff too. That's what I came here to say. I'm sorry if this sounds all blackmaily or something, but it honestly kind of hurts when you use something that's special to put me in a box."

It's just sex was the answer that hovered on the tip of my tongue, but it would have been a lie, and I was tired of lying. To him and to myself. With Toby there was no just anything, however hard I tried. "I never want to hurt you, darling."

"Then trust me. Not just with your body." His hand settled over my chest, missing my heart as usual, because he was both sentimental and hopelessly inaccurate, and for some inexplicable reason that...moved me.

I leaned into him, into his touch, and just breathed him in, the heat and the traces of his day, cooking oil and washing up liquid and Toby. Oh, Toby. Yearning unfurled into a vast and fathomless swell, swept me against him, and I broke.

I broke, and it felt like peace or hope or love, and I didn't care. "Anything. Anything you want."

"Everything."

Sweet, greedy, impossible princeling, he could have me.

Because, truthfully, he already did.

We sat there for a long time, doing nothing except holding each other, Toby's body curled into mine, utterly quiescent, almost as if he slept. But he was wide awake, and I sensed his eyes upon me, never straying. I half wondered what he was thinking. What he made of this man he had just made his.

———

Later, much later, we were hungry, so I pulled out the collection of takeaway menus Robert and I had long ago begun collecting and dumped them all in Toby's lap, where they shone like a neon rainbow.

"Do you have a favourite?" he wanted to know.

Once. I shook my head. "Why don't we... Why don't we find one?"

The smile he gave me. God. As bright as a pinwheel against my skin, and I submitted myself to it, not perhaps gladly but without hesitation, and let it spark every nerve I possessed.

He picked up a couple of the menus. "How do you feel about wok puns? Do you, in fact"—he pulled out finger guns—"wok them?"

"I was about to say I could go either way on wok puns, but I've changed my mind." I sat down on the floor at his feet, propped an elbow on one of the sofa cushions, and rested my head against it, which allowed me to look up at Toby as he sorted through take-away menus. It wasn't a particularly, or intentionally, submissive act. It was simply where I wanted to be right then.

"Not even...Woking on Sunshine?"

"That's a lie. You made that one up."

He laughed. "Yeah, but there's some strong competition here. Wok This Way? Wok 'n' Roll. Wok Around the Clock. This one's just called Wok 22, I don't even know what that's a pun of. It's just a really random reference. Anthem for Doomed Woks."

"The Grapes of Wok?"

In the end we settled on the Tasty House because Toby said he was susceptible to really blatant advertising. He stroked my hair and told me a story about being lost in Brighton after a night out clubbing, desperate for sustenance, and ending up in an eatery called FOOD simply because of the name. He rambled on easily enough, half hypnotising me with his voice and his fingers until I was helplessly content and as completely his as I'd ever been.

"Laurie?"

"Mmm?"

"Tell me something about you."

I half opened my heavy eyes. "What sort of thing?"

"I don't know. Anything."

"That's not helpful, Toby."

"Well"—he pouted at me—"neither are you."

"How do you mean?"

"You don't talk."

"What do you call this?"

He tugged playfully at my hair. "I mean, like, you say things but you don't *volunteer*. You don't tell me stuff. I don't really know much about you at all."

I opened my mouth to protest, but then I realised he was

right. My friends had all known me for years, and to the sort of strangers I met, I told only my preferences, my hard and soft limits, my safeword. Somehow, I'd lost the habit of talking in the way he meant. Of sharing myself like that. It was a rather frightening thought. And lonely too.

My mouth had gone dry. "I'm not trying to keep anything from you."

"So talk to me."

Oh God. I had no idea how to begin. And suddenly, I found myself wishing I played the alto sax. Was that why Dom had told me that? Because he felt like this as well? "I can't... I don't... I want to but..."

What I wanted to say was *help me*. But I couldn't quite form the words. I didn't like to beg outside the bedroom.

Then Toby grinned and helped me anyway. Granting mercy when I needed it most. "What's your sign?"

"My...oh, Leo."

"Your favourite colour?"

"Blue."

"Your favourite ice cream?"

"Vanilla."

He gave a whoop of laughter. "Seriously?"

"What did you expect me to say? Mint choc pain? Rum and suffering?" He was still giggling, so I went on, "Look, I'll have you know that proper vanilla ice cream, the sort with the pods in it, is really good." Oh dear God, I sounded pompous.

But Toby leaned down and kissed my brow. "It's okay, I'm into cooking. You don't have to defend vanilla to me. It's awesome."

For a little while, we were quiet, his hands still moving tenderly in my hair, and I wondered if he was satisfied with the talking we had achieved. But then he asked, "Do you like your job?"

I shrugged, my shoulder nudging his knee. "I'm not sure 'like' comes into it."

"That's your answer to everything." There was an edge of laughter to his voice.

"Just sex and work."

"Is there anything you do like without making it really complicated?"

I smiled up at him, soothed and absurd and undone. "I like you."

He went a little pink. "Now you're just avoiding the question."

"I..." I wanted to answer, but I didn't know how to begin, so I lost myself in silence, while his impatience gathered around me.

"See, this is exactly what I mean. You're fine to talk to me about ice cream but not what you do every day?"

"I'm not...I'm not trying to push you away. I'm just"— frightened of frightening you—"wondering how to explain."

"What's to explain?"

The truth was, most people didn't understand what I did and why I did it and how it made me feel. If I was lucky, they would tell me they thought I was very brave. If I wasn't, they would shake their head and say, *I just don't know how you can do something like that.* As if I were an alien or a serial killer. I sighed. "I don't like what I do, Toby, but I need to do it, and it's part of who I am. I think...I think there's a strangeness or some dislocation inside me that makes me perfectly designed for it."

He blinked, but he kept on touching me, and I pressed into his touching. *Don't lose me. Don't let me get lost.* "I don't think there's anything weird about being a doctor. About helping people."

"I don't really help people in any sense you'd recognise. I just stop them dying."

"That seems pretty helpful to me."

That was how it always started: trying to make light before understanding set in. There would be a few minutes, at least, when Toby might look at me and believe me some kind of hero. But I wasn't. I wasn't brave. I wasn't noble. I was just a man who made decisions.

"It's not benevolence," I explained. "It's detached from that, just like I am. When I arrive at an incident, that's the first thing that happens. The adrenaline hits me, and everything slows down, and all of me is gone, shunted away to I-don't-know-where, so there's only the things I know how to do and the clarity to do them. It's how I can do it. Know which bodies I can fight for, which ones I can't, or won't."

His eyes held mine, not yet flinching. "That sounds kind of like a big responsibility. I freak out when I have to do the weekly egg order for the caff. Does it scare you?"

"No, it...it thrills me." I closed my eyes for a moment, hiding from my own truths and his reaction to them. "It's a profoundly powerful thing to stop someone dying in such a direct and individual way. Most medicine is an extended negotiation, but prehospital medicine... It's the thinnest imaginable line between life and death. It's where I can do something that matters."

"Wow." He let out a rush of breath, as if he'd been holding it. "Laurie, that's amazing. *You're* amazing."

It was desperately tempting to let him think that. To snatch up his admiration like a greedy child. I couldn't do it though. I couldn't take what wasn't rightfully mine, no matter how much I wanted it. "But you see," I said softly, "it's only afterwards I remember. Only afterwards I remember it's lives. Not just bodies and statistics and probabilities and triage."

For a little while, Toby said nothing. I had absolutely no idea what he was thinking. Another thin line, but this time I was powerless, waiting for him to choose his side. Choose me. He slithered off the sofa and came fully in my arms. His answer was a kiss.

And we kissed for a long time, softly, Toby's tongue sweeping mine. The last time we'd brought our bodies together on (well, in the vicinity of) my sofa, it had been in passion, our kisses clanging cymbals, so different from these. But in some strange way they felt the same, kisses that were their own journey. I'd forgotten it could be like this, but each and every time, whether it was fast or slow, rough or sweet, Toby reminded me.

At last, we parted, but he stayed close, both of us still on the floor—which should have been ridiculous. Oh, why did I care? Who was here to judge us, except me?

Toby tucked his head against my shoulder and wriggled his hand into mine. "It doesn't matter how you do it. Just that you do."

I smiled, grateful for his stubborn affection, his conviction that, whoever I was or whatever it meant, it was right for me to be that way. It had been such a long time since I'd talked about any of this. I hadn't thought I needed to. With Robert it had been accepted as part of me and therefore part of us, just like everything else, as unchangeable and irrelevant as the colour of my eyes, my inability to roll my tongue, or my preference to suffer and his to make me.

It wasn't long before Toby stirred again, peeping up at me through his lashes in what he clearly thought was an appealing fashion. And he was right. "Can I ask something else? And don't say you just did, because that shit isn't funny."

"Um. Yes?"

"Even if it's weird?"

"Especially if it's weird."

"You don't like...what you like...because of, like, stuff, do you?"

I ran the words through my head a few times trying to make sense of them. "I don't like what I like because of, like, stuff?"

I felt him laughing before I heard it. It was an unexpected intimacy. "Thanks for making me sound like a moron. I meant... the sex thing, the kinky sex thing."

"Oh, I see." Another reasonably familiar question, though rarely asked as bluntly. "You mean, do I want to be hurt and shamed and denied because I'm stricken with terrible guilt for all the lives I can't save?"

He stared at me. "I guess that's a no."

"That's a no." I slid a hand under the hem of his T-shirt and up his back, wanting the simplicity of his skin under my palm. He shuddered a little, his spine shifting against me as he uncurled beneath my touch. I stroked him, smiled, felt light. Content. "This is where you reassure me that you don't have some trauma to avenge upon my not-particularly-reluctant flesh."

His eyes flew wide. "God no. I want to hurt you because I ☆ love you."

And, as some potent mixture of anticipation, tenderness, wanting, and fear flooded me with heat, I believed him.

———

Our takeaway arrived a few minutes later, and despite the fact I had a perfectly serviceable dining room just across the hall, we ate on the floor of the living room, surrounded by plastic bags and foil containers.

"You know"—Toby wagged a wooden chopstick at me—"I've been reading the internet—"

"You should never read the internet, Toby."

"Ha-ha. But, yeah, if we were doing this properly, you would be like naked and on your knees and eating from my hand."

I went still with apprehension. "Um, is that something you'd like?"

He laughed. "No. Not at all."

"Thank God."

"Why?" He gave me a wicked, curious look from beneath his lashes. "Would you, if I wanted?"

I groaned, unable to easily articulate or understand the complexities of my reaction. "I–I don't know. I've never done that with anyone. I don't think I'd like it at all, but there's part of me that stirs to...to...do something I hated that much for you."

Toby was quiet, watching me, his fringe falling maddeningly across one eye. How could he stand it? My fingers itched to push it away. "No," he said finally, with all the conviction I lacked. "No. I'm kind of so totally turned on by the idea of you doing something you hate for me, but I want it to be something I really want, not something I don't care about."

Relief swept over me gently. I hadn't precisely anticipated his answer, but oddly enough it didn't surprise me. "You know you can do anything you like with me."

"Yeah, I do." He grinned. "That's why I've got to make it count."

"Also, I'm not sure cheap takeaway was what the internet had in mind for those kind of dominance games. It's not exactly anyone's idea of sexy, is it?"

He flicked his hair out of the way. "Oh yeah?"

So to prove my point, I ended up licking a splash of kung pao sauce from the centre of Toby's hand—sticky-sweet, full of MSG, and underneath it, the taste of skin. I lost myself in a matter of moments to the unexpected roughness of his palm, its collection of small scars and its deep grooves. It was a worrier's hand, a worker's hand, passionate and restless, though temporarily quieted by my clasp. I slipped my tongue between his fingers, which made him yelp, and circled back to trace the fleshy mound at the base of his thumb. Thenar eminence. Mount of Venus.

He made a half-swallowed guttural noise, which came out something like *ngh*.

I kissed lightly over the planes of his palm. There was nothing but Toby now, his scent and his taste, his raspy, suddenly shallow breathing.

"Holy shit. Now I know why the Elizabethans got so freaked out about paddling with the palm of the hand. That's, like, fucking lewd, man."

I gave him my smile too, left there against his skin, in his hand, like a secret. Then I let him go and sat back against the sofa, trying to ignore our now present and matching erections. "Point proven?"

"I wouldn't say—" he still sounded shaky— "proven. You eviscerated your point. That is absolutely my idea of sexy."

"I'm not sure that had much to do with the food."

"Huh. Maybe we'd better check."

He held out half a prawn cracker, and I eyed it dubiously. But it was Toby, and pleasing him pleased me, so I leaned forward and accepted it. As his fingers slipped past my lips, I recognised the charade and took them as though they were his cock, sucking and licking until he was moaning unabashedly.

When I let him go, he shoved me onto my back and stretched out on top of me, and we unravelled each other gently, kissing and touching and pushing our bodies together through too many layers of clothing. It was far from the most erotically charged experience of my life, but it felt so good, so profoundly, quietly good in a way I would have been hard-pressed to explain.

On my living room floor, time stopped mattering. There was

only Toby, hot and sharp-boned and wriggling, his T-shirt riding up and his jeans halfway down as he rubbed himself against my thigh and occasionally my cock. His hair was in his eyes and his kisses were sloppy, and the scent of sweat and arousal muddled awkwardly with the scent of half-eaten takeaway. Denim chafed my skin, and my partially undone shirt was too tight under my shoulders, but still, I came before he did, almost without realising I was going to, the pleasure cresting from some deep, half forgotten place inside me.

Toby dissolved into his usual litany of love and obscenity, jerked, tensed, and erupted all over me. While he made a cursory attempt to clean us up with a handful of napkins, I stared at my ceiling, slightly stunned, wondering how and why dry humping had suddenly come back into my life.

"Oh man"—Toby draped a possessive arm over me—"that was awesome."

We drifted for a little while in satiation and silence, and I came perilously close to falling asleep, but then Toby tilted his head back so he could look at me and asked, "So, when that red helicopter is whirring overhead...that's you?"

"Occasionally. At night we use a car. But I only do a couple of shifts a month. Mainly I'm at the hospital, seeing patients there or doing tedious things like paperwork and training junior doctors."

"Do you only work a few shifts because it's so...I was going to say 'stressful'...but I guess 'intense' is better?"

He was right; *intense* was better. After a moment, I nodded.

"What sort of stuff do they call you out for?"

"All sorts of things. Car crashes, stabbings, shootings, industrial accidents, cardiac arrest, falls. We go wherever we're needed. I was there after the London bombings."

"Seriously?" He pushed himself onto an elbow. "Oh my God, I was, like, at school."

"Thank you for the reminder of your appalling youth." I gazed up at him, less shocked than I should have been at the evidence of the distances between us. Perhaps it was because, right now, there were none. We were simply each other's, in a world of our own making.

"It felt totally weird, like the day before you break up for the holidays, except the opposite of that."

I pulled him back into my arms, where he fit and I could keep him safe.

"We were off for the rest of the week." He sighed, and for a moment he didn't seem quite like Toby. Smaller somehow, a little bit faded. "I was really fucking scared for ages. And everyone kept saying how brave we all were. Like you have a choice not to be around if someone blows up part of your city using the thing that takes you from one bit of it to another."

He fell quiet again, and I had nothing to say either. I was too busy being uncontrollably afraid of the world and all the ways it could hurt my Toby, and how little I could protect him from any of it. It was a foolish impulse, selfish and slightly patronising. Pain was simply an inevitability of living, and I had to learn how to trust him with his own, as I trusted him with mine.

"I remember it too." The words came out hesitantly, almost against my will, an offering of a kind.

His head snapped up. "Yeah?"

"Yes. I remember...I remember walking along the tracks to get where I needed to be. I was walking past people, people who were injured, probably dying, calling out to me and to each other and to God, all of them lost in the dark. And I was ignoring them because...because they would *probably* die without me, but beyond them were the people who *definitely* would. And beyond them there were people for whom I wouldn't even try."

"But aren't there, like, secondary explosions and stuff when bombs go off?"

"Sometimes."

"And you went down there anyway?"

"It's my job. I was probably terrified, but I didn't really think about it."

"You're one of my favourite people in the universe." He nuzzled under my chin like an overly enthusiastic, slightly amorous cat. "And you totally blow my mind sometimes."

For lack of any other response, I cleared my throat, pleased and embarrassed and slightly overwhelmed. What was I supposed to say? Ditto? Because he did, with his honesty and his playfulness, his unexpected strength.

"You know what else blows my mind?" he asked.

"What?"

"Just other people's lives generally. How fucking real they are sometimes. Like, take my great-granddad. He was in the war, right? He doesn't think he was brave either because it was just what he had to do, you know?"

His voice had grown a little husky. I stroked his hair a bit, letting its wayward strands fall softly between my fingers, and then he began to speak again.

"We used to do Poppy Day together every year and—"

"Used to?"

"Yeah, he's not well. We missed last year. Had to watch it on the telly. We're not religious or anything, but we always used to go to a service with his army mates. And I'd get all kind of...tight inside...when I saw them, always one or two less than the year before, shuffling and limping and hobbling into the church, all these frail and, like, totally valiant old men, you know."

"I know." I kissed him close-lipped and still tasted salt.

He sniffed rather wetly into my collar. "Once in Africa, Granddad's whole unit got killed or scattered so there was just three of them left, starving and ragged and desperately trying to get back. But there was this minefield between them and the British Army, and they were all like, 'Well this is it, curtains.' But he was like, 'No way. I'm a Jacobs; I'm going to be first against the wall when the Germans catch us.' So he just, like, leads them over this...this fucking minefield, y'know. This kid from East London whose name nobody is going to remember but me."

Oh God. Toby, my Toby. I held him tightly, though really, I was the one who felt held. Surrounded by him and all his deep, fierce love. "Toby..."

"Yeah?"

Yeah what indeed. "Let me take you to bed."

He blinked, damp eyelashes scraping my neck. "Why are you even asking? Hell yeah."

We untangled, stood—in my case rather stiffly. I held out my hand, and he took it, and we went upstairs together.

I stripped him, laid him out, and covered him with my body, and he lifted his knees and wrapped his legs around me. "I don't think I'm ever going to do anything amazing."

"You're already amazing," was the last coherent thing I said to him that night.

He woke me the next morning with a kiss, a cup of tea, and a plate of his inexplicably delicious scrambled eggs. We were both a little shy after the intimacies of the night before, but even that was pleasure of a kind. I'd shuffled away, bruised, almost satisfied, and slightly shamed, from so many semi-anonymous encounters that I could no longer differentiate them, but I couldn't remember the last time it had been like this. If it should even have been possible to be thirty-seven and feel so new.

"Laurie?" Toby was sprawled naked on his stomach, his feet swinging in the air, the silverish sunlight pooling on his back and shining on the curve of his arse. He was entirely at ease, beautiful, some Wildean wet dream given form. Just for me. God. Was this my taste now? Hyacinth boys? Or could I say my taste was simply Toby?

"Yes?"

"What's in the Bluebeard room?"

I should have expected it—he never let anything go—but, nevertheless, the question hit me hard enough to make the blood roar in my ears. "Nothing. I mean, almost nothing. Just some relics. It's mostly empty."

He propped his chin on his hand and eyed me slyly. "Mostly empty except for a single rose in a glass case, wilting slowly, petal by petal, and, like, waiting for you to learn to love again."

For a moment I thought I was angry, but it turned out I was laughing—a slightly odd laugh, edged with pain. Was that really how he saw me? My love as abstract and ridiculous as a fairy tale? "Fine. You can look if you want."

He bounced off the bed, an entirely different creature to the shivering boy who had clung to a towel and refused to let me see him, and claimed my dressing gown. Somewhat more reluctantly, I cast aside the *Times*, pulled on some trousers, and followed him down the hall.

The room was exactly as I'd left it. The first memory that surfaced was not of Robert, but the night I'd met Toby. When

I'd stood here, shamefully weeping, for myself, and perhaps for Toby, if only I'd known it then.

Right now he looked confused, his face turned up to the skylight. "Um...I was kind of expecting...not like a dungeon...but... like something..."

"I told you there was nothing here. Once, it was a space we used. Now it's just a room I don't."

"There's that." He pointed to the wooden chest shoved against the far wall. "It's not got a body in it, 'as it, Mr. Todd?"

I wasn't in the mood to be playful. "It's full of things, Toby. Things I used to use with Robert, all right?"

"We don't have to do this. I was just interested, but not if it's going to make you pissy."

God. I could hear the hurt in his voice. "No. No, it's fine. Sorry. Here." I crossed to the chest and threw it open, revealing... everything. Topped by the cuffs I'd given him when he'd asked to tie me up and I'd...let him. Even thinking about what he'd done to me that night made me hot with fear and humiliation and bliss.

Toby crept over, peered inside, and gasped. I hadn't been particularly careful. I'd simply bundled up the ropes and chains and floggers and toys and dumped them into the box, and now they lay tangled up together, neglected, stripped of context, frankly peculiar. I'd been vaguely intending to throw them away for years, but somehow I'd managed not to. It hadn't felt like I would be moving on. It'd felt like I would be giving up hope. Not for Robert, but for something.

"I don't even know what half this stuff is," said Toby. I couldn't tell if he sounded horrified or awed.

"Well, you can ask me, and I'll tell you." I was so far away, so very far away, right now.

"You've got a lot of rope."

"Yes. Robert... He...he liked it."

He glanced over his shoulder. "That was your boyfriend?"

"He wasn't my boyfriend."

"You've got a serious bee in your bonnet about that word."

"It's facile. I mean, he was my friend, but he was my lover and my partner, the man I would have chosen to live my life with."

Toby straightened and the lid of the chest fell shut with a muted crash. His face was oddly still, reflecting nothing, his eyes flat and stripped of their brightness. "You're seriously not over him, huh? After...how long?"

"Six years, almost. Together for twelve."

"You don't think that's edging on...y'know...pathetic."

I was too weary to even be angry with him. "Probably, Toby. Very probably."

There was a long silence.

"What? That's it?" One of his arms flapped in a gesture of frustration so profound it was almost comical. "That's all I get?"

I could have pretended I didn't know what he meant, but I did, and he was right. He deserved more. "It's not him I'm not over. I mean, I loved him, and love doesn't just go away when it becomes inconvenient. But it's the loss of...a whole life, I think."

I sat on top of the chest. Too late, Pandora.

After a moment, Toby squeezed on next to me, pulling up a knee and hugging it. "Plenty of people have multiple successful relationships. Some divorcées even get married again. Crazy shit like that."

"No, I know that. But"—I patted the chest—"there's this. Early on, I told myself it didn't matter. It was just sex. So I went out, and I tried to meet people I could fall in love with. But it always came back to this."

"Because," he asked uncertainly, "you need it?"

I'd never liked to think of submission as need, because it stripped away too much agency and reduced to helpless compulsion everything I craved and wanted and thrilled to. What I *needed* was the choice to share these things, not simply to have them fulfilled. How long since I had thought about this? And longer still since I'd had to articulate it to someone else. But then, usually I didn't offer, and people didn't ask.

Except today I'd come as close as I ever could to offering, and Toby had asked.

"Because," I explained, "it's part of me, and if I deny it or ignore it, it feels like I've had to give something up for someone else. Even if it's something that some people would consider, I don't know, unimportant in the grand scheme of love and desire."

He grabbed my hand and gently uncurled my fingers. "It's not unimportant."

"I think it's almost incomprehensible sometimes. The truth is, somebody could be perfect for me in every way, but if he didn't want me on my knees occasionally, then I couldn't be happy with him." I looked down at our hands, at Toby's skinny fingers and knotty knuckles, his pared-down, slightly ragged nails. I could imagine them on my skin. "That's when I got into the Scene, where everything is about this." Another tap on the chest. "And I realised I was going to have to choose, so I did, but it was just another compromise really."

He twisted round so he was facing me, and since it felt a little odd to be in profile to him, I turned too. Perhaps this had been his plan all along, because he slid his spare hand round to the back of my neck and pulled me close, his gaze intent on mine. "Is that how you see me? A compromise?"

I swallowed.

Yes. And no.

And maybe. And no.

No. But perhaps that was just the answer I wanted to give him, and it wasn't fair to lie.

"I don't know," I said.

He still didn't flinch. "Because you aren't any sort of compromise to me." He leaned in and kissed me lightly. "You're perfect."

I blushed. I actually blushed. All because of a chaste kiss and a childish compliment. "Nobody's perfect, Toby."

"Well, okay, if you ever felt like actually believing in me. In us. That'd be nice. And, like, someday you could maybe make it easy, instead of making me fight for every scrap of you like you're the fucking Somme."

His thumb swept back and forth over my wrist. I hadn't realised I was sensitive there, but my pulse quickened at his touch. "So not perfect, then."

"You could work on it." He smiled. "Wouldn't take much. And then I'd have a sexy, clever, kind, and interesting guy who'd be willing to love me back." Before I could answer, or—more likely— protest, he went on. "It doesn't have to be this or that with me. Because all *that* stuff and all *this* stuff"—he tapped his chest, missing his heart as usual—"they're the same, y'know. They're just reasons I'm into you."

I couldn't afford to think about any of that right then. Toby had too many ways of making me naked. I shuddered suddenly, remembering being on my knees for him, remembering wearing chains for him, suffering for him, begging for him. The wild light in his eyes. The way I made him gasp and moan and come apart, just by being helpless. By being his.

"All right," I said.

He let me go, laughing. "Someday you're going to stop being the Somme and be...like...Zanzibar."

"Um, I'll last thirty-eight minutes?"

"You'll just stop fighting." He leaned in and nudged my nose with his. "You can occasionally and voluntarily say something nice to me, you know. I won't expect you to marry me after."

I kissed him instead. Concession, apology, promise.

Afterwards, he grinned at me. "Hey, since we're here, can I have another look in the magic box?"

I couldn't think of a reason to say no, so we climbed off, and I unleashed Toby. I stared out of the window at the grey morning sky as he rummaged, trying not to pay too much attention to the clinks and thumps.

"Laurie?"

"Yes, darling?"

"Will you come back? I don't have a fucking clue about any of this."

Which was how I ended up sitting on the floor with Toby, surrounded by sex toys like the most depraved Christmas morning imaginable. Most of it, thankfully, was self-explanatory and Toby was a child of the internet age, so it never quite became a show-and-tell. But there was no denying that it felt good—some impossible, shiver-inducing mixture of anticipation, fear, and pleasure—to watch him there and imagine myself at the mercy of Toby and all these things.

"This," he announced, "looks like something you'd use in the kitchen."

Oh God, help me. "It's not something you use in the kitchen."

"Like one of those really complicated things people buy for separating eggs that never work properly because that's what hands are for."

I gave him a look. "And verily the Lord beheld Adam, who He had fashioned in His image, and thought to Himself, 'I had better give him some appendages for the separating of eggs,' and thus he gave man two hands for that purpose, and, lo, eggs were separated, and it was good."

Toby giggled—it was a giggle, there was no other way of describing it—and I smiled at him, helplessly pleased to have inspired it and how natural, how easy, it felt to be with him now I wasn't constantly on my guard against any show of affection. Even if part of me still balked and called it foolishness.

"What's it for, then?" he asked.

"It's just a type of cock ring, Toby."

He jangled the thing. "Cock rings, you mean."

"They're called 'The Gates of Hell.'"

Suddenly he grinned at me, just like he had at Pervocracy: too big, too bright, too goofy, the tip of one incisor peeking out of the edges of his smile. "You'd look gorgeous in it. Can I put it on you?"

"What, now?"

"Easy, tiger. I mean, like...at some point."

My cock hardened self-defeatingly, as if in masochistic expectation of future restriction. "You know you can."

"Yeah, I know. I just like hearing you say it." He traced the circumference of the widest ring with a finger. "Does it hurt?"

"Yes, but I don't mind. If you like it."

He tilted his head curiously. "Could you come with this on?"

"Probably. If you"—my careful tone wavered a little—"forced me."

"I'd like that. I'd really like that. God." He was a little flushed as he put the Gates of Hell back down, which filled me with the most terrible desire to kiss him, to please him, to hurt for him.

And to tell him all these things.

To admit that I'd always been Zanzibar.

"Now this"—he picked up something else—"this is definitely kitchenware. It looks like it's one of the bits from under the sink."

"It's an anal hook."

"Jesus...does that...go where I think it does?"

"No, Toby, it goes—" I tried to think of some sarcastic alternative, but then I realised how pointlessly petulant it would sound. "Yes. Yes, it does."

He ran a hand gently over the curving steel. "You're into some seriously hardcore stuff."

"I wouldn't say *into*. More sort of *own*."

"How am I supposed to live up to this?"

I reached out, pulled the damn thing off him, and cast it away. "You're not."

"Wow." He frowned, his face pulling into a sequence of tight, hurt lines.

"That wasn't supposed to sound negative. The thing is, it's not what you do that matters, it's"—I paused a moment, not quite sure what I was saying—"what it means."

Oh. Oh God.

In the rush to console him for my carelessness, I'd stumbled over a piece of truth that was fundamental to me, held so deep in my heart I'd forgotten it was there. On instinct alone, I'd tried to give it to Toby, and instead given it back to myself.

It's not what you do, it's what it means.

For a moment, I was dizzy with rediscovery. Then there was only pain. A flood of interchangeable memories accumulated over three years' worth of hopeless, pointless hookups. Necessary at the time, but so very much not what I had ever wanted and nothing close to what I needed. And how hollow it seemed now that I was with Toby. A wretched past to bring to this beautiful boy.

I didn't think I did anything or said anything, but there must have been some trace of what I felt reflected on my face or revealed by my body because suddenly Toby was in my lap, in my arms, kissing me.

"I'm so glad I met you," I told him.

And I meant it. I meant it as deeply as I'd ever meant anything.

———————

Later, we piled everything back into the box, except for a flogger Toby was still holding. He was letting the falls run gently through the fingers of his opposite hand, and the rasp of skin and deerskin seemed both unbearably loud and unbearably sensuous in the quiet, almost empty room.

"What if I wanted to hurt you?" he asked.

"Well, you'd be unlikely to succeed with that. It's very soft."

"Yeah, I know. I guess I thought..." He looked flustered.

"I take it you've never used a flogger before?"

He shrugged. "What can I say? Comprehensive school. Just wasn't on the curriculum."

"Then you've got the right instincts because this one is a good choice for you." That banished some of his sulkiness, his lips tipping into a little smile. I stepped closer. "You're not...particularly tall so I'm afraid it's going to be a bit annoying to find floggers that work for you."

"All the world's against me." He put a hand to his forehead and staggered melodramatically.

"I'm afraid so, darling. Most whips will be designed on the assumption you're not...um—"

"A short-arse?"

I nodded. "But this should work fine. The tails aren't too long, and the handle should be comfortable." I put my hand over his and showed him how to find the balance point, and then I adjusted his grip so he was holding the flogger correctly. "It's all in the wrist."

Toby made an odd, breathy sound.

"Too much?"

"No, it's just...insanely hot. You showing me how to...so I can...*on you*. You have no idea how fucking horny I am right now."

I slid my free hand into the dressing gown, discovering his cock throbbing among folds of flannel. "I have some notion."

Then he was wriggling and laughing, and I was laughing too, layering this moment like fresh paint over a lot of cracked, old memories.

"Mind you"—he pressed shamelessly against me—"I'm still not sure I'd have the balls to use this on a person."

"Do you want me to show you?"

There was a pause. "Um...uh...this probably sounds weird, but I don't think I go that way. Like, not at all. Same as I know I don't want to sleep with girls, even though I haven't tried. Sorry."

"I'm not asking you to submit to me."

He twisted his head round to give me an incredulous look. "You're going to tie me up and hit me with something, and somehow that's not submissive?"

"I wasn't going to tie you up."

"Oh, well, that's cool, then."

"It's up to you, Toby, always. But I suppose it comes down to whether you think dominance and submission are about acts or about people."

He was quiet for a moment. "I guess I think...power is where you put it." He looked down at the flogger, his expression slightly wary. "So how would it work? I...I'm kind of pathetically scared of being hurt."

"I wouldn't hurt you. I'll make you feel wonderful."

"By hitting me?"

"I promise."

He sighed and slapped the flogger into my outstretched hand. "I must be fucking nuts."

"Thank you. Can I take off your dressing gown?" After a moment, he nodded. "Okay."

I undid the knot and pushed the fabric off his shoulders, letting the whole garment flump onto the floor in a pile. It wasn't cold, but Toby shivered instinctively in his nakedness, and gazed up at me with slightly widened eyes, kittenishly blue, I realised, in natural light.

"Just so you know," he said, "I'm not feeling all that dominant at the moment."

I dropped the flogger, took him into my arms, and kissed him. First, his mouth, then his throat, his shoulders, his collarbones, soft and steady worship to remind him that I served him, adored him, wanted only to please him.

When he was hard, gasping, and shivering for quite different reasons, I turned him to face the wall and had him brace himself upon his hands. He made a slightly unhappy noise, almost a whimper, and tightened his shoulders, his enthusiasm visibly flagging. I covered him with my body, caressing him, loving him with my hands and my mouth, until the position felt natural and he was warm and pliant beneath my touches.

I didn't think he even noticed when I stepped away to pick up the flogger, but when I drew the tails slowly up his back, he jerked and then let out a long, shuddering breath. I did that for a while, letting him grow accustomed to the feel of deer hide against his skin, the weight and drag of the tresses.

"You know where it's safe to flog someone?"

"Yeah." His voice was pleasure-thick and husky. "'S'on the internet. Back, arse, not spine, not kidneys."

It had been a while since I'd held a flogger, longer still since I'd used one on someone. It felt comfortable in my hand, though, its weight familiar, and its movements predictable. I practiced a little against the air until my arm and wrist remembered how to make the tresses fall as I wished.

And then I hesitated, staring at Toby's naked back, awkward in a way I hadn't anticipated. Standing there, completely unrestrained, a flogger in my hand, and needing—of all things—reassurance. "This... You would... It's all right, isn't it?"

"Yeah. Totally. 'S'nice." He pulled his shoulders back, opening his body to me. "I trust you. In, like, all the ways."

"Try to keep still in case...I—" Miss. Wrap the tails. Hurt you.

"Promise."

I moved close behind him and kissed the nape of his neck, because I knew he loved to be touched there. He responded with a little moan, but—true to his word—he didn't move. Then I stepped away, steadied my hands, and began. It was a tease, a seduction, another act of worship, this time with thirty buttery soft pieces of deerskin free-falling against his upper back.

Toby had tensed initially, the muscles in his arms tightening as he braced himself for the pain I would never give him. But as soon as he got used to the steady rhythm of my strokes, the brush and heavy, caressing thud of leather, and the heat gathering under his skin, he relaxed again, his head falling forward between his outstretched hands.

"'S'good," he mumbled. "So good."

His pleasure settled inside me, as warm as whisky, and banished the last of my uncertainties. I was completely out of practice, but this was so gentle—simply the weight of the flogger and the guidance of my wrist—I could probably have kept it up for as long as he wanted. As it was, it took only about fifteen minutes until my Toby was flushed and supple and moaning softly with every fall of the flogger.

He was beautiful. And as usual, I was desperate for him. For his pleasure. And utterly humbled by his responses, his honesty, everything he gave and made me want to give.

I switched to figure eights, letting the tails land more firmly now on each side of his back. The first strokes drew a deep, blissed-out groan from him, like the first time I'd taken his cock into my throat. I didn't know how long we lasted, the air full of soft swishes and slaps, my harsh breath and Toby's, but it was long enough to make me sweat and ache a little. Which felt right too, so very right.

"Laurie...Laurie...I need..." Toby sounded almost drunk.

I dropped the flogger, and he pushed himself away from the wall, swaying into my waiting arms. The skin of his back was burning against my chest, but he was utterly pliant, a molten boy, cast in the shape of all the pleasure he'd taken from me beneath the falls of a flogger.

He caught my wrist with trembling, clumsy fingers and dragged my hand to his cock, which was as hot as his back and straining towards his belly, damp-tipped. I made a fist round him, and he came against the wall a few seconds later, his face turned into my neck, his mouth painting *yes* and *Laurie* and *I love you, I love you*, against my skin.

We finished in a sweaty, sticky pile on the floor, both of us barely able to move. I was half-aroused, half-content, wholly Toby's.

"Oh my God," he said finally. "I need to be able to do that to you." He sat up, still naked and come-splattered, his hair shiny with perspiration and sticking up hedgehog-style from the top of his head. "Teach me how."

I groaned. "I'm an old man. I'm exhausted."

But nevertheless, I staggered to my feet and taught a very eager and quick-learning Toby a few basic strokes, including the ones I'd used on him, and quite a few harsher ones he could... use on me.

"Man." He inscribed several perfect figure eights in the air. "This should have been on the syllabus. I'd have been at Oxford by now with my four As in Kinky Sex and Further Kinky Sex."

"Toby, why *aren't* you at university?"

There was a long silence. Even the flogger was still.

"Meh," he explained.

And then nothing more.

"'Meh'? What does 'meh' mean?"

"It means I don't want to talk about it, okay?"

I could have pointed out that Toby could be oddly reticent for somebody so insistent on the necessity of caring and sharing and etc. But I didn't because his eyes begged me not to.

He twirled the flogger loose-wristed, his technique definitely improving. "So. What's the next step?"

"I'm afraid it's terribly unglamorous. But you practice."

"You don't mean on you, right?"

"On a pillow. Or a wall. Until it's all muscle memory and awareness, and you can make those tails land exactly where you want, every single time."

"Wow, that's not on the internet. Bunch of doms hitting a wall."

"I'm sorry, Toby. But the truth is kink is no different to any- ☆ thing else. If you want to be good at it, you practice."

"You say that but you have no idea how long it took me to

make a soufflé that didn't implode." He flashed a big smile at me. "I've totally got this. Uh, I mean, unless you want the flogger back?"

"No, keep it."

"It's not weird, since it was, y'know, your bloke's?"

"I don't care if you don't care."

"Only thing I care about is all the stuff I want to do with you." He sidled up close. "Besides, there's plenty of ways I can hurt you without needing special training."

"Yes." It was a sigh of longing and surrender.

He curled his hands into claws, put them against my chest and dragged his nails across my skin. They weren't sharp, but the touch was still too harsh to be a caress, its message unmistakable. I looked down in time to see the white lines he had given me fading slowly.

Which was when he did it again. And again. Until his fingers left a wake, a cold burn that gathered and deepened with each new journey.

"Please." I didn't even know what I was asking for. It certainly wasn't cessation.

He leaned in and licked fresh fire over the places he had left raw. "Something to remember me by."

I gave him a startled look.

"I mean till next week. Sorry, that came out way melodramatic."

It must have been that promise of pain, making me light-headed. "You're in me deeper than my skin."

He pressed himself against me, bringing his lines into hot, bright life. "I wish I didn't have to go. But, y'know, boy has to earn a pittance."

I almost told him to quit his job, take a sick day, anything really. Just stay with me. But I was nominally supposed to be the grown-up here, so I kissed his brow and watched him scamper away in search of clothes.

I picked up his discarded dressing gown. Nothing had changed, the box was back in its usual place, but the room felt different. It smelled of us.

"Oh, Laurie," Toby called out, his voice drifting up the stairs, "I forgot to say. You've got a letter. I think it's from the Queen."

I went down to the bedroom. "What?"

Toby was wriggling into his jeans, an activity that took a while and tended to be diverting. "It's on the side. Like, who sends letters these days?"

"Is that what led you to conclude I'm in correspondence with the Queen?"

"Hah. No. It's just all fancy. Gold and shit."

He'd left the letter on top of the chest of drawers. I recognised the style and laughed. "It's not the Queen. It's an old friend of mine."

"You've got weird friends, dude."

"Tell me about it. He's an academic." I sat on the end of the bed, eased open the wax seal on the envelope, and slipped out the invitation. It wasn't the first I'd received, so I knew what it would say: *Dr. Jasper Leigh requests the pleasure of your company at High Table*, and so on.

Toby pulled his T-shirt over his head, emerging from it, if possible, even more floppy and tousled, and padded over. "What is it? A wedding?"

"Just dinner."

"That must be some dinner. Can I see?" I passed him the piece of card, which was tastefully cream, edged in gold, and embossed with the college crest. "Um, is this for real?"

"I'm afraid so."

He gave me an odd, slightly anxious, slightly hopeful look. "It says you can bring a plus-one."

"Yes, but—"

"Can I be your plus-one?"

"You don't want to come to a college dinner," was my instinctive answer.

"With you? I totally do."

I gazed up at him and offered rather pleadingly, "It'll be boring, Toby."

"'It'll be boring, Toby,' or"—he glared—"'I'm ashamed of you, Toby'?"

"God, I'm not ashamed of you. If I'm ashamed of anyone, it's me."

He put his hands on his hips, like a very small but very determined fishwife. "That doesn't help. I don't want you ashamed of anybody. I just..." He sighed, the anger fading from his voice, leaving it full of tenderness and a kind of yearning. "I just want you to be as happy to be with me as I am to be with you."

I could too easily imagine Jasper's smirk as I turned up at college with Toby on my arm. The malicious bastard had a face designed for smirking, all thin lips and glittering eyes. *Why darling*, he would say, *how terribly Uranian of you*. And then I would have to remind myself he was one of my oldest friends. It was that or punch him.

A stricture that, in the past, had not always been successful.

But that was the strange comfort of long-standing friendship, ribbons of familiarity and old love woven through your life.

I took Toby's hands, tugging him closer. "You mustn't blame me if you hate it."

"I won't," he breathed. "Hate it or blame you."

"Also, it's black tie so you'd better let me take you to—"

"Oi, I'm not a complete pleb. I can do black tie."

"Really?"

He laughed and kissed me. "No need to look so scared. I won't embarrass you."

"And," I went on sternly, "you'll need a note from your parent, teacher, or guardian because we'll be staying over."

"In Oxford?"

I nodded.

"Like a minibreak?"

"No, Toby. Like spending a single night in a different city."

He squirmed between my knees. "That totally counts. And you'll show me all the sights, right?"

"Yes," I heard myself say. "Yes, I'll show you all the sights."

He turned up in good time the next Friday afternoon, carrying what looked like a bundle of clothes in a Tesco's carrier bag. I leaned in to kiss him and recoiled, eyes watering.

"Good God, you smell like my father." I sniffed cautiously, and wood and citrus assaulted my nostrils. "Why are you wearing Old Spice?"

He shuffled his feet. "I don't know... Well...I thought it would be cool to have like a signature scent or something?"

"So you chose Old Spice?"

"It reminds me of my granddad. Also, wasn't there adverts? Isn't it cool again?"

I took his hand and pulled him into the downstairs bathroom. He didn't protest as I tugged off his hoodie and his T-shirt and gave him a hasty sponge bath until he smelled, well, something like my boy again. "I'm sorry, Toby, but Old Spice will never be cool. And it really doesn't suit you."

"Oh."

One very small monosyllable from a very small Toby. Fuck. I'd crushed him. If there was ever a time for disastrous stylistic and sartorial experiments, that time was being nineteen. "Maybe I overreacted. It just...took me by surprise."

"No." He hung his head. "You're right. It's weird on me. Maybe I put too much on."

"Everybody's skin and body chemistry react differently. You might just need to try a few things before you find one that's right." I smiled in what I hoped was an encouraging manner. "It's a good idea, though."

"Really?"

"Absolutely. You know, if we left now, we'd probably have a bit of time before dinner, so...if you wanted...we could..."

"Yeah?"

"Go shopping?" I offered. "Try to find you something."

"What? Both of us? Together? You and me?"

No, Toby, someone else. "Yes. Both of us. Together. You and me."

He gave me a smile I'd never seen before. It was so shy it nearly broke my heart. "You'd do that with me? You wouldn't mind?"

"No, not at all. It'll be fun." For some reason, the nakedness of his joy made me slightly awkward. "Also, it's mainly selfishness on my part because I really can't stand Old Spice."

He scampered gleefully out of the bathroom. "Um, Toby... shirt..."

He came back for it, laughing, and then ran upstairs mysteriously to get "something," but finally we had our coats on, our bags in hand, and we were ready to go. We took a taxi to Paddington because I wasn't in any mood to wrestle the Tube, and despite Toby's best if somewhat sheepish efforts to contribute, I got us two first class tickets to Oxford. Which was possibly excessive for an hour of travel and made Toby's eyes get very wide indeed, but one of the advantages of having a well-paid job and very little free time was that certain minor luxuries—like travelling in moderate comfort—became incidental.

"Y'know," said Toby, as we got ourselves settled on the train, "I've literally never travelled first class ever."

"Well, it's hardly the Orient Express."

"No, but there's leg room, arse room, and a table. Which"—he frowned—"now I think about it are pretty basic facilities."

"Yes, first class isn't so much about extravagance as not being completely miserable."

He grinned at me over our decadent table. "All the same, I'm still excited."

"They'll probably bring you a complimentary cup of tea in a bit."

"High life, here I come."

As we pulled out of Paddington, Toby leaned over the arm of his seat and peered down the aisle. There was a suited gentleman with a laptop at the other end of the carriage, and a woman who seemed to be, if not asleep, definitely on the verge of it, but otherwise the place was ours. Quiet but for the clatter and rumble of the train.

I wasn't sure if Toby would be a talkative traveller, but he seemed content with his phone, and that suited me perfectly. I liked the emptiness of travel, peace and blank time, and there was something unexpectedly pleasant in sharing it with Toby. A companion in my silence.

My own phone was full of diversions—books I could have read, emails I could have answered—but instead I let myself gaze out of the window, partly at the greenish-grey countryside, but mainly at Toby's wavering reflection.

I usually rationed my looking, not wanting to reveal too much of my foolishness, my fondness, but now I indulged. Revelled, even. He looked different in daylight, paler and brighter and sharper all at the same time, as though he was finally fully in focus. I could even see traces of the man he would become in the set of his jaw and the curve of his cheek. But for now, he was just Toby, my Toby—blue-sky eyes and fading acne, his generous smile, his slightly retroussé nose.

He was slumped right down in his seat, looking every inch the stereotypical teenager, but then his stocking-clad foot slid purposefully up the side of my calf.

I froze, swallowed whatever undignified sound I might have made, and turned away from the window.

Toby's face was the picture of innocence as his foot crept higher.

"*Open your legs,*" he mouthed. I shook my head frantically.

"*Open. Your. Legs.*" Every silent word deliberately framed. Command. Undeniable. Irresistible.

I did it. Of course I did. And hidden beneath the table, Toby spread me wider, caressing with surprisingly agile toes the inside of my thighs and...oh God...the shaft of my helplessly hardening cock.

His eyes gleamed, intent on mine.

"Tickets from Paddington, please."

I stared up at the ticket inspector, wordless, mindless. Toby stilled but did not pull away. Heat gathered between my legs, heat and the promise—or the threat—of his touch.

"Tickets from Paddington, please, sir."

"Oh, yes. Of course."

My hands were shaking so badly Toby had to help me with my wallet. He offered up the tickets with a sweet and effortless smile. The inspector smiled back as she put the little paper stubs into her clicker, punched, and returned them.

And I felt…naked, Toby's flushed and flustered creature, as though whoever I was the rest of the time—a careful, controlled, and competent man—was just a skin I wore.

"Would you like a complimentary tea or coffee?"

Toby was still smiling up at her. "I'd love some tea."

The words blurred about me. Faraway sound. Close to meaningless.

"What about you, sir?"

"I'm fine, thank you."

"Orange juice? Water?"

"I'm really fine."

I couldn't hear my own voice properly. Did I sound impatient? Normal? As though I were nothing but a single point of contact, a star going supernova where Toby's foot was resting?

She nodded, and continued down the aisle. *Tickets from Paddington, tickets from Paddington, please…*

As soon as she was gone, Toby grinned. Wriggled his toes. And I let out a long, slow breath that might as well have been a scream.

He got his complimentary tea, and biscuits he picked from a basket, deliberating endlessly—wickedly—between chocolate brownie cookies and raisin oatmeal crunch. As though I wasn't his captive, leashed by his lightest touch.

He tormented me nearly all the way to Oxford, holding me on the most maddening edge of desire, never enough, never too much. Watching my face for the reactions I couldn't always suppress and occasionally moving against me more explicitly—a firm nudge to keep me spread, the arch of his foot slipping beneath my balls—just to make me blush or gasp or shake.

He made me powerless, desperate, debauched. His suffering plaything.

I loved it.

He pulled away when the driver announced we were approaching Oxford, which gave me a little time to recover what was left of my mind and my dignity, but even so, my legs felt absurdly shaky as I descended to the platform.

Toby bounced after me. Not a care in the whole damn world.

We could have taken a taxi, but we were in good time, and I'd promised Toby shopping. He stopped for a moment on the steps of the station.

"Everything all right?" I asked.

"Is this it?"

"Not what you were expecting?"

"I thought it was the city of dreaming spires, not, like, a really bad traffic junction and a random bronze bull."

I was used to Oxford, but Toby was right. This corner of it wasn't particularly impressive. The squat grey station, the mess of the Botley Road, the Said Business School with its sandstone aspirations.

☆ "That bull was nearly Margaret Thatcher, so don't knock it."

He gave me a slightly blank look—as though he'd heard the name, but couldn't place it, or remember if it was important. Which was, frankly, terrifying.

"Ready to go?" I asked, so I didn't have to think about it.

He nodded, and we set off, past the random bronze bull and the really bad traffic junction, heading towards the centre of town where grey surrendered everything to gold and green.

Toby was big-eyed and eager. Adorable. I wondered what it would be like if we actually went travelling together. Somewhere a little farther afield than sixty miles up the M40. I didn't care where. How good it would be, just to be with him. To have his silences and his touches, his cruelty and his joy.

Foolishness. It was all foolishness.

Robert and I had kept intending to go away together—for twelve years we'd intended—but we were both too busy and life kept getting in the way. And here I was daydreaming of running off who-knew-where (Prague, Venice, Paris) with a nineteen-year-old I'd known for barely a handful of months.

"I lived down here for a bit when I was a student," I said, as though I could drown out my own thoughts by talking. "My bedroom looked directly out over the train tracks."

"Room with a view, huh?"

"Actually, I really liked it. Especially at night, when it was just moving lights and the shadows of people. Gold walls and green grass are nice, but the railway used to make me feel part of something."

"What, like, industrialisation?"

I smiled. "Life."

"Aww, man." Toby's tone was strangely exasperated.

"What's that supposed to mean?"

"It means I fucking love you."

"Thank you."

He snorted. "That's slightly better than 'all right'…so improving steadily."

"Well, what do you expect me to say?"

"'I love you too, Toby' is kinda traditional. Would be nice."

"You can't nag someone into falling in love with you."

He gave a sad little smile. "Yeah, I noticed."

We walked up George Street, between the interchangeable pizzerias, in not-quite-comfortable silence. It was probably fortunate we were not in Prague, Venice, or Paris.

At last, Toby tugged on my arm. "It's just you let me feel you up all the way here, even though it looked like you were going to actually die, and then you said all that stuff like you'd peeled it off your soul just for me. And my heart got so, like, big and heavy and squishy that I thought it might literally explode if I didn't tell you I loved you. Don't you ever feel like that even a little bit?"

"I–I don't know." It was a cowardly answer. And it wasn't even true.

"Okay."

God. That was his crushed voice. "I mean, yes, sort of. A bit. I mean, I wouldn't put it quite like that. But that's not love. It's just happiness and…and the moment."

"And that," said Toby triumphantly, "is just semantics."

I shoved him, and his little grinning face, into Debenhams, and we rode the escalator up to the cosmetics section. The perfumes and colognes were arranged in long, brightly lit aisles, separated by designer.

Toby turned bewildered eyes up to mine. "I don't even know where to start."

Truthfully, neither did I, but I set off as though I did, and soon we lost all our inhibitions, picking up outlandishly decorated bottles largely at random, spraying and sniffing, and bickering. Toby was fatally drawn to heavy, woody musks, which he was at least self-aware enough to recognise were wrong for him.

"I'm different in my head," he explained, reluctantly setting down something redolent of sandalwood and cedar. He went up on tiptoes, leaning into me, and inhaling deeply against my neck, before I pushed him away in case we got spotted canoodling like teenagers in the middle of Debenhams. "What do you use? I like that."

"Uh, nothing. That's just soap and me." I grabbed for the nearest bottle and shoved it at him, hoping to distract him. His merciless attentions on the train had left me...reactive. "What about this? Cool Water."

He held out his hand and pointed at an unscented spot on the back of his wrist. We went through the now familiar ritual of spray, shake, wait, and sniff.

"Actually"—surprise and relief, along with peppermint, orange blossom, and sandalwood rolled over me—"that's quite pleasant. Inoffensive."

"Is that how you see me? Quite pleasant and inoffensive?"

"How about this, then?"

It was childish of me, but I handed him a tester of Vera Wang's Princess, in its purple crystal, heart-shaped bottle. Laughing, he pushed me out of the way as if intending to put it back on the shelf. Then spun, at the last second, enveloping me in a sticky-sweet mist of sugar and flowers.

"You little bastard."

He blew me a kiss, utterly unrepentant, and disappeared into the next aisle. Soon we'd lost all ability to smell or recall what we'd smelled previously. We were sense drunk. Slightly giggly.

"I liked one of these... I'm sure I liked one of these..." Toby was running his nose up and down his bare arm like the world's most peculiar code cracker. "Was it Eternity?"

"Or the Givenchy?"

"No, you said that one smelled like I'd been lying on the floor of a public lavatory and a nice attendant had poured disinfectant on me."

"Right. Um. How about Cool Water?"

"But I don't want to be pleasant and inoffensive!" he wailed.

Oh I was laughing again. "Believe me, you're in no danger."

We'd run out of Toby, so I sprayed the sample from the next bottle onto my own wrist. It was too sweet for me, floral but not feminine, the top notes deepened by a hint of those woody base notes he loved so much, lending it balance and just a hint of machismo. "Toby. This one."

I lifted my hand for him, and he breathed the air over my pulse point, his eyes closing as he savoured. He hadn't even touched me, but somehow, it was shockingly sensuous. I might have gasped. At last, he looked up again. "Yeah. That one."

I dabbed a little against his neck, to make sure it wasn't going to react badly with his skin, but it didn't. It suited him perfectly—sweet and dark and spicy. I glanced surreptitiously around us and stole a quick, clumsy kiss.

"You do know," he said, as I pulled back, "the Sexual Offences Act was passed in the sixties, right? We're allowed."

I blushed. The truth was, Robert and I had not been particularly public with our affections. But I was touch-hungry around Toby, touch-hungry and silly, as though no years stood between us at all. Seeking some kind of physical distraction, I picked up the biggest bottle of Burberry London that they had and looked around for a till point.

"Uh...uh..." Toby's hands fluttered. "I can't... I don't need... The small one's great."

"It's on me."

"I can't let you do that."

"Why not?"

"Well...because I'm broke and I can't—"

"Then it makes sense for me to be the one paying, doesn't it?"

"I guess..." He scuffed at the ground, hands buried deep in his pockets, hair falling hopelessly into his eyes. "Um. Thank you. Nobody's...um—"

"You can make it up to me later." Oh God. "I mean, not in a prostitute way."

"I wouldn't mind." His eyes shone like the bottles that surrounded us. "It's kind of hot, actually."

"I'm ignoring you now and going to pay for this."

He sidled up too close, his hip knocking against me. "So, am I like your kept boy?"

"Stop it, Toby."

He was giggling as we approached the counter. I put the bottle down and pulled out my wallet. "Just this, please."

To my surprise, the cashier—a pretty young woman with soft brown eyes—smiled at us. Warmed and a little flustered, I smiled back.

"Hey"—Toby's hip nudged me again—"this was really nice of you."

"He's very generous, your dad." The cashier's words bloomed in the silence like jellyfish.

I felt the upward curve of my mouth turn rigid.

"Oh my God!" Toby was actually laughing. "He's not my dad! He's my boyf—errr...lover."

I was starting to wish I hadn't objected so strenuously to *boyfriend*. *Lover* sounded particularly seedy when I was holding my credit card.

And Toby was still talking. "He's thirty-seven, I'm nineteen, so while he could technically be my father, he would have had me irresponsibly young."

The machine jammed on my receipt. I stared at it ferociously because there were no more smiles for us.

"And also," finished Toby, "he's gay. So. No."

I'd thought *Get out and run away* were the only words left in my universe, but then I heard myself say, "It's very rude to make assumptions, Toby. I could have had you with a lesbian."

I put my wallet away, picked up the bag, and walked off, Toby pressed tight to my side. The ridiculous boy would probably have tried to hold my hand if I'd had one free.

———

I took him the scenic route to college, down Broad Street, not Cornmarket, golden towers springing up on all sides, our horizon filled with spires and domes.

"You're freaking out, aren't you?" he asked.

After a moment, I nodded.

"Can't you just...laugh? It's not a big deal."

Easy for him to say. "She's right, you know. I am old enough to be your father."

"So?"

"So it's not appropriate."

We walked along awhile in silence. "Look." Toby pointed. "A giant gold boob!"

"The Radcliffe Camera was built in 1737 by James Gibbs. It's very much admired."

"Yeah, it's a good boob." He was quiet a moment, and then, almost pleadingly, "Oh, Laurie, please don't freak out on me. This is my minibreak."

"I'm sorry... I just—"

He cut me off. "Okay, you know what I think is ina-fucking-propriate? People who don't love each other. People who hurt each other. People who stay together out of fear or habit or apathy. We're in love, how is that wrong?"

"The disparities between us. It's an abuse of pow—Ow." He'd kicked me sharply in the ankle. "What was that for?"

"Because you're insulting me, right to my fucking face. Do you think because I'm poor and little and nineteen, I don't know what I want?"

He was shouting, now, in Radcliffe Square, his free arm wind-milling wildly. To be honest, it was probably the place to do it. A student standing by the railing and smoking a cigarette with an air of artistic panic barely gave us a second glance.

"Do you think if I felt abused or exploited or taken advantage of, I'd be with you? Do you think I can't tell the difference? Do you think I don't know what love feels like?"

I was going to reply, but he kicked my ankle again.

"Fuck you." The anger faded from his voice, leaving only pain. "You believed in me. At that club, you believed in me. The only person who's ever. And you didn't laugh, and you didn't judge. You just got on your knees, and it's the most romantic thing that's—"

I dropped everything except the cologne, and that was only because I was afraid it would break. But my bag, my suit, the jacket I'd had on my arm because it had been hot in Debenhams—all went tumbling to the ground. Then I dragged Toby into the mess, wrapped him up tight, and kissed him with everything.

When I finally gave him his mouth back, he went on without missing a beat. "The second most romantic thing that's ever happened to me." And then he smiled his smallest smile, the secret one, the one with all his pain in it.

"I'm sorry," I told him. "I do believe in you. It's just..." I'd been about to say I didn't believe in me, but with Toby in my arms—smelling pungently of far too many things—it wasn't a moment for doubt. Just this.

So I kissed him. Again. Again.

Afterwards, we stood wrapped in each other, surrounded by cobbles and centuries and stone. And a gaggle of slightly startled tourists, some of whom were pointing phones and cameras at us.

I glanced at them warily. "You do realise this is probably going to end up on YouTube, don't you?"

"Then"—he shrugged—"I'll find it and Like it a gazillion times."

I gathered up my things again, but as I started walking, Toby slipped his arm through mine. And I didn't shake him off or pull away.

———

☆ College, when we finally arrived, blew Toby's tiny mind. His exact words. "It's like...a fucking mansion just off the street. Like that's normal."

"Welcome to Oxford, darling."

He stood in the archway, staring at St. John's quadrangle, a small, out-of-time figure, cast in pale shadow by the silver-gold towers. "I'm in goddamn Hogwarts."

"No, that's Christ Church."

I stepped into the porters' lodge to pick up a room key and almost immediately ran into trouble.

"Well, well, well. Mr. Dalziel."

☆ Oh God. Behind the desk was Bob, immortal, unchanging, terrifying Bob, who regarded me today with the same too-knowing, slightly disdainful affection he had shown some twenty years ago.

"Hello, Bob," I muttered, quiet and lost and eighteen again.

Toby had hustled in behind me, and now he glanced between us with blatant fascination. "You know him?"

Bob's eyes glinted. "Laurence Jennings Dalziel, 1995, Medicine. Of course I know him."

"I've booked a room," I tried, before anything worse could happen.

"I suppose you're here to see Dr. Leigh."

Dr. Leigh? He'd never called me that even when it was my correct title. Always "mister" and always in this tone of faint exasperation. But I found myself nodding meekly.

"Charming gentleman, Dr. Leigh." Bob pulled a large, leather-bound book out from under the counter. There was a computer two steps away, but of course it would be the book. He opened it and began squinting down page after page of spindly, handwritten entries.

"How's Mrs...." Fuck, I'd forgotten his surname. "How's your wife?"

"Why, she's dead, Mr. Dalziel." There was an awful silence.

"Oh my God, I'm so sorry."

"I'm only joking. Sheila's doing very well." He turned a page. "Ah, yes, you're in the New Building, third floor."

Toby had both hands fisted over his mouth, but high-pitched little giggles were escaping anyway.

Bob turned to the vast grid behind him and with great ceremony lifted a key from its hook. He turned the tag over, subjecting it to a level of scrutiny probably not witnessed on earth since Moses got his hands on some sort of tablet. And finally he slammed it down on the counter.

Heaven forefend he actually give it to me.

I sighed, picked up the key, and pocketed it. "Thank you."

I had my hand on the door handle and my foot on the step when he called out in a nasty sort of singsong. "Oh, Mr. Dalziel?"

"Yes?"

"You wouldn't be having an overnight guest, would you?"

I spun round. "For the love of God, I'm thirty-seven. I'm... I'm...I'm allowed." In my head, that had sounded more assertive and less pathetic.

Bob blinked, just once, and then waved me off imperiously.

This time I was almost out of the door. "Oh, Mr. Dalziel?"

I gritted my teeth. "What?"

"Welcome back."

In the quad, Toby had hysterics, and I waited with what I thought was impressive forbearance for him to calm down.

"This place," he gasped, "is fucking nuts."

"It has its ways."

He wriggled his hand back into the crook of my arm. "You really like it, huh?"

"There's always going to be a part of me that calls Oxford home." We walked across the quad, past the chapel, and into the honeyed gloom of the cloisters, our steps echoing together upon the flagstones. "It's where some of the most important things of my life happened to me. I grew up here. Learned who I was here. It's where I first fell in love. Had sex. Got drunk. Took drugs. Stayed up all night talking with people who understood me."

"Jesus." Toby was staring again. The last sunlight of the day was spilling down the stonework and across the pristine lawn. "This is so beautiful it hurts. I'm never going to have any of this stuff, am I?"

"Oxford?"

"Everything you said."

My heart squeezed painfully. The truth was, I didn't know how to have a conversation like this with Toby. I'd been alive for longer—a lot longer—so I should have had some answers for him, but I didn't. And regardless of what had been said in Radcliffe Square, trying to offer him...what? guidance?...felt perilously close to parental.

"Those things aren't about where you are," I said, as gently as I could. "They'll happen naturally because you're nineteen and your whole life is waiting for you."

He ran his fingertips along the wall. "I don't feel like it's waiting. I feel like it's fucked off."

"Why? What happened?"

He just shrugged.

And I didn't want to ruin our—Damn it, it was *not* a minibreak or a holiday of any kind. But I still didn't want to ruin whatever-we-were-having by insisting on answers he didn't want to give me. There was no rush, after all. I could try again some other time.

We emerged onto the New Building lawn, and Toby drew in a sharp breath. "That's the 'new' building?"

We gazed across yet another gleaming grass-scape to the Georgian symmetry of the New Building, with its arches and its tall, leaded windows. "Well, compared to the fifteenth century, the eighteenth century *is* new."

"This place." Toby shook his head again. "Fucking nuts."

"If it would help, I could show you Waynflete. It's across the river, behind the Sainsbury's, although in my day it was behind an off-licence."

"Is that where you lived?"

"Yes, for my first year. It's a concrete monstrosity from the sixties. All the colleges have them, but some hide them better than others."

Toby smiled, and something that had knotted itself inside me unravelled again.

As we trooped along between the glass-smooth lawns, heading for the building, he muttered, "'Water, water, everywhere, nor any drop to drink.'"

"Hmmm?"

"All this grass you're not allowed to walk on. Doesn't it just make you want to like…run all over it?"

"I've never thought about it."

"What happens if you do?"

"Go on the grass? I don't know. Bad things probably."

He slipped away from me and ran towards the grass in exaggerated slow motion, humming "Chariots of Fire", "La-la-la-la-laaaaah-la. La-la-la-laaah!"

"Toby, don't." It was hard to sound stern when I was laughing. "Behave yourself."

Reaching out with straining fingertips, he very carefully brought his toes down on the edge of the lawn and froze, as if expecting the heavens to rain down thunder and retribution. Then he relaxed. "I seem to be okay."

"Yes, well, it's a slow-acting poison, you little git."

Finally, we found the right staircase and located our room. This building was primarily reserved for fellows—and Jasper, who had God's own luck in the room ballet—so it was quite luxurious compared to what I remembered of student life. It was, however, fairly basic in its facilities.

I put down my bags. "You know, I should have booked a hotel like a normal person. I just didn't think."

"No way. I love seeing a piece of your past. And the view... holy shit. Look at the sky. I've never seen anything like that. That's crazy sky."

There was a large desk in front of the window, and Toby was stretched almost all the way over it, streaked gold and orange and pink and purple in Oxford's brightest, boldest light.

"It is a spectacular view," I agreed.

He spluttered, scrambling off the desk, and returned his arse to its usual position. "How long do we have before dinner?"

"Well, if we want to see Jasper before the reception, about an hour."

"About an hour?" He tapped the side of his chin thoughtfully.

I nodded, anticipation, yearning, and pure, simple lust pooling slickly in my stomach.

"I want you over this desk." He slid aside to make room and smiled invitingly.

I hesitated because I always did. A different dom would have snapped at me, or forced me, but Toby never did. He never made it easy. He made me choose.

Made me choose submission. The quiet humiliation of doing something simply because he had told me to.

I crossed the room. Step by step, step by step, and bent over the desk, bracing myself on my elbows. Instinctively, I turned towards him seeking, oh, who knew? Reassurance. Approval. Just his eyes upon me.

"Yeah." His hand drifted gently over my hair. "Just like that."

He'd barely touched me, barely asked anything of me, but suddenly I was shuddering, my cock aching. I forgot how to care about anything except Toby and whatever he wanted me to give or have taken.

He pushed away from the desk and came round behind me, his fingers trailing the length of my spine through my shirt, and then ghosting across my arse. I dropped my head between my arms and pushed up against his touch.

I heard his breath catch, and then his hands were sliding under me, fumbling with my belt and the buttons of my trousers, tugging them down with my boxers.

God. Oh God.

Half-naked always felt so much more naked than naked. I swallowed a moan, rested my cheek against the desk, letting gold burn softly behind my eyelids.

"Hey." Toby's body curled over mine, his breath warm against my ear. "I kinda...brought something with me."

"What?"

"From the magic box. Just a tick."

I couldn't tell whether it was organisation or disorganisation that made him leave me there on the desk, partially undressed and unrestrained by anything but his wishes—but, regardless, it was exquisitely mortifying. I was too hot and too cold and too covered and too exposed all at the same time. And aroused, unbearably aroused.

He was back in moments. Something thudded onto the desk. I opened my eyes and—

"Toby. No, I—Ah."

His fingers, warm and slippery with lube, parted, and then pressed into me. It was a shock—he rarely took me with quite such confidence—but the relief of that swift, certain touch after the day's teasing was sublime. I arched off the desk, fucking back against his hand, groaning shamelessly.

As if he hadn't just put a vibrating butt plug down beside me.

"Fuck yeah." Toby. All husky and breathless. "Fuck me."

And I did, driving myself not-so-slowly mad on his fingers, while the meadows and cloisters of Magdalen shimmered pink and bronze beneath the last rays of the setting sun.

"More?" he asked, curling his fingers deep inside me, making me burn and twist and want.

"Yes. God, yes."

But he pulled out. Leaving me gasping, empty and bereft. "Okay, good, so here's the deal."

"No, please... I need—" He wasn't holding me down, but some-how—in that agony of loss and longing—I forgot, and struggled frantically, as though he were.

"Shhh." He leaned over me again, pushing sweaty hair back from my brow. "This is the deal. I let you come now and you wear that for me tonight. Because...because I think it'll be totally hot. Or you say no, and that's okay too, but you don't get to come till I see you next week."

I slumped over the desk, defeated. "Toby, I can't."

"It's your choice, love." He kissed the top of my ear, and I trembled helplessly, as though he'd whipped or cut me.

"Please don't make me."

"You don't have to."

I writhed in an anguish of lust, pushing my cock clumsily against something that was probably a drawer handle.

"Don't hump the desk." One of his hands closed around me from behind, and it felt so good, so perfect, so exactly what I needed that I couldn't stop the rush of tears. "Have me."

My mouth tasted of salt. God. I was actually crying.

He'd made me cry with nothing more than a choice. "I don't want... I can't let you—"

"Yeah, you can." His palm was still slick with lube, gliding over too-taut, too-burning skin. "Tell me what you want."

"I want to come." Weeping. Shaking. Pressing into him.

Afraid if he stopped touching me, I'd stop breathing. "Okay."

He put his lips against my shoulder and bit—not hard, just enough to feel the blunt pressure of his teeth and the heat of his mouth through my shirt. I cried out, claimed. And then he slid his fingers back inside me, and tightened his grip, and claimed me again.

It was surely a devil's bargain, but oh, he made it sweet.

He didn't tease me, but he drew it out, forcing pleasure upon pleasure, working me with his hands, his mouth, and words that soothed and inflamed me all at once.

I was gorgeous. He loved me. It was okay.

And I believed him. Sprawled over a desk, trousers down,

arse up, ruthlessly finger-fucked in a pool of my own tears and sweat and pre-come, I felt...cherished. It was that, in the end, that sent me flying. Surrender and release, the accompanying orgasm almost incidental.

I was still bliss-struck and gasping when Toby rolled me over, straddled me, and kissed me hard. I probably tasted dreadful—raw and bitter from my tears—but his tongue took me even to the deepest corners of my mouth. He was ferociously hard and smelled musky with sex and too many colognes.

I reached for him, but he caught my hand and bore it down to the desk. Leaned over me, flushed and smiling, damp-haired, his eyes blurry with desire. "That was just for you."

I could barely move my lips. "Thank you."

☆   We lay on the desk, neither of us wanting to move despite the discomfort. It was dark now—a tawny, Oxford dark, fat-mooned and starless, the night sky gleaming with silhouettes of spires.

Then I caught a glimpse of the time—oh fuck—and limped off on wobbly legs to shower. When I came back, Toby was sitting in the room's only chair, one leg crossed over the other, and for a tiny shocking second I almost didn't recognise him. He was also freshly washed and wearing a double-breasted tuxedo with a satin shawl collar that wouldn't have looked out of place in a film from the forties. It gave him a strangely timeless look. All he needed was a cigarette between his fingers, and I could have been on a date with the young Dirk Bogarde.

"You look—" I didn't know how to finish, and then I did. "Stunning."

He blushed and was Toby again, his hand drifting self-consciously towards his perfect bow tie. "Yeah? Not like a knob?"

"Not even a little bit like a knob." God help me, I couldn't work out if I wanted to lick the shining patent leather shoes of this elegant young man, or just fuck him senseless. Maybe both. "Where did you get a vintage tuxedo?"

He shrugged. "Granddad."

I finished towelling my hair and began unzipping my suit carrier.

"Uh, Laurie..." I glanced over my shoulder to find the elegant young man holding a most inelegant object and grinning. "Forget something?"

I froze. "Toby, do I have—"

"No, you don't have to." Relief. "But you'd kind of be wriggling out of a deal."

My thoughts turned anxiously. Maybe I could renege now, and he could punish me later. That would be fair? And then I wouldn't have to... Then he wouldn't... "What if I do?"

"Nothing." He shrugged. "I just didn't think you would."

Fuck. "Fine. Give it here."

I strode towards him, making him tilt his head back to meet my eyes. A power game, a pathetic one, but Toby just looked up at me as if he didn't care and pulled his hand back. "I'll do it." His gaze flicked briefly about the room and then settled on his own knees. For a terrible moment, I thought he might have wanted me over his lap, and that might have been too much. I wasn't sure I could do that for him...or maybe I could... I didn't know— But then he jerked his head towards the window. "Over the desk again."

And that, of course, had its own resonances. My body stirred a little under the memory of his touches, and I hesitated, staring at the space where I'd lain before.

Not a word from Toby. Not even an unsteady breath.

In a welter of furious ambivalence, I arranged myself for him, braced again on my elbows, legs spread, though perhaps not far enough. Not enough to seem willing.

Of course, I could have stopped him. I wasn't restrained. Even if I was. And his little deal was nothing but a smoke screen.

I hated plugs. I hated how they made me feel. Humiliated. Out of control. Weak in the most specific of ways. Nothing like a cock.

I had trained...forced...willed myself to a kind of carelessness for scenes with strangers. I hadn't given them this, this vulnerability, this fear, this raw shame.

But I gave it all to Toby. Because he wanted it.

There were a thousand ways this could have gone, all of them more or less annihilating. He could have made me beg, he could have made me hold myself open for him. But, instead, he came up behind me and kissed his way down my spine, soft touches that made me tremble and feel almost like weeping again.

Because he was going to do this to me.

Because he had made me want to do it for him.

He slid the thing into me easily enough, everything prepared, and I knew my own body too well to allow it to struggle or resist.

I couldn't quite hold back a sound of distress, and Toby groaned in answer, deep and rough. Then he helped me up, turned me round, and stared at me, lust-drunk, not so urbane now.

"All right?" he asked, quite serious suddenly.

The plug wasn't uncomfortable. It was just there, unyieldingly, undeniably there, a constant reminder of Toby, and myself, the things we did, and were, together. Damn him. It was a far-too-stirring thought.

I glared down at him. "Not remotely. I'm manipulated... violated...mortified—"

"Now you're just trying to turn me on."

Trying? I followed the hectic flush as it slipped down his throat and under the wing collar of his dress shirt. "Oh, yes. I'm not going to suffer alone."

"I might've"—he choked on an indrawn breath—"misjudged this."

I gave him what I hoped was a haughty look—well, as haughty a look as a man with a foreign object lodged up his arse could manage. "Live with it, Junior."

Toby grinned and casually smoothed the breast pocket of his tux.

It must have been where he'd secreted the remote because the fucking plug began to vibrate. I was still a little sensitive, so it was on the edge of pain...but oh God...the good edge, flinging me into an intense, tingling state of full-body awareness. It made my skin dance. My head fell back, and I moaned, surrendering to sensation, to Toby's will and caprice.

"Shit." I felt Toby's eyes upon me. "That seriously didn't help. You're not going to do that at dinner are you? Because, Jesus, it's a little bit *When Harry Met Sally*."

"No." I smiled down at him. "That was just for you."

He put a hand between his legs. "You fucking bastard. Fuck, you're hot."

I was thirty-seven years old and wearing nothing but a butt plug. But there was 1940s film-star Toby, looking about to spontaneously combust from sheer desire. It was probably hysterical, postpubescent hormones, but still, it felt so good. So ridiculously good.

We were running late, of course we were, so I had to dress in something of a rush, which meant several fraught minutes in front of the mirror, my bow tie getting worse and worse and worse as I tried to make it better. Then just make it not awful.

"Dude, what are you doing?" asked Toby, in a tone of profound pity.

I turned away from the mirror, two bands of crumpled silk

hanging loose around my shoulders. "What the fuck do you think I'm doing?"

"I honestly have no idea. It looks like a car crash from here."

"Why," I snapped, "is yours on a string?"

"No way. Some of us are classy and know what we're doing." He crooked his finger at me. "C'mere."

Infinitely worse than the plug was kneeling between Toby's legs as the classy nineteen-year-old expertly tied my bow tie for me.

Except it wasn't embarrassing at all.

It was intimate. Toby's fingers at my throat, his breath against my cheek, like the moment of a kiss.

It didn't stop the little monster buzzing me as I stepped into the hallway, making me gasp and steady myself on the wall.

It was going to be an interesting evening.

Jasper had rooms on the next staircase. We should have been there twenty minutes ago, so I knocked and pushed open the door without really paying much attention to whatever was happening inside.

"Um," I said, "hello, Jasper."

Toby came in after me, and then came to an abrupt halt. "That"—his eyes had gone comically wide—"is so not black tie."

8

TOBY

So I guess I'm expecting somebody like Laurie. Or somebody sort of teachery. Or maybe somebody sort of grandfathery, since I think academics are supposed to be old.

What I'm not expecting is a guy slumped in an armchair wearing a pair of grey silk boxers and drinking something that's probably brandy straight from one of those crystal decanter things they have in costume dramas.

And Laurie is all, "Hello, Jasper," like this is normal.

Oxford, man. Fucking nuts.

He stares at us a moment, totally not freaking out that he's sitting there practically naked. "Oh. Laurie. And your plus-one. I didn't know pederasty was a vice of yours."

Laurie has his stern face on. "My vices are both well documented and none of your business. This is my... This is Toby."

My Toby? I can live with that.

Jasper gives me this sort of pale, graceful hand, limply palm down, like I'm supposed to bow over it and kiss it. Which I'm totally not doing, so I ignore it. "Uh. Hi."

"Delighted, I'm sure, Tobias."

I scowl. It takes a special kind of wanker to call you something that isn't the name they've been given. "It's Toby. And it's not Tobias, it's Tobermory, *actually*."

I hate my name. Words cannot express how much I hate my name. But right now I'm really fucking pleased my mum's a nutcase so that when he says, *Ah, like the city*, or maybe, *Ah, like the whisky*, I can be all smug and, *Actually no*.

He's looking at me again, which is when I realise he's wearing glasses as well as underwear. I don't know if that makes it worse or better. And, finally, what he says is, "'Here and there among cats one comes across an outstanding superior intellect, just as one does among the ruck of human beings, and when I made the acquaintance of Tobermory a week ago I saw at once that I was in contact with a "Beyond-cat" of extraordinary intelligence.'"

Which kind of takes the wind out of my sails because it means he gets it. Gets a little piece of me. Some bloke I'm not sure I'd trust to open a can of beans. But that's when he smiles at me, and it's like he's totally delighted, and weirdly, I feel okay again.

"Am I missing something?" asks Laurie.

☆   "Only something sublime, darling. Go back to your skulls and your stethoscopes." Jasper's diction is a bit too perfect, the way you only get when you're a Beyond-drunk of (probably) extraordinary intelligence. "You know, Toby, if I was called Tobermory, I would never let anyone call me anything else."

All my instincts are screaming at me that I'm in the presence of a complete arse-pot, but when he's looking at me and smiling at me like that, I feel like the centre of an amazing, shiny universe. My mum does that sometimes. It scares me that some people have that much power, and half the time they don't even care.

I don't really notice until I've done it, but I've gone and stuck my hand in Laurie's, like an idiot. I'm totally expecting him to pull away, but he doesn't. Just closes his fingers tightly round me like he's never letting me go. It's only *his* universe I really want to be part of, and I think he's telling me it's okay. He's not going to leave me floating in the cosmos of someone else's random charm.

Jasper leans forward. He's really pretty. Not hot like Laurie is hot, but if he walked past me in the street, my head would totally turn. The truth is, I love Laurie to bits, and I can't imagine wanting to look at anybody more than I want to look at him, but he's not a head-turner. He's a magnet to me, but I think if I wasn't me, I wouldn't give him a second glance. Not that he's a minger or anything, but Jasper is...something else.

He's younger too, but I'm not good at guessing that stuff, so I don't know by how much. Kind of this English rose of a man, all porcelain and soft pinks, greeny-brown eyes and shiny brown hair, like something out of an old portrait. I get an impression of height from him, but he's not muscular at all. He's just bone and skin and elegance. And now I'm taking in the view, I see there are nail marks and bite marks and red blotches fading all over him.

And my not-gaydar suddenly does its little *ping*.

"May I call you Tobermory?" he asks.

Of course I say yes. Because he's made it seem so special, like it's this secret we share. And Laurie gives my hand another squeeze, like he's telling me it's still okay. And because I trust Laurie, I relax a bit. Maybe it's safe to be just a little bit charmed by this drunk, naked...enticingly vulnerable guy.

Laurie reaches for the decanter thingy and pulls it away. Jasper makes this soft protesty noise but doesn't actually try to stop him. "You know, J, you should probably think about putting some clothes on."

"Oh, what's the point?"

"Social custom? Personal dignity? For heaven's sake, we'll be late for dinner. Where's your gown?"

"I don't know." Jasper gestures in his languid way. "Somewhere."

And Laurie makes this little growl at the back of his throat. Sexy.

Then I think...wait, *gown*?

"I was dressed earlier," Jasper offers. "It can't have gone far."

"For fuck's sake. Toby, help me find his clothes."

Laurie lets me go, steps back, and something crunches under his foot. He jerks away, and there's a few pieces of blue china strewn on the rug.

Now I'm paying attention, the place is kind of trashed. It's an amazing room, vaulted ceiling, wood panelling, huge windows with velvet curtains. And books, so many fucking books, though lots of them are on the floor. There's a lot of stuff on the floor.

It looks like something seriously violent happened in here.

"Um," I ask, "did you get robbed?"

Jasper stares straight at me. "In a manner of speaking." I don't know if it's his glasses or the light or being pissed or what, but his eyes are really vivid, gold in the green and grey in the brown, all these pieces of colour.

Laurie's found some trousers and a shirt, both pretty crumpled, and he flings them over. "Where's Sherry?"

"He's gone."

"Isn't he coming tonight?"

"Not with me, he isn't. Ignorant colonial cunt."

I gasp. "Ohmygod, you don't use the c-word as an insult."

"Colonial? What else do you call Yanks with delusions of grandeur?"

"No, the other one... It's misogynistic because, like"—I try to remember what Mum says—"there's nothing inherently unpleasant, threatening, or offensive about female genitalia."

Jasper has sneery brows. They're very thin and arched, like they're designed for making you feel bad. Right now he's got one tilted at this really fucking devastating angle. "Have you actually seen one, my little eromenos? A cunt?"

I'm so cross with him I say without thinking, "Yeah, I've seen ☆ my mum's."

Whoa. Welcome to Silence: population everyone.

"Not like personally," I add quickly. "But she paints it a lot. She's an artist."

The truth is, I'm not thrilled about the fact half the world has seen my mum's...y'know...in really intricate detail and in various stages of...jouissance, to use her word, but it's her...y'know...so I guess she's got that right. I can't really get past the fact that it's a...y'know...and my *mum's*...y'know...but if I try really hard I can see it's kind of...beautiful down there, sort of fantastical like a maze, in all these rich colours... *Arrrgh*, no, my mum, nonononononono.

Jasper's staring at me again. I think he's just worked out who my mum is. Fuck.

This is why I like Laurie so much. He has absolutely no culture. And he comes to my rescue, without even knowing I need rescuing, throwing the rest of Jasper's clothes at him and insisting he get dressed, in the same voice he uses for me when I'm being naughty.

I bet Jasper finds it hot as well. And he does actually start pulling his clothes on in this incompetent, half-arsed way. In the end, we have to help him, which he seems to kind of like, leaning against Laurie while I do up his shirt and try not to think how fucking smooth his skin is. It's like he was made to be hurt.

He's drunk like nobody I've ever seen before. Like you wouldn't know he was drunk...except he is, if that makes sense. Drunk in this deep, cold, empty way.

I'd feel sorry for him, except it's too confusing.

As soon as he's semi-dressed, he sinks back into the chair like there's not a single bone in his body.

Laurie dangles a white bow tie at me. "Better you than me."

I sigh. It's true. I don't want to watch Laurie butcher a bow tie again. But I also don't want to get up close and personal with Jasper. In case...well...because I might like it.

I try various non-embarrassing positions, like leaning over him or going round the back of the chair, but they don't work at all. And even though he doesn't say anything, I can *feel* mockery gathering inside him, like he's going to wait for the worst possible moment and then be all *Oh, don't bother.*

Well, fuck that. I climb into his lap.

"You'd better let me," he drawls. "If this is the best you can do, we'll be here all night."

"Toby, what the hell are you doing?" That's Laurie. He sounds seriously ticked off. "Get off him."

I ignore both of them—because I am tying this bad boy, I am tying it now, and I am tying it right—grab Jasper by his choirboy curls, fling the bow tie round his neck, and tie it. Perfectly. I tie it fucking perfectly.

Then I disembark the good ship HMS *Inebriated Wanker*, and I hit the remote I've got tucked in my jacket pocket because I am peeved with Laurie and his little *What the hell are you doing?* routine and...also because I want him to know that there's only him, only him for me, and that's the only way I have to tell him.

He takes a sharp breath. His shoulders tighten, his hands

clench, and he frowns. But he's kind of a tight and frowny man, so I don't think anyone would notice a change but me. It's so fucking hot. Because I know behind his careful posture and his calm(ish) expression, he's suffering—pleasure and embarrassment both—and that there's part of him that hates it and a part of him that loves it, and none of it matters anyway because he's doing it for me. It's like I'm touching him, right now, in the most intimate possible way.

And oh fuck. *Don't get a boner, Toby. Do not.*

When I decide to have mercy on him, he glances my way very briefly, all soft and kissable and sorry and mine.

Good.

He clears his throat. "Come on, J. Time to go."

Jasper doesn't move. "I don't want to."

"Because of Sherry?"

"I don't want to see him." He leans back in his chair and ☆ drapes a wrist over his forehead like he's dying of consumption. I didn't think people actually did that. He looks pretty and silly at the same time, a bit of his inside wrist exposed under his shirt cuffs. I'm kind of fascinated by how blue his veins are.

"What's he done this time?" demands Laurie. No sympathy whatsoever.

Jasper mumbles something.

"What?"

"He. Published. A. Paper."

"That's his job."

"Yes, but—" Jasper shifts forward and curls slowly in on himself like a wilty flower. "But it's brilliant," he finishes in this voice of utter despair. "It's so...clever and engaging and insightful and... original. So fucking bloody original. The bastard. I hate him." Then, very softly, "I admire him."

"You're in love with him," growls Laurie. "And you have been since he took the top first at prelims."

"Which should have been mine."

"Oh, for fuck's sake." Laurie grabs his arm and hauls him upright. Jasper sways in this willowy way for a moment, and then he's rock steady. "Buck up, you dick. And, anyway, you invited him."

Jasper nods sadly. "I wanted to...to...congratulate him."

Laurie and I sort of exchange Looks. Mine says, *I love you.* I can't read his, but I decide it says, *I'm so glad you're basically normal, apart from wanting to put things up my arse.*

"I congratulated him very intensely. Several times." Jasper sighs, and for a moment he genuinely looks confused and kind of hurt as well. "And then I couldn't stand the sight of him. He was just so...so...beautiful. He gleamed. How dare he fucking gleam?"

I glance round at the carnage. "So then you had a massive fight?"

He blinks. "Fight?"

For a moment I'm confused by his confusion. And then I get it and...Jesus.

Wow. That's Olympic-standard fucking.

Laurie's got hold of what looks like an opera cloak and is pulling Jasper's arms through it and muttering under his breath. Finally, he steps back. "That'll have to do."

I can't help staring. Everything's changed now Jasper's got his clothes on. He looks like he was born to stand around in a suit, a white bow tie, and a cape, austere and monochrome and all untouchable, like the grass.

As soon as we leave his rooms, Jasper's a completely different person, leading us briskly down the stairs and across the quad, his shoes resounding on the flagstones and his cape thing flapping behind him. I've barely known him half an hour and I've got so much emotional whiplash it's a wonder my head hasn't fallen off.

But then Laurie takes my hand. Voluntarily. And it turns out that's all I need to be stupidly happy.

We end up in the SCR, which stands for Senior Common Room, and believe me there's nothing common about it. It's sort of half library, half how you imagine a super-exclusive gentlemen's club might look (like, not the strip-joint sort): books, oak panelling, antique furniture, red leather armchairs by the actual, real *fire* fire. It's not just another world; it's another fucking century. It's full of people—mainly men but there's some women too—about half of them dressed like Jasper in the robes or whatever. And there's this table where there's glasses of champagne laid out for people to just have, like at a wedding.

I make a beeline for it, tugging Laurie along behind me.

He's frowning—in his worried way, not his angry way. So cute. "Toby, there's going to be a lot of drinking tonight. Try and pace yourself."

"But champagne. Free champagne."

Jasper makes this sound that I think is a laugh he's trying to pretend is a cough. "Tobermory has the makings of an academic."

Yeah, except for the whole going to-university part. "Not my thing."

"Agreed." Laurie hesitates for a moment, then takes a glass for himself and chinks it lightly against mine, making them both sing.

I smile at him like a goofball because I love him so much, just for touching our two glasses of champagne together like that. *Our. Us.*

"It's much better to know an academic," he's saying, "and then you get to experience all the advantages of academia—like free champagne—with none of the disadvantages. Like being an academic."

"Excuse me, I think you've got"—Jasper leans forward and brushes a finger against the corner of Laurie's mouth—"a touch of smug on you there."

Laurie just shrugs. But he's a little bit pink, and his lips are twitchy like he wants to smile.

"Urgh." Jasper shudders in this gay, theatrical kind of way. "What have you done to him, Tobermory? I recognise that soupy-eyed look. You've only gone and made him happy, haven't you?"

Wow. For a moment I just stare at Jasper, overwhelmed by the gift he's given me so carelessly. I'd barely have believed it before today, but he's right. I do make Laurie happy. He's given me that power too. And, what's more, other people can see it. See that we're right together. I'm so ridiculously thrilled that I have to downplay it. "Yeah. Is that a crime?"

"Not at all. I'm just"—he sighs, and I can't tell if he's playacting or not—"terribly, terribly jealous."

Before I can answer, we get sucked into the whole posh-people-party thing, and I lose track of all the names and faces, and which names belong to which faces, in about three seconds flat. But it's okay because Laurie knows some of these people, and Jasper knows nearly everyone, so I just stand there chuffing champagne and smiling like an idiot. I briefly meet the president. Not like of the United States, of the college. He calls Laurie "Laurence," which makes him sound like an alien I've never met, and afterwards he looks all flustered.

Eventually, though, we settle into a corner by one of those big, big windows, and I stare down into the cloisters, feeling like a king. Jasper's on his third glass of champagne. I'm still on one because I genuinely don't want to embarrass myself or Laurie.

It's good shit though, whatever they're serving. Sweet and dry and sort of buttery soft and filled with so many tiny bubbles

I'm armoured in them. They fizz around my tongue stud, and I desperately want to kiss Laurie like this, with our mouths all full of light.

Instead, I take the opportunity to buzz him, and he leans against the stonework, his fingers tightening on the stem of his glass.

God, I'm so fucking horny.

He idly puts an arm across my chest and draws me in to his body. It's so nice, because we're sort of nestled together in the window arch—me in front, Laurie holding me tight. Tight against his erection and his hard-beating heart.

He lowers his head like he's kissing my cheek, but he's actually whispering, "Behave, damn you," all unsteady into my ear.

I wriggle. Because sadist. And Laurie's arm turns vicelike.

Jasper's eyes kind of skitter away from us, like he guesses a bit of what's going on. Oops. I should probably stop.

Just in time. Because then we're hailed, an American accent cutting way too easily across the roomful of politely murmuring Brits, and this man, dressed like Jasper but in this slapdash, careless way, all his layers out of control and his bow tie skew-whiff, comes bounding over.

Jasper's whole face freezes into this awful sneer, but his eyes are kind of hot and desperate.

"Sherry." Laurie sounds genuinely happy though. "It's good to see you."

"Hiiii!" The American hugs us. Both of us, since Laurie's still not in any position to let me go. But that doesn't stop the newcomer. He just enfolds us both in these huge monkey arms and squeezes, me stuck in the middle like I'm Baby Bear.

"Uh," says Laurie, when we can all resume breathing, "this is Toby. Toby, this is Sheridan Hunter Fitzroy III."

"It's okay, laugh it up. And call me Sherry, all right?" He's staring at me like he's expecting something.

"Uh, okay."

"So, you're the new guy, huh? I've been dying to meet you!"

"Really?"

"Course! So, come on, Toby, tell me all about you!"

He kind of talks in exclamation marks, and he's...he's sort of the most golden person I've ever met. I think he's crazy hot in this clean-cut, very square-jawed way, but he's also kind of...y'know, the shiny, transparent coat you put over nail polish to stop it getting chipped or rubbing off. He's like that, but all over. And there's this generosity to him that's *scary* because it's like he really believes you're the best person ever, and he's madly thrilled to be with you. Except it just means that you feel like you're going to disappoint him at any second because you're not the best person ever. You're just you.

Which is exactly my problem. "Um...uh..." I really don't have a fucking clue what to say, or how to be interesting enough for him. "I'm just..."

"He's Coal's son." That's Jasper, out of nowhere.

I'm pissed he knows, even though it's my own fault he knows, but at the same time, I'm kind of relieved because now I'm irrelevant again.

Sherry's eyes go wide, so blue they're dazzling. "Seriously? Oh my God. I *love* her. I saw *White Ink* in Tokyo. Stunning."

I shrug. That's always the best answer. But there's also Laurie to lean into, and he cuddles me.

"What am I missing?" he asks.

Nothing is what I want to tell him, but then the president clinks on his glass, and I brace myself for some kind of speech, but we're just being called in to dinner.

Jasper grabs and knocks back another glass of champagne. And then we go through a little door and onto—I am not fucking kidding—the roof. There's a wooden walkway covered in chicken wire, and we all troop along it very carefully like a bunch of penguins. And all around us, the towers and walls glow in this pale and ghostly way against the night. It's completely surreal, and I'm glad I only had one glass of champagne.

Sherry's gone up ahead, so we go on either side of Jasper. He's pretty steady on his feet, but it feels safer that way. He's staring at Sherry's back like he's trying to burn a hole straight through him.

"How can you love him and be jealous of him?" I wasn't actually intending to say that aloud, but apparently I do anyway.

And Jasper actually answers. "Because if I wasn't...I'd be abject."

That makes no sense to me.

We make our way down a twisty little staircase and through a teeny tiny door, and then we're in another world. It's not a massive room, but it's seriously oak-panelled, with sort of flying buttresses across the ceiling and stained glass windows like in church. There's lamps and candles on the tables, but that's it, so it's very close to being gloomy, but the light flickers and catches on all the silverware and makes it magical instead.

We're at the back on a raised platform, and everybody else stands up as we file in. It feels really scary, and I'm so sure I'm going to fall over or do something wrong, but it's fine. Once we've all found our places—I'm safely squished between Laurie and Jasper—the president bangs a hammer on the table and rattles off something in Latin.

Then there's a screeching of chairs, and we sit down.

I must have a funny look on my face because Jasper pats my

hand. "Next time, come on a Sunday and grace will be sung from the gallery."

I'm not sure I want to hear grace being sung from the gallery—my head might explode from sheer weird—but I love that he says it so casually. Like it's obvious I'm coming back.

Sherry's opposite, next to this dark-eyed, intent man who tells me his name so softly I totally miss it, and a younger guy in a really rubbish cape who looks absolutely fucking terrified to be here. I think the quiet guy is some kind of librarian and the other one is some kind of graduate student.

Jasper's pouring us water. I have at least three separate drinking glasses in front of me, and I count up four forks, so this is definitely going to be the awesome kind of dinner. Even my bread roll is delicious-looking, and there's a saucer of individual butter florets.

I totally love this shit.

I lean over to Laurie and whisper, "Thank you for bringing me."

And he gives me what Jasper calls his soupy look and whispers back, "Thank you for coming."

I spot a discreet little card hidden behind the candelabra, which I guess has to be the menu. It's gold-edged and topped off with the college crest, just like Jasper's poncy invitation.

I nudge Laurie. "Dude, listen to this: roast squash soup with toasted pumpkin seeds and crème fraîche."

"Um, yes?"

"What's wrong with you? Doesn't that sound delicious?"

He looks around at the people who are closest. "I do actually feed him."

"Anticipation is part of the pleasure."

"Of food?"

"Of any sensuous activity," purrs Jasper.

Across the way, Sherry chokes on a mouthful of water, and I kind of cheer inside for Jasper because it proves the guy isn't completely invincible.

Jasper twitches the menu out of my hand and reads it out in something that can only be called Sexy Voice. Promises of seared Cornish sea bass, roast venison loin, and apple crumble tart roll over me in a way that gets me all eager and quivery.

Yeah, I'm a glutton. I just really like food. Any food, honestly, as long as it's good—even really simple stuff like scrambled eggs and cakes. But it's sometimes nice to know you've got Calvados foam in your future. Even though I'm a bit dubious about foams in general. Sometimes they end up looking like you've spit all over the plate. Not good.

"How's your anticipation now, Tobermory?"

I cough a bit. "Yeah…it's getting…there."

"And now you know"—Sherry smiles at us—"why Jasper has a fan page on Facebook."

"Undergraduates." Jasper makes a dismissive gesture.

"They adore him. They tweet about what he's wearing and what he says. He has his own hashtag."

For a moment, I think he's taking the piss, but then I realise he's not. He *likes* Jasper. He just likes him, in this completely uncomplicated way. And I get a bit sad for them because it feels like that ought to make everything simple.

Except for all the ways it isn't and doesn't.

Then a waiter slides some roast squash soup in front of me, and I cheer right up again. Because shallow. It's good soup, rich and creamy and a little bit spicy. The pumpkin seeds give it texture. Nom. All the nom.

I let the conversation drift away from me while I concentrate on the food. I think it's got nutmeg in there. Ginger definitely.

☆   When I next look up, Jasper seems to be randomly torturing Terrified Guy by complaining in this horrifically eloquent way about DPhil students who don't do anything useful for society or humanity or the university, until Terrified Guy looks like he wants to drown himself in his soup. "Uh, what do you do, Jasper?" I ask as they're taking away the bowls, just to get him off the guy's case.

He tosses his head haughtily. "I work primarily on historiographical writing of the High Middle Ages, in Latin, French, and English." I've no idea what that means, but I *hmm* intelligently. "Like Dr. Hunter," he adds in this tight little voice.

Sherry nods. "I'm writing a book on the development of English national identity in postconquest England."

"A book?" Jasper squeaks.

☆   My mum has parties; I know how to handle conversations like this. I turn to Terrified Guy. "And what about you?"

He mumbles something.

"Sorry, what?"

"I'm a researcher at the Department of Oncology."

"Like...cancer?"

He looks miserably at his place setting. "We're trying to better understand the molecular basis of tumour cell resistance to radiation treatments."

"Oh, wow, yeah, that sounds totally useless."

Laurie and Sherry both laugh, and Jasper drinks off an entire glass of white wine he's been given at some point. Then Laurie sort of pounces on Terrified Guy, and they end up having a really intense conversation about BKM120, perfusion CT scans, and 18-F-something-or-other PET-CT something somethings. Jasper and Sherry start getting into it over a manuscript from some monastery in St. Albans.

And I just prepare myself for seared Cornish sea bass with crab and sesame sauce.

God, yes. Bring it on.

I don't actually mind not being part of the conversation. First off, the food is nice enough it deserves my attention, and I like being able to soak up the atmosphere in peace. It's noisy because of all the wood and the clattering of plates and cutlery, but at the same time oddly intimate: little bubbles of conversation in these pools of hazy candlelight. Waiters, confusingly also in black and white, weave in and out of the shadows, keeping the wine flowing.

I'm deep into the venison loin with bacon, cabbage, chestnuts, and the butternut purée when I suddenly notice Sherry is talking to me. But what he really wants to know about is my mum and what she's doing at the moment, so I tell him about the new exhibition in the railway arch. It's kind of hard to talk about because it's called a symbol...I mean the title of the exhibition is a symbol...because that's not confusing or anything.

It's probably genius or something. But what the fuck do I know?

There's this sort of ripple going down the table now. People's heads are turning, and I hear my mum's name on strangers' lips.

Shiiiit.

"Toby?" Laurie frowns. "Is your mother someone...famous?"

Jasper sniggers into his venison.

"Lil bit, my friend," says Sherry. "Teeny lil bit."

The quiet librarian glances up. He's very pale, his eyes all shadowy in the candlelight. "She's an artist, Laurie. Sh-she's collaborating with my ex. Or they were w-when...before..." His hand tightens on his fork, and he seems to run out of words.

"Who's your ex?" I ask.

"M-Marius?"

"Oh, I remember Marius." Tall, hot, and Byronic-looking, like most of Mum's beautiful, arty young men. God. I hope they aren't fucking. "He seemed very...passionate?"

He gives me this stricken look and then stares at his plate, and I feel terrible, and I don't really know why. Then somebody else whose name I can't remember leans over Laurie. "Is it true you have three fathers?"

"Err...no." I give it a beat because I've done this a lot. "I've got five."

Laurie turns so sharply he almost puts his elbow in the butter. "What the hell?"

"It's not a big deal. My mum was sleeping with a bunch of people when she got pregnant, which was probably for the best, in a way, because she was fifteen, so nobody went to prison."

"Good God," Laurie mutters. I'm kind of worried about how he's taking this, but I've started so I have to finish.

"Anyway, a bunch of them came forward afterwards, because it was all scandalous and cool, and about five of them stuck around on a sort of irregular rotation."

"And you didn't think to get a DNA test?" I don't like the careful way Laurie says it.

"Why? I didn't care about whose spunk it was, I just wanted someone to stand up and say, 'Me.' When I was like nine or something, I was so sick of it I called everyone together, and I was like, 'No more part-time dads. Choose.'" I need something to do with my hands, so I take a big gulp of wine I don't want. And then I grin as I deliver the punch line. "So none of them stayed."

Afterwards I went to Granddad. Cried my eyes out. Looking back, I don't know why I was upset. I had him.

"What about your mother?" asks Laurie.

"She didn't care either way. They were all sort of friends by then, but she was basically done with them." Everyone is looking at me, all curious and eager. So I sigh and give them what they want. "She doesn't believe you should have sex more than once with the same person. Because...it'd be like photocopying a piece of art."

Laurie actually rolls his eyes. "Your mother doesn't believe in photocopiers?"

"She doesn't believe in the mechanics of mass production." ☆ I take a breath and recite in a monotone, "'Even the most perfect reproduction of a work of art is lacking in one element: its presence in time and space, its unique existence at the place where it happens to be.'"

So that's how I start a riot, everybody talking at once about art and the meaning of art and the nature of authenticity and all the usual shit.

Laurie isn't saying anything. I try to catch his eye, and when I do, he mouths, *Who are you?* at me.

I mouth back, *Yours*.

And we hold hands under the table until the apple-and-quince crumble tart arrives. The Calvados foam looks okay and tastes amazing. I want to lick it from Laurie's fingers.

God. Laurie and food. My two favourite things.

"And what about you, Toby?" comes Sherry's voice into my private gastric-lust haze.

"Huh?" Oh God, they better not be asking me about art, because I don't give a fuck.

"Are you an artist too?"

"Uh, no." I deploy my best *duh* voice. "It's not genetic."

He smiles so nicely I feel a bit of a dick for snapping. "I just thought you might've had an interest."

"No, I work in a caff."

"How terribly bohemian of you," drawls Jasper.

God. You just can't fucking win sometimes. "Yeah. Apparently the Kray twins used to throw people through the front windows way back when."

"Let me guess, by day you study the human condition, and by night you write your novel?"

"At night I see my granddad and wait for the weekend to roll round so I can be with Laurie." And now everyone looks disappointed. Well, everyone except Laurie. I sigh. "I used to want to be a poet, okay?"

"What changed your mind?"

I'm kind of losing track of who's looking and who's talking.

I shrug. "I like poetry too much."

☆   Jasper pushes away most of his crumble tart—a serious waste, if you ask me—and pulls his wineglass closer. He rests an elbow on the table, which you're not supposed to do, and cups his chin in his hand as he looks at me with his pretty eyes and this faint, unreadable smile. "I've decided I adore you, Tobermory. Which poets do you favour?"

He makes it easy to forget there's a whole world beyond him. "All sorts, really."

"Don't play hard to get. It doesn't suit you."

"Oh, all right. I like...the metaphysical poets, especially Donne and Marvell. And the Earl of Rochester. And François Villon. And Byron. And Gerard Manley Hopkins."

"You like your verses rather rough and rugged."

"Like I like my men."

Laurie chokes.

"I just like it when the way it sounds is part of how it looks, y'know?"

"I do know," Jasper tells me gravely. And I think he means it.

"I like Wilfred Owen too. And Mina Loy, she's the only modernist I can stand. And Brenda Shaughnessy, and Li-Young Lee, and Eduardo C. Corral." I'm starting to feel a bit self-conscious now. Like bits of my insides are suddenly on the outside. "Oh, and Don Marquis."

Jasper laughs, but it's so gentle I'm kind of shocked. "'*Toujours gai, Archy, toujours gai.*'"

I guess I lose track of the time a bit, because the next thing I know that isn't poetry or the soft rhythm of Jasper's voice is Laurie tugging at my elbow.

As we get to our feet, the rest of the room stands up as well. And it just goes to show how quickly things get normal because I don't even blink. Soon I'll be expecting people to jump up and down depending on what I do.

I can tell Laurie's tense, but I don't know why.

"The next bit is also a tradition." He sounds a bit snappy as he yanks me through the side door. "We'll all sit in a circle and drinks will be handed round. Always pour to the right and pass to the left. The drinks will be served until you don't replenish your glass, so for God's sake, remember to stop or we'll be there forever."

"Okay. Pass left. Stop drinking. Got it." I smile up at him, but he doesn't smile back.

"And I'm afraid we won't be sitting together."

"What? Why?"

"I don't know. It's just how it works."

I hope he's pissy because he's not going to be able to drink brandy and hold my hand, but I'm not sure. I don't *think* I've done anything to embarrass him.

We all huddle into another room—not oak-panelled for

a change, but it's got a chandelier. All the chairs have been arranged in a horseshoe round the fire, and as we come in we're sort of funnelled off in different directions like passengers on the Titanic.

I really want to cling to Laurie, but I can't. I'll look like a knob.

I think it's meant to be some sort of special social alchemy thing, because I'm shown my place like it's supposed to be awesome. There's a guy already settled into the seat next to me and he shakes my hand as I sit down, telling me his name is Harrison Whitwell.

He's another American, which I could have guessed from the interchangeable first name/surname thing he's got going on. Why do they do that over there? I mean, really, why? Turns out he's a lawyer and an honorary fellow. I'm not sure what this means, but he seems pretty pleased about it. And he's wearing a different cape to everyone else—it's got some hardcore scarlet trim.

At first I'm a little bit...not shy of him, exactly, but uncertain. It's kind of scary to just be *given* to someone you don't know with the expectation they'll want to talk to you. Except he *does* want to talk to me—or, at least, he gives a very good impression of it. He's really nice, not too intense, and he seems happy he got me. He asks lots of questions, and tells a lot of stories that make me laugh. He looks after me when the decanters come round, pours out little glasses of sweet white wine and ruby-red port. I remember what Laurie told me, though. I remember to stop and I pass to the left.

The best thing, though, is when the bottles reach the far side of the horseshoe. There's actually this...machine thing that slides them back across.

The decanters rattle on the wooden rails, and I'm fascinated.

"It totally boggles me that somebody actually sat down and, y'know, invented that."

His eyes twinkle at me. "Considering where we are, it doesn't surprise me at all."

We laugh and then his hand sort of drifts onto my knee. I wonder if I'm being sexually harassed, which is kind of exciting, honestly. I'm not used to thinking of myself as the sort of person someone would *want* to sexually harass. I guess Harris (as I'm allowed to call him) is flirting with me a bit, but in this really gentle, courtly kind of way that...I, uh, really like. I don't feel threatened at all. I just feel special. Not the same way Laurie makes me feel (sometimes anyway, when he forgets I'm not supposed to be special to him), but it's still good.

So his hand stays, and we keep talking, and the decanters go round, and the whole thing is sort of hypnotic. We talk about everything, and I kind of play up to him. He's older than Laurie, and it's not as if I've got an age-inappropriate fetish or anything—which Laurie isn't, he's just Laurie—but there's a lot about Harris I like. Confidence and warmth and interest in me.

I guess I'm kind of a total slut for that last one.

They send round fruit and chocolate as well as the booze, and near the end, a pretty box Harris flips open for me. "Snuff?"

"Oh my God, for real?" I guess that had come out louder than I meant, because there's kind of a lull in conversation.

"You want to try?"

Well. Never let it be said Toby Finch wasn't willing to try. "Uh, maybe, but I don't know how."

He does, and I get a snuff-for-beginners talk before he dabs some into the hollow between his thumb and forefinger and offers his hand to me.

What in Rome, right? I lean over and sniff. I'm a bit

tentative—and you're definitely not supposed to snort it—but the stuff goes up my nose, so I guess I don't mess it up. It's a pale flash in the front of your brain, like just the right amount of wasabi.

I get a little round of applause for my bravery, which is cool.

Except Laurie doesn't seem happy at all. His eyes are so cold and stormy he sort of doesn't look like my Laurie anymore. He looks like he did when I first saw him, remote and wild and totally out of my league.

Maybe I shouldn't have taken snuff. He's a doctor; he probably feels strongly about addictive substances. But it's not like one pinch is going to turn me into a snuffhead.

Eventually we're allowed to stop drinking and start mingling again. Harris gives me his business card from a silver box of them and says I should call him if I ever find myself in Chicago or if I fancy giving the law another shot. He tells me he thinks I'd be a good lawyer, which is nice, but fuck no.

Then Laurie grabs me by the shoulder and spins me round.

"Laurie, what are—"

"Outside. I need to talk to you outside."

He doesn't actually give me any choice about it, just drags me out of the room and into the silence of the cloisters.

I can hear him breathing, harsh like when we're fucking. "What the hell, Toby? Just what the hell?"

I think...I'm almost scared of him. And that's a *weird* feeling. Also, he's seriously riled up about nicotine. "You mean, the snuff?"

"I mean all of it."

"I only took a bit."

"Not the fucking snuff...the...the..."

I blink at him. "The what?"

"Do you have some kind of...queer Electra complex? Older man fetish? Unresolved daddy issues? What?"

My mouth kind of drops open. I can't decide if I'm angry or hurt. Well, I'm both. But I can't decide which is bigger. "Jesus, Laurie. That's not okay."

"And flirting with half my fucking college is?"

"I wasn't—"

I don't get a chance to finish because he shoves me up against the wall and pins me there and presses his mouth to mine. Fuck, he's strong. And anger is coming off him like heat, and his kiss is sort of mean and frantic and tastes of sweet, heavy things.

Talk about mixed messages. Except. Wait. No. Oh my God.

I can't really get away from him—not sure I want to, anyway—but I pull my head to the side, which makes it hard for him to keep kissing me. "Laurie, are you jealous?"

The silence gathers itself again, and the pressure of his body against mine sort of eases off a bit. "Fuck." One word, but he sounds so defeated.

"It's okay." I lift a leg and hook it round him, dragging him in, hoping he'll get the message and start aggressively molesting me again. "I mean, I wasn't *trying* to make you jealous, and it's totally baseless because I'm all yours, but it's so hot you are."

"It's not hot, Toby, it's fucking adolescent. God, what's wrong with me?"

"What's wrong with you is you like me, and you don't like the idea of anyone else having me."

His touch is gentle as he pushes the hair out of my eyes. "You were enchanting. No wonder they all want you."

Maybe it's messed up, but I'm so fucking proud right now that my heart is spinning round the top of some spire somewhere. I think he's exaggerating in the madness of being jealous and not knowing how to deal with it, and obviously I genuinely don't want to upset him, but I like how much he wants me. How much he can't deny it right now.

"Well, they can't have me. Because I'm yours."

He nods.

I tip my hips into his. "Say it."

He hesitates. Longer than he ever has, even when I've made him beg for something he doesn't want to want.

It makes me anxious, the way his other waiting doesn't. I guess because this time it's not a game.

"Because..." It's hard to read someone in the dark. I can only catch the gleam of his eyes. "Because..." The word kind of rasps the second time he says it, like he's almost in tears. "Because... you're mine."

"I am, I so am." I throw my arms around him and nearly fall over because that only leaves me one leg for me, but he holds me up, safe between him and a five-hundred-year-old wall.

His cheek rubs against mine. His jaw's a bit rough. Calvados foam and centuries of civilisation, but Laurie still isn't tame. "Oh God, Toby. I'm so sorry I—"

"Don't you fucking dare. I loved it."

"Did you now?" There's a different note in his voice now, playfulness and a hint of threat I find insanely sexy.

I grin. "Yeah, because I'm a dirty little flirt, remember?"

He catches my wrists and drags them over my head, cradled in his palms so they don't catch on the stone. I'm not really into being restrained, but when it's Laurie, it's somehow still something he's giving me, all his strength for whatever I want to do with it.

I give him what I hope is a dirty-little-flirt look. "It's how I bring powerful men to their knees."

He groans in this deep, helpless way, and it echoes in the

cloisters, this suddenly far-too-intimate moment. And then he's pulling me away from the doorway into the shadows, and we're kissing again, fumbling in the dark, everything reduced to touch and sound and secrets.

Laurie's rough with me, but in a good way, a little bit out of control. His body traps me against the wall again, but I keep my hands free so I can twist them in his hair, span them over the tight-pulled muscles of his back, dig them into his arse. Grope my way up to the remote in my breast pocket and hit the button, so he shakes and grinds against me, muffling his cries in my shoulder. And he's even wilder now, turning me round and bending me over the ledge of an archway.

My hands come down on cold stone. Laurie leans over me, his teeth scraping the back of my neck, and I make a guttural, shuddery sound.

We must look fucking amazing. Framed in filthy tableaux in the moon-drenched cloisters.

I love doing this: imagining us together while we're together, all the ways we're different and the same, all the ways our bodies fit and all the ways mine can make his yield.

Laurie's fingers are under my cummerbund. The button on my trousers comes loose with a *snick* and bounces away—*plink plink plink*—and then, in one ruthless tug, I'm bare-arsed in an internationally renowned institution of higher education.

It's honestly kind of thrilling—I've come a long way from the boy who thought being fucked facing the foot of the bed was way out there—but at the same time, a bit nervous-making.

Except we're right at the back and it's dark and I'm pretty sure Laurie wouldn't be doing this if there was any danger.

So I just wriggle at him and arch my back, loving how powerful it is to be the dirty little flirt he thought I was.

He groans again, and then I hear him spit, which is so out of place here, so obscene and exciting. Also terrifying, because Laurie is, uh, sizeable and I'm kind of a lube fiend. And I definitely don't think I'm a sufficiently high-level sodomite for him to cruise in on saliva and a fair wind. His hand lands between my shoulder blades, holding me down, and he drags his slickened cock over the crease of my arse, which—considering his cock has been in my arse—shouldn't be as shocking as it is. But I guess my arse is kind of vulnerable at the moment, and I stifle a little whimper, knowing how hard and hot he is for me, wanting this urgency and this exposure, this weird little edge between threat and desire.

Then he shoves his knee between my legs and his cock between my thighs. And holy shit, that shouldn't feel like anything, but it does...it really does. There's just something really basic about it, this make-do conjunction, and it sends my stomach all wibbly and my legs all shaky. The skin of my thighs is wet and tender around his cock, like it's my mouth or something, like he's inside not outside, and I squeeze around him, tight enough to make his fingers curl and his breath catch. He thrusts... against...*into?* me, and his shaft rubs the underside of my balls, not entirely gently, but it makes startled little tingles ricochet through my whole body.

Sliding his arm around me, he lifts me off the ledge and reaches down to my cock. I guess I've had a pretty intense day— teasing Laurie on the train, fingering him into a pleading mess over the desk, knowing there's a plug inside him because I put it there, and now this—and I'm honestly not very good at restraint at the best of times. I've been a bit proud, actually, at how well I've controlled myself, but the moment he touches me, I sort of lose my mind. He gets his other hand over my mouth just in time to catch my scream.

Fuck. His hand. His cock. His body and the stone around us. His hot breath. The cold air. The *cloisters*.

His hand tightens over my mouth because I can't even breathe quietly. I'm making these funny little raspy, moany noises as he jacks me off and fucks between my legs, and everything is sweaty and sticky and a little bit awkward, but that's what makes it perfect. It feels raw and dark and a little bit ugly, and I come, biting his hand and sobbing because it's just so good, so fucking good.

He doesn't even let me catch a breath, just pushes me down again.

"Say it." A hot growl in the darkness.

"Say what?" I'm not messing with him. I'm just genuinely, fucked-out delirious.

There's this pause. Tiny but infinite. Eye-of-the-storm type thing. My brain finally finds enough spare oxygen to make a thought happen. I'm about to tell him I'm his, or he's mine, or something, when he whispers, "Tell me you love me."

"I love you." I think I might be scary close to actually crying. I know he wants me in a sex way, but this is so much more than that. He wants *me*. "I love you."

There's a remote in my pocket with a button that lets me implode him. I was kind of meaning to press it the moment he got close, but I just forget. I forget everything except what he needs to hear from me, and he comes, not in a wild roar, but so gently, trembling, as he holds me and I tell him over and over that I love him.

We don't exactly get an afterglow. We get a hasty pulling up of trousers and an inept deruffling of hair. We're both kind of wobbly, and not quite embarrassed, but self-conscious. Still open to each other, like we're still having sex.

Laurie has to use his pocket square to clean me up and mop the spatters from the stonework, and as he bends down, he winces.

"Toby, I have to... Please, can I...? I'm kind of sensitive."

"Oh God. Yeah. Sorry."

"No, no, it's fine. I just need it out."

He limps through the archway towards the New Building, and I trail after him, a bit guiltily. There's a toilet hidden in the bushes—like, for real—and he dashes into a stall, slamming the door behind him.

"Uh, can I help?"

"No. Absolutely not. Can you wait outside?"

"Sure."

I wait outside, and in a few minutes Laurie emerges, looking close to normal.

I gaze up at him anxiously. "You're okay, right? I didn't do anything bad?"

"You made me wear a butt plug to a formal dinner. Yes, Toby, you did something bad." I think he's smiling. "But it's all right."

"I didn't hurt you?"

"No. It's just having you watch me remove a butt plug crosses a line."

Suddenly, I notice something. "Uh, what happened to it?"

"I've thrown it away, darling. I'm not walking around with it in my pocket."

I slide my hand into the crook of his elbow as we wander through the moonlight. "You're just trying to get out of wearing it again."

"You got me."

Yeah, I think. *I do.* I lean against his shoulder, sleepy and content, but not wanting to bring my magical night of ancient traditions, good food, and cloister-banging to an end.

He untangles us and puts his arm round me instead, and that's even better.

"Is it over?" I ask. "Are we supposed to go back?"

"We can if you like. Most of the guests will have drifted away, but not everyone."

"No. It's okay. I like this more."

We make our way back through the cloisters and into the front bit. Our footsteps ring against the stone.

"There's a lot I don't know about you, isn't there, Toby?" His voice as he says it is quiet, just for me.

It's odd, because I've been kind of desperate for him to be interested in me, and now that he is, I'm not ready. I've got too much to lose now. He's *given* me too much to lose.

Today has been...better than anything. Being with him. Being part of his world, his life. Being someone he wants enough, values enough, to be jealous of.

Yes, it's not love. But it's near enough, right?

But what happens when he realises he has nothing to be jealous *of*? What if the truth about me—about my crappy little life—changes everything again? When we're finally close to where I want us to be.

So I flash a grin at him. "Then ask me sometime."

"You could have, at least, told me about your mother."

"Well, maybe I like just being Toby to you."

"How could you be anything else, you stupid boy?" He sounds kind of annoyed, but something else as well. Something I have no clue about. He stops walking and swings me round. "You see, the thing is—"

God. He looks so fucking serious. And I'm so afraid he's going to start demanding answers—Why aren't you at university? How did you fuck everything up so badly? Am I really dating some guy who cooks eggs for minimum wage? How can someone as everyday as you possibly be the kid of this famous iconoclastic genius?—that I panic and burst into the quickstep.

His face is kind of a picture as I jump about. "What the hell are you doing?"

"I don't know... I just felt happy, and the stone is all tappy, so I started dancing."

"This isn't a movie from the Golden Age of Hollywood, Toby."

I hold out my arm and the moonlight spills over my tuxedo jacket. "We are in black and white."

The shadows move over his face as he laughs. "I didn't even know you could dance."

"I'm not a barbarian. My granddad taught me."

I offer my hand, but he just stares at it like it's a dead fish and then actually backs away from it. "Oh...I can't. I can't dance."

"What, not at all? Not even when you hear ABBA?"

"I do my very best not to hear ABBA."

"I'll show you. It's easy."

He shakes his head. "I really can't, Toby."

I slow-quick-quick-slow my way round the...what's it called... quadrangle in the arms of an imaginary partner. Since he's watching me, I throw in a couple of rumba crosses, showing off, and eventually, natural turn and progressive chassé my way back to him. I'm a little bit breathless, but it's a big space. "And you call yourself a gentleman."

"I've never called myself a gentleman." He sounds stern, but then he smiles and kisses me lightly. "I like watching you dance."

"Dance with me. It's way more fun."

I try the hand thing again, and this time Laurie takes it. He's really hesitant, and his palm is a bit sweaty. He's scared? Oh my God. Too adorable. Getting him into the right position is like trying to move the Tin Man without an oil can, but I get him there. He's not going to win any competitions, but it could be worse. By which I mean I can hypothetically accept that there could be a less comfortable, less graceful way for someone to look. Though I can't actually imagine it.

I was going to have him lead since he's so much taller, but there's no way that's ever happening. He's stiff as a board, and his hand holding mine is a terrified claw.

Just when I thought I couldn't love him any more.

So I soothe him like I do when we're fucking, like when I have him in chains, and he quiets. I tell him it's going to be okay. I tell him he's beautiful. Because to me he is, and never more so than when he's doing something he doesn't entirely want to do.

God. I'm a sick puppy.

But I wouldn't change it for the world. Not when I get this.

I talk him through the basic steps and then guide him into them. At first he doesn't trust me, doesn't trust himself, won't relax, or can't, falls over my feet, his own feet, bits of perfectly flat ground, and he stands on my toes, like, *a lot.*

I'm just starting to think I've made a terrible mistake when he...there isn't another word for it...he surrenders, and we're dancing. Slow, slow-quick-quick-slow, slow-quick-quick-slow, slow-quick-quick-slow. He even lets me throw in a couple of natural turns and a back lock without freezing or stumbling or mushing my feet into the dust.

I speed it up. Because it's a quickstep, not a worried-and-quite-slow-actually step, and Laurie's laughing a little bit as we gallop round the quad in each other's arms. We're about five percent graceful and ten percent competent, but fuck it, we're dancing. And the faster we go, the closer we get to flying.

Eventually he falls over, and we come to a giggly, gasping, cuddly halt.

"Now you've just got to do it to music," I tell him.

"Now I just have to have a lie-down somewhere. Maybe with a cold flannel on my forehead."

I mock-scowl at him. "It wasn't that bad."

"I told you, I can't dance."

I pull him back into hold. "Nuh-uh, you *don't* dance. There's a difference."

"Not to me, there isn't."

I try to think of something that would be good for a quickstep and hum the opening of "Walking on Sunshine."

Laurie turns into marble. "And certainly not to Katrina and the Waves."

Apparently not. I peer up at him—the man I love and can't call boyfriend. I think of him on his knees. How he touches me. How he looks at me. The sadness in him and the secret joy he gives only to me. All the ways he makes me powerful.

All the ways he doesn't really know me.

That's when I know what we should dance to. "'Dear, when you smiled at me, I heard a melody...'"

And Laurie smiles, and we dance, and it's a fucking disaster. Since I kind of have to concentrate a bit on singing, I can't count at the same time, and so Laurie keeps getting lost, and it's like our bodies have completely forgotten how to move together.

I'm just about to call the whole thing off, when—

"'*Zing*! Went the strings of my heart.'"

Another voice joins mine. A way better voice, an effortless tenor belonging to someone who can actually sing. It's Jasper, leaning in the archway that leads back to the cloisters, wineglass in one hand, cigarette in the other.

Laurie and I collide. Stare at him. He gives us an airy little *carry on* gesture, like this is totally normal.

So we put our arms around each other again. I lead and Laurie follows and Jasper sings, and there's moonlight, and we dance and dance and dance until we fly and my heart is so *zing*. I can't even.

9

LAURIE

Toby didn't come back.

At first I thought he was just late, then I thought I'd confused the day, and then I realised he wasn't coming at all. I told myself that it was entirely his right, that it was inevitable, that it was probably for the best. But I was frantic.

Was my dancing really that bad?

But he'd told me he loved me. You didn't say that to someone, and then—Oh God. Not again. Not again.

It had only been a couple of hours, but suddenly my house was full of empty rooms, and I didn't know what to do with myself. I couldn't bear to be in it, but I didn't dare leave in case Toby turned up. I kept half hearing the doorbell. He would tumble over the threshold and into my arms, just like always, and there'd be some story, some mistake, some misunderstanding, and we'd laugh, and I'd feel angry and foolish at the same time, but I'd forgive him. I'd forgive him because I was desperate to feel angry and foolish.

Instead of alone. And bereft.

And still foolish, for having let this happen. For having known all along that this would happen, or something like it, and made myself naked for him anyway. It wasn't even masochism. It was a basic failure to learn.

Toby would have called it hope.

I kept thinking about last weekend, searching compulsively for the hint, the hint that surely had to be there, of what was to come. The moment it had gone wrong, and I hadn't noticed. But I couldn't find anything. We'd been happy. Hadn't we? Wandering hand in hand through golden streets. If people had been inclined to look askance at us, I hadn't been inclined to care. Perhaps Toby had?

On Sunday, I called Grace. I didn't ask her to, but she came over anyway and kept my futile vigil with me. It helped. It meant I couldn't cry. She wouldn't have judged me for it, but I'd never liked doing that in front of other people. Without the excuse of sexualised suffering, anyway.

I tried to explain what had happened, but I couldn't because I didn't know. There was only Toby's absence.

She could have confronted me with all the nonsense I'd told them over pancakes, but she didn't. She just put a hand on my arm and asked if he wasn't answering his phone and what messages I'd left him.

Which was when I had to admit I'd never asked for his number.

Grace blinked. "Okay. Well, there's no need to panic. Toby's a young person. He probably lives on the internet. Google him."

"Isn't that basically stalking?"

"Public domain, and you wouldn't be reduced to stalking him if you'd communicated with him properly in the first place."

The truth was, it simply hadn't occurred to me. I'd been so resigned to the notion that something like this was going to happen anyway that I'd practically engineered it. And now it had and I was devastated and I had only myself to blame.

"Even if he is on the internet," I said, "what am I supposed to do? Sign up for Facebook so I can Like him? Twitter at him?"

"Tweet, love. It's tweet." She turned on my laptop and opened up Chrome. "What's his name again?"

Fifteen minutes of dedicated Googling later, we had comprehensively established that Toby was not on the internet except for the occasional fleeting reference connected to his mother or his school life.

"Sorry." Grace put my computer aside and curled up on the end of the sofa. "I thought it was worth a shot."

"I wouldn't have known what to say, anyway."

She shrugged. "How about, 'Are you okay?' Something might have happened."

A hundred and seventy—no. No. I closed my mind to statistics. "Or he might simply have decided to stop coming. I did nothing to keep him, really, except quietly fall in love with him while telling everyone—including him—I wasn't and wouldn't."

"You're...um...you're in love with him?"

I dropped my head into my hands. A ridiculously melodramatic gesture, but one in keeping with a ridiculously melodramatic statement. "Oh, I don't know. I don't know anything anymore. Maybe. Probably. I've forgotten what love feels like, so how would I recognise it?"

She shook her head, sympathetic and exasperated as only an old friend can be. "You think way too much."

"I know. The world makes most sense to me when I'm working or..."

"On your knees."

We sat in silence for a while. I knew I was being poor company, but I was selfishly glad I wasn't alone.

"I don't like not knowing," I muttered, finally. "Did he just wake up on Friday morning and fall out of love with me? At least with Robert, I understood."

"See, I never did quite figure out what went on there. I thought after what happened, you'd be the one to leave, not him."

"My forgiveness wasn't even in question. He just couldn't forgive himself."

"I live in abject terror of that, you know." She drew in a sharp ☆ breath. "Hurting someone in the wrong way."

"It was a couple of fractures. They healed." I realised I was holding my wrist protectively, my own hand a cuff. I wanted Toby's touch. "I would have trusted him again, if he'd ever let me."

"But he dropped you, Laurie."

"So? His horrible aunt once called me unnatural at a family dinner party. He dropped me then, as well, when he laughed it off."

She frowned. "It's not the same, though."

"Isn't it? It's just love and trust. Hurt and kinky sex is neither here nor there." I took a deep breath and let the truth slip out. "God, I miss him."

"Robert?"

"Toby. For fuck's sake, I've only had two relationships. It shouldn't be hard to keep up."

"Sorry." But Grace was laughing.

And then, so was I, though it hurt a bit, this helpless, sharp-edged mirth that had to cut its way through tears.

She stayed until close to midnight and then left, and I was alone again, without Robert, which didn't matter, and without Toby, which did.

I was grateful for work the next day because it gave me focus, but it was surprisingly difficult to put Toby's absence from my mind, and took far more energy than I would have expected. Perhaps I needed a holiday—a feeling-sorry-for-myself holiday. Pathetic. But I couldn't remember the last time I'd taken annual leave, and I was tired and sad and unfairly angry with Toby for doing this to me. I told myself I'd been resigned to my compromises, but he'd promised me everything, throwing love around like Smarties, and I'd believed him. Then he'd dropped me, just like Robert. And just like Robert, he'd run.

It was wrong to make comparisons, wrong to feel this hurt and empty, but I did. I did.

I kept imagining the alert, the swoosh of doors and the clatter of footsteps, and the body, the far-too-familiar body, being whisked past me to the operating theatre. It was ridiculous, of course. Nothing so dramatic had likely taken place, and even if it had, there was no guarantee it would be my hospital or my shift.

I would simply never know where Toby's life would take him. Had already taken him.

I was so miserable, I began to worry about my performance, and that was something I couldn't afford, so I booked two weeks off. One of my colleagues actually said, "Good for you." I wasn't sure what I was going to do with the time. Going away seemed both painful and pointless without Toby. But I had to do something.

Get through this somehow.

Surely it had been worse after Robert. But the strangest thing was I couldn't remember that pain at all.

———————

On Friday night—twelve days since I saw him last, not that I was counting, except that I was—I came home and found him in a black suit, sitting on my doorstep. And just like that, all the anger, all the fear, all the misery washed away, leaving me perfectly cold. Safely indifferent.

I regarded him a moment. "Hello."

He didn't look up. "Hey."

"I didn't think I was ever going to see you again." I was actually pleased—darkly pleased—to sound so calm.

"Why? Because I didn't show up once? Isn't that a bit of an overreaction?"

"Well, what was I supposed to think?"

There was a long silence. It was an odd moment. He was right there, in front of my house, but he seemed far away, sullen and young, an unlikely cause of all that hurt. Perhaps I'd gone a little mad, investing so much in whatever it was I'd thought we'd had. A relationship? With a teenager?

"My granddad died," he said.

Oh fuck. The worst of it was that my immediate reaction was a brief flare of resentment, as if he had somehow engineered the whole situation to make me react to his absence and then render my reactions—my distress, my annoyance, my sense of betrayal—invalid. It was as if he had deliberately set out to make me look foolish. Which he hadn't, of course he hadn't. It was simply that his pain had left no room for mine, and he hadn't even thought to let me know.

"Funeral today," he went on. "He missed the snowdrops. He's supposed to come with me. That's what we do. Every year."

"I'm so sorry." I tried to push everything aside except concern. "Do you want to come in?"

He shrugged. "I don't know. I really wanted to see you. It's all I've been thinking about all day, but now I just feel weird about it."

"I missed you too." It seemed a safe enough thing to say. It didn't remotely cover the mess he'd left me in, but it wasn't a lie either. I reached down and gave his shoulder an awkward squeeze, but he flinched away from me. "Toby?"

"I didn't miss you. I wanted you to be there." At last, he looked up, his eyes dark-shadowed, almost bruised. He was very pale, and his acne had flared up, blurring his jaw, his brow, the top edges of his cheeks with red and white stars. "Don't you get it, Laurie? I wanted you to be with me, but here I am as usual, sitting on your doorstep, waiting for the corner of your life I'm allowed."

On a rational level, I knew it was grief that made him speak like that to me, but the sheer *unfairness* of it struck at my good intentions like a pickaxe. "For fuck's sake," I snapped, "if you'd bothered to tell me or ask me, I *would* have been there." Then I gasped and covered my mouth. That hadn't been what I'd meant to say at all.

"Wow, yeah, okay." Toby wrapped his arms round his knees, pulling himself into an impossible ball. "How the fuck was I supposed to tell you, Laurie? Get myself shot in the hope you were the one in the helicopter?"

My whole body went cold. My worst fear, flung at me by a grieving child: arriving on some scene of terrible destruction to find, not a problem to be solved, but the body of someone I loved. "Toby, don't even joke—"

"It's not a joke. I literally have no way to contact you. You've never got round to giving me any. Because it's always on your terms. Everything is always on your terms."

Oh God. I deserved every word. He'd been alone, and in pain, when I could have—*should* have—been with him, and that was my fault, not his. All this week fretting because I didn't have his number, and I'd never even thought he didn't have mine. "Oh God. I'm—"

"If you say you're sorry, I'll scream." He looked at me, his eyes all shadow and shiny with unshed tears. "My granddad's dead, Laurie. The person I love most in the whole world. And I spent his funeral thinking about you. How fucked is that?"

If he didn't want my regret, could he at least accept my consolation? "It's not fucked. Funerals are...funerals. Grief is grief. There aren't any rules about what you should be thinking or feeling."

"Oh, fuck you, that's not the point."

"I know." I was almost glad, in a way, to bear his anger without flinching. It was something I could do for him. "The point is, I wasn't there for you."

His fingers knotted restlessly. "Well, at least you get it. But why's it always me?"

"Why's what?" It felt wrong now to be looming over him, so I hunkered down in front of him and linked my hands together.

"Why do I always have to ask for everything? Why do you never just...give...or offer?"

"I'm sorry I wasn't there for you, but I'm not psychic. I didn't know."

"Yeah, but you never ask either. Do you know how fucking hard it is to be the one who's always asking? Why do I always have to roll my heart between us like it's a fucking marble?" His voice lifted, then broke. "How the fuck am I supposed to know?"

"Know what? That I'll be there for you?" I tried to keep my voice gentle, but there was something unexpected and unexpectedly painful about his uncertainty. "Darling, how could you doubt it?"

Again, that cold, bright stare. "Because you've never given me a reason to believe it."

His words slid into me like pieces of glass. "That's...that's not fair."

"Well, neither are you."

I had no idea how to answer. Everything he'd said was true: I hadn't been fair. And *sorry* was so inadequate as to be insulting.

I didn't know how long he'd been sitting out there, so I stood up, took off my coat, and draped it across his shoulders. He didn't react, but at least he didn't shake it off. Then, I sat down next to him, and we stayed like that for a while, locked in our silences. He smelled faintly of the cologne I'd bought him, a hint of spice and tears, and I ached to be back in Oxford, where it had briefly seemed possible that we could be in love. Where it had been the easiest, simplest thing in the world.

He was right, though. Asking was difficult. Incredibly diffi-cult. But there was such a lot I should have asked and asked for, such a lot I should have given, instead of pretending and telling myself I didn't want any of it. I hadn't given him freedom. I hadn't even managed my own expectations. All I'd done was place every burden of love and trust on Toby, made it impossible for him to ask for something as basic as my presence in his life, and sen-tenced us both to nearly a week of hell.

Perhaps it was already too late to begin building certainties. But the least I could do—at last, at long last—was try. Ask. "Toby?"

"What?"

"I know I should have done this weeks ago, but there's some-thing I need to ask you, and something I need to give you."

"Too late. I don't want your dead-granddad pity."

"This isn't pity." I crushed my own impatience. I knew, like my anger and my hurt, it was just a form of emotional distrac-tion—a way for me to feel less on edge, less vulnerable, less fuck-ing guilty. "When I didn't see you last week, and I had no way to contact you, I was...I was..."

"What?" He sounded so sceptical. My fault again.

"Distraught. Devastated. Heartbroken. The thing is, I've been telling myself for weeks that you have the right to walk away from me at any time. Well, you don't have that right." His head turned sharply, and I reached out without thinking and pushed his fringe out of his eyes. "I mean, you do have the right, I'm not insane. But you have to break up with me first."

"Y'know," he said softly, "that sounds like you want to be my ☆ boyfriend."

"I do. It wasn't what I was going to ask, though."

His lips curled into the smallest smile. "I'm still counting it."

And I smiled back, just as tentatively. "All right."

We were quiet again as I struggled with my incredibly banal, yet utterly necessary request. It should have been so simple, but somehow it wasn't. I'd pleaded with him shamelessly for all manner of violations and all manner of mercies, but the sexual vulnerabilities I allowed were nothing to sitting on my doorstep with Toby, admitting everything I wanted—and needed—from him.

He nudged his shoulder gently against mine. "What did you want, Laurie?"

I took a deep breath. "Your phone number?"

"Course. And text me, so I've got yours." Somehow he managed to say this as though it was perfectly normal. As though we weren't months overdue.

I reached into my pocket, plucked out my phone, and added Toby to my address book. Texted him my contact card.

Then I pulled out my house keys and slid Robert's old key off the ring. I'd put it on there for safekeeping when he'd finally moved out, and never got round to removing it.

Initially it had been sentimentality—it was somewhere we were still together, two keys nestled against each other on my key ring—and then just apathy. I handed it to Toby. "This is what I wanted to give you."

His eyes widened. "Jesus, Laurie."

"No more sitting on my doorstep, okay? Come whenever you like, whether I'm here or not."

"Seriously?"

I nodded. "Again, it's something I should have done weeks ago."

He arched his hips off the step, wriggled his own set of keys out of his pocket, and added mine to the bunch, where it vanished among the other bits and pieces of Toby's life. "So what do I get when my next family member dies?"

"I ask you to marry me."

"That's so not funny." It wasn't, but it was, the way only terrible things can be sometimes. Toby leaned in and kissed me chastely, a little sadly. "Thank you."

"Will you come in now?"

"Yeah."

I left him on the sofa, looking a bit like a stranger in his funeral suit, and made him tea and hot buttered toast, because it was the only thing I could think to do for him.

In grief, Toby's living far outstripped my own, for I had never lost anyone I truly loved. My parents had not been close to their parents, so the death of grandmothers and grandfathers had always been an abstract thing to me. And though I would surely mourn the passing of my own parents, our relationship was one of form and custom, love through duty, and complete mutual incomprehension.

It was strange the way some generations felt unreachably distant and others not at all. In so many ways, I had met all their expectations, but there was still one where I hadn't and couldn't. They'd never reproached me for it. In some ways, it might have been easier if they had, because then it would have given me a reason to dislike them.

I suddenly remembered a birthday—twenty-first? twenty-second?—breaking beneath their silence. "Why don't you ever ask about him?"

My mother had looked momentarily embarrassed, not because of the question, but because I had raised my voice. "I didn't know you wanted me to," was all she'd said. And, after that, at the end of every phone call, always and without fail: "How is Robert?" To which I could only ever answer, "Fine."

The most ironic thing, the cruellest, was that Robert should have been perfect—attractive, well educated, well brought up, ambitious, charming—but for the fact he was a man. All the trappings of civilisation, of good living and eligibility, meant nothing. For he would not bear children. And, while we were together, he could not have married me.

What would my parents think if I ever introduced them to Toby?

And how mortifying—how loathsome and cowardly—to be thirty-seven and still afraid of their disappointment.

I sat on the floor, my head against Toby's knee, as he nibbled the toast and sipped the tea. I didn't know what to say to him or how to comfort him. I only knew he was in pain, and that there was nothing I could do to take it away.

The hospital, of course, was full of pain, full of loss, but there I was merely a ferryman. This was different. I had no role to hide behind. There was only the nakedness and helplessness of love.

"You know what sucks?" He put the plate down—he'd hardly eaten anything. But he kept the tea, cradling the cup too tightly, the skin of his hands blotching pink and white.

"Tell me?"

"Nobody liked my granddad except me. He was kind of a ☆ horrible person."

I wasn't quite sure what to make of this, but perhaps it made it easier for him to dwell on bad memories instead of good. "That doesn't seem to fit what you've told me."

"No, he was nice to me. But his daughter, that's my grandmother, hates him—I mean hated him—because he was really strict with her when she was growing up. He used to hit her and stuff. It wasn't meant to be abusive or anything. It was just the way he'd been raised."

"He didn't...?" I wasn't sure how to finish, or what I would do about the answer.

"God no. Never. Not with me."

Relief rolled through me, and then I felt like a hypocrite. I was quick enough to react to the possibility of other people hurting Toby, noticeably less so when it was me.

He stared blankly at his tea. "My grandmother married really young just to get away from him, and she wouldn't let him near my mum when she was born. But then when she got pregnant—my mum, I mean—and they threw her out, suddenly he was there, supporting her, taking care of me. He had one of those...baby carrier things you strap to your chest. Used to carry me everywhere like a little monkey."

I reached up and peeled his fingers off the cup. He didn't resist when I took it away and put it down, just held my hand instead. "People change. There's nothing strange or wrong about it."

"I guess. He had to have this operation, you know, in like the sixties or seventies. He was injured at Dunkirk and shrapnel got in his heart, so this doctor came all the way over from America to get it out. It took like nine hours or something, and he had this massive scar running all the way down his front and his back. Everybody thought he was going to die. My mum thinks that's what changed him."

"Does it matter?"

For a moment or two, he didn't say anything. Then he shrugged. "I guess not. Not anymore, anyway."

It was harder than I would have imagined possible to see him like this, so uncertain and so sad, but he was still my boy, my Toby, still so full of light. I could picture him in some churchyard, a small splash of dark beneath a grey sky. And I should have been there beside him. He shouldn't have had to mourn alone. I hated myself for that. "The fact he treated other people badly doesn't change the fact he loved you."

"No, I know. It's just"—he squeezed my fingers—"kind of lonely."

I swallowed, guilt and shame, pain and love twisting together inside me like wire wool until I wasn't sure how I could bear it or keep it all contained.

"Like normally," he went on, "all the love and loss and all the rest of that shit is spread around, but there's just me. He was there for me my whole life. How the fuck am I supposed to make that matter enough?"

I pressed myself against his leg, my face usefully hidden against his thigh, and tried to give him some sort of answer. "You grieve and you remember and you live."

My voice must have betrayed me because his free hand curled into my hair and pulled a little, as if he wanted me to look at him. "Laurie, are you crying?"

Fuck. I was. Horrible, sticky tears that burned in my eyes. "I don't know what's wrong with me."

"Are you really crying for me?"

Apparently so. As if it could somehow ease his pain. Another tug made me lift my head, and I glanced up at him, embarrassed and wet-eyed, helplessly hurting for him.

"God." His thumb swept under my lashes, gathering caught moisture. "Wow."

"I know it's not about me," I mumbled, "but I'm sorry I wasn't there with you, and I'm sorry for your loss, and I'm sorry it's been difficult for you, and I'm sorry it's probably going to be difficult for a while. I wish I could make that better, but I know can't." I took a deep, ragged, teary breath. "And I'm really sorry I'm crying like an idiot, because I have no fucking idea why I'm doing that."

"'S'okay." He tumbled off the sofa and into my lap, and kissed me through a mess of hopeless words and salt. "It's...nice. It helps. Everything kind of comes and goes. Like sometimes I feel so nothingy it's almost like I've forgotten he's dead, or maybe I'm dead or something." He curled into my arms, and I wrapped him up as tight and safe as I could. "Cry for me, okay? Since I can't right now."

So I did, just for a little while as I held him, and Toby told me stories of his grandfather—a man who had fought a war, made terrible mistakes, and learned so very late in life how to love.

Later, I carried him upstairs, undressed him, and took him to bed. At first we simply lay, our bodies entwined, but then we came together more certainly, more urgently, seeking each other in kisses and touches, some scattered words and a few more tears, and Toby mastered me with nothing but himself.

———

I woke in the early hours of the morning to discover I was alone. My first reaction was a wave of panicky abandonment followed by visions of a grief-stricken Toby wandering the streets of London in the middle of the night. Common sense reasserted itself as sleep receded, and I realised it was far more likely he was just somewhere else in the house. So I slipped out of bed, pulled on my dressing gown, and went looking for him.

I found him in the living room, cross-legged on the floor, his hands full of rope. In the flicking light from a black and white movie, he seemed to be practicing knots from a battered copy of *The Boy Scout Knot Book*.

He flinched when I put a hand on his bare shoulder. "Couldn't sleep?"

"Sorry. I didn't want to wake you."

"Always wake me." I knelt down next to him. "What are you doing?"

He shrugged. "Dunno. Thought it might help or something. Give me something to do with my brain that isn't think about Granddad. It's...it's like the emotional equivalent of having a tooth out, y'know? I keep touching the space with my tongue to make sure there's really...nothing there."

"Oh darling."

He rubbed the heel of his hand across his eyes. "Wish I could cry. That'd be normal, right? And then I could get better."

"There's no normal in grief."

"Yeah..." He glanced at the rope spilling across the living room carpet. "I think I got that memo."

"Is it working?"

He sighed. "Not really. Mainly, it's just annoying the crap out of me."

"What's the problem?"

"Well, I need my hands to tie the knots, but I need something to tie the knots *around* like, for example, my hands."

"Ah yes, a common manifestation of the infamous chicken-and-egg problem." I didn't know what else I could give him, how else I could help him, so I offered him my wrists. "What are we watching?"

His eyes met mine, sad and silver-touched by the screen. "You don't have to do this. I'll be okay."

"I want to. Will you let me stay? Be with you?"

A long shuddering breath, as if it was his yielding, not mine. Then he took my wrists in his cold hands and began—inexpertly—to bind them. For whatever reason, he'd chosen nylon rope. I shivered a little as it slid against my skin, a cool, silky whisper of mingled promise and danger.

"It's *Swing Time*. Found it on iPlayer."

"I've never seen it."

"One of Granddad's favourites. Sunday-afternoon-type viewing."

It was hard not to watch Toby's fingers working to immobilise me, but I glanced at the screen where a man and a woman were singing irritatedly at each other in the snow. Toby was whispering the words under his breath, interspersed occasionally with instructions from the book. My heart ached helplessly for him, and my body—God help me—my body was a whore.

I shifted, trying not to draw his attention, but I should have known that was foolish. His eyes flared, his face losing some of the stillness that made him almost a stranger in that eerie half-light.

And then his hand pressed between my legs. "Are you getting hard in front of Fred Astaire? That's so wrong."

"I'm sorry." I squirmed even more. "I can't help it. You're tying me up. I know it's not what you need right now."

He grinned. "It's exactly what I need."

"And I'm probably ruining all your happy childhood memories."

"Or..." He drew the knots tight, keeping a thumb beneath for control, and I moaned. "Making new ones."

I closed my eyes, everything disappearing except Toby and the rasp of rope across my skin. "If this is what you want."

"I don't know what I want."

I didn't know what to tell him. For a little while, we sat together without speaking, Toby's head bowed over my captured hands, Fred and Ginger bickering in the background.

Robert had liked to bind me. Severely, decoratively, lovingly, humiliatingly—I had thrilled to all his moods, to the strange liberty of constriction, and the peace of being so mercilessly held.

This wasn't like that at all.

I was worried for Toby. Grieving for his grief. But in a strange way, content. He was with me now, and I was going to...do better and be better. I was going to be there for him in every way I hadn't been before. Make him safe and happy.

As he did me.

He cursed softly as a knot slipped and unravelled. "I think I really suck at this."

"It's just practice." I struggled a bit and most of the rigging held. "Why the sudden interest in ropework?"

"Something to do? I don't know. I thought it might impress you."

"You don't have to impress me, Toby."

It was the wrong thing to say. I could tell by the downturn of his mouth. "Yeah, well, maybe I want to."

"You already have me." There was some...anxiety, some uncertainty in him, and I didn't fully understand where it had come from, let alone how to alleviate it. I tried a more teasing note. "You don't need ropes to keep me."

"But your last boyfriend..."

It was neither something I expected nor wanted to hear. I didn't want to talk about Robert with Toby, not because I was trying to keep anything from him, but because I'd already wasted too much of my present on my past. "It was one of his things, yes. But I'm with you now. We have our own things."

"Okay." He tucked his knees up to his chin and huddled.

And I wished for my freedom so I could touch him, reassure him with my body if nothing else. Finally I looped my hands over him and drew him in close. He made a startled sound—almost a giggle—and then settled against me.

"Are you really worried about the ghosts of boyfriends past?" I asked.

"I'm worrying about everything." He tucked his head against my shoulder and let out a long sigh. "I know I should be thinking about Granddad, but all I can think about is me. It's messed up."

"I told you, there's no normal here. Whatever you feel is okay."

"Fretting because"—he touched his jaw self-consciously—"I'm really scrofulous right now? That's normal, is it? Not completely shallow and selfish?"

"Not at all. And I'll get you some tea tree oil tomorrow."

"Oh God. I'm grotesque." He hid his face against my neck.

"Acne is susceptible to stress and emotional distress."

"Not helping, Mr. Doctor."

"How about this." I rubbed my cheek against the edge of his jaw, nuzzling into him, awkward without hands to touch or anchor me. "You're beautiful."

He twisted and looked at me, his eyes wide and a little tear-blurred. "I'm really scared, Laurie. I'm scared of being alone, and of...of the whole of my life." He took a deep, shuddering breath, and then the words came rushing out: "And then I get really angry at my granddad for leaving me. And then I feel like a shithead. And then I get stressed out at something completely irrelevant like acne or not being able to tie a double slipknot. Or that I can't live up to some guy you were with like ten years ago."

"All of that's understandable," I told him soothingly. "Except for the bit about Robert, which is nonsense."

I kissed his cheek. On the screen, the credits rolled, bathing us in flickering light.

"But..." Ever persistent, Toby ducked out of my embrace and wriggled away. "You were with him for ages, and when you couldn't be with him, you didn't want to be with anyone and—"

"I want to be with you."

After a moment, he nodded. "Okay." I hoped that might be the end of it, but he went on. "It's just everything feels so fucked up right now. I don't want to fuck this up as well."

I wanted to reassure him, but I was wary of forevers. Robert and I had promised each other so much. Possibly too much. "Let's not jump off bridges until we come to them."

Toby blinked moisture from his lashes. "At least tell me why you broke up with him, so I know not to do that."

Oh God, how to explain. How to condense all that pain and loss and confusion into a single, useful parable. "Well, you could try not to tie a slipknot on a sole load-bearing suspension line, causing me to fall and break my wrist and fracture my pelvis." I heard Toby's startled gasp, but I pressed on, wanting to be done. "And you could try not to be so consumed with guilt about it that you stop having sex with me."

I knew I was being unfair to Robert. It had been complicated, and we had both been hurt in our different ways. I'd become a permanent reminder of a single moment of failure—no wonder he hadn't been able to bear being close to me.

My voice had lost something of its careful modulation, so I took a few calming breaths before I continued. "Then you could not start going out to clubs, and doing all the things you used to do with me with other people. And when I confront you with it, you could not tell me it wasn't cheating because it wasn't sex. Because it was. Sex. Cheating. It was."

There was a long silence.

Toby's arms came round me and held me so very tightly, my already-trapped hands trapped between us, making me feel at once safe and unbalanced and exposed. As Robert had once done with rope. "I won't do that," he said fiercely. "I won't ever do that."

"Please," I said, realising I was weary beyond reckoning, "can we go back to bed?"

He nodded and began to undo his knots.

I would have already been leaving had it been a workday, so it felt a little strange—chronologically dislocating—to be shedding my dressing gown and crawling under the duvet in the greyish half-light of an incipient dawn, my wrists still hot from Toby's ropes.

But I slept regardless, with sudden and terrible ease.

———

I woke again in what had to be the early hours of the afternoon. I was relieved to find Toby still in the bed with me, but he was awake and watching me, and I didn't know how much he'd slept.

I reached out to fluff his hair. "Are you all right?"

"I–I don't know. It's weird waking up with you like this."

"But you often wake up next to me."

"Yeah, but you're usually hustling me out of the house because you have to go to work."

Another unwanted but entirely deserved reminder of what a dick I'd been. "It'll never happen again. And for the next week at least, we can do whatever you like. I'm... Well...I suppose I'm on holiday."

"You...you"—his eyes widened—"took holiday? For me?"

I couldn't lie. "Um, technically, I took holiday to get over you because I thought you weren't coming back."

"It's about me. Still counts." He nipped at my shoulder, possessive and playful at the same time. "I'm counting it."

Here, at last, I had an opportunity to prove myself. To give him everything I had—for one reason or another—withheld. "Would you like... Would it help...if we went away somewhere? Together?" I heard his breath catch. And remembering his excitement at a night in Oxford, I couldn't resist teasing him gently. Anything to reach him in his loss and bring him back to me. "You know, a minibreak."

"Oh, Laurie." He sounded heartbroken rather than amused, and I was conscious of yet another failure. "I'd love to, but I can't."

"Why not?"

He gave me a watery smile. "You may be on holiday, but I have to work."

"Straight after your granddad's funeral?" I frowned at the ceiling.

"It's okay."

It was not okay. He was surely entitled to some sort of compassionate leave, paid or...ah. "Is this about the money?" I hadn't meant to ask it so baldly or abruptly, but concern made me clumsy.

"Like, hello. Tactless."

"Sorry."

He sighed. "It's not about the money."

"What is it about, then?"

"Um, it's my job."

I felt just a little bit like shaking him. His stubbornness, endearing though it was, came perilously close to destructiveness sometimes. "You work in a café, Toby. Jobs like that are two a penny." It was obvious from the silence, the sudden rigidity in his body, that I'd said the wrong thing. "I just mean, you have rights, and you've suffered a bereavement, and you shouldn't push yourself."

"It's not what you said, though, is it?" he muttered. "Look, it might not be worth anything to you, Mr. Consultant, but it's what I have, and that means something to me."

"Well, if it makes you happy, then of course—"

But this wasn't the right thing either. "Now you sound like my mum."

He was nineteen. Confused. Grieving. *Patience, Dalziel.* "I don't know what you want from me right now."

"How about not pissing on my life?"

"How is suggesting you take some time to deal with the loss of your grandfather pissing on your life?"

He rolled away from me onto his side, his body curving like a comma. A comma that didn't want me touching it. "You were sneery," he said, in a small voice.

Very tentatively I laid my hand across the smooth dip at the top of his flank, and he didn't shake me off. "I'm sorry, Toby."

"Nobody gets it. Nobody I knew at university bothered to keep in touch, and all my school friends who went to university think it's weird."

"If it's what you want to do, then"—I smoothed my fingertips lightly over his tender skin—"fuck them."

"Hah. Easy for you to say. Bet nobody thinks you've wasted your life."

Well. No. At least, not professionally speaking, although how I came to it had been an inextricable mixture of my parents' determination, my own temperament, and an early recognised need for purpose and stability. It hadn't precisely been a choice, but I wouldn't have chosen otherwise. "You can't compare yourself to what other people are doing. Only you can know what's right for you."

"I don't want to talk about it."

Once again, I was obliged to remind myself that it wasn't appropriate to lose your temper with the grief-stricken. "But—"

"Laurie, like, seriously. What part of 'don't want to talk about it' are you interpreting as irrelevant?"

I gave up. We didn't have to do this now. I slid an arm over him, and curled myself around him so that we were two commas now—quotation marks, perhaps—and gradually he relaxed into me.

I was just on the verge of falling into a doze when he said very softly, "I'm sorry I can't go away with you."

"There'll be another time." I kissed the tops of his shoulders, where the skin was rough and sweet beneath my lips.

"Where would we have gone?"

"Anywhere we wanted. Paris, maybe."

"Because that isn't at all clichéd." His voice wavered as he spoke, which made me think he was more likely trying to hold back tears than rebuff me.

"We still have the weekend."

He sniffled. "I guess."

I put my lips to the back of his neck and felt the shiver move through his skin. "Two whole days, just for us. We can do whatever you like with them."

"Really?" His hair tickled my nose as he shifted.

"Yes."

He seemed to be thinking about it. "I–I want to make you a lemon meringue pie."

Not quite what I expected. "All right."

"And have some seriously filthy sex."

That seemed more like it. "As you wish."

"And...and...okay, I can't really think of anything else right now."

"I'm sure other things will occur to us." My ridiculous, beautiful boy. I would have found a way to give him the moon if he'd wanted it.

He pushed his arse against my cock, making me gasp. "Is there anything you want to do?"

I wasn't sure I could top filthy sex and a lemon meringue pie. I was about to say so, when I realised there was something else I owed him. "I'd like to take you on a date."

He squeaked. "What? In public?"

"No, in a nuclear bunker." I fiddled idly with the arrow through his nipple, gently moving it back and forth until he was panting and wriggly. "Can I take you out to dinner?"

"I don't know." It was a pathetic attempt at indifference. I could hear the excitement in his voice. "I'll have to think about it."

"Please."

"Well, maybe, if we can have all the courses, including aperitifs."

That afternoon, we went shopping together. As soon as supermarket deliveries had become a thing, Robert and I had signed up, and never looked back. Our lives, our time, had seemed so much better spent elsewhere. But this was pleasant in the most ordinary of ways, and I trailed along after Toby, pushing the trolley, and it didn't seem like a waste of my Saturday in the slightest.

He bounced all the way home.

"Do I just leave you to it?" I asked, once we'd unpacked and my kitchen work surfaces were covered with purchases.

The look he gave me was downright wicked. Downright terrifying. "No way. You're totally going to be part of this process."

"In a...loading-the-dishwasher capacity?"

"Nuh-uh." Oh God. "But first I need to make pastry."

So I sat at the kitchen table and read the *Times*, not entirely successfully, as Toby got to work. He was humming under his breath—"Zing! Went the Strings of My Heart"—and seemed a little more like himself.

At last, he was rolling out his pastry and using it to line a pie tin I didn't even know I owned. "Okay." He popped everything into the fridge. "Now I just need to grab some things from upstairs."

"For the pie?"

"For you. Give me like...five minutes. And"—he flashed his toothiest grin—"take your clothes off."

I froze. "When you said you wanted a lemon meringue pie and filthy sex, I didn't think you meant together."

"That's what you get for underestimating me."

He vanished upstairs, leaving me paralysed with awkwardness. The kitchen was warmer than the rest of the house because of the AGA, and nobody would be able to see me unless they scaled the garden walls and came right down onto the patio. But there was still something a little terrifying about stripping myself in the middle of my kitchen. I felt disproportionately vulnerable for how safe I was there. It was something about the way the light fell, bright but without heat, across my skin, illuminating and revealing me. All my desires undeniable and laid bare beneath the winter sun.

Nervous anticipation stirred the hairs on my arms.

I wasn't sure how to wait for him. On my knees? On the hard floor. Would that help? A piece of fantasy. But he hadn't said...

In the end, I rested my hips against the table and folded my arms, as though this was perfectly normal.

It seemed like longer than five minutes. It seemed like forever.

But finally I heard footsteps on the stairs, and Toby reappeared, his arms full of...things. He paused in the doorway, his eyes sweeping up and down my body with such unabashed and possessive eagerness it made me hot and flustered and a little bit shaky. I wasn't sure a nineteen-year-old should have been able to do that to me, but there was an absurd sort of gratification in knowing he found me worth looking at, that he liked me naked and at his pleasure.

He dumped a couple of pillows on top of the table, his hands tracing the worn-smooth surface. "This is so awesome."

"It's actually a magistrate's bench. I got it at an antique sale."

"That must be why I keep having kinky daydreams about it." He patted the wood. "Up you get, on your knees."

On the table? I'd be so...exposed. Little shivers chased themselves over my skin, turning me hot and cold at once. "Oh, Toby, really?"

He gazed at my hardening, traitorous cock. "Yeah, really."

So I climbed onto my kitchen table, aroused and embarrassed, or aroused because I was embarrassed, which was its own sweet-sharp torment.

"Spread."

I made a noise that was most certainly not a whimper and

obeyed, sliding my thighs apart, and then further still, until Toby was satisfied.

He tucked a pillow under each of my knees and smiled up at me. "So fucking hot."

I tried to come up with something grumpy to say in response, but it was hard to think, hard to breathe beneath Toby's gaze. "The things I do for you," I managed.

"I know." Gleeful was how he sounded as he skated his nails up the inside of my legs, while I shivered helplessly at being so defenceless and tried to hold position, cock and adductor muscles already aching softly. "Okay. So..." He released me briefly from his attentions and rummaged again in his pile of ropes and cuffs and God knew what else. He held out his hands to me, the Gates of Hell in one, the anal hook in the other, and grinned again. "Choose."

That was easy. I pointed at the Gates of Hell. "Cool." He threw them back into the pile.

For a moment I groped after meaning, and then I understood, and then I groaned. "You mind-fucking little bastard."

He nodded, utterly unrepentant. "Hands behind your neck."

It occurred to me—as it always did at some point—that I could simply refuse. I could get off the damn table and not allow him to do anything to me. The only power he had was power I'd given him, and I could take it back at any moment, with a look, a word, the simplest of gestures.

But I didn't want to. I wanted him to have me, to have everything, my pleasure, my pain, my pride, and my shame. I wanted to lay it all at his feet until we were both free, until I was his and he was mine, and everything else was tatters.

I put my hands behind my neck, and he cuffed them there. His fingers ruffled through my hair, tugging it lightly so that hot sparks slid all the way down my spine.

"Okay," he said. "Down."

I didn't want to do it, but I wanted him to make me. I needed him, I needed his hand—firm and inevitable—to control my descent. He was so gentle that I nearly wept with mortification and a kind of terrible longing. I could feel the scars and whorls in the table beneath my cheek. Toby was just a haze of warmth behind me, standing at the delta he'd made of my body as he debased and opened me.

I shuddered and yielded to him, impaled on his merciless, lube-wet fingers. Someone moaned, but it was Toby, the sound as naked as I felt. And I answered, pushing my hips up, needing him to know anything he wanted, I wanted too. That I wanted this. For him to do this to me. For me. With me.

His hand closed around my cock, and the sheer pleasure of his touch burned through me like the brightest sunlight. My sudden cry echoed on the kitchen tiles, too loud, too harsh, too desperately revealing. He bent over my back and kissed his way down the straining, suppliant arch of my spine. My fingers knotted against each other, but there was nothing for me to hold on to. There was just Toby, his mouth on my skin, and everything he made me feel. The truth was, pleasure frightened me more than pain. It demanded a deeper surrender.

It was almost a relief when he moved away.

But then came the blunt pressure of the anal hook, stretching me wider, pushing into me. It was a dull sort of violation. It didn't hurt, but it seemed like it might, and that was somehow worse, holding me on the edge of a gasp.

Until Toby whispered, "Breathe," and then the damn thing was inside me, my body struggling round it like an oyster with a pearl.

I hated it. Loved it. Loved how much I hated it.

And how safe it was to be in that place with Toby, who somehow saw the spaces between all my blurred lines far more clearly than I did.

He used the chain between my cuffed hands to draw me upright again. He was careful, but even that slight movement... jostled, reminded, pleasured, tormented. A few drops of sweat slipped between my shoulder blades, and I was so sensitive, so lost in my skin, I half thought I felt the heat of them, the scratch of salt within each sphere. My mouth gaped open, and a sound came out, wavering and unformed, a muddle of misery, need, arousal, and submission.

Yes.

Please.

This.

There was a chink of chain as Toby fed it through the ring, then the click of a snap hook as he connected it to the cuffs, and there, I was bound. I tugged, because it was always my first instinct, and the curve of the hook twisted on the threshold of my body, reminding me of its invasion, intensifying my sense of restraint. I swallowed a gasp, my pulse fluttering fearfully. Robert had often put me in more demanding bondage, but for all its crudity—perhaps *because* of its crudity, the harsh mixture of exposure and penetration—this stripped me, flayed me, and left me raw. My cock strained upwards obscenely between my spread thighs, pre-come slicking down the sides, and dripping onto the table.

"Oh God. Laurie." Toby scrambled up next to me, pushing between my legs, and buried his hands in my hair. For a moment, his wild, shining eyes were my whole world, and then, with a little growl, he kissed me savagely. I didn't dare move, not wanting to feel that awful tug and pressure deep inside me, but he had me braced—as long as I didn't struggle, as long as I didn't do anything but let him shove his tongue deep into my mouth, and take me, take everything.

He tasted like the tea he'd drunk earlier. Then of me. And it was so beautiful, that cruel and hungry kiss.

We were both dazed and breathless when he pulled away.

His hands skimmed across my body, stroking, scratching, owning it, while I shivered and moaned softly, tethered and untethered at the same time. The pads of his thumbs circled my nipples, stirring pleasure like glowing ashes until it flamed in me afresh, and I threw back my head, arching into his touch, heedless of anything else. The movement dragged against the cuffs and the hook, and the shock of those harsh adornments jolted through me, a cry catching at the back of my throat.

Toby leaned in to me, and put his mouth where his hands had been, covering too-sensitive flesh in a wash of exquisite heat. What little breath I had shuddered out of me, and I choked on Toby's name, a fly in honey, trapped and drowning in sweetness. Just when it became almost unbearable, he caught my nipple on the edge of his teeth, and that rougher touch sheared through me like lightning, and I almost came in the rush of knowing myself so utterly controlled. So utterly his.

He looked up, smiling, moisture glistening on the lips that had kissed me and hurt me, and reached below the level of the table, where I couldn't easily see. When he brought his hands back up, he was holding a set of clover clamps connected by a steel chain. They glittered between his fingers, promising pain.

I was damp with sweat and spit and ecstasy, powerless to resist, wanting and not wanting, and waiting for him to deny me the choice, to give me whatever he chose to give. His fingers fumbled against skin—once, twice—as he clamped me. And each time, his eyes held mine, the lust in them its own caress, as I hissed at the chill, sharp bite. Breathing through it and knowing it was nothing to the burning agony that waited for me when he took them off.

"There." Toby stepped back. Surveyed me, his subject, his kingdom. He was flushed and a little sweaty too, as breathless as me, the ridge of his erection outlined against his jeans. "Fuck. Wow."

I'd done that to him. Made him hot and hard and hazy-eyed. And in that moment, any pain, all indignity was worth it. No. Part of it. Inextricable from it. Inseparable, indistinguishable from joy.

Toby seemed to be having trouble looking away. "Okay. Right." I loved the harshness of his voice when he was like this, fiercely turned on and full of cruelty. "I've got a lemon meringue pie to finish."

"And..." My lips were dry, my body spread and aching, pain gathering intimately both inside and out. "What do I do?"

There was nothing but love in him as he told me, "You suffer for me."

Which was what I did while Toby put his crust in the oven and began to work on the filling, talking to me all the time about what he was doing, the words blurring with the pain and the discomfort, until everything was Toby and all the ways he touched me and loved me, hurt me and delighted me. I floated, the edges of my world turned as soft and frayed as feathers. It was strange to be so physically abject, and so completely happy. Toby's.

God. I hurt. I hurt.

There was something relentless about it, the steady heartbeat of pain and the slow *drop-drop* of time. Moving brought no relief, just a reawakening of harsher agonies, unwanted pleasure, the thrust and press of metal inside me, the sway of the chain, and the tightening of the clamps on my nipples. Even breathing stirred the air too much, made it rasp against skin grown tight and hot and thin.

Sometimes I could not hold back my sounds.

Sometimes my eyes would sting with helpless moisture.

And sometimes Toby would come to me, put his mouth to my mouth or against my eyes, and take my groans and all my tears.

I liked being able to watch him. My restraints, in that respect, had set me free. There was nothing for me to do but look and revel in my looking.

He seemed happy, moving around my kitchen with the same confidence he had learned in touching and taking me. The muscles of his back shifted under his T-shirt like the memory of wings as he worked, and every now and again I'd catch the flash of his forearms, all pale skin and sinew, dusted only faintly by dark hair, the occasional freckle. He was leaning most of his weight on one leg, so his arse was tightly nestled against the denim of his jeans.

Perhaps a stranger would look at Toby and see little more than a skinny postadolescent with a shockingly bad haircut. But he was my boyfriend, my dom, my fragile prince, and he was nothing less than beautiful to me. I loved the tender spot at the back of his neck and all the whisper-soft hairs that would stir beneath my breath. I loved his narrow feet and his disproportionately large toes. I loved the small, flat mole that lurked beneath his left earlobe. I loved the place between his collarbones and the hollows beneath his clavicles where sweat gathered and gleamed. I loved the slim and gorgeous cock that tasted so much of salt and him.

☆   These were the rosary beads of my submission. Though my only god was love.

"I've got about five minutes before the crust's done." He

came and stood in front of me, and his fully clothed proximity suddenly reminded me of my own nakedness, my own vulnerability. He brought with him a waft of wholesome smells: flour and sugar and baking pastry. "Wonder what I should do with it?"

He ran his hands over the straining, sweat-slick muscles of my abdomen, and I flinched from his gentleness, which only jostled the hook and the chain and made me sob a little. He hushed me, soothed me, strung soft kisses across my body like fairy lights. I was too raw to even think of resisting. I just leaned into him, lost, seduced, begging for his touch, letting the pleasure fill me like the pain.

He gave me that as well, his nails and his teeth leaving reddened tracks and marks, gifts across my skin. By then, it was all sensation, and me all yielding. He found the tender places—the underside of my arms, the edge of my ribs, the crease of my groin, the side of a knee—and ignited them like touch paper, until I was nothing but fire and lightning, made and unmade by his harsh breath and his trembling hands and all his frantic, whispered words of wonder and gratitude, love and desire.

Then there was silence, stillness. Toby's eyes locked on mine as his fingers closed around the clamps. A tug, and they were gone.

An infinitesimally tiny fraction of a second roared through my ears. And, after, everything was pain. Engulfing, all-consuming, inescapable. A red-hot, skin-deep rush. The taste of copper in my mouth. I couldn't move. I didn't dare. I could only shake and endure. Surrender. Stare into the too-bright mirror of agony until there was no fear left. Only the sharpest light and a pure, deep peace.

I heard a feral, rough-edged screaming. Me?

"Holy God. Holy holy *fucking* God." Toby's head was thrown

back, his throat rippling, his mouth stretched in a helpless gasp. His hands—which, I now realised, had held me throughout—tightened on my legs. Another shudder jolted through him, and then he doubled over against the table, moaning and clawing at me.

My throat hurt, but the rest of the pain was fading.

Traceless as frost in sunlight. The world looked different, clearer, cleaner, slightly photoshopped, as if I'd inhaled pure oxygen. And I felt, strangely, like laughing.

Toby uncurled slowly. "Fucking hell." He sounded shaken. "I just...fucking hell."

I carefully looked down at him. Though I still didn't precisely like them, even my bonds troubled me less. "Are you all right?"

"I...just like"—he was already flushed, but somehow he turned even redder—"totally came. When you screamed...it was... just so fucking beautiful."

"Thank you," was all I could think to say. But it wasn't just a dominance game. I meant it. Thank you for the pain. Thank you for letting it mean so much to you. Thank you for believing I'm beautiful. Thank you for making me feel so powerful. Thank you for loving me. Thank you. Thank you.

"Fuck." He undid his belt, peeled down his jeans and boxers, cleaned himself up with the boxers, and then tossed them between my legs. The familiar scents of sex and Toby swept over me like the brush of his hands. "You didn't even have to touch me."

His fingers glistened slightly with the traces of him. It made my own cock drip and ache with wanting. "Can I..."

He grinned. "Fuck yeah."

He wriggled back into his jeans, one-handed, and held the other out to me. I drew his fingers into my mouth and lapped up the taste of his pleasure, earned with pain. His eyes fluttered, and I made him moan for me, and I revelled in it. The power of pleasing, in this place where only pleasing mattered.

At last, he pulled away.

"Thank you, again," I said.

"Yikes, your voice is wrecked. I'm going to get you some water."

He refastened his belt and hurried over to the sink. I could have reminded him there was a water filter in the fridge, but I just didn't care. On his return, he climbed onto the table, nestling between my legs, and held the cup to my lips. It was an awkward angle, but it was still the best, slightly lukewarm, slightly chalky tap water I'd ever tasted. And it turned out I was thirsty—which probably shouldn't have been surprising, but there was something a little startling about being given exactly what you needed before even recognising you needed it.

Afterwards, Toby put the cup carefully to one side, and curled up against my sweaty, still slightly throbbing chest. An odd cuddle, perhaps, but I liked it. There was something comforting about it, the sense of closeness, even though I couldn't put my arms round him.

He reached up and ran a hand lazily over my shoulders. "Do you need out?"

"Need?"

"It's been about half an hour."

I stretched—and winced. I was going to *ache*. But I couldn't lie to him. "I–I don't...need—"

"Good." He smiled up at me, sleepy-eyed, soft-mouthed. "I like you like that, and I still have to make the meringue."

"Oh God."

He tipped his head back and kissed me under my chin. "Besides, I want to reward you."

"By leaving me tied up on a table with a hook up my arse?"

"Pretty much." He slithered down onto the floor.

"I'm sure this sort of thing is against all food hygiene regulations."

"I'll wash my hands really carefully." He took the cup back to the sink and scrubbed himself thoroughly before taking his pie crust out of the oven.

Once again, he talked to me about what he was doing, but I was too far gone, too deep, too high, to be able to hold on to much of the meaning. There was just the rhythm of his voice washing over me, keeping me close.

His lemon filling was the colour of sunshine as he poured it into his golden pastry crust. And whatever went into meringues, the making of them was a vigorous business. The thin muscles of Toby's mixing arm stretched and flexed.

"You seriously need to invest in an electric whisk. I'm getting wanker's cramp here."

But through determination and some strange alchemy, what had started as a bowl of thin white liquid thickened and formed glossy Alpine peaks. A few minutes later, Toby's lemon meringue pie was fully assembled, and he was putting it back into the oven.

"The trick," he explained, "is not letting your curd get cool." He put the two bowls down on the table beside me. "You sometimes get this weird wet layer between the lemon and the meringue, but if the curd is still warm, then it cooks the meringue from the bottom so the layers stick together better."

I'd seen Toby passionate before; I'd seen him certain and in control. This was the first time it hadn't been sexual. "You're really into this, aren't you?"

He nodded. "Yeah. It's cool." Then he ran a finger round the rim of the bowl, gathering some of the gleaming, yellow curd. "Want to try?"

"I want to suck your fingers. If they've got lemon curd on them, I can live with that."

"If you don't respect my pie, I'm putting those clamps back on."

I thought he was joking, but the terror was real enough and dizzyingly sweet. "I'm sorry. Please don't."

"It's all about the combination anyway." He dipped his finger into the second bowl and scooped up a floof of white foam. "Ready?"

"Yes."

Toby's finger slid between my lips, filling my mouth—which already tasted of him—with sugar and lemons. "*Oh.*"

"It's good, isn't it?" He sounded smug, but he deserved to.

I nodded, twisting my tongue around his finger, chasing up the last few streaks of curd.

"More?"

"Yes. Yes, please."

He wriggled, pushing against the table. "God, Laurie, are you trying to make me come again? I love it when you beg."

And I loved it when he made me beg.

He swept up another fingerful of curd and frosting and smeared it across my parted lips before swooping in to kiss me.

It was a sticky mess of tongues, the flavours sweet and tart and Toby-warmed. Perhaps with anyone else, I might have hated it. But not with him. I was as powerless against his playfulness as his cruelty, and just as hopelessly enchanted, as desperate to please. My pulse quickened, the tight thrill of submission jumping again inside me, as he licked lemon from the corners of my mouth and left me breathless, moaning softly.

He tugged the bowl of curd a little closer and dipped in once again. "Oh, whoops." He didn't even try to sound convincing as he twisted his wrist on the way up to my lips and flicked lemon across my already too-sensitive nipples.

I screamed.

Fuck, it was fucking *searing*. And I was so hard my cock hurt too.

Toby leaned in and very gently cleaned me up, the tip of his tongue tracing the golden spiral across my skin, leaving a shimmering wake of damp heat, soothed pain, and gathering pleasure.

God, the sounds I made for him. I had no control. No desire for it.

He looked up, smiling. "I always knew you'd taste good with lemon."

"Oh, Toby, please."

"Please what?"

I writhed, hurting myself now and not caring. He steadied me with his hands. "I don't know...just...just...*please*."

I had no notion what I was asking for anymore, but Toby seemed to know the answer anyway. He came up on tiptoes to kiss me. "Yeah. I promise."

He reached into the bowl of frosting and swirled a little up my thigh. It felt like clouds, warmed by his mouth as he chased them down, scooping up the sticky flecks with his agile tongue. He kept caressing me long after all the frosting was gone, kissing and nibbling his way towards my groin. Though studiously ignoring my cock.

I closed my eyes. Unfurled beneath his attentions. Pain had burned away self-consciousness and any hint of shame, leaving me as pliant as the restraints would allow. All that remained was need and a kind of soaring exhilaration that made me laugh aloud and say, "I thought you were supposed to be converting me."

"I *am* converting you." He bit me about as hard as I deserved for that. I imagined, with a dark thrill, the blunt imprint of his teeth on my thigh. He'd left marks on me before. I'd worn them with secret pride. Pressed my fingers into them sometimes for the memory of pain. Then he lifted his head and collected another dollop of frosting.

We both watched as the foam hung tantalisingly from his fingers in pale, soft-edged stalactites. He brought it to my cock and let it slide over me, a few flecks drifting onto the tabletop.

He leaned in again, idling his other fingers up my shaft. "How do you like my lemon meringue pie now?"

I pushed into his touch. "I love it."

"It's delicious, isn't it?" His breath swirled over my cock. "Best you've ever had."

Then he slid his lips over me and my "Yes, oh yes" was as sincere as it was absolutely frantic.

He'd never done this to me before. He'd admitted once, a little awkwardly, he didn't think he was very good at it, so I told him he didn't have to do anything he didn't want to do, and we'd never discussed it again. I liked to suck him though, on my knees with his hands knotted in my hair. Or lazily in the morning, pinning his writhing hips to the mattress. On my back, with Toby standing over me, his hand resting against my throat so he could feel his cock inside me.

But now he touched me without hesitation, lapping up the frosting, teasing me with his tongue, drawing me a little way into his mouth. My fingers twisted against each other, seeking some kind of purchase against the pleasure, but there was no defence. There was only something else to suffer for him. This terrible bliss. The helplessness of it, the intimacy.

I gasped out his name. Spread myself wider. It drove the hook deeper, but even that pressure was part of this now, subservient to Toby, another way he had chosen to fuck me. Everything tangled up together: freedom, restraint, pain, humiliation, rapture, fear, love. One of Toby's hands curled round me, his grip tight, so perfectly tight, my skin sliding tenderly against the roughness of his palm. And just when I thought he couldn't give me any more, he sucked in a shaky breath and took enough of my cock to meet his own hand. Sealing me in wet velvet warmth.

I rocked forward, heedlessly, and the ball inside me nudged my prostate.

"GodpleaseTobyIcan't—"

I came uncontrollably. So hard I saw nothing at all. Just a flawless, unending dark.

I only got back to myself when I heard Toby coughing.

He looked up from my cock, semen and saliva dribbling down his chin.

"I'm so sorry, I tried to warn you."

He gently released me and wiped his mouth on the back of his hand. "It was hot."

I was starting to shake, and I couldn't control that either. "Th-thank... It was... You..." My words came out as slurry as my thoughts.

I didn't quite follow what happened next, but Toby took care of me. Unchained me. Drew the hook out as gently as he could. Held my hands through the sullen agony of stiffness and returning blood flow. And then we lay entangled on my kitchen table, Toby holding me tightly, until I was done with tears and I had skin enough to face the world again.

"I love you," he whispered. "I love you. Shit, my pie." He only left me for the time it took to rescue it. He put it on the counter and rushed back into my arms. "Final secret of a good lemon meringue pie: wait till it's cooled before you cut it."

"Good to know." I turned my head and surveyed the result of his labours: a picture-book lemon meringue pie, perfect golden pastry topped by an immense swirl of baked meringue. My boy really did have talent. So many talents. Beautiful, clever, merciless Toby.

"You do realise there's going to be a test later, right?" he asked.

I mustered a pale shadow of outrage. "Toby, that isn't fair. I'll fail."

He propped himself on an elbow and peered at me with narrowed eyes. "I bet you've never failed anything in your whole life."

"I excel at standardised tests. Which is hardly a skill to boast about."

"Oh, man." He lay back down, resting his head on my shoulder. The table was not comfortable to lie on, but right now it was as perfect as Toby's pie. "I fail even at the shit I'm supposed to be good at. I got a D for my English Lit GCSE. I was like totally the teacher's pet. A*s all year. Still came out with a D."

"What went wrong?"

He sighed. "There's this bit where they give you a poem and ask you a dumb-arse question about it. The poem was 'The Jaguar' by Ted Hughes. Do you know it?"

"No."

"Sorry." He ran his fingers over one of the reddened patches he'd left on my skin, sending little shivers through me. "It's earlyish Hughes, so nature shit, basically. I only really like *Birthday Letters*. I mean, that's just him wanking off about how sad he is his more talented wife killed herself, but at least it's sincere, y'know? Anyway, 'The Jaguar' is about a zoo full of, like, stultified animals. Except there's this jaguar who's going all crazy in his cage. And the question was, right, get this: what does Ted Hughes think about zoos?"

It was absurd. We'd just had sex and pain and lemon meringue pie, and my standardised test impulse still leapt to life. "It doesn't sound like he likes them."

"Oh great. Well done. A*. Fuck you."

"Isn't that the answer?"

"Well, yeah, I guess, but the poem isn't about fucking zoos. It's about people. All the animals are anthropomorphised. Like the parrots who are cheap tarts or whatever. Because don't we... *in a very real sense*"—his sarcastic voice was starting to sound increasingly similar to Jasper—"live in a social zoo. And the jaguar is a poet, because even though he's surrounded by bars, he still sees freedom. And that's kind of his madness and his salvation all at once."

"That's all very well," I said, "but it doesn't answer the question. Which was about zoos."

Toby ruffled a hand through his hair. "You are *so* not a jaguar."

"You're missing the point. Standardised tests are simply about demonstrating your understanding of the question. The answer, to a degree, is irrelevant."

"Well." Toby pouted. "I care about the answer. And if that means I suck, then...I guess I suck."

I brushed my thumb over the sulky curve of his mouth. "You don't suck, Toby. But if someone puts a hoop in front of you, the quickest way to get past it is through the middle."

"Wow, you're on their side. You're supposed to be on my side."

He sounded a little confused, and genuinely hurt. It had been such a long time since GCSEs had even remotely figured in my thinking that I hadn't stopped for a moment to consider that they might still be important to Toby. I was about to apologise when Toby sat up.

"Can you hear...buzzing?"

I'd half convinced myself it was just in my head—a side effect of too much demanding sex—but no. It was my front doorbell. "Just ignore it, and whoever it is will go away."

Whoever it was did not go away.

The buzzing went on and on and on. Someone was clearly leaning against the bell.

Fuck. I looked down at my thoroughly ravaged and still naked body, groaned, and tried to sit up.

"Wait." Toby put a hand on my chest and kept me down. "I'm sorta dressed. I'll deal with it."

He gave me a quick kiss on the nose, scrambled off the table, and disappeared up the stairs. It was probably just a really zealous Jehovah's Witness, but clothes were rapidly becoming a good idea. I sat up and swung myself onto the floor.

God. Maybe I was getting too old for this. Everything hurt, inside and out, and I was a mess of marks and semen and lemon curd. I must have struggled against the cuffs a little, because while they hadn't bruised me seriously, they'd left me with a matching set of rough red bracelets. I stroked my thumb over my wrist and smiled. I was tired and wrecked, unable to even answer my own front door, and I was so very, very happy.

Though, as I eased myself painfully into my trousers, I was rather glad Toby wasn't around to see this particular indignity.

"Uh, Laurie." His voice drifted down the stairs.

"Yes?"

"It's, um, your friends."

Shit. *Shit*. Who? Why? I reached for my shirt and pulled it—wincing—over my shoulders. "I'm...I'm coming up."

Grace and Sam and Toby were arranged in a tableaux of awkwardness in my hallway. I chose not to think about how I must have looked to them.

Grace stared for a while. Then stomped over and slapped me in the shoulder. "I was worried about you, you dick. Next time, answer your goddamn phone, and I won't come barging over at what is blatantly a really bad time."

"It's okay," offered Toby, unhelpfully. "We'd pretty much finished."

Sam clapped a hand over his mouth, entirely failing to stifle his yelp of laughter.

Grace flicked a glance at Toby. "Don't think being cute is going to stop me being cross with him."

I sighed. "Look, I'm sorry I didn't call. Are you staying?"

"We've just hoofed it across London," said Sam. "Course we're fucking staying."

Grace led the way into my living room, and while everybody was getting comfortable, I made the introductions.

Toby nodded. "I remember you from Pervocracy."

"Believe me"—Grace smiled—"we remember you too."

"Why were you worried about Laurie?"

"That's not important," I interrupted. "Does anybody want some tea?"

"Because you'd fucked off," Grace explained. "He was in a state."

"Really?" Toby hustled across the sofa and practically climbed into my lap. "Really really?"

I brushed his fringe out of his eyes. "Yes, really. I told you. And you know, it's bad manners to get excited when you hear about someone being miserable."

"Yeah, but I was miserable without you too, so it's comforting. And for the record"—he turned back to Grace and Sam—"I didn't fuck off. I had, like, a thing, and I didn't have his number."

I could feel my friends' attention on us like heat. It wasn't intrusive, but it was certainly intense. I could understand their curiosity and their concern, and I was tired of hiding. Since Robert, I'd been so wary. I'd lived like a jackal, hoarding my happiness as though it could be stolen from me at any moment. I slid an arm round Toby and drew him tight against my side where he belonged. "He had a funeral, and it was my fault he couldn't contact me."

"Well, I'm just glad I don't have to worry about you anymore because frankly"—Grace gestured illustratively at herself—"I have better things to do with my time."

Sam nodded. "Yeah, now worrying about Laurie is off the agenda, you've got space for a whole new hobby. You should... What's the name you Poms have for that thing where you jump up and down and hit each other with sticks?"

"Sex?"

"Gardening?"

He snapped his fingers. "Morris dancing. You could do that."

"I will not," said Grace coldly, "be doing that."

I cleared my throat. "I'm sorry you felt you had to worry about me."

"Oh, you know." She shrugged. "Love. Friendship. Comes with the territory."

"And thank you for coming round."

"Well, I wasn't going to watch *When Harry Met Sally* with you while crying into a tub of Häagen-Dazs, or anything like that. I was going to take you to a party tonight and try to get you laid."

"Well, thank God he came back."

I gave Toby a grateful little squeeze, but he clearly had other ideas. "Ooh, party. I like parties."

"I do *not* like parties," I said firmly.

"Hey, look." The unexpected seriousness of Sam's tone

startled everyone. "I'm sorry, but I've got to mention it. The elephant in the room." He leaned forward, interlaced fingers hanging between his knees. "Laurie, you reek of sex, and there's... lemon sauce, I think, in your eyebrows. Can you go take a shower, mate?"

I ran out of the room, leaving them laughing.

When I came back, Toby had made tea, and his lemon meringue pie was sitting in the middle of the coffee table.

"We've been promised," Grace said, "that you had sex in the vicinity of this pie, involving only the components of the pie, and not the pie itself. So we've consented to eat it. Though apparently we have to wait awhile until it's cooled."

The afternoon passed pleasantly between my friends, my lover, and a lemon meringue pie. I thought Toby was a little nervous—as he had been initially at Oxford—but he soon relaxed. Sam was so laid back he was generally believed to be impossible to dislike, and Grace was Grace.

And, as it happened, Toby's lemon meringue pie was incredibly good. *Foodgasmic* was Grace's word. Though I'd liked eating it from Toby's fingers better.

They left around seven to get ready, furnishing me—at Toby's insistence—with the party details, in case I changed my mind.

"Are you being ashamed of me again?" he asked, as soon as they were gone and we were clearing up the tea things. "Not wanting to take me places?"

"No, it's just going to those kind of parties was what I did before I met you."

"*Those* kind of parties?"

I cleaned a stray fleck of meringue from the pie plate. "Private parties, Toby."

"What, you mean like sex parties?"

I nodded, hoping that would be enough to shut him up

"If we go," he asked, undeterred, "do we have to like...do anything?"

The idea of it turned my stomach. It wasn't that I had any objections to the principle—after Robert, I'd shared and been shared willingly enough—it was just...Toby was mine and I was his, and I never wanted to choose between sex and intimacy again. "Absolutely not."

"So"—Toby made his eyes very big and gazed at me imploringly—"can we go?"

"I don't understand why you want to."

He gave me one of his *duh* looks. "So I can say I've been to a sex party, obviously."

"And that's something you expect to come up in conversation, is it?"

"Maybe." He shrugged. "I just can't see any reason not to go."

I could have given him twenty, but I could also see that my resistance, rather than discouraging him, was only contributing to his curiosity. And I'd promised him only that morning: anything he wanted to do. So I surrendered. "All right, we can go." He squeaked excitedly. "But, Toby...I need... I'm sorry... Can we talk about some things?"

"Laurie, we can talk about anything."

I closed my eyes. This felt juvenile. Embarrassing. Something I should have been able to navigate with more sophistication. Toby was young. He deserved his adventures. But I knew, on instinct and from experience, I wasn't the right person to share them. "Toby...I can't... I don't want you... Look, you have to promise you won't...give me to anyone."

His mouth dropped open. "You're not a box of After Eight mints."

"I know, but I'm your...you know..." I didn't even want to say it. I hated those words. Sub. Dom. Lovers, we were lovers. "The expectations can be different."

He gazed at me solemnly. Eyes so very blue. "Laurie, I promise. That's totally not me. Thing is, I'm a greedy little shit. You're mine, and I'm keeping you."

I hoped he was right, and I was wrong.

———————

But from the moment we arrived at the party, I knew it had been a mistake to come.

As I'd warned Toby, it was a room full of strangers fucking and hitting each other. Everything smelled rather heavily of disinfectant. But Toby glanced round curiously and without repulsion, which made me wonder what he saw that I had long decided was mere façade.

Sexual liberty. Twenty-first century decadence. Exploration, acceptance, fulfilment.

The whole of the moon?

We picked our way through the moving bodies until we found the chill-out space. Toby's hand was tucked into mine.

"Are you all right?" I asked him.

"I think so." He frowned, his nose wrinkling. "It's just kind of weird, isn't it? Like, you know, when you're sober and everybody else is drunk? It's like that except with bonking."

I found a corner and drew him down onto a mound of brightly coloured cushions. "It's less weird if you're involved. But it's not really my thing."

"I'm feeling way too sheltered right now." He stretched out, resting his head in my lap. "Obviously there was stuff going on at Pervocracy as well, but it felt like a nightclub with sex. Whereas this is just people wandering around, sometimes with their bits hanging out."

I ran my fingers idly through his hair. "I know it looks like sexual anarchy, but there's etiquette and rules and boundaries. You don't have to be...a...be an all-you-can-eat buffet. You can just be with your partner or your friends. Nearly all of these people already know each other. It's actually a pretty exclusive group of perverts."

He hummed at the back of his throat, pressing into my touch, I think for comfort as much as pleasure. "Do you know them?"

"Most of them a bit. Although I wouldn't call them friends."

Grace and Sam found us a few minutes later. Sam was shirtless, fresh nail marks glowing on his arms and shoulders, and Grace was wearing a polka-dotted halter neck dress that looked eminently removable. She put her hands on her hips.

"Oh wow, look at you two. You look like the old guys in the box in *The Muppets*."

"Statler and Waldorf," I supplied.

"Toby, just because Laurie is one of life's hecklers doesn't mean you have to be." She held out her hand to him and pulled him to his feet, away from me. "This is your first time, right?"

He shuffled his feet, nodding.

"Okay, here's the thing, grasshopper, all parties are basically the same, whether they involve sex, or kinky sex, or drinking, or playing group Scrabble, for that matter. Fun is where you find it. If you just ignore Laurie's tortured little face and crappy attitude, you can totally have a good time tonight if you want."

Toby, to his credit, cast an anxious look at me. I didn't think he was as comfortable ignoring my tortured little face as Grace was. But then, he hadn't known me as long.

She drew his arm through hers. "You've discussed limits and boundaries, right?"

"Oh yeah." Toby nodded eagerly, as though he was sitting a test and he knew all the answers. "We don't want to do stuff with other people, and I'm not supposed to give him away, which I wouldn't do anyway. Because...just no."

"So you can fuck each other." She flashed her tomcat grin. "I think a lot of people, myself included, would enjoy watching that."

Sam put his hand in the air. "Me too! Me too!"

"We...we didn't talk about that." Toby had gone very red. I couldn't tell if he was embarrassed or flattered or some combination of both. "I'm...not sure—"

☆   "It's fine. Freedom is being able to say yes *and* no."

He gave her one of his crookedest smiles, and I tried my hardest not to be hideously jealous. Maybe I should fuck him—or let him fuck me—in front of everyone. Prove he was mine. And, oh God, which one of us was nineteen? I couldn't think of a less healthy reason to have public sex. Grace was right. I did have a crappy attitude.

And I wanted to be at home. With Toby.

"Have you ever seen sounding?" Grace was asking, as if that was a perfectly reasonable thing to say to someone else's boyfriend.

"Seen...sound—"

"Oh, Toby!" She bounced—a slightly dangerous action in that particular dress—and tugged on his arm. "It's amazing. Come on, my friend Alice was talking about doing a demo."

Which was how we ended up standing around, watching some guy get a surgical steel rod shoved expertly up his urethra. At least, that was what Toby watched. I watched Toby. He was rapt and bright-eyed, leaning close to Grace so she could tell him how it worked and how to do it safely.

My own feelings were impossibly conflicted.

I didn't want to stay, but I wanted to please Toby. And right now, he seemed excited to be here, though his burgeoning friendship with Grace was likely to prove dangerous for me. Not because I had any real cause for jealousy, but because she tended to be...inspiring.

The stranger was babbling ecstatically, begging Alice to take it out, don't take it out, let him come, please, please, please.

In spite of myself, I shuddered. I could too easily imagine Toby's hands upon me, the slick-slow invasion of metal.

Robert had never done that to me. He liked control, but Toby liked to be under my skin. He wanted to be inside me, in my body and in my mind. In my heart. So similar in some ways, so utterly different in others, the two men I loved.

We left Alice and her partner—or partner of the night—to each other and moved into another room. We were in the basement, which our host had lavishly transformed into a series of smallish dungeons. I might have whispered something to Toby about the sheer lack of imagination on display down here, but I didn't want to be the play-party heckler Grace had claimed I was. Besides, Toby was still talking enthusiastically about what we'd just seen, bombarding Grace and Sam with questions. They were walking a little ahead of me so I couldn't hear much of what they were saying over the usual noises—leather against skin, the clank of chains, the occasional gasp or broken cry.

Suddenly Toby stopped. "Oh my God."

Without even a premonition of misfortune to protect me, I turned to see what he saw: a man, tall and broad-shouldered, gleaming with sweat, wielding two floggers against a blood-flushed back with such consummate skill he made it look effortless, the tails flying and falling in that harsh, wild rhythm that had once been his gift to me.

"That's amazing." Toby was still staring at the two men locked in their cycle of give and take, trust and acceptance. "That's totally fucking amazing."

He sounded positively worshipful. My own voice seemed to come from some distant place. "It's called Florentine flogging. Like anything else, it's just practice."

"Um." Grace tried to draw him away. "Maybe we should go somewhere else."

But Toby was still transfixed. "No way, I want to watch this. It's like poetry. Who is that guy? Can I talk to him after? Do you think he'd show me how to do it?"

"His name's Robert," I said.

He was using the matched pair of black-and-green bull-hide floggers. He'd had them specially made. I'd been there. I knew them as well as I knew Robert, those rough extensions of his touch, his dominance, his love. His...lover...was bound to a Saint Andrew's cross, his arms spread wide. I knew how that felt too, that physical openness at once powerful and vulnerable, the sense of waiting to be transformed. His body had the laxity of deep surrender, as if he was falling into every stroke, as if they were part of him now. I didn't think he was even aware of the sounds he was making, low purring moans, not pain, not pleasure, just the intoxication of pure sensation, liberty and submission, barely audible beneath the swish and slap of leather.

I missed the end of their scene, lost in the torn-open spaces between past and present. When next I looked their way, they were embracing, Robert enfolding his new partner as he had once enfolded me, his heaving chest pressed to all that burning, gorgeously reddened skin.

The intimacy of it was almost unbearable.

But before I could turn away—get away—do anything—Robert looked up, met my eyes, and smiled.

So I had to smile back.

I had to wait for him to uncuff his lover. I had to wait for them to kiss, exchange love whispers, touch each other gently, familiarly. I had to wait for them to walk over and join us.

At some point, we'd become a crowd. Since he'd begun playing in public, Robert always drew a crowd. It was easy enough to understand why. He was so good at what he did, and the chemistry between him and...Noah, the man's name was Noah...was undeniable. They were beautiful together.

"Laurie." He was still smiling as he greeted me, sweat glittering on his brow, arousal still hot in his eyes. "It's been ages. How are you? You remember Noah, right?"

He always said this. I didn't think he meant to torture me, but it seemed unlikely that the man who possessed everything I had once so deeply cherished would just slip my mind. "Yes, I remember, Noah. I... You... That..."

I had run out of everything it was possible for me to say.

Toby cleared his throat loudly. His hand wriggled into mine, and I folded my fingers tightly around his.

I took a deep breath. "Um, I don't think you know... I don't think you've met... Um. This is my...partner, Toby."

I waited for shame, triumph, pride, anything. But there were just these truths, stark and undeniable: Once Robert and I had loved each other. Now Robert loved Noah. And I loved Toby.

A ripple of *something*—surprise, curiosity, amusement—went round the assembled kinksters. Toby and I were nothing like Robert and Noah. We were mismatched, implausible, absurd. My tastes were well known, as was my availability, my preference for casual encounters. For Toby's sake, I wished there wasn't that familiarity.

I wished I didn't have that history. It made me feel washed up and well used, a poor exchange for all his passion and sincerity.

I was afraid I reflected badly on him. I was afraid I made him laughable.

And that made me hate myself.

Robert touched me—he touched my arm—as though we were friends, as though he had the fucking right to do that. "I'm happy for you. And good to meet you, Toby."

I still couldn't think of anything to say. I wanted him to leave, disappear into his fucking happy ever after with Noah, and leave me alone with whatever I had with Toby.

"Thanks," said Toby into the silence. I had no idea what he was thinking. If he was all right. If he hated me. "I loved what you were doing with the two floggers. That was awesome."

Robert smiled his easy smile. Everything was easy for Robert. "You should try it on Laurie. He loves it."

I gazed at Robert, mute and pleading. *Please. Don't. Just don't.* The worst of it was, I didn't think he was trying to be cruel. He was just so far away from me, so far from *us*, that none of this even mattered to him.

But Toby was laughing. "Mate, I'm worried about fucking up with one flogger, let alone two."

That turned the laugh general. Most of the doms here would never have dreamed of admitting something like that. And there was little Toby, who either knew too much or too little to be ashamed of his fallibility, his uncertainty, his beautiful, imperfect humanity.

"You mean," asked a different voice, someone I maybe recognised, maybe didn't, "you've never flogged him?"

"They haven't been together very long." I thought that was Grace.

"Oh, Toby," said Robert, "you have to. He needs it." I shook my head, hating to be so discussed, revealed, made public, but nobody seemed to be paying attention to me. "He's beautiful under the whip. Beautiful."

"He's beautiful all the time." My Toby. So ridiculously loyal. Ridiculously stubborn. "And we'll get round to it, y'know, when I'm sure I'm good enough."

"I can give you some pointers, if you like."

I was dimly aware of audience approval. Everybody liked a little theatre.

"I'm sure he's fine." Grace again.

"Come on, lad." That was a stranger, someone I'd probably subbed to or slept with. "Don't be shy. Show us what you've got."

Various other comments followed—most of them fairly well-meaning, but humiliating nonetheless, in their certainty that Toby had something to prove or stripes to earn.

His hand was sweating, or mine was. I was desperate to tell him he didn't have to listen to these people, that he was everything I wanted and needed, exactly as he was, but I didn't know how. Not without making him look weak—weaker—in their eyes.

"Look." I heard the anxious waver in his voice. "That's...uh... really nice and everything, but it's up to Laurie."

He couldn't have said anything worse if he'd actively tried. ☆ I had to do something. I didn't care what these people thought about me, but I cared what they thought of him. Or rather, I hated that he would show them who he was—his fearlessness, his vulnerability—and they would think less of him for it, blind to the power in him, his tenderness, the sugar-twist of his cruelty, everything that made him worthy of the truest submission I could give.

I found words, and made them carry. "I'll do anything you want."

Which was taken as assent from both of us.

I didn't protest. I'd meant what I'd said. I'd do anything for Toby. I'd do this. I wouldn't let them shame him or dismiss him. Dismiss us.

Everyone cleared a space around the cross. I stilled my shaking hands, unbuttoned my shirt, and shrugged it off. It was probably nothing they hadn't seen before, but still my skin crawled.

Robert handed Toby one of his floggers. Toby's grip was awkward—the weight and length were probably all wrong for him. Whatever he did—perhaps he was trying to find the balance point, perhaps he was just trying to get used to the feel of it—sent the falls spinning chaotically until they wrapped around his wrist.

He yelped. "Ow, fuck. Um... Look... I don't..."

Don't laugh at him, you fucking bastards. Don't fucking laugh.

"This is kind of heavier than I'm used to," he muttered. Robert reached out and expertly untangled the tails.

"It's bull-hide—heavy thud, with a bit of weight behind it. It used to be one of Laurie's favourites. It's a bit long for you, but I'll show you how to compensate."

"Or"—a different voice—"he could just use something better suited to his height and build." Dom-the-dom eased out of the crowd. He was leather-clad as usual, holding a short-handled flogger, and I wished to God he wasn't here to see this. But perhaps I deserved it. I hadn't treated him well, after all. "Try this one... Toby, isn't it?"

Somewhat hesitantly, he swapped floggers. Then he grinned up at Dom. "This feels super nice."

Toby's smile should probably have been government classified. Even Dom went a little pink. "It's, uh, elk, Scandinavian elk."

"Oh wow, I'm glad I know where the elk came from."

Dom chuckled. "Yes, his name was Sven. I'm afraid it's all I've got with me with a shorter handle, and it's shot-loaded so the balance should suit you. It's a little bit softer than bull-hide, but it's still got a decent thud."

"Right. Thanks." Toby adjusted his grip and threw a couple of figure eights.

To everyone's ill-disguised surprise, they were perfectly competent. The tails went were they should, his wrist action was loose and fluid. For the first time since Robert had put a flogger in his hand, he looked comfortable. In control. But only I caught the curve of his lips, the glow of his eyes. He genuinely *liked* this.

There was a spattering of applause.

Then he crossed the dungeon to where I was waiting for him, went up on his tiptoes, and kissed me. "Are you all right?"

No. I nodded.

He peered at me doubtfully. "Are you sure? We don't have to do this. I don't care what they think. I only care about you."

"I care."

"Okay. Um..." He glanced past me, at the cross. I wasn't sure how I would bear it if he chained me to it in front of Robert and Dom and all these people who had already done far worse to me. But I would. I would find a way. For him. "Can you just hold on or something? Like when you did me?"

I could hardly breathe. So I nodded again, turned, and obeyed. I tried to make myself open, receptive, like Noah had been, but my muscles were twisted into knots, tight with painful reluctance, and I couldn't.

Toby must have sensed something wasn't quite right, because he ran his palm over my shoulders and down my back.

I loved his touch, but just now I couldn't bear it. It was an intimacy I couldn't afford. It certainly wasn't something I wanted to share with a crowd of onlookers. "Do it," I told him. "Just do it."

He stepped away, leaving me alone. I'd let strangers do this before even bigger crowds. There was no reason to be afraid now. No reason to be heartsick.

I rested my head against my upper arm, waiting.

10
TOBY

Laurie's ex looks like I wish—and sometimes imagine—I look. Tall and strong and stern and Daniel Craigy, all jaw and cheekbones and piercing blue eyes.

I think maybe Laurie has an unacknowledged thing for blue eyes.

Mine aren't as good as Robert's.

Nothing about me is as good as Robert.

I probably ought to be a puddle of insecurity and despair... except I'm just not. For once in my life I'm okay. And this is a fucking weird time for it because I think we're kind of in a pickle.

I don't know how I got us into it, and I definitely don't know how to get us out of it.

I've been practicing with the flogger Laurie gave me and daydreaming about what it'll be like when I hit him with it, the sounds he'll make, and how much it's going to totally get me off. But I'm pretty sure none of those daydreams—and there's been *a lot*—included an audience and Laurie's ex telling me all about what Laurie likes.

Because fuck it—I know what Laurie likes too, and I wasn't the one who ran away like a coward because I fucked up. I want to tell him: *you don't get to say this shit anymore*. But he's tall and hot and invincible and really amazing with those two floggers, so I don't have the balls.

Which I guess makes me a coward too.

Besides, I don't want to embarrass Laurie in front of all these people. I know they probably just think I'm a clueless kid—and let's face it, I *am* a clueless kid. But not when it comes to Laurie, because I love him and I trust him and I know him. I do. I *know* him.

But if I don't do this—and I have to do it without fucking up—then nobody will believe I'm right for him. They'll feel sorry for him. Or like he said to me all those weeks ago: like he's indulging me. I think he'd hate that. He's proud, is Laurie.

☆ And the way he gives that up for me—the way he lets me take it from him—is *private*. In public, it's my business. I have to look after him.

The good thing is, I'm pretty sure I'm not going to fuck this up. The flogger I'm holding is heavier than the one I'm used to, but it's nowhere near as bad as the one Robert gave me, and I just kind of like it. It's thrilling and humbling at the same time, and above all deeply sensuous. The handle tucks into my hand really neatly, and the chevron pattern is comforting under my thumb, like the creases in someone's palm. When I stroke my fingers through the tails—there must be like forty of them—I can feel the grain in the leather, tiny dents and bubbles, also oddly personal, warming from my touch.

I really, really want to make them dance against Laurie's skin. Two beautiful, powerful things I'm going to bring into conjunction, pain and pleasure, skin and leather, and ohmyfuckingGod. *Ngh*. I'd be hard, except my cock is a bit scared because a bunch of people are ogling it.

I glance at Laurie. His gorgeous back, all strong and markable, goldenish in the dim light. I love him so much, and I'm so fucking desperate to hurt him.

Except...this isn't how it's supposed to be. This isn't for other people; it's for us. And I think Laurie's shaking. Not like he usually does, but in this tight, frantic way, as if he's trying to control it but he can't.

I head over to him. I guess everyone thinks I've lost my nerve, but I don't care. I put my hand flat between his shoulders, and he jerks like I've stuck him full of needles. He's clammy with cold sweat.

"You know what." I turn to the crowd. "Fuck this."

"Toby..." A tiny whisper from Laurie.

"No, seriously. This is...like...important. It's ours. And I'm going to do it my way, nobody else's. So...show's over. Sorry."

I give the flogger back to the guy who gave it to me. He gives me this weird little nod, like he's saluting me. I guess he gets it.

Everybody else is still sort of staring. What part of "show's over" don't they fucking understand?

Well. Tough. I ignore them. Go back to Laurie and try to get him off the cross, but his hands are clinging to the wood, and embarrassingly, I can't reach, and I can't get him to let go.

I tug pathetically at his shoulder. "Come on, love. I want to go home."

And that gets through to him. He unlocks his death grip and turns round. He kind of doesn't quite look like my Laurie. He's trembling all over now, eyes like a wild horse.

Jesus. I'm fucking glad I didn't hit him. But in a weird way, I also know I didn't even come close. But I guess Laurie didn't know... Fuck, I've fucked this up. I was just confused and trying to do the right thing. And fuck.

I back off a little bit, trying to entice him after me, like he's some shy, feral creature and I'm a totally inept trapper. But he does follow, step by step, and then—suddenly—he just crumples to his knees at my feet. It's awful and graceless and kind of helpless, and I hear him hit the floor, and I can't imagine how much that must have fucking hurt. Then he kind of pitches forward onto his elbows, hands outstretched towards me, and I think what he's saying is "thank you, thank you, thank you."

And, Jesus fuck, this isn't for the rest of them either. So I throw myself down beside him and gather him into my arms. I hold him and he holds me too, and we hold each other so fucking tight. I don't know for how long, but when I look up again, we're alone.

That's one good thing.

And Laurie's warm again, and he's not trembling anymore.

So that's probably another.

After a bit, he pushes my hair out of my face, which he's kind of obsessed with for some reason, but it's how I know he's getting to be okay. Which God, I'm so fucking relieved about. Then he gives me this shy little smile and says, "Banoffee pie."

And then we're laughing. It's shaky, and I'm not sure if I should be crying, but whatever, it's what we're doing, and it feels right.

There's no reception down here because basement, which means we can't ring for a taxi, so we go stumbling for the stairs. On the way, we meet the guy who lent me his awesomely nice flogger, and he's got Laurie's shirt.

It takes both of us to get poor Laurie into it. He tries to help, but his fingers are basically incompetent.

God. What have I done to him?

It's Nice Flogger Man who calls us the taxi, and all three of us end up sitting on the doorstep waiting for it to come. The cold air is really good because it was comfortable-when-naked hot in the house, which meant it was basically uncomfortable-hot. Laurie rests his head on my shoulder, like he's completely exhausted, and I suddenly realise I feel kind of the same way—inside, not outside—and we slump against each other. "Oh, Toby," Laurie says, in this slightly slurry, dreamy way, "this is Dom. He plays the alto sax."

This is clearly some kind of in-joke or something, but Nice Flogger Man—Dom, I guess—looks thrilled. I think he's probably kind of hot, but he's so not my type it barely registers. Total lack of ping, and I'm starting to accept I'm all about the ping.

"Uh, do you, like... Are you in a band or something?" I ask.

"I sometimes jam at the North Star on a Tuesday night."

Laurie stirs a little. "We should come, hear you play."

"I'd like that." Dom smiles and stands up, trousers squeaking. "I think you two can take it from here."

And then, totally out of nowhere, Laurie is like, "I'm sorry I never called you," and I'm like, *Wait, what?* but I don't say it aloud, thank God.

But Dom just shrugs. "I'm glad you found what you were looking for," is all he says, as he goes back inside.

I call after him, "I hope you do too," but I'm not sure he hears me.

I mean it though. He seems like a good person.

Our taxi comes, and we're quiet all the way home, holding hands in the back. As we pass under streetlights, they paint Laurie in orange stripes, like he's a tiger. A very tired tiger who needs looking after tonight.

"Y'know," I say, when we finally get home, "let's not do that again."

Laurie gives me this look. "You know, let's not."

We still aren't talking much, but it's not the bad sort of not-talking. It's not Laurie-keeping-me-out not-talking, it's not needing-to-talk not-talking. It's still early, but after Laurie has some water, we go to bed anyway, and just sort of lie there, being with each other.

It's totally romantic in this quiet, unexplainable way.

I roll onto an elbow and stare at him all goofy-like, and he stares back—entirely ungoofy—but the greys in his eyes are soft as swan's-down.

"'He's all states, and all princes I,'" I whisper to him.

I don't think Laurie really knows what I'm on about, but he smiles up at me anyway.

"I'm sorry I fucked up tonight."

"You didn't."

He sounds like he genuinely means it, but I'm not sure I deserve to get off that lightly. "I nearly did. I didn't know what to do, and I got in a mess."

"It was my fault too." He glances away sheepishly. "I got caught up in everyone else's ideas about what was important. Thank you for, err, not."

☆ I'm kind of bummed to learn that's still a thing that happens in your thirties. "But what if I'd... I mean, would you have let—"

"I know my own limits, Toby." He reaches for my hand and presses it tight. He's all warm and strong and unshaken. "The worst it would have been was stupid, since neither of us wanted it."

"I didn't want to let you down."

He gives me his uncertain smile. "Ditto."

That's how we leave it. All equitable and mature and shit.

Except it's fake, isn't it? Just like me. I'm trying to cling to how I felt at the party—all strong and sure and shit—but we both know what happened, or what nearly happened, is all my stupid fault.

I was the one who pushed to go in the first place. If I'd listened to Laurie, and what he wanted, instead of being lost in my own messed-up head, I'd never have come so close to hurting him.

The truth is, I just can't bear to...to...think right now. Not about Granddad. Not about myself. What Laurie doesn't realise is that no matter how kind he is, no matter how much he holds me or fucks me or tries so hard to understand me, this weekend is just a way station. What's waiting for me on the other side is life without Granddad.

Just greasy café days spiralling the same into forever. And I'm scared and alone and I don't know what to do.

I thought grief would be kind of cool and lofty: this rarefied sadness. But it's the most ignoble thing I've ever known. I feel like a wild animal, lost and scratching. And all I want to do is see my granddad again. I want to look into his eyes again and see that love there. That unchanging, unflinching love. Why the fuck didn't I realise what a gift that was? Why wasn't I grateful for it every day of my shitty little life? Instead of taking it for granted.

Like the sun and the moon.

The moon waxes and the sun rises and my granddad loves me and everything will always be all right. And now only some of those are true. And thank God Laurie's asleep so he can't see these pathetic tears I'm crying in the dark for myself.

He'd want to comfort me, of course, but I don't know how to be comforted by him.

This man I know so much about and so little that it all kind of blurs in my head—these tiny details like how he likes his eggs or the sound he makes when he comes, and this huge stuff like thinking of him walking down the Underground tracks towards a bomb and this whole relationship he had when I was barely alive.

And the fact he doesn't really know me either. Only thinks he does.

And so I lie there, stifling my sobs in my hands, wondering how long until he leaves me too.

I must fall asleep at some point, but I don't sleep so well. I just haven't been lately.

I like being next to Laurie though. I still don't sleep, but it sometimes stops my head spinning. I concentrate on all the little things, like the heat of his skin and the beat of his heart and the deep, steady rhythm of his breath. It seems so eternal, so ceaseless, the physical business of being alive. It's hard to imagine that it'll just stop one day. For all of us.

I wasn't there when Granddad died. I don't know if that's the sort of thing that's supposed to matter. They told me it happened in his sleep. Apparently it was peaceful, but I bet they always say that. It's what you want to hear.

The last thing I said to him was, "See you tomorrow, Granddad."

Which turned out to be a lie. A really banal fucking lie.

But it's all lies, really, when someone dies. The whole business of consolation. I don't think I even really believe in God, but I did find myself sort of...hoping. Because there's nothing like being handed an ornamental pot of your loved one to make life just a little bit fucking pointless. Ninety-something years and all that's left is ashes and a boy who can't even mourn you properly.

Because what I'm really thinking as I watch Laurie sleep is: I wish he would try lying to me. Just a little bit. He could, for example, say *I love you*. And I don't care if it's real or not. Just want to hear him say it. So I'm not so fucking alone.

But people don't fall in love with mopey, needy idiots, so I'm determined to be shiny by the time he wakes up. I bring him eggs and the Sunday paper, and curl into the crook of his arm while he reads and eats, and in a weird way it does kind of work. I half convince myself that I'm okay. That Monday is another country I may never have to visit. And maybe now I have Laurie's phone number and a key to his house, that this is enough. That we're *something*. Boyfriends. Whatever.

We take it easy for most of the day. After yesterday, I don't think we're up for anything super kinky so we just sort of have sex. Except there's no *just* about it when it's Laurie. He takes me apart with this incredible fucking tenderness and then stretches me out on top of him like a wanton slut, takes my cock deep into his throat, and slides his fingers deep into my arse, and oh God, turns me into this pleasure circuit. I last no time, as usual, fucking myself crazy in two directions at once, while Laurie bathes me in all his muffled moans. Doesn't take me long to get back in the game though. Ten minutes sprawled over him, with him hot and hard and desperate and denied, and then I pin his wrists to the pillow and ride him like the rodeo until I fountain wildly over both of us and he pours himself into me in a warm, familiar flood. And for a little while, I can pretend that maybe I'm where I'm supposed to be.

———

In the evening, Laurie takes me out on this date. This actual motherfucking date. Which turns out to be something I want so badly I haven't even dared admit I want it. And for once, I don't even have to ask for it.

I haven't been home, and when I've been with Laurie I've been mostly naked, so I've only got some jeans I've come in and my funeral suit. It's not my funeral suit in any real sense. It's just a suit. But since I wore it to Granddad's funeral, that's basically what it is now. Laurie thinks I should just go in the jeans, but this is *a date*. And he's supposedly taking me somewhere nice.

I don't want to be someone who looks awful at nice places.

Laurie tries to convince me that everyone would just think I'm an eccentric millionaire or something.

But I think I'd look like a rent boy. A cheap one.

So funeral suit it is. I leave the collar undone and the tie behind, so at least it's kind of smart-casual funeral. Laurie's in dark blue. It makes the grey in his eyes all pale and pearly, more than usually wolfish. I love it.

He takes me to this place in Mayfair. It has a Michelin star. I have no idea how he's managed to get a booking at such short notice, but he just gives me a mysterious look and tells me he knows people. I don't know if he's feeling nostalgic for Oxford, or if it's the only place he could get into, or if he thinks I'll like it, but it's very...brown. Wooden floors and oak panelling gleaming darkly under this huge skylight thing. The tables are all squished pretty close together, but soon we're seated at one, and nobody has made any comments about me looking like a rent boy or Laurie looking like my dad.

So it's all good.

I disappear into the menu, and Laurie lets me order for him. He's indulging me a bit, and even though we only do kinky stuff in a sex context—honestly, it's the only context I want to do kinky stuff in, the rest of the time I want a boyfriend—I think we're sort of flirting around the edges of it right now. I'm pretty sure it's as far as we're ever going to take it, but it's kind of obvious to both of us we're each getting our own thrill out of it. I like choosing for him, and he likes being chosen for.

Laurie blushes a little bit as I engage the waiter, but the guy is either really well trained or a really nice person or just really used to accepting the dynamics of other people's relationships, because while he talks to both of us, he defers the decisions to me and answers all my questions. Because I've got loads.

We have pork belly with snails. The crackling is crisp and velvety at the same time, and the snails come with carrot purée and roasted garlic, and they're kind of this perfect earthy contrast. I practically swoon, and Laurie faffs with the napkin over his lap and hisses at me to stop having sex with the food.

That kind of sobers me up, not because of what he says, but because I shouldn't be allowed to be this happy right now. Not with my granddad being dead and Monday coming at me like a train down a tunnel.

Laurie spots it, though—the shift in my mood—and holds my hand over the table. In public and everything. I cling to him and let him make it okay. He tells me the stuff he's been telling me all weekend: it's natural, and not wrong at all, and sometimes I'm going to feel bad, and sometimes I'm not, and there's no rules. It doesn't mean I loved my granddad any less if I'm not sad all the time.

I get it. I do. Rationally what he's saying makes sense. But it's like there's something between us, between me and the world, this...crust I know is there but can't break through. I try to remind myself that Granddad wasn't, like, a psychopath. He wouldn't want me to be miserable. But that's somehow worse in a way because all he is anymore is dead. And he can't want anything for me or from me ever again.

And I don't know how I'm supposed to deal with that. I'm kind of dizzy but in my brain, all the time. Like I'm going to fall over. I don't want to go back to work. I want to stay with Laurie. I want him to take me to Paris. I want him to hold me until my world stops spinning and I'm strong enough to stand on my own again.

Which is so completely fucking pathetic.

Besides, if I don't go in, Joe will probably fire me, and then I'll have to figure out what to do next. And I can't. I just can't do that right now.

We have the bouillabaisse for our mains, which Laurie—I think trying to make me laugh again—confesses he would never have ordered on account of not being able to pronounce it and not knowing what it is. So I go on about Marseille bouillabaisse for a while, showing off basically, until I feel a bit like me again. It's a portion for two, and it comes in this huge copper pan thing, along with croutons and rouille sauce, and it's weirdly romantic, sharing this vat of stew on a chilly winter-spring evening.

I think the main fish in there is hake, not rascasse, but the amount of saffron in the stock is so completely wonderful I pretty much *do* want to have sex with it. Even Laurie seems a bit dazed about how fucking good the whole thing tastes.

We finish with honey ice cream and crushed honeycomb, which I'm slightly dubious about because I'm convinced it's going to be too sweet. But it isn't. Somehow it's subtle. I guess that's the sort of shit that gets you a Michelin star.

I'm discussing this with Laurie as we're crunching through honeycomb, and somehow...I don't know...but somehow I'm too relaxed, or not paying attention properly, or love struck and food hypnotised, but what he says is, "Are you going to have your own restaurant some day?" and what I say is, "Yes."

And then I'm completely terrified.

Because once you've thought something like that, or said it, all you've done is given yourself something to fail at.

Or have taken away.

We don't have sex that night. It's kind of the first time ever. But I'm too happy and sad and scared of tomorrow and, on top of that, scared of not having sex in case Laurie minds, but he doesn't seem to. He just holds me while I'm very, very small. Too small for everything.

All because my weekend with Laurie is over, and I have to go ☆ back to Greasy Joe's and the life I've kind of accidentally made for myself that I don't know how to live and don't know how to change.

I wish I could stay in the circle of Laurie's arms where everything's all right.

Which is probably why I forget about tomorrow, and don't even set the alarm on my phone, and I sleep, at last I fucking sleep, deep and dreamless and stupidly happy, in the world Laurie makes for me. Until Greasy Joe wakes me up with a phone call at half nine, because I'm late, I'm so late, and Luigi's sick, and Bella's had to go home, and everything's a mess, and I'm a fucking irresponsible kid, and what the fuck do I know, and I need to get the fuck down there, right the fuck away. For fuck's sake.

Like insanely angry is his modus operandi.

I know he doesn't *mean it* mean it.

But the shock...after everything...after being so safe and cared for...practically rips my skin off.

And suddenly, everything with Laurie seems like bullshit. A soap bubble, fragile and floating away from me. And I'm so not a prince. I'm a kid, a fucking irresponsible kid who can't keep a shitty job at a shitty caff properly.

This is how it really is.

Not...this...this fucking bullshit soap bubble with a man who's going to wake up one morning and see how fucking crap I am.

And he's been awake since the call. Greasy Joe has volume, even over the air waves, so I don't know how much of that Laurie caught before I got out of bed and out of the room. None I hope. I'd fucking hate it if he heard.

"What's the matter?" he asks as I start scrabbling around for my clothes and yanking them on.

"Forgot work."

"Was that your manager? Does he usually talk to you like that?"

I shrug. Try not to look at him.

He stirs in his cloud of Egyptian cotton. "Are you sure you're well enough?" He hesitates a tiny second before he says *well*. Like there were other words he had to discard first. Strong enough, maybe. Or capable. "You've had so little time."

"Well, it's what I got. And you're the last person to talk to me about what I want versus what I get."

I yank-zip my hoodie so hard I nearly hit myself in the face and run downstairs to find my shoes. Truthfully I'm almost glad to get away from him. I don't want to talk about this, and the more he's nice to me, the more I want to cry.

So, no.

When I finally get to Greasy Joe's, sweaty and late, it's total carnage. I don't know who's been in the kitchen while I've been away, but it's…it's not trashed, but it's not right. It's not been cared for and everything's kind of higgledy-piggledy, stuffed wherever, and I know this makes me sound like a freak, but systems are important in a kitchen. It feels like somebody's been wearing my pants and had them on backwards all the time they were wearing them. What the fuck's with the ordering? There's way too much bacon and way not enough eggs and no tomatoes at all and the mushrooms look kind of oogly and argh, argh, argh.

And that's just the back. Up front…I have no idea what's going on up front, because there's only Ruby serving, and she's really nice, but she smokes a lot of weed and you can tell. There's customers, and some of them have food, but nobody looks happy, and there's a bunch of American tourists standing in the doorway kind of laughing in a mean way about how lousy service must be part of the authentic British experience.

I know it's just a caff and just a job and it's not my fault and I shouldn't care so much, but it feels really overwhelming right now, and I do care, because if I don't, I'm just wasting my life. Everything is really bright and loud, and everywhere I look there's something I don't know how to deal with, and out of nowhere, all I can think is my granddad is dead and I wish he wasn't. But there's nothing I can do about that *either*.

There's nothing I can do about anything.

My hands are shaking so hard I can't even tie my apron properly, and I'm just standing there in the kitchen like a stunned moose when Joe barges in and tells me I'm a worthless fuckup who's fucking up his caff. He goes on and on, getting louder and louder, as if it's not enough that all the diners can hear him, he wants to make sure the street can hear him. Laurie back in bed in Kensington can probably hear him. The whole fucking world.

He finishes with, "Sort it out, or get out, or I'll throw you out," before he's off, in this immense ripple of fat and muscle, like a Spanish galleon under full sail.

Ruby's got her elbows propped on the service hatch, watching the show. "Wow, his dander, it's like so up today."

"Yeah." I try to act like...like I'm okay. Anyway, it doesn't matter. It doesn't fucking matter. All I have to do is cook some shit for some people. That's *it*. There's scraps of paper blowing about on one of the surfaces. "Uh, what's this?"

"Which?"

I point. "This!"

"Oh, that's orders, babe."

I paw through them crazily, this shipwrecked sailor looking for a message in a bottle. "Which comes first? What tables?"

"Oh yeah, forgot. Soz." She's chewing absently on a piece of her own hair. I seriously want to rip it out of her mouth.

"It's fine," I say, and I don't recognise my own voice. "It's fine. Just...sit those Americans."

"Which Americans?"

"Jesus, Rubes, the ones in the fucking doorway."

She turns really slowly. "Oh yeah, lol."

"Like, put them on six."

"Which one's six?"

"Put them anywhere. Just put them anywhere."

She drifts off, and I'm left in my wreck of a kitchen. I try to stack up the orders based on how and where they've flown, but it's hopeless. In the end I go for one I can read and whizz it along the grabber as if this is the same as being even a little bit in control of what's going on.

I tell myself: *one thing at a time.*

Except there's a lot of things, and they're stacking up faster than I can do them, which means...I'm never going to get on top of this. I've failed before I've even tried.

And I feel weird, like hot and cold at the same time, and I still can't seem to stop shaking, which is really bad when you're supposed to be preparing food. But it's not like I have a choice.

One thing at a time.

Full English. Okay. I can do that. I can do that.

I wash my hands, fire up the griddle...and realise about half the stuff I need is piled up in about six inches of stagnant water in one of the stainless steel sinks.

Fuckfuckfuckfuck.

I try to wash up while I'm cooking, but that just means I do a shitty job of both. And more orders come blowing in through the service hatch, and Ruby can't remember how to use the coffee machine, and I drop a stack of plates and I don't have time to clean the shards up properly so I just have to kick them under one of the counters, and while I'm stressing about that, I burn my eggs, which takes real fucking skill because, Jesus, they're *eggs*. And while I'm scraping them off the griddle in a torrent of grease and charcoal, I burst into tears, and then I'm weeping my heart out into someone else's breakfast as Stevie— one of our regulars—sticks his head in, and is all like, "I can see you're up against it, son," and tells me he's going to come back tomorrow.

I know he's trying to be nice. I know he's trying to *help*.

But I've lost a customer. I've fucking lost a customer.

And I can't stop crying.

In the end I go to the back of the kitchen, and I crawl into ☆ a space under one of the work surfaces where we keep the industrial-sized tubs of mayo and ketchup and mustard, and I make myself about as small as I can get—disappearing small, like I did for the bad year I had at school when everybody knew I was gay.

I don't even know if what I'm doing is crying anymore. There's some tears, but mainly it's noisy and weird and sounds more like hiccoughs, and the more I do it, the more I keep doing it, even though it's starting to hurt a bit because my mouth and my throat are all dry and I can't seem to get enough air.

I'm so lost and stuck in this loop of breathless-cry-hiccoughing that I don't even hear footsteps, I don't even know there's somebody with me until Laurie's drawing me into his arms, whispering my name, calling me darling, and gently brushing the hair out of my sticky eyes.

At first I think I've gone bona fide nutters. Like I'm so miserable I've hallucinated him.

But, no, he's really here. Laurie is here, in Greasy Joe's, with me. And that's so incredibly, well, incredible that I forget what a mess I am. So I'm just pathetically happy to see him, which I mainly demonstrate by covering his shirt with snot and slobber.

Eventually he manages to coax me upright, and I manage to ask him what he's doing here.

"I was worried about you," he says.

That doesn't exactly make me feel brilliant, but since he found me cowering behind a tub of Hellman's, it's not like I can claim I'm fine. I scrub at my face since I've basically abandoned all hope of pride and dignity. "I don't know what's wrong with me. Everything's a mess."

I squint up at him, looking for wariness or disgust or shock, but there's only Laurie, my Laurie, frowning a bit, but in his thoughtful way, not his angry way. "Come home, Toby. Let me take care of you."

Home. That sounds so nice. So does the bit about taking care of me.

But I'm supposed to be able to take care of myself.

I grab a bottle of water from the fridge and drink it scary fast. "I can't. I know it's rubbish, but this is my job and we're understaffed and if I go away there's nobody to cook. I just..." Looking round at the chaos makes me want to run away and hide again. "I don't know...how to..." I give up. I can't even finish a sentence right now.

Laurie doesn't say anything for a moment. Then he goes, "All right." And I have no idea what that even means in this context. He leans in and kisses me lightly.

Then he's unhooking one of the spare aprons off the back of

the door and putting it on. And while I'm gaping, he strides out of the kitchen, sweeping the crumpled heap of orders with him. I hear the clatter and click of the filter coffee machine and then his voice cutting easily over the disgruntled hubbub of the caff.

"All right, everyone, we've had a technical hitch with our ordering system—"

"What sort of hitch?" asks one of the Americans.

There's a teeny tiny pause. And then Laurie, at his driest, "They fell off the slider."

And people are laughing. But not, like, in a bad way. "So, we're going to give you all a free cup of coffee while we double-check your orders, and then we'll get your food to you as quickly as we can."

I've been working at Greasy Joe's for nearly a year, so I know the place, and I feel the atmosphere shift. I'm kind of stunned. A free cup of 99p coffee shouldn't make people go from not-okay to okay just like that, but there's something about Laurie, something I've only ever seen sort of banked before or maybe only in the way he focuses it on me. Somehow he makes you believe in him. And it doesn't matter if it's a big thing or a small thing, you just do.

It's so weird watching him like that, just being Laurie, in this grotty little caff.

He's probably going to encore by turning a pumpkin into a carriage for me.

He's talking to Ruby now, agreeing to—or basically, telling her—a numbering system for the tables. It's not the one we normally use, but honestly, it's probably an improvement. And the next thing I know, Ruby's back in the kitchen, sleeves rolled up, and she's doing the dishes in a slightly haphazard but still better than nothing way. And I can hear Laurie's voice in the caff, like I'm attuned to it, even if I don't know exactly what he's saying.

He appears at the service hatch, jug of coffee in one hand, a stack of orders in the other, which he feeds into the grabber. "Two full English, one with no black pudding, one with extra sausage. One cheese-and-bacon omelette. One chips and a portion of hash browns."

For a moment, I'm frozen. And then...I'm not.

Everything is simple again.

Two full English, one with no black pudding, one with extra sausage. One cheese-and-bacon omelette. One chips and a portion of hash browns.

I can...I can do that.

And I do. And while I'm cooking I tug on the slider, so I can occasionally glance at the little piece of paper fluttering above my head. I don't actually need the reminder, but I like having Laurie—okay, yeah, his handwriting—so close to me. He's neat for a doctor, but maybe he's just being extra specially careful. He's put the table number in a little box at the top right, all precise.

☆ The next orders come in quickly, Laurie calling them out to me as he sends me the slips, but it's okay, I've got this. The truth is, with Laurie around I feel I can do anything.

And that's kind of scary too, in its way.

When the first order is ready, I arrange the plates in the hatch and ding the bell, and because I'm feeling almost whole enough to be silly, I call out, "Service!"

Laurie's over in an instant, and for a moment our eyes catch over a pair of full English breakfasts, and he smiles at me.

This man I tied up on his kitchen table while I baked a lemon meringue pie. Who nearly let me hurt him in public. Who can't seem to stop finding ways to give me himself.

I...don't know what I've done to...get this. How I can possibly be what he wants? Especially now that I've basically had hysterics into some mayonnaise. Well, near some mayonnaise, but that doesn't exactly make it better.

The thing is, it was just easier to believe in good stuff when Granddad was around. But he's gone, and now there's just me, and who's going to be proud of me when there's nothing to be proud of? The pieces of me and the pieces of him are all in boxes at the hospice. I need to go pick us up, but I don't want to see what two lives look like.

Things are running pretty close to normally after an hour or so. I'm knackered and sweaty, and I still want to be...God... Laurie'd called it *home*.

So yeah. I want to be at home with Laurie.

Home sounds even better than Paris.

I can't quite believe Laurie's the same guy who freaked out at taking me sixty miles up the country. But even if he does still want to sweep me off somewhere, there's no way I'll be able to get time off. Also, I have exactly £57.29 in my bank account right now.

I really have been living in a crazy bubble, so obsessed with wanting Laurie and winning Laurie, I didn't stop and think how it was going to work. Like, he wants to go on romantic holidays, and I can barely afford to take him to KFC.

At one point, Greasy Joe stomps downstairs, ready to rip me a new one, discovers everything's fine, grunts, and then goes away again, totally failing to notice there's a complete stranger working in his caff. Because that's how he rolls.

Once we've dealt with the breakfast/brunch rush, Laurie sends Ruby to clear and takes over the washing up. And I feel fucking terrible.

He's a doctor—no, a *consultant*. He went to Oxford. And now he's up to his elbows in dirty plates and Fairy Liquid. All because of me.

I leave the griddle, so horribly aware I'm flushed and spotty and deeply unattractive right now. "You don't have to do that. We're okay."

"I'm not going until you're coming with me."

"Yeah, but..." I tug on his elbow, trying to stop him. "You shouldn't be doing that shit. You're like...too good for it."

"Toby, do you think I got to the age of thirty-seven without ever washing dishes?" He turns and piles a few bubbles on the end of my nose. Should be cute, right, but it just breaks what's left of my fucking heart. "I can work a menial job for a day. It's fine."

That's the thing, though, isn't it? I nearly tell him I work this menial job every day, but then Ruby's at the hatch.

"Somebody wants to know if you can, like, make...a..." Her brows pull together.

"A what?" I ask eventually.

"Oh, sorry, um, a root beer float."

"Not without any root beer or ice cream, no."

A second or two later, she comes back with, "What about cream soda?"

I think about putting my head in the oven, but I have to prepare for the lunch crowd, so I don't. Laurie powers through the washing up, and I chop all the things, and Ruby goes out for a smoke, and finally we scrape a few spare minutes to hang out by the service hatch, having toast and tea.

The thing is, while there are rubbish things—*menial things*—about my job, and I'm not a big fan of being paid £5.03 an hour, there's also stuff I really like. Working with food and people. And these quiet moments when you feel you've been through something and created something. Even if it's just some awesomely fried eggs. I kind of dither between being glad Laurie's here and horrified and terrified about what'll happen when he realises this isn't Take Your Awesome Older Boyfriend to Work Day. That this is my life. For real. And this is really who he goes to his knees for, surrenders his body to.

Most of our regulars have set times they come in—usually just before, or just after, the normal times most people are thinking about breakfast or lunch or a cup of coffee and cake. It's how they always get to have the same table and get their orders in before the rush. It amuses me in a way—because it's a bit daft, deliberately choosing to have your lunch at 11:45 a.m. every day—but it sort of makes me sentimental too, the way people will structure their lives around the stuff they feel is important. Even if it's just an omelette done exactly the way they like it.

Is that what's happening with Laurie and me?

Except what I'm doing to his life is dragging it down with mine.

Even though we're just standing next to each other, not really saying or doing anything, I guess there's something about us. Or maybe I talked up my boyfriend too much because everybody guesses straight away that he's the guy. I mean, the ones who aren't uncomfortable with the gay thing, which some of them are even though they try to be nice about it. But I get shoulder-squeezed and cheek-patted and hair-ruffled a lot, and Laurie gets told at least twice that if he hurts me, folks will find out, and then they'll break his kneecaps.

So that totally helps all my concerns about what a shitty deal our relationship is for him.

But he seems okay and hasn't run away screaming yet, even under the threat of actual physical violence. He just smiles through the...I think...fairly well-meaning ribbing he gets about being a cradle snatcher. I'm scared though, because I remember how upset he was when that woman thought he was my dad that time. I really don't need to give him any more reasons to run.

So I blurt out desperately, "Hey, maybe he's not a cradle snatcher. Maybe I'm a grave robber."

In the explosion of laughter that follows, Laurie puts his arm around my shoulders. "Toby, darling, please stop helping."

The rest of the day kind of bobs past pretty much normally.

Apart from Laurie, who gets on with things like he's been there for years. It should be funny or something, right, how hard I try, how much I want to be good, and he just comes in and makes it look easy. In the afternoon lull, I phone in tomorrow's food delivery and bake up a storm because nobody's been keeping up with the cakes. And, after Ruby leaves, I give the kitchen this epic clean. You have to be consistent with standards, and I'm worried it's been neglected while I've been away.

I can't make Laurie leave. He gets down on his hands and knees with me and cleans up the broken plates and scrubs under benches. He helps me do the coffee machine and the grill hood and behind the fridges. And finally he kind of peels the marigolds off me and chucks my cloth into the bin and says in this scarily gentle voice, "If you scrub any more of this kitchen, there'll be nothing left. I think we're done."

I'm slightly dizzy and a bit confused, like I've just been woken up, except I'm pretty sure I wasn't asleep. I check the clock on the wall and it's half eight. Fuck.

The kitchen is cold and silver all around us.

"Toby," Laurie asks me, "why on earth are you doing this?"

"It needed cleaning."

"No, not that." He gestures around the caff. "*This.* Why are you here? Why aren't you at university? Or catering college? Anything would be better than this."

I shrug. I don't want to have this conversation. I just want him to take me home like he promised, and make me feel safe and powerful and loved. Instead of all the things I really am. "Does it matter?"

"It matters to me." I don't want to look at him, but I know he's looking at me. The steady warmth of his eyes.

"Well," I snap, "it doesn't."

"For God's sake, Toby." Laurie's hands close over my forearms, and I don't like it. It's too close to being trapped. "Walk your fucking talk."

I try to pull away, but he's too strong. "What do you mean?"

"You won't let me hold anything back from you, and that's all right. I don't want to anymore. But you won't even answer a goddamn question for me."

There's something in his voice, under the anger. But I can't make my head quiet enough to figure out what's happening. I don't feel...anything. I just want him to take his hands off me and stop asking me stuff. I stare blankly at the wall over his shoulder.

"Why won't you look at me? What's wrong with you?" ☆

I'm not going to cry. I'm not going to cry. I carefully turn my head. Meet his eyes. Nearly cry anyway, because he looks so confused. "There's nothing wrong with me, Laurie. It's just...this is who I am. It's who I've always been. Someone with a shitty job because it's all they can get."

He leans in like he's going to kiss me, but I flinch back, so he doesn't. Folds his arms instead, maybe so he won't be tempted to reach for me, but it just makes him look faraway and unassailable. "This is what you're doing, but it isn't who you are. You're a clever and talented young man with a lot of potential—"

"You sound like my English teacher before I got that D. You

sound like one of the dads when they can be arsed to pretend to take an interest."

He steps away.

And I immediately wish he hadn't. I'm so fucked up right now that I can't even work out whether I want my boyfriend to hold me.

"That's not fair," he says in this too-calm voice. But I totally got to him. I can tell from his mouth, the flush on his cheeks. "I'm not trying to be some...sort...of father figure here, and I don't think that's what you want either."

It's not, but he's taken away what I wanted, which was what we had when he didn't know about this stuff and I could be who he thought I was.

He sighs. He's not angry, he's *disappointed.* Yeah, yeah. Aren't they always? "Toby, I just want you to talk to me. Please."

"What's there to say?"

"I want an explanation." He knows how bad that sounds because the flush deepens. "I mean, I want to understand."

"Why?" I give him a hard stare. "Because all of a sudden who I am and what I'm doing isn't good enough for you?"

"It's not good enough for *you.*"

My heart's this red-hot lump. I think I'm going to be sick. "How the fuck do you know what's good enough for me?"

"That's not what I meant."

But everything I've ever heard about me is in what he just said. *Tobermory is clever, but doesn't apply himself. Tobermory has potential, but doesn't live up to it. Tobermory needs focus. Tobermory needs discipline. Tobermory needs to decide what he wants and work for it.* I tuck my hands into the pockets of my hoodie to hide the fact they're shaking.

"I just meant," he goes on, like this is supposed to help, "you could do so much more than this." I've heard that before too. The thing is, nobody's ever told me *what*, or *how*. "You told me last night you wanted to have your own restaurant."

I wish I hadn't. It's going to hang over me forever. "So?"

"Is that why you dropped out of university? To go into catering?"

People are always so fucking desperate for you to have some sort of plan. "Not really."

"Then what happened?" I can tell how hard he's trying to stay patient with me.

But that just pisses me off even more. Makes me stubborn and petulant and like I don't want to give him anything. Which on some level, I know is stupid and unfair. The problem is I don't know how to stop. "I didn't like it."

"What—I don't—" He sighs, and I definitely don't like this Laurie. This exasperated adult who doesn't get why it matters that Ted Hughes doesn't give a flying fuck about zoos. Who doesn't get *me*. "What does that even mean?"

I kind of explode. "It means I didn't fucking like it. What don't you get? Two terms in, I realised I didn't care about the law, I didn't like studying it, and I certainly didn't want to be a lawyer. So I dropped out, and here I am, working at the only place that'd take me."

Laurie doesn't say anything. That makes me almost happy in this awful, nasty way like I'm saying *I told you so* to myself. And it totally kills me at the same time, because there's some deeply sad and pathetic part of me that wants him to see all this and love me anyway.

"Isn't," he tries at last, so carefully he might as well just stab me in the face and have done, "isn't there something else you're…interested in or want to do? You could study something. Or develop your cooking? Start working towards that restaurant?"

Does he have to keep coming back to that? I mean...yes...maybe...? "I don't know." My voice bounces off the stainless steel. "I just don't fucking know, okay? I've never known. My entire life is just me pretending—not very well—that I have a clue what I'm doing. But I don't. I just don't. I don't have, like, a dream or a goal, and I don't know how to get one, or what's wrong with me that I don't."

Great. Now I'm crying again. Just to make me hate everything a little bit more.

Laurie's hand reaches across the space between us, but I don't feel like touching it. "There's nothing wrong with you. You're nineteen. It makes perfect sense that you aren't sure what to do with your life yet."

"Oh yeah, and what were you doing when you were my age?"

At least he has the grace to look sheepish. "Well, I was studying medicine, but—"

"When she was my age, my mum was already famous. She'd had two massively successful exhibitions. *Two*."

"You don't have to be your mother."

"Easy to say when it's not actually an option." I wipe my eyes and try to glare at him through the wet, grey haze. "This is bullshit, Laurie."

It's going exactly the way I've always been terrified it would. He's trying to be kind and understanding and all this crap, but basically what he's seeing right now is a lost and confused teenager who needs his help and guidance.

And, yeah, okay, I am lost and confused, but I'm his boyfriend, not his project. I don't want to be rescued. I want him on his knees. In my arms. In my body. I want him laughing and crying and hurting and happy and whispering his secrets to me in the dark like I'm worthy of them.

I want to be his equal.

But I can't be. Because I'm not. How the fuck am I supposed to be his prince when I'm just a pauper?

And I really want to be with my granddad. I've always told him everything. Like when everybody was calling me names at school or when my friends stopped speaking to me or when I got that fucking D, which meant I wasn't allowed to do English at A level. And we'd go to Hyde Park, or to Primrose Hill, or any of the other eighty gazillion places he liked to go walking, and sometimes the snowdrops would be out or the daffodils or the world would be gold with autumn, and he'd tell me that I was the best part of his life, and if I was good enough for him, I was good enough for anybody.

And I'd believe him.

Every.

Single.

Time.

"Toby, please." Laurie's talking to me like I'm standing on a ledge. Like I'm a hamster he's trying to get out from behind the sofa. And I hate it. "Talk to me. I can help."

"I don't want your fucking help, and I don't want to fucking talk about it." Oh God. I'm yelling. Yelling and crying and ugly and raw. "You don't get it. I knew you wouldn't get it."

He draws in this breath. Willing himself to be patient with the crappy, lunatic teen. "You haven't given me a chance to get it. You've never trusted me with...with anything."

"Yes, because I knew you'd be like this."

"Be like what? I'm trying to—"

"Yes, yes, you're trying to help me." Fuck. I'm a monster. And

I can't stop. "So, what, you can pack me off to university or get me some differently crappy job and congratulate yourself on having saved me before you leave me?"

His eyes get wide, all the gold in them consumed by grey. "Who said anything about leaving you?"

"Because you've been leaving me from the moment I met you. And now you know the good stuff is stuff you made up. And the real stuff is"—I gestured at the kitchen, pile of egg boxes in the corner, the carefully cling-filmed cakes—"this."

"It's all real, darling. And I'm sorry—"

"I had it right that very first night. You're always sorry. What the fuck use is sorry?" I reach into my pocket and pull out my keys. The teeth are embedded in the seam of my jeans I hear something tear as I yank them free. Getting his key off the ring takes ages. My hands are shaking too much. Kind of ruins the gesture.

"Toby, what are you doing?" There's an edge to his voice now. Fear maybe. And in some twisted, miserable way it feels good to hear it. "I'm not leaving you. I don't want to leave you. Why are you acting like this?"

The key finally comes free from the ring, and I throw it at him. His hand comes up, and the key slaps against his palm, hits the floor with an unimpressive *clink*. Something I wanted so fucking badly—nothing but an unimpressive *clink*.

☆   I stare at Laurie, who looks pale and shocked and confused and hurt and all hazy through my tears. "You don't even have the bollocks to tell me you love me." This is meant to sound devastating. But it sounds what it is. What I am. Small and broken. "And I'm sick of waiting for you to be done with me. I'm done with you."

Next thing I know, I'm running for the fire door like the

building is on actual fire. I just can't be here right now. I don't know where to go or what to do, but I can't be here.

"Toby. Don't." Laurie catches my arm as I rush past him, but I yank hard enough that he'd have to hurt me to keep me, so he doesn't.

I hear his footsteps behind me.

"Get away from me," I yell. "Go away."

He stops.

"Please." Laurie's voice is this distant swirl of panic and fear, cracking a bit. "Please don't leave."

I shove through the door and into the night, and I don't look back.

11

LAURIE & TOBY

☆

Toby was gone. He'd run.

My first instinct was to go after him, but he'd...told me to get away from him. That he was done with me. And I wasn't sure I could bear to see him flinch from me again, his eyes full of something far too much like fear, far too much like hatred.

I'd argued with Robert. All couples argue. It was something you learned over time how to do without destroying everything. How to navigate each other's anger and pain. But I'd somehow forgotten how...how searing it could be, and how easily vulnerability to love became vulnerability to hurt. Toby had lashed out at me like some wounded creature, not just careless of my feelings, but deliberately striking where he knew he'd do the most damage, and it had come out of nowhere when I had only wanted to help him. I tried to muster self-righteousness and resentment, but I was too worried for him, and too afraid for myself.

What had I done? Had I lost him?

I tried to detach myself from panic and pain but—for once—it didn't come naturally.

Stay calm. Assess the situation.

If the patterns of his previous behaviour were anything to go by, Toby would come back to me. Even that very first night when I'd made him leave and he'd been unable to get home. That should have been reassuring. It meant I could reasonably rely on his common sense. He wouldn't do anything stupid. All I had to do was wait.

But I feared for him anyway and for myself.

What if it was different this time? What if he truly was sick of waiting for me?

And, oh God, why had I never told him I loved him? I'd thought it to myself often enough. Even noted the absurdity of it. Of being so helplessly, irresistibly, and undeniably in love with a nineteen-year-old boy. But giving Toby the words had seemed at once too much and too little, too easy at his feet and too difficult in the quiet, and so I'd kept my peace. And so he'd fled from me.

In case he came to his senses sooner rather than later, I decided to stay a little while in that shining, unfamiliar kitchen. When it became clear he wasn't coming back, I rang him. Went straight to his voicemail: "This isn't Toby. I'm too fucking busy or vice versa."

I didn't know how to say what I needed to say, so I hung up.

And then rang again, a few seconds later, in the hope he would pick up. When he didn't, I blurted out something tangled about needing to talk to him, amid apologies and pleas. It wasn't dignified—it probably wasn't coherent—but I didn't care. I just wanted him to answer his phone.

So much for detachment. So much for calm.

Not wanting to get him into trouble, I checked the café was properly locked up, turned off the lights, picked up my door key from the floor, and let myself out of the fire door, making sure it closed behind me.

Maybe if I went home, Toby would already be there. Sitting on the front step just like always. He could have been on the

Tube now, for all I knew, which was why I kept going straight to voicemail.

As I walked briskly towards Bethnal Green, I struggled with various burgeoning annoyances. I was annoyed at Toby for running away from me, and I was annoyed at myself for being so upset by it. But my mind kept throwing up images of loss and destruction—of Toby alone or frightened or hurt in the dark—and, much as I tried to rationalise them away, my heart had become a shrieking hysteric that wouldn't listen to reason.

It was an awful journey. I tried phoning a few more times, and still there was no answer. On the Tube I fretted constantly he was trying to phone *me*, but when I emerged there were no messages, no missed calls. And I still went straight through to his voicemail.

I texted him. All I wrote was, Toby, please.

I practically ran down Addison Avenue, not really expecting anything, but hoping.

The house was dark, and there was no Toby.

Inside, I phoned him again. Silence.

What was the point of giving people keys and phone numbers and all these promises if they were going to mean nothing?

And what if something had happened to him? A moment of distraction was all most accidents came down to. And would anybody know to tell me?

God. God.

I tried to remember if it had been like this with Robert and me, back at the beginning, before we had settled into the patterns of love. We'd surely had our own dramatic moments? Heart-crushing uncertainties?

But it was so long ago, submerged into my past like Robert was now, that even if I could scrape up incidents, they felt too distant to be real, the emotion that had led to them or under-pinned them entirely lost to me.

There was only Toby and this hurt and this fear, this loss and helplessness.

As the empty hours dragged by, I dug up further frustrations to comfort me. What had I done or said that had been so terrible? He should have been thanking me, not running away from me. The problem here wasn't me. It was him, and his immaturity.

What was I thinking? It wasn't that he was immature—simply that he was young. His experiences and expectations of life were shaped differently to mine, but that didn't mean they were inferior or misguided. Had I ever recognised that before? Had I told him? Or had I just questioned, lectured?

Had I failed to get him, just as he'd claimed?

If I'd said the words—if I hadn't taken it for granted that he must have known I loved him—would he be with me now? Safe in my arms and I safe in his? If he had truly understood how I felt about him, if he had known he had dominion over my heart as well as body, he could never have feared I would think less of him for...anything. But I had never given him reason to trust me. And everything I had given had been too little, offered too late, at a time when the world had already stripped him of too much.

I deserved this pain. I deserved his anger and his mistrust.

I'd just...thought I'd have more time to prove myself to him. To show he was loved and treasured and valued. But then I'd thought that with Robert too. Waiting to heal, to change, to move on, to find ourselves again, and he'd already left me.

I found myself—of all places—in the kitchen, where the warmth from the AGA Toby loved so much wrapped around me like a hug. Still clutching my phone, just in case, I sat on the table and waited. This room was full of Toby. To say nothing of the depraved and imaginative things he had done to me in it. I'd cleaned the table afterwards, blushing and aroused, but the memory was whorled in the wood now, as it was in my skin.

There were other memories too. Everyday ones. Toby telling me some slightly incoherent story, gesticulating wildly with one hand, as he put on the kettle for tea. Coming down with him at midnight for toast. Watching him lick shiny, melted butter from between his fingers. Carrying him back to bed again after.

And this was where he'd told me about his D.

Something else I'd handled badly, assuming it wasn't important. No wonder he hadn't wanted to talk to me about any of this. *You're supposed to be on my side*, he'd said then. And I hadn't been. I hadn't really listened or tried hard enough to understand. Which meant I'd treated his choices as if they were mistakes, and his fears as if they were nothing.

And now...I didn't even know where he was.

I tried phoning him yet again, mortified to think my name was probably in double figures on his missed-call list. But I didn't know what else to do. What if he didn't come home tonight? What if he didn't come tomorrow? What if he never answered his phone to me again?

All because of one conversation?

Or did it go deeper than that?

The truth was, the years between us mattered. Not—as I had thought—because of how other people would judge, but because while some of the bridges between us were instinctive and effortless, love and sex and faith, others had to be carefully built. And I'd failed not just to build them, but to notice they were needed.

I put my head in my hands, hating myself, terrified that it was too late. It was true he'd always come to me before, but maybe this time he wouldn't. And I didn't know how to go to him. It might almost have made me laugh, remembering how enormous asking for his phone number had seemed. But it was nothing, a string of numbers that no more connected me to Toby than a flare shot into the sky.

I run for the Tube in case Laurie follows me.

He doesn't.

Of course he doesn't.

Why would he? After everything?

And I'm such a fucking mess because all I want is for him to hold me. Which he was doing until I shouted and cried and threw things at him like the insane freak I am. But I want him to fight for it too, even if that means fighting me. I'm just so...tired of everything being so careful. Uncertain. Fragile. A compromise. Everything that isn't sex, anyway. It's not so much the kink I want, but the way it feels. Like we fit and I'm his and this is right and I can do anything.

But right now I don't know where I'm going or what I'm doing, and nothing's right, so I go home.

Mum's there and so's Marius. When we'd moved in, we couldn't figure out how to get a sofa up to the loft so we have these silk scatter cushions that drive me mad, and he's sprawled over them, looking gorgeous and fantastical, like something from the *Arabian Nights*. And Mum is, well, Mum.

I must look completely wrecked because the first thing she says is, "What happened to you?" in this slightly bewildered tone.

I tell her because...why not? I'm too miserable to pretend anymore. "Broke up with my boyfriend."

"Probably for the best, love. You know relationships are ultimately an ideological construct designed to limit our freedom."

This is so not what I need to hear right now. "I know."

"Far better to live a whole and self-determined life than lose yourself in the illusionary transcendences of romantic love."

"Yeah." Why the fuck can't she just...like, hug me or something? But it's not what she does. Granddad does...did that stuff. Mum's the one who yells at teachers about Key Stage 4 being intellectually moribund. She's the one who bursts into PTA meetings when she decides the school is unconsciously reinforcing homophobic paradigms. Kind of embarrassing really, except embarrassment just sort of doesn't happen to her. My mum in action is like nothing any normal person could prepare for: imagine the Toni Collette role in a Britflick, played by Eva Green. That's my mum.

"In other words," she was saying, "fuck him. Are you cooking tonight or shall we order in?"

I give her a blank look. "Maybe get a takeaway?"

"How long were you together?" I've almost forgotten Marius is there until he speaks.

I don't want to be having this conversation with a stranger who may or may not have fucked my mum...but that's all I've got right now.

"Um, depends how you count it." Three months since he first threw me out of his house. Three days since he gave me his door key.

"He's been mooning about since before Christmas."

Great, *now* Mum notices stuff? "Yeah, well. Won't be doing that anymore, will I?"

"I don't know." She gestures as if to encompass my general mien. "What do you call this?"

"How about"—my voice goes all shrill and adolescent—"having a broken heart?"

There's this silence. Which I eventually break by sniffing.

And finally Marius says, "I'm sorry. I take it he was your first boyfriend?"

I nod.

He sits up and he's looking at me, so I kind of have to look ☆ at him back. He's got this overt, effortless sexuality to him—or maybe that's just his very pointy shoes—that makes it hard to imagine him with the quiet librarian. But then I remember that guy had an intensity to him as well, just inward-turned, rather than extrovert. They'd have made a scarily hot couple. Smouldery types smouldering at each other.

So I tell him out of nowhere: "I think I met your ex in Oxford."

"Edwin?" His eyes—which are sort of honeyed, like whisky in candlelight—go wide behind those long, dark lashes. "How did you... I mean... How was he?"

I shrug. "Seemed okay. We didn't talk much."

To my surprise, that makes him laugh, though not in a happy way. "No, I don't suppose you did." His mouth curls into a crooked half smile, the shadow of a dimple flickering in his cheek. "You should be careful of first love, Toby. It's very powerful and very dangerous."

"Sure. Whatever."

I just can't be doing with people right now. I retreat to my room, but then I realise I'm going to have to hear them all night, talking and laughing and being passionate about art and shit. And God help me if they get creative. When Mum's on an inspiration kick, you may as well cry havoc and let slip the dogs of war.

I sit on my bed and take out my phone, which is old and crappy and ran out of battery midway through Sunday. I think about plugging it in, but why bother? He's not going to call me. Why the fuck would he? Laurie doesn't do that. I'm the one who frets and begs and demands and waits and pushes and needs and loves.

He's just...there.

Through the partition that's supposed to be my bedroom wall, I hear a cork pop. Voices. Footsteps. The clink of glasses.

Fuck. I don't want to be here. But I don't have anywhere else to be. Nothing in this whole fucking city belongs to me.

So I go to the last place I remember feeling okay. The last place I knew I was loved. The last place that felt like home.

I get the last Tube to St. Anthony's.

I wanted to cry, and it was ridiculous. Probably in a day, or a couple of days, I'd hear a knock on the door, and Toby would be there, a little bit hurt, a little angry, and ready to talk.

But that didn't feel like an answer. It felt like no solution at all.

"*Why's it always me?*" he had asked me.

I hadn't realised at the time, but it cut both ways. Now I wanted to be the one who acted, not the one who waited. But I didn't know how.

Detach. Think. Stay calm. Assess the situation.

If not here, if not me, where would Toby go? To a friend's place, perhaps? If so, I had no way of finding him. But he was vulnerable and upset, and he'd want to go somewhere he felt safe. From what he'd said, I wasn't sure he had many close friends at the moment. Home, then? To his mother's? That seemed most likely.

I checked my watch. It was late. Probably too late.

But fuck it. I wanted Toby, and I wanted him to know how much. He'd sat on my doorstep enough. Now it was my turn. My turn to fight for him. To show him he could depend on that. Depend on me. To show him he was loved.

And that we weren't done.

That we were only just beginning.

I was sure he'd told me where his mother lived. Not specifically, but there'd been enough passing mentions for me to work it out. If I could only remember.

Detach. Think.

A loft? In a converted factory.

A tobacco factory? In Shoreditch.

Tabernacle Street?

I nearly cried again, but this time it was pure relief. I turned on my computer and fired up Google Maps, squinting at satellite images until I managed to locate what I thought was likely to be the place.

I called a cab. Stuck a note for him on my front door just in case. *Toby, my darling, I have gone to find you in a city with eight million inhabitants. If you're reading this, please call me. I'm sorry.*

The taxi driver wanted to know where in Tabernacle Street I was going and eyed me a little dubiously in the mirror when I said he could just drop me anywhere. That was when I realised I'd left the house without a coat, and it was cold. My reflection in the window stared back at me with hollow eyes.

This was such a bad idea.

Nevertheless, I tipped the man apologetically and scrambled out onto a narrow, poorly lit road, lined by an architectural miscellany of offices and warehouses.

I hurried up the street, looking for something I recognised from the map, hoping inanely that Toby would be walking the other way or looking out of his window, and we'd rush in slow motion into each other's arms, and everything would be fine again.

My footsteps echoed in the silence. Some of the more modern buildings had mirrored windows that reflected a haze of moonlight. There was no sign of him.

I passed a corner pub, offices to let, a pizza place, everything already closed and locked up tight. And then I found it. An old tobacco factory that had been converted into trendy flats.

This had seemed a lot more romantic and a lot less awkward in my kitchen. For long minutes, I did absolutely nothing. I just waited in an empty street, trying to find the courage to do something stupid. Then I stepped up to the door, found the buzzer for the top floor, and pressed it.

Sweat prickled on my spine. My heart pounded.

"Hello?" came a voice that certainly wasn't Toby's.

"I...I'm looking for...Toby. Toby Finch." Oh God. It sounded bad, on the wrong side of midnight, stripped of all context. Had our positions been reversed, I might have seriously thought about calling the police.

But after a moment, the answer came: "You've just missed him. I think he's probably gone to his boyfriend's."

Which meant this husky, East London voice belonged to Toby's mother. Fuck. "Um, I am his boyfriend."

There was a crackly pause. Then, "You'd better come up."

It was a long climb, but I took the stairs two at time, and arrived—hot and aching—at the loft in a matter of minutes. The door was ajar, but I knocked anyway, not wanting to barge in on Toby's mother when she was at home by herself.

"It's open."

"Sorry." I stepped inside and—"Oh God, you're naked." Except for a curl of paint over one breast.

"Why, do you have a problem with the female body?"

"N-no...I was just startled." I still wasn't entirely sure where to look. If it would be more or less impolite to look at her or away from her. "Do you, um, not believe in clothes?"

"Not when I'm painting in the privacy of my own home, no." Toby's mother put down her palette and brush and sighed. "I'll put on a robe."

There was something long and silk and vaguely oriental in pattern tossed over a nearby chaise. She picked it up and draped it over her shoulders, which more sort of framed her nakedness than covered it.

I couldn't help searching for Toby in her face, but I couldn't find him. Coal was tall and long-limbed, willowy even, whereas he was short, restless, and graceless. She shared his colouring though, pale and dark, except her eyes were sloe-black to his blue, and her hair was darker too, falling almost to her waist in loose, paint-and grey-streaked waves. Truthfully, she was beautiful in all the ways Toby wasn't, her certainties and carelessnesses implacable somehow.

"So," she went on, regarding me with only the laziest interest, "you're the boyfriend."

I nodded, feeling helplessly gauche, and wondering if I should offer my hand. "Laurence Dalziel."

"Yes, he said." She strolled across the loft to the corner kitchen, dragged a carton of milk out of the minifridge, and drank it straight from the container. "He didn't say, though, that you're older than me."

Ah. I glanced away from Toby's naked mother to the canvases of Toby's naked mother, and—since there didn't seem to be any available escape routes—back again. "Uh...yes...I know it's unorthodox, but I can assure you..." God, I sounded so desperately pompous. "The thing is, I really love him," I finished piteously.

She dropped the empty carton in the sink. Toby would hate that. "I had Toby when I was fifteen. Who am I to judge his choices?"

"Um, his mother?" I offered.

She gave me a look, proud and fierce and bright-eyed, and all of a sudden I saw Toby there. "Considering you're fucking my son, I don't think you get to tell me how to raise him."

God. I deserved that. "I'm sorry."

She shrugged. "My parents were bloody strict with me. Wouldn't let me do or say a damn thing I wanted. No way I was doing that to my own kid. Speaking of which, where did he go, if he's not with you?"

"I don't know," I wailed. "We had a...a...fight, and he ran away, and now he's not answering his phone."

"Oh, then he could be anywhere."

I stared at her. "Doesn't that worry you?"

"Not really? He's got a mobile, a credit card, a brain."

"So," I asked impatiently, "you have no idea where he might be?"

"Well, neither do you, so stop judging." She swept back to the canvas she was working on, which took up most of one wall, and gazed at it, her head tilted slightly quizzically to the side—something else that reminded me of Toby.

After a moment or two, when it became evident she wasn't going to say anything else, I tried, "Isn't there someone I could call or something? A friend? A family member?"

She glanced over her shoulder. "I can't tell if you're sweet or clingy."

The worst of it was, neither could I. "It was the first time we've argued quite like that."

"Yeah?"

She sounded profoundly uninterested, but I was terrified

and confused, so I told her anyway. "I just wanted to know why he was working at that horrible café instead of...doing something more suited to his talents and abilities."

"I always assumed he liked it."

"I...um...I'm not sure he does."

"Then he should stop." She picked up her brush again. "Now ☆ unless you want to be the man from Porlock, I'd like to finish this."

I had no idea what she was talking about, but I recognised dismissal, and my heart shed its last few hopes. "I'm sorry. Um... could you maybe tell him I stopped by? Or...ask him to... I don't know..."

"You should wait for him. As long as you wait quietly and stay out of my way."

"Really? I... Yes...thank you."

"Shh."

I put my hand over my mouth before an instinctive "sorry" could escape.

Coal's loft was mainly a space and a view. Spectacular, but I wasn't sure I would have been entirely comfortable living here. There was a tiny kitchen tucked into one corner, what looked like a portioned-off bathroom, and a curtain that I tentatively drew aside to reveal what must have been Toby's bedroom. I felt awkward for trespassing, but there wasn't really anywhere else I could go.

Toby's little bit of home was surprisingly austere: just a rack for his clothes, a futon to sleep on, a little bookcase stuffed mainly with poetry and cookery books, and a cuddly honey badger sitting on top of his pillow. The walls were haphazardly plastered with the accumulated passions of all his nineteen years. From the number of starscapes and earth rises and maps of the solar system, it seemed that once upon a time Toby might have wanted to be an astronaut. Or perhaps, from the dinosaur evolution charts and fossil guides, a palaeontologist. There was also a biodiversity poster of Western Australia's deep sea, a National Geographic spread of angelfish, and a cross section of a coral reef from what was presumably his marine biologist phase.

Oh, Toby. Toby.

Less easily classifiable were the cover art for the Penguin *Dorothy Parker*, a film still of Fred Astaire and Ginger Rogers I recognised from *Swing Time*, a concert poster for *Rufus Wainwright—5 Nights of Velvet, Glamour, and Guilt* at the Royal Opera House, and a Dr. Seuss verse: "Today you are You, that is truer than true. There is no one alive who is Youer than You." And finally what turned out to be a detail of Saint Sebastian from Titian's Averoldi Polyptych—something I only knew because it was written on the bottom of the print. It showed a particularly muscular and slightly wild St. Sebastian struggling with the arrows that pierced him.

I could see why he liked it.

I took off my shoes and sat cross-legged on Toby's futon, staring at the image and wondering if he had stared at it, dreaming of a man on his knees and yearning for the real thing. I reached into my pocket and checked my phone. No messages. No missed calls. Tried Toby again and got only his recorded voice while I sat in his empty room.

Time passed slowly. The sky through Toby's sloping window turned pearly grey.

Eventually I lay down. The pillow smelled of his hair product.

I thought maybe I could cry now, but I was afraid that might constitute a disturbance of his mother, so I cuddled his honey badger instead and waited for him to find me.

_____

I end up at Granddad's room before I remember it isn't his room anymore.

The door is slightly ajar, which is what stops me barging in on some strangers. It's like looking into Narnia or something. This unfamiliar world, full of wrong things, when I'd got used to it being his. Ours.

There's someone asleep in the bed. This frail, person-shaped outline, breathing too faint, too shallow. I recognise that fractured rhythm. It's the way you breathe when your body thinks every breath might be the last. And there's two women, hand in hand, waiting there, one of them dozing in an *oh fuck, your neck is going to hurt tomorrow* slump, and the other reading on a Kindle. She glances up, and I'm stuck standing there, feeling awkward and intrusive and creepy as fuck. I mouth *sorry* and she smiles, and I back away.

I wander the silent, shadowy corridors a bit and end up in the sunroom. It's empty, of course, since it's gone two. It's weird in there at night: surrounded by dark glass and the sheen of moonlight. I grope my way over to the chair I'd sat in when Granddad was having a super-good day. What with him dying during the winter, we'd never actually got much sun in here, but it was light and he liked being able to look at the garden. Not much to see there, either, to be honest. Dark soil and bits of green. And right now, nothing at all.

I take off my shoes and curl up.

My own reflection in the windows makes me look like a ghost.

I guess I fall asleep. I don't really remember, but the next thing I know there's a hand on my shoulder, shaking me gently awake.

"Wuzzat," I say. Someone's switched on a lamp and even

that's enough to dazzle me. Eventually though, I knuckle my eyes clear and discover Marwa—one of the nurses—leaning over me.

"What are you doing here?" It's a fair question and she doesn't ask it unkindly.

Unfortunately, I don't have an answer. "Um...I just... I..."

She doesn't say anything for a bit, and I wonder what I'll do if I get thrown out since the Tube isn't running and—as usual—I've got no money. But then she holds out a hand to help me out of the chair. "I was going to put the kettle on. Do you fancy a cuppa?"

I nod and follow her to the staff kitchen, and she makes me the sort of tea you're not supposed to like, all full of milk and sugar. Except I do like it. And even holding the mug feels good, my hands coming slowly to life in the warmth. Then we sit down at this rickety little table, and for what seems like ages we don't do anything. Just drink our tea in the quiet.

"Must feel strange," she says. "Not coming here every day."

I shrug. I hadn't come every day. Just most days. And it wasn't a chore.

She gives me this wicked little smile. "And what are we going to do without your cakes?"

I used to like her smile—she was Granddad's favourite—but now it just hurts in this unexpected way. I don't know what to do, how to handle it, and shrug again.

"I know you miss him."

There's part of me that wants to be all like, *Well duh.* Except that part's a dick. So I just nod. And then the words start squeezing out of me. "I do, I really do. He...he wasn't just my granddad, y'know? He was almost kind of...my dad, except I don't know what that would be like, so more kind of...my friend. Which is totally pathetic, but...it is what it is, and...I-I don't know what to do." Whoa. Breathing. I should try that.

She picks up my empty mug and takes it to the sink. Glances over her shoulder and tells me, "It'll get easier."

"What will?"

"Living, Toby."

I think of school. University. My moved-on friends. Laurie. And mumble, "I'm not very good at that."

"Well." I catch the edge of her smile as she turns back to the washing up. "You've got a lifetime to figure it out."

"I guess."

"It's good you stopped by, though. Most of your granddad's things have gone into storage, but there's a box I was wondering how to send to you."

Death: how to turn a life into pieces. Granddad is...in storage. In boxes. In an urn. On a memorial stone. Nowhere. "Thanks."

"You can wait in the staff room until morning."

I'm too tired and battered to put up any sort of fight. I let her lead me off and tuck me up on a sofa.

She pushes the hair out of my eyes. "Don't take this the wrong ☆ way, Toby, but I don't want to see you here again."

I just yawn. It feels wrong and empty and scary, but she's right, of course. There's nothing for me here.

I don't really sleep. I more sort of drift through a couple of hours, vaguely aware of people trying very hard not to disturb me. Every now and again I sneak my hand out of the blanket and let my fingers brush the edges of the box Marwa left beside me.

I peek inside the next morning when I'm on the Tube heading back to Shoreditch. It's very neatly packed, lots of stacked papers and smaller boxes. I rummage a little, and then I see:

Frogs
Leaping in and out—

And I feel this...crack, right in my heart. For a moment, I can't breathe. But then I can. And I realise my heart is okay.

It always was.

☆   Because love is strong. Stronger than death.

Mum's out when I get back, but she's definitely been working. You can tell from the carnage—the paint and the empty bottles. The half-finished canvas of...actually, I'm not going to look at it too closely. I think about tidying up, but the urge to fall face-first into my pillow is too great.

I pull back the curtain and have an epic Three Bears moment—assuming the three bears screamed camply and threw their shit on the ground—because there's someone sleeping in my bed.

"Oh God." Laurie sits up so suddenly he nearly hits his head on the eaves.

"Jesus, Laurie. You nearly gave me a coronary."

There's papers everywhere. And I'm so knackered that it takes a moment before it hits me.

Laurie. Laurie's here. In my room.

Waiting.

For me?

I stare at him. Just stunned. "W-what are you doing here?"

☆   Laurie rolls off my bed and stands carefully. My corner of the loft isn't massively welcoming to the less sizeably challenged gentleman. He looks tired. Worried. Gorgeous. "You know what I'm doing here."

"Um..." I'm not ready to start hoping again for nothing. "I might need you to tell me."

He reaches into his pocket and pulls out the key I threw at

him yesterday. Takes my hand and folds my fingers round it. "I think you dropped this."

"Did I?"

"Yes."

I have to look up to meet his eyes. His gaze is so steady, so certain, I almost start crying. I don't know why being on the brink of—maybe—getting everything I've ever wanted should be bad, but my stomach is so fizzy I'm afraid I might be sick.

"I've made a lot of mistakes," he tells me. "I tried to provide solutions when I should have listened. And let things go when I should have fought."

"'S'okay." I shrug. "I didn't really want you to know what a loser I am."

"You're not a loser, Toby. You're just lost. And it's okay to be lost."

I try to laugh, but it comes out shaky and weird. "It doesn't feel okay. Feels fucking awful."

He reaches for me, his hand closing over mine where I'm still holding his key. "Then we'll be lost together, and we'll figure it out together. Whatever that means. Whatever it takes. I'm with you, and I'll be with you for as long as you want me."

God. After everything, he still doesn't fucking get it. This bullshit isn't what I want at all. I don't want to be his project. I don't want him to take care of me. I want us to take care of each other. "That's, err, mighty charitable of you, but—"

"I'm not finished."

I pull on my hand. "Well, I think I am. Like I told you yesterday."

"For fuck's sake." Something flares in his eyes. A kind of savagery that I shouldn't like. But it reminds me of when I first saw him, so distant and cold and desperate. Like he was waiting to be tamed. To be mine. Not this patient grown-up person who wants to fix my fucked-up life. "This isn't charity."

And he goes to his knees.

Hands behind his back like the very first time.

I make this embarrassing choking sound. Because he's so perfect like that, and—even tired and sad and confused and messed up—I want him so badly it burns. But I don't know what it means that he's giving this to me now. Maybe he's telling me it's all he *can* give, and, yeah, I guess the last time he offered, it was all I knew how to want. But I'm done with working with what I've got. "Laurie, I—"

"This isn't submission."

"Isn't it?"

"No." He looks up at me, tired as well, but he's never looked more beautiful to me than in this moment, strong and open and unafraid like when he surrenders his body. "It's love."

———

It took Toby such a long time to respond. He was naturally such a graceless, restless boy that there was always something a little terrifying in his stillness. No more so than now.

When he'd first arrived—so pale and fragile in the thin morning light—there'd been no time for anything but reaction. But now that I was capable of thought, I was beginning to wonder if everything I'd done had been in any way...sensible. If it was too much. If it was what he wanted. If he would understand. Or if all I had done—running across London, waiting in his room, throwing myself at him like this—was play the fool.

But what did it matter? Some actions were worth their consequences, whatever those consequences might be. And of everything that had ever been spoken or written about love, I couldn't

remember a single occasion on which it had been described as
sensible.

I tried again, offering myself to him, without shame or hesitation, in the simplest, purest terms I knew. "I love you."

Toby drew in a breath so deep and shuddering it made
his whole body shake. And then he was in my lap, his wet face
pressed against my neck, his arms twined about me as tight as
ivy. "Really? Oh my God, really? You love me?"

He was all edges and angles, but I gathered him up and
held him close. "Yes. For a long time now. At least since Oxford.
Probably before."

He pulled back a little and managed a faint, teary grin. "From
the first moment you saw me, right?"

"It seems unlikely, darling. You were far too young and very
rude."

"Must have been my magnificent grounds at Pemberley,
then. Oh God..." His laughter vanished swiftly, and I regretted
it, the shadows settling in his eyes afresh. "Laurie, are you sure?
Like really sure? You've seen...well...you've seen my life. Is this
honestly what you want?"

"I want you. Who you are. Not what you do or don't do."

He made a soft sound, almost a sob, and the relief in it pierced
me with fresh guilt. But then he twisted his fingers possessively
in my hair and mumbled, "Thank you," and happiness swept
through me like summer heat.

"For what?" I couldn't resist asking.

He laughed, but when he spoke, his voice was steady, his
expression utterly serious. "For getting me."

It was becoming uncomfortable on the floor, whatever the
pleasures of being entangled with Toby. I made him stand and
tugged him over to the bed with me. Even that small parting

seemed to unsettle him, and as soon as we were seated, he curled into my side with a muffled sigh.

"But, Toby?"

A very small voice: "Yes?"

"You have to talk to me. You have to trust me."

"Isn't that my line?"

"Not anymore." I turned him gently. Wiped his tears and brushed the hair out of his eyes. "I mean it. You'll never have to wait for me again. And when I ask about your life, I'm not trying to be your parent or your friend or your careers advisor. I'm asking as your...boyfriend, lover, partner, the man who wants to be fucking you, the man who loves you."

"I just thought you wouldn't want to be any of those things if you knew what a mess I'd made of everything."

Some part of me was faintly irritated that some part of him thought I was such an utter monster. But then I had spent the last three months finding any excuse to push him away and hold him at bay, so perhaps I deserved it. And it was something I could only heal with time, with devotion, with unfettered love. For now, I kissed the damp tip of his nose. "That's because you're an idiot."

He scowled, but his eyes betrayed him. There was amusement there and hope. And after a moment, he pushed me onto my back, climbed on top, and kissed me so hard he ground my lips against my teeth. But I didn't care. The pain was beautiful, welcome, because it came from Toby. And we kissed for a long time, deeply and far too intimately on his childhood bed.

Afterwards he tucked his head against my shoulder again. "Um...Laurie...?"

"Yes?"

"You know that stuff you were saying about it being okay to be lost?" He tilted his face up to mine, his eyes as wide and blue as the sky beyond his window. "Did you mean it? You'll really help me figure this shit out?"

"I promise."

"Like...you really want to do that with me?"

"Yes. I want everything."

For some reason that made him smile. "Even the rubbish stuff?"

"Everything." I kicked his ankle gently. "But no more of that. That's my boyfriend you're talking about."

He rolled onto his stomach, watching me lazily from beneath his lashes. "Good point. Someone as awesome as you would never date someone rubbish."

"You said it, Junior."

We lay for a while in each other's arms, warm and quiet, and I came perilously close to falling asleep. Which, in turn, reminded me of something I had meant to ask. "Where were you last night?"

"Oh...uh. I kind of went to the hospice."

"You what?"

"I know. It was daft." He sighed. "But at least I picked up some of Granddad's stuff. I mean, before I threw it all over the floor."

"Sorry. I take it you didn't expect to find me here?"

"Hell no, but feel free to do it again. Whenever you like."

I gave him a slightly wry look. "How about the next time we argue, you just make me sleep on the sofa like a normal person?"

"How about we don't argue?"

"Oh darling, all couples argue. It's how you handle it that matters." He didn't seem entirely reassured, so I went on. "We'll figure it out."

He snuck his hand into mine. "Okay. But I can't imagine ever wanting you to sleep on the sofa."

I nearly said, *Give it time*. But love held my tongue.

After all, what harm did it do to believe him?

"What did you bring home?" I asked instead.

"Oh, um, mostly it's his medals and crap I made for him." His eyes skittered shyly away from mine. "Uh...I could...I could show you, if you want?"

"Of course I do."

We sat on the floor together so that Toby could gather up everything that had fallen and put it carefully back into the box. Sometimes he would pause over something or other to explain it to me, letting me hold, for a little while, these treasured pieces of his life he had once shared with someone else he loved.

12
TOBY

It's a couple of days before I find the courage to go back to Greasy Joe's. I'm expecting it to be carnage, like it was the last time I wasn't there, but I arrive in the middle of the afternoon lull and it's pretty quiet. I can even smell baking coming from the kitchen. It can't be Hairy, because he's in the caff itself, with his foot up on one of the chairs, so it's probably Luigi.

There's a few regulars around and Ruby hovering by the big kettle. And Greasy Joe, who's chatting to Hairy. He's wearing an honest-to-God apron, and holding an actual motherfucking coffeepot.

Holy shit. I'm dead.

I've never seen him do that...like, ever.

When I sidle over, he turns death-ray eyes on me.

"Um." My voice has reached the sort of pitch usually only registered by dogs. I cough. "Can I have a word?"

He huffs out this gale-force sigh and makes a show of checking a nonexistent watch. "What the fuck day do you call this?"

"The wrong day, but—"

"Then get in the fucking kitchen, and we'll hear no more about it."

I think of Granddad. And Laurie. And me. I think about me.

And what I want. What I deserve. I've got down from canine to castrato as I force the words out. "My granddad's dead. I'm entitled to unpaid compassionate leave...so...so...I'm taking it."

Greasy Joe inflates like a puffer fish. He's already a big man, so it's fucking awful. "If you don't do your fucking job, there won't be a fucking job for you to do."

There.

Everything I've been scared of. And actually, it's not so bad. All that's happening is I'm losing a shitty job. And Laurie's right. I can get another one.

Or...I can try to get a different job. One that isn't shitty. Or I can be Laurie's live-in cabana boy. Or whatever. The point is... the point is...the future is terrifying because it's full of stuff, not because it's empty.

I dig my nails into my palms. What I mean to say is something dignified and professional about accepting those terms and consequently tendering my resignation. What comes out of my mouth is, "Oh, go fuck yourself."

I'm in the process of sweeping out of there, not that I'm a natural-born sweeper, when the applause starts. I spin round, and the whole caff is clapping for me. Greasy Joe too.

He comes after me, and I think he's going to punch me in the face or something, but he just claps me on the shoulder—nearly dislocating it. "Take your fucking leave, son. You'll always have a job here."

"Then—" My head is spinning. It must be adrenaline. "I think you could do a bit better than £5.03 an hour."

He laughs this crazy Tim Curry laugh. "Don't push your luck."

I get out of there, texting Laurie with trembling fingers to tell him I'll be back soon.

I still can't quite believe how easy that was. How simple.

Greasy Joe got it wrong, though. I'm starting to think you should always push your luck. *No*, you can deal with. *Don't know* is the most frightening thing of all.

When I get back to Laurie's, I babble the whole story. I don't lie, but maybe I make myself a bit bolder and a bit less squeaky. I can tell he's proud of me. Hell, I'm proud of me. When I'm done talking, he drops to his knees and gives me a celebratory blowjob. And I don't just feel like a prince. I feel like a fucking king.

––––––––

It's a good week. Just me and Laurie. Together. In love.

We do have another argument. He gets sick of my pants on the floor, so he gives me a drawer—a fucking drawer, like this is supposed to be enough. I don't make him sleep on the sofa though, and the next day he offers me a room.

Like a whole room. In his home. Just for me. He says I can do whatever I like with it. Make it my own space. I take the Bluebeard room, of course. The light up there is beautiful, and Laurie's mine now.

But basically, things are good. So good I sometimes feel guilty for falling so easily into happiness. We watch black and white movies and have all the sex and eat takeaway every night, and talk about...everything.

And when I'm ready, we talk about me.

I tell him how I wanted to be an astronaut, then a palaeontologist, then a marine biologist, then a spy, then an explorer, then an artist, then a poet. About how I had so many dreams, and they all just went away, one by one, until there was only me left.

It's kind of a relief, in a way, to get that out there.

But I'm also terrified because this trusting-people shit is

hard. It's this naked feeling like when he kneels for me, and part of me can't quite believe it's me he wants. Still wants.

The reality of me.

He tells me how being a doctor wasn't his dream, either. How his parents put a lot of pressure on him to live a certain kind of life and be a certain kind of man, which is an odd thing to learn about him, since I have sort of the opposite problem. It's one of those moments when I realise that the gaps between people ☆ are always less than you'd imagine. Though I've honestly been hoping there comes a point in your life when you stop worrying about what your parents think.

"So, you see," he says, "my career was just something to work towards to please my parents. And now it's just something I'm good at and helps me be...useful."

"But are you happy?"

He gives me this smile. "Deeply."

When he puts it like that, in his straightforward way, it doesn't seem so terrible a way to live. We can't all be my mum, after all.

I'm not sure I've ever wanted to be. I just wasn't sure if there was an alternative.

My mum's never really cared what I've done—to her there's art, and there's everything else. No difference between a lawyer or public lavatory attendant.

Laurie does care, but only because I care. And it turns out that's just the right type of caring. The truth is, he'd probably be okay if I just kind of...lived with him. But I'm not the househusband type. I want my own life, whatever that means, and Laurie understands, and we spend ages trying to figure out what that might look like.

I've never had someone to do that with me before. I've always just been trying to figure it out by looking at what other people were doing and hoping nobody noticed I was just miming.

We come back to the cooking a lot. The restaurant and the Michelin star. I don't know how or when it happens, but somehow—just by loving me and believing in me—Laurie nurtures this little flame inside me until it remembers how to burn on its own. I get that cooking is a tough thing to make a career out of—long hours and hard labour—but it's still the thing I love most in the world.

After Laurie and Granddad, of course.

Laurie disappears onto the internet and comes back with lists and lists of catering colleges, some of them in Paris, for fuck's sake. He tells me I shouldn't be curtailing my life to be close to him, and if this is what I really want to do, he'll wait for me. But I don't want to go to Paris. It's full of French people. That's a joke. Well, kinda. But *mon français est très mal.*

And, besides, I've seriously had it with school and all that hoop-jumping learning. Whatever Laurie thinks, it's not for me. I'm not getting another D because I quenelle with my left hand, not my right. So that's out.

I do some internetting of my own, and it turns out if you're willing to start at the bottom, the staff turnover in kitchens is so ridiculously high that somebody will probably take you if you ask them nicely. It's a fucking terrifying idea, but Laurie thinks I'm brilliant. We make this list of all the places I like best in a reasonable commuting distance, and then I bottle it for a while.

Laurie doesn't push me. In a strange way, that's what gives me courage.

So, one day, while he's sleeping, I ring the first restaurant on the list. They don't have any openings, but they don't treat me like I'm insane for asking, so I don't immediately die of despair. It doesn't happen at the second restaurant either, or the fifth, but I get through to the chef of the eleventh (it's the place Laurie took me a week ago), and she asks me a bunch of questions about who I am, and what I want, how much experience I have, and when I can start. I kind of babble, but it seems she really likes the answer "Whenever" to the last question, and she ends up asking me to come in the very next day for a chat—and suddenly, I have a job.

Like a bottom-of-the-ladder job, with a salary to match, but Melissa Lake—that's my *boss*, who has a Michelin star—thinks I've got potential. Or maybe she's just saying that so I'll wash dishes and sweep floors and peel potatoes, but who cares?

I've got a job. And potential.

Laurie's so happy for me, he wants to take me out to dinner again. But I just tell him to take me to bed.

Once we're both naked—something we accomplish in about two seconds of desperate handsy tugging—I shove him down and straddle him.

Mine, mine, mine.

I run my fingers down the line of his throat, hearing his breath hitch as I go. He tips his head back, offering himself, and this hot thrill of possession goes through me as I close my hand around his neck just like that very first night. I'm not ready to do anything super hardcore, but I think we both like the idea that I could. His hand comes up, takes my wrist, and he guides me so my thumb and first fingers settle on either side of his neck, against...I guess...the artery. I feel his pulse so strong here it's like I'm holding his heart in my hand. It gets me hard as fuck, and kind of tender at the same time, and the rush of his blood is this red rush of power all through me.

"Toby?" I feel my name in his throat under my palm. "Yeah?"

"Would you... Do you think... Would you like to flog me?" His pulse jumps. "Please."

I totally fail to play it cool. "Oh hell yeah."

I let him go, and we sit up in bed, and I'm kind of fluttery and nervous and excited in this first kiss, fairy tale way, and Laurie is a little bit flushed as well, so we're kind of shy suddenly. Then I say, "Um, so—" at the same time he says, "How do you—" so we stop and go "No, after you," and then we both start talking again, and I say, "What's the best—" and he says, "Shall I—" and then it's such a mess that there's only one thing left to do, and that's laugh.

Once that's over, we eye each other cautiously.

"Well, that was..." I say.

"It was," he agrees.

"I really want to do this." Like my ridiculous hard-on isn't giving the game away a bit, but after the party, I want to make sure he knows this is for me and for him and for both of us. And fuck anybody else.

His eyes have gone all smouldery, smoky grey and hazy gold, like when he's on his knees, or when he's fucking me. "I know."

"So, how do we do... What's best?"

"I used to have...um...furniture, but not anymore. Lying, standing, or kneeling covers most of the basics. And it depends if you want to"—his flush deepened—"restrain me."

"Do I need to?"

"I can be still, if you want."

I grin. The thing is, I like tying him up. The question is...how and to what? And then I remember the hooks in the bed frame, and I know exactly what I'm doing. I tell him not to go anywhere, because I'm a dork, and go grab stuff from...*my room*.

I've got the deerskin flogger, and there's a few more in the magic chest, but since Robert left them behind, they're probably not favourites. Also, I'm kind of limited by which ones aren't going to knock me off-balance. There's one, but the tails are rubber and even throwing them against the air feels whippy and scary, so I pass. There's also a single-tail coiled up like an adder, but I'm like, *Fuck no.*

Then I find...I don't know...I think it must be horsehair. It's really beautiful—this shining white-blond fall that feels both silky and rough against my fingers. The handle is smooth wood, just as shiny and fits my hand, warming against my palm, like it's saying, *Meant to be here.* It's so light, but when I swing, fuck, those strands pack a wallop.

I practice a bit until I'm pretty sure I'm comfortable. It's weird because it's totally different to the deerskin flogger, but it's like my brain has learned how to compensate without me. I'm not really thinking at all, just letting my wrist do its thing.

I also whack my own thigh a bunch of times. Not quite as hard as I can go, but less than half as hard as I can go is making me yelpy and eye-watery. It's heavy and sharp at the same time. I guess that's what they call "sting."

So I take that, the deerskin, some cuffs and snap hooks because my ropework—even with *The Boy Scout Knot Book*—is arse. And let's face it, it's probably always going to be arse. I recognise it's an art, and it's a perfectly reasonable thing to be into, but when I want Laurie tied up, I want him tied up and fuck faffing around.

In the bedroom, Laurie is waiting patiently, sprawled out on the covers, all strong and leonine and hurtable. He springs up as soon as I come in, his eyes lingering on my kinky swag.

I put everything down on the chest of drawers out of his way. Maybe I should have blindfolded him... Actually, maybe I *should* blindfold him. He's scared of it (which, naturally, I like), and it makes him all raw and open and frantic.

That gives me an idea. But first things first.

"So...I thought you could maybe stand at the bottom of the bed and hold on to the frame?"

He hesitates. Always, he hesitates. And then he nods and obeys, stretching himself between the bedposts like Samson.

He looks...perfect. I spend a minute just kind of climbing him with my eyes, up his calves and thighs, knotty muscles and rough dark hair, over his gorgeous, gorgeous arse, which is kind of this smooth, gleaming curve, and then there's his back, which is all these stark and powerful, pristine planes...and also sort of towering above me.

Shit. All my walls and pillows have been basically me-height. Shit.

I'm an idiot.

"So..." I try to keep my voice exactly the same as it was the first time. "I thought you could maybe *kneel* at the bottom of the bed and hold on to the frame."

I can't see his face, but somehow I know he's trying not to smile. Something to do with the pull of his shoulders, I think. And I'm smiling too, even though he can't see that either.

He goes to his knees in that graceful way of his, like he belongs on them, just while we're like this, and I crouch next to him, and fasten the cuffs on his wrists. I make a bit of a ceremony of it because I...can, I guess, stroking my thumbs over the skin first, kissing the long vein. It makes him shiver, just these small touches, and the leather closing round him.

I do the other side and clip the cuffs to the hooks set into the bed frame—and there he is with his arms outstretched, all sacrificial and magnificent and so clearly turned on by it. I slip my hand between his legs and idly palm his cock, forcing a little moan out of him.

Then I let him go, and that's a kind of power too, all the ways—and things—I can make him want. It's like love, this power—surprising, endless, warm. It makes me dizzy and soft inside. (Not outside, obviously. Outside, it does the exact opposite.)

Cock first, I head back to the chest of drawers. I don't know if this is normal, but Laurie keeps his ties in there, all snarled up together with his socks. I thought you were supposed to have a special rack or something, but Laurie's ties are crap anyway. They're mainly blue and grey and crumply; ties that say, *I'm only wearing this because it's, like, required by my job or whatever, and given the choice I'd rather be naked at my boyfriend's feet.* Err, well, maybe not the second bit. I'm looking for the one he was wearing the night I forced myself back into his life and he...with his tongue. God, even thinking about it makes me all hot and embarrassed and fucking thrilled.

☆ Anyway, I can't find it because all his ties suck, so I just grab one and go back to him. He tilts his head back, just a little bit, to help me slip it over his eyes. I like his hesitations and his struggles, but I like this too—this trust that's effortless sometimes. Surrender that slips through him like light. He gives this soft, soft sigh as the darkness takes him, and he bows his head.

I put my palm flat against the space between his shoulders, feeling the heat of him, the strength, the way those big muscles are held wide for me. He's not tense, but he's not relaxed either—it's something else, something more like readiness, or openness, as if his body is a door to some deep, lonely part of me, which I guess is whatever it is in me that wants to cause pain to the man I love.

Except with Laurie, I don't even have to give myself the side-eye. He understands and makes it okay.

He makes what I have to give beautiful.

I pick up the deerskin flogger and dance the tips of the falls over his shoulders. It's a caress, pure and simple, a kiss from closed lips. I don't even have to think about it much. I know where the tails are going to go and they do. My hands are a bit sweaty, but they're steady, and I'm not afraid. He trusts me, so I trust me.

The thing that kind of shakes me a bit is not so much what I'm doing—or the ways I could fuck it up—but all possibilities of it and in it. Like when his body is stretched out over me or under me and the ways of touching each other are...forever. This is the same, except I've got a flogger to be my hands and my teeth. I keep my wrist loose and twirl the thing a few times, just getting sure of myself. And then I–I...do it. I hit him. I hit a person. I hit... ☆ Laurie. Gently, because we're warming up, but I'm still hitting him, over and over again with these underarm strokes that fan the tails across his back as they fall.

And it's weird because it doesn't feel wrong at all. It feels... amazing. I kind of live in those strokes, in the rhythms of them, and the soft sound of leather against skin. It's its own universe somehow, this cycle of reaction, reaction, reaction, him and me, flogger and him, flogger and me, all connected. The best thing, though, is when the falls land, the impact travels all the way from his body to mine, through the leather, then the handle, through my arm and to my heart. We're so...together.

At first I don't think I'm really doing anything, but then these pinkish lines rise to the surface of his skin, and then they stop fading away, and then his whole upper back is flushed. And, okay, it's not a big deal, but I did that. I put myself all over him, and I'm there in all that warmed skin.

And I want...to do it more.

"How... What's it like?" I ask.

Because I want to know everything. I want to touch him in all the ways.

"Warm." His voice is rough but intent somehow. "You."

Not exactly coherent, but it's all the answer I need.

I switch to figure eights. Even with one hand, I'm not as good as Robert, but there's still a rhythm here—two firm strikes, one left, one right—and the moment the first one lands with this glorious *smack*, Laurie chokes out this sound of pure, ragged longing. And fuck, I just love his noises. I think it's because he's a quiet man, really. Not like in the obvious way of not speaking much, or speaking softly, but in the way he is. All these still places in his soul that he disturbs for me.

When we're together, I collect his groans and whimpers, his muffled cries and the ones he can't muffle. I fucking cherish them. This is all new, though, the way he is beneath my flogger, and that first little noise he makes is like the first time he put his mouth on my cock. Leaves me full of this sweet, shuddery joy and something darker, something that wants to make him struggle and hurt and yield.

I hit him harder, the same spots, over and over again, putting my arm into the blows as well as my wrist, until the flush deepens, gleaming under a patina of gathering sweat. I'm sweating too, and my breath is coming a bit hard. It's partly excitement and partly that this is...demanding, in the same way sex is demanding: blunt physical effort muddled up with pleasure and intimacy and the closeness of being against and inside someone, of *sharing* something.

Laurie murmurs a sound like *yes*.

My confidence is flying with the tails now, so I can sort of vary what I'm doing. I've been performing my steps like a dancer—to a pattern—but now I guess I'm free-forming. I nestle my harder blows in with softer ones, claiming all that gorgeous expanse of glowing skin in all the ways I can throw a flogger. I jolt him sometimes with the force behind my strikes, but he doesn't try to twist away from them. Just gives me some naked sounds—a little bit shocked, a little bit hurt, a little bit blissful—and takes the next one. And the next.

His breathing is edged with groans when I stop and swap to the horsehair thing. Its lightness is kind of a surprise, as I swing my whole arm in a circle above my head, keeping the tails from wrapping round the handle. And then I throw the tips against his back with all my strength and anything gravity can give me.

It makes a completely different sound: soft and swift, rustling like sharp-winged birds flying past me.

And...Laurie...God...he kind of screams, not exactly pain, just the suddenness, I think, of a new sensation, and while he's lost in that moment, I cover his upper back and shoulders with all these stinging little flicks, watching the impact points flare and vanish like a trail of comets against a red sky. Laurie's moving now, not in a way that throws me off, but sort of into me and into my strokes, so we're one, our breath harsh and mingling with the scratchy whisper of horsehair on skin and Laurie's occasional frantic moan.

I *love* this. I fucking love it. I love that I'm hurting him, and I love him.

I'm gasping and sweaty and my heart is thundering and I'm not sure if I'm going to come or laugh or cry or...or...what.

I turn my body sideways, gather up the tails, and fling the flogger at him with everything I've got, sending them crashing into him like handfuls of needles. He jerks and cries out, sounding so powerful and powerless at the same time, this chained-up man who is taking pain for me, who isn't afraid to be weak for me or ashamed to be afraid. The bravest, strongest, most beautiful man I've ever met.

And then I'm throwing the flogger aside, and I'm wrapping myself around him, pressing myself against all the hot, hurt places I've left on his body, and he's, "Oh God, yes, Toby, touch me, please," so desperately that I only really hear because it's what I'm thinking too. And I kiss him and bite him and tear at him with my fingernails, and I'm sort of actually really crying, but it's good crying somehow, and makes Laurie hiss when I spill salt all over his abraded skin. But he's still leaning into me, still arching to my touch, still answering my tangle of snarls and sobs with "please" and "yes" and "Toby."

It's crazy because even though I'm crying everywhere, I'm not sad. There's just all this feeling pouring out of me, but it's wild and fierce and rapturous, like I've been waiting for it my whole life and everything makes sense now. And it's not that I'm complete, or some shit like that, because I always was, but there's a bunch of pieces of me that fit together in a way they didn't before.

With Laurie. Because of Laurie.

The urge to have him and take him and revel in all the ways he's mine is clawing me to shreds from the inside out.

Shakily I unclip the cuffs. Concern for his knees and his arms kind of vaguely flits across my brain, but I don't think he's been there long, and when I tell him, "Up," he lets me use his own weight to pull him and shove him over the bed. There's no resistance in him, no struggle, he doesn't even put his hands out to protect himself—just falls, surrendered, blind and helpless, his upper back this blazing testimony to all my love and savagery.

"Don't move."

My cock feels like it's going to explode if I touch it, but I somehow manage to slaver myself in lube.

I don't do Laurie, though. I want *this* to hurt a little bit too. I want him to carry it with him, like the marks on his skin. I want to give him this gift. Because with him I can be fearless too.

I kick his legs wider—which makes him groan in some muffled mixture of eagerness and shame—but I don't touch him. Not yet.

He shifts a little against the bed, pushing his hips up, so I catch a glimpse of his tightly drawn-up balls, the shadow of his eager cock. "Please?" he tries, a little hesitantly.

I love it when he begs, but it's not what I want. I lean over him, shoving our bodies together, and rub myself over his back until he gasps and writhes. I put my lips to his ear, and I whisper, "Spread yourself for me, and I'll fuck you."

And then I stand again and wait, shuddering with lust and ☆ power, cruelty and love, tears drying on my face and sweat on my back.

Laurie makes a mortified little noise and hesitates for a long moment, though I have no doubt he'll do it, no doubt at all. Then reaches back his hands and pulls himself open—exposed, vulnerable, inexpressibly needy, and completely beautiful. I last about a cool, controlled nanosecond before I slam into him like a really short, skinny juggernaut showing serious commitment to getting into some guy's arse.

It's... Well...I make it. There's a moment when I think I might not, but Laurie kind of lets out this sharp, pained breath, and suddenly, fuck, he yields, and I'm in. He's tight, but there's enough lube that I don't think I'm going to actually do any damage. I like the charade of violence, the pretence that I could actually overpower him, his flogged and hurting body forced into subjugation by mine.

I push his hands out of the way and pull his hips back to meet my thrusts. He claws at the bed, as a kind of instinctive reaction to loss of physical control, but I'm in him deep by then and I sort of know how to do this now. His body goes pliant when the pleasure hits, and the sound he makes is one for my trophy cabinet: ecstasy and relief and gratitude and submission.

I dig my fingers into his flanks, and I fuck him like I've never fucked anyone. I wouldn't have dared. But the marks I've left on his skin are singing to me, urging me to use him, and take him, and bring us together like that again. The less care I seem to show, the more Laurie responds, twisting under me, crying out with helpless passion for every harsh thrust I give him.

It *is* like flogging. Rhythms and patterns and control, and the sheer power of having someone respond the way Laurie responds to me. Everything we give and take from each other in those moments of pure and perfect connection. I know how to take him to the brink and how to pull him back, how to please myself and deny him, until he's practically weeping with longing, begging me to touch him, to fuck him, to let him come. And when I don't, when I'm cruel, he wails and protests and loves me even more. And I'm humbled and honoured and touched and so fucking happy he can find this thing in me to love.

I want to be like this forever, but it's too much for me: the pleasure and the power and Laurie being Laurie. So utterly gorgeous when he's all undone, no control or pride left, stripped back to nothing but this. Because beyond shame, fear, and vulnerability, there's only true things: sex and love and us.

I fall over his back, still buried deep inside him, and sink my teeth into his shoulder, into all that red and tender skin. It's not... planned.

Because all I'm thinking is *mine*.

And Laurie bucks up, into my bite, against my body, and comes with a hoarse, wild cry, just from my teeth and my touch and my cock.

I almost come too, but with some world-record-type effort of will, and probably some serious internal damage to my bollocks, I hold off. Instead I pull out of him as carefully as I can. I barely need to touch myself—just the sight of him lying there in a shuddering heap, hurt and fucked, and covered in all the ways I've had him, is enough. I spray myself across his back, white over red, and Laurie takes that too, with the same grace, the same generosity, the same courage and eagerness he takes everything I give him: my cock, my cruelty, my kisses. Me.

I just about manage not to fall on top of him and ruin my handiwork. I land on my side next to him, and he lies where I've left him, as though I've still got him in chains, his body heaving a little with the aftermath of everything we've just done. Reaching over, I push the tie out of his way, and he emerges, blinking and wet-eyed.

"Oh, Toby," is the first thing he says, with his voice still rough from all the noise he's been making. "You've been crying."

I'd sort of almost forgotten I'd done that, and swipe at my face with my elbow, feeling like an idiot. Because who cries when they're flogging someone else?

Laurie eases himself up a bit gingerly, rolls over, and then pulls me against his chest. I'm about to protest that I'm fine, I don't need him to look after me, but the moment his arms enfold me, it's like I'm trying to climb inside his skin.

"Darling," he murmurs. "Darling."

He calls me darling like eighty times and holds me really tight, and I nearly cry again, but thankfully I don't.

"It was just...really good," is the best explanation I can give him.

But it doesn't matter. I know he understands.

The rest of our holiday kind of gets away from us, and we don't really do anything except be together, but that's okay. We talk a bit about going away, but in the end we don't.

There's plenty of time for that stuff, and all I want is to be with Laurie in a place we both call home.

That last Sunday, the day before I'm meant to start work, and he's due to go back, he tells me he's got a surprise for me. I guess I've been pretty love-spoiled over the past couple of weeks, but we deserve this, Laurie and me. He's sleek with happiness, somehow, like the man I fell in love with lives on the surface now, not hidden deep inside, and it blows my mind to think that's for me and because of me.

It's this crystal-bright day, when it feels like winter is cracking like an egg and spring is spilling everywhere.

We get on the Tube to South Kensington, and Laurie still won't tell me where we're going, but he's excitable like a little kid, so I don't mind. I like him like this. I like all his secrets, innocent and not-so-innocent.

It turns out he's taking me to the Chelsea Physic Garden, which wasn't one of Granddad's places, though maybe it should have been because I learn it's the oldest botanical garden in London, founded way back when for trainee apothecaries.

It's closed during winter, but it's open on special occasions, and this is one of them.

Laurie says it's called a Snowdrop Day.

And I can see why. The woods are so thick with tiny white flowers that it genuinely looks like snowdrifts. I've never seen so many, and they shine in the fresh-made sun.

I've cried a lot recently, mainly for myself, but this is the first time I've really cried for Granddad.

We sit under a tree, and Laurie holds me, and it's not so grim.

Because, at last, all the bad stuff—the fear and the anger and the pain and the guilt—is gone, and this is just grief stripped of everything but love. And I'm okay to cry for love.

I really am.

When I'm out of tears, I kiss Laurie and thank him, and I tell him how in love with him I am.

"I love you too," he says, so easily it's hard to believe he used to freak out at the very idea of it. "You make me very happy."

I smile up at him. I'm so proud that I can do this. That I can make a man like Laurence Dalziel happy. "I intend to do it for a long time."

I guess that's kind of the wrong thing to say because he frowns. "Toby, I don't have...expectations."

"Oh man, don't start that crap again. Not in the middle of our totally romantic day, which I've already cried in."

He colours a bit and laughs, but the shadow is still in his eyes. "I just mean...Toby, you're nineteen, I'm thirty-seven. We fit each other now, but the time might come when we don't. When you're thirty, I'll be nearly fifty." I'm about to cut him down with a scornful "So?" because, honestly, I don't want to love anyone except Laurie, but he goes on before I have a chance. "Our perceptions of time and distance aren't consistent. Sometimes the gap between us will seem nothing, sometimes it'll seem enormous. The day might come when we don't know how to bridge it."

Sometimes, for a clever man who's supposed to be older and wiser than me, he's kind of a doofus. "That's just relationships, Laurie. They aren't consistent either. You found a gap you couldn't bridge with Robert, and that had nothing to do with what age you were."

"I suppose, but—"

"Maybe the day will come when you cheat on me or—"

"I will *never* cheat on you."

"Okay, okay." I scramble to my feet and brush the soil off my arse. "Maybe the day will come when you go off my lemon meringue pie or decide my feet smell or find my insecurities annoying instead of adorable. Point is...let's worry about it when it happens."

He smiles up at me, squinting through the sun dapple. "I can't imagine any of those days."

"Neither can I, so let's just be in love today."

"All right." He rises from the ground, with all that grace and power he doesn't hesitate to lay at my feet for the asking.

Everywhere around us the world is green and white and gold and waiting.

I hold out my hand, and he takes it, and we walk together into the spring.

BONUS MATERIAL

Enjoy both beloved and brand-new behind-the-scenes material as Alexis Hall takes you on a tour of the world of *For Real*, including:

Toby's Kinky Lemon Meringue Pie
A Note of Acknowledgement
Author Annotations
"In Vino"

Toby and Laurie will return for their aftermath in a future title.

TOBY'S KINKY LEMON MERINGUE PIE

Makes: 12 servings

Time: Approximately 2 hours plus chilling [and shagging] time

Ingredients

Crust

1¼ cups all-purpose flour

1 tablespoon sugar

½ teaspoon salt

6 tablespoons unsalted butter, chilled and cut into ½-inch
  pieces

¼ cup shortening, chilled and cut into ½-inch pieces

2 tablespoons vodka, chilled

2 tablespoons water, chilled

Lemon Filling

⅓ cup cornstarch

¼ cup granulated sugar

⅛ teaspoon salt

1½ cups water

½ cup lemon juice, strained from 2 lemons

2 teaspoons lemon zest from 2 lemons

4 large egg yolks

2 tablespoons unsalted butter, cut into ½-inch pieces

Meringue

    4 large egg whites

    ½ cup granulated sugar

    ¼ teaspoon cream of tartar

    ½ teaspoon vanilla extract

What to do:

1. Preheat the oven to 200° Celsius / 400° Fahrenheit. **[Make sure your boyfriend has a food processor or electric whisk. Seriously.]**

2. Add the flour, sugar, and salt and pulse to combine. Add the butter and shortening and pulse until the mixture forms pea-sized clumps. Add the water and vodka and pulse until the dough starts to come together, about 6 pulses.

3. Form the dough into a ball, flour a surface, and then roll out to fit your pie tin. Press the dough into the tin and cover in foil. Refrigerate for 30 minutes.

4. Add dried beans to fill the pie tin. Blind bake 20 minutes. **[This is a really good time to torment anybody you might have tied up and suffering for your wicked dirty pleasure.]**

5. Remove the foil and bake an additional 5–10 minutes or until crust is golden. Set aside while you make the filling. Lower the oven temperature to 160° Celsius / 325° Fahrenheit.

6. In a medium saucepan over medium heat, whisk together cornstarch, sugar, and salt. Whisk in water, lemon juice, and lemon zest. Whisk in the egg yolks until no yellow streaks remain. Stirring constantly, add butter and allow to cook for 1–2 minutes. The mixture should be very thick.

7. Pour the filling into the pie crust and cover with plastic wrap while you make the meringue.

8. In a stand mixer, beat egg whites, sugar, and cream of tartar on high speed until fluffy, soft peaks form. Beat in the vanilla.

9. Remove the plastic wrap and put the meringue on top of the lemon filling. Bake for 20 minutes. **[This is another really good opportunity to have your way with your wildly hot and submissive boyfriend—just sayin'.]**

10. Cool on a rack for 1 hour and then chill in the refrigerator until cold, at least 4 hours.

A NOTE OF ACKNOWLEDGMENT

Toby's lemon meringue pie recipe was devised and written by Elisabeth Lane.

AUTHOR ANNOTATIONS

Look for the star symbol as you flip through the book to discover what Alexis Hall was thinking while writing *For Real*.

1. Epigraph
   Alexis: The thing I love most about Donne as a poet was that he wrote mostly about sex and then found faith. And still wrote mostly about sex. Just, like, about God?

   But, seriously, I go weak at the knees for the words and forms of secular passion used in a divine context. Or do I mean the other way round?

   Or both. I probably mean both. I usually mean both.

Chapter One

1. *Paragraph begins with:* I turned to make my escape...
   Alexis: Honestly, what makes a "realistic" portrayal of a kink club is a pretty vexed question, given (depending on where you are in the world and who you know) they run the gamut of club night to sex party. I think the fancy dress/cabaret night with some alcohol and some play represents a very specific end of the London kink/alternative scene that existed

when I was writing this book. (God knows what anything looks like post-pandemic.)

I do know, however, that I wanted to steer away from what strike me as heavily fictionalised portrayals of BDSM clubs. Don't get me wrong, all fiction is fictionalised and I don't believe it's the point (or the job) of fiction solely to represent reality as accurately as possible.

But secret kink clubs run by gorgeous twenty-eight-year-old billionaires feel like they're pretty thin on the ground outside the realms of romance and erotica.

2. *Paragraph begins with:* It had been the best part of a year...
   Alexis: Gosh this feels a bit of a wild reference even for me. But I do actually find Powell a fascinatingly human and surprisingly accessible writer, despite his very long sentences and very many books.

   The context of the quote is the narrator thinking about Poussin's *A Dance to the Music of Time* (after which Powell's very long book sequence is named). Being an upper-middle-class white man who grew up between the wars, and bore witness to all the changes that were wrought across the twentieth century as a whole, he's obviously thinking about the figures from his past who have woven like dancers in and out of his life as Time controls the movements of all.

   But honestly? It's also very what belonging to a relatively insular subculture can feel like.

3. *Paragraph begins with:* I was also supposed to have brought a shtick of some kind...
   Alexis: Hell yes. Fuck nice.

4. *Paragraph begins with:* I scanned the gathered revellers.

    Alexis: This image is another nod to Donne (one of his secular poems this time, 'A Valediction Forbidding Mourning'):

    > *If they be two, they are two so*
    > *As stiff twin compasses are two;*
    > *Thy soul, the fixed foot, makes no show*
    > *To move, but doth, if the other do.*

    This image of the twin compasses, moving eternally together, has stayed with me all my life as an image of love (secular or divine, depending on your Donne Context).

5. *Paragraph begins with:* Sam blinked. "Wow, man, that's a seriously dated reference."

    Alexis: And now even more dated. *weeps in old*

6. *Paragraph begins with:* "Kink crowds are the same the world over."

    Alexis: This is, of course, Laurie being cynical. But also I secretly think he's got a point.

7. *Paragraph begins with:* "But we could get him a little kennel."

    Alexis: Oh no, even the non self-consciously dated reference, that Laurie is too old to get, is now dated.

8. *Paragraph begins with:* "A popular beat combo," explained Sam, smirking.

    Alexis: I sometimes wonder if this is one of those British cultural references that does not translate for U.S. readers.

    There's no confirmed attribution but the urban legend goes that "a popular beat combo, m'lud" was the answer offered by a barrister to a judge when the latter asked him who The Beatles were.

It's usually used as a semi-ironic shorthand for "you are not down enough with the kids to get this".

9. *Paragraph begins with:* He wasn't particularly attractive.
   Alexis: Ah yes. Romance heroes with traces of acne. Why don't we see more of these?

10. *Paragraph begins with:* I gazed down at him, into his oddly dark blue eyes...
    Alexis: Apparently I have a weakness for eyes like this. Although, to be fair, in *Boyfriend Material*, Luc's eyes are blue-green. Whereas Toby's are, um, *blue* blue? Yes. Definitely distinct. Uh huh. Moving on.

11. *Paragraph begins with:* His hair had flopped again...
    Alexis: I am secretly fond of this detail, even all these years later. That Toby would passionately press his hand to his heart, except in the wrong place, and Laurie would notice he had.

12. *Paragraph begins with:* Because I knew what he meant.
    Alexis: I think kink as part of identity is *complicated*, especially as it intersects with marginalised identities like queerness. On top of which, there's always this worry that you're accidentally doing capital-R representation—or you'll be perceived as doing that—when you're just trying to depict a certain POV that some people hold, but that is absolutely not the only possibly POV to have. In any case, this feels right for how both Laurie and Toby think about themselves.

13. *Paragraph begins with:* "It's like," he went on tormentedly...
    Alexis: Bluntly, this is kind of the whole heart of the book for me. Why I wrote it. Obviously I am not dissing the dom/me fantasy Toby articulates here, but our ideas about sexual power are entwined so deeply with our ideas about social power—perhaps more deeply than they should be—that I wanted to tease those things apart and see what we got. And what we got was Toby Finch.

14. *Paragraph begins with:* "Anything. Any of it."
    Alexis: This also speaks to complex ideas about attractiveness and power. I mean, don't get me wrong, I think it's just as enthralling for someone in the submissive role to possess none of these traits (other than the wanting to do it, of course). But even writing these annotations in the 2020s, years after I wrote this book, there's still a degree to which we view power as masculine and, therefore, the surrender of power as anti-masculine. And so I guess I wanted to explore that as well. Push back against it a little maybe.

15. *Paragraph begins with:* I didn't know why I did it.
    Alexis: This is the kind of bullshit I only get away with in Spires. That ambiguous hanging "it" of whatever Laurie does. The fact he refuses to (or can't?) tell us what the "it" actually is for several paragraphs to follow.

    Although I feel that the narrative evasiveness speaks to where Laurie is right now, as regards both his emotions and his capacity for submission. It takes him a while to work up to submitting in text as well as in person.

16. *Paragraph begins with:* There was a stillness in the room.

Alexis: For some reason, this line from Laurie makes me even more excited to get to write Dom the Dom's book. I think I'm just kind of obsessed with writing complicated subs. Especially since being complicated often feels like it's the prerogative of the dom.

17. *Paragraph begins with:* But he only grinned...

    Alexis: I tried to walk this line with Toby as regards his confidence. I didn't want to make him invincibly assured or have him just instantly become what we'd recognise as "a dom" as if by magic. But I did want to give him first rate instincts. Especially for Laurie. And especially for Laurie's bullshit.

18. *Paragraph begins with:* Oh God. I was so hard for him. For this.

    Alexis: Normally my anally retentive attention to detail (or mental unwellness) would not allow me to end two sentences so close together with "for this" and "from this" since it can create a sort of visual/aural clashing. Like the wrong kind of echo.

    However, in this specific case, it is the *right* kind of echo. Given how far Laurie and Toby are apart emotionally, I gave them a lot of linguistic mirroring during their sexual encounters to keep reinforcing the idea that these two are, in fact, in sync. If they can let themselves be.

Chapter Two

1. *Paragraph begins with:* I don't know where I found the courage to do this.

    Alexis: Oh Toby. He was *such* a hard sell at the time of writing. He may be still, I don't know. But I remember getting emails from readers telling me how they just couldn't "buy" him as a dom. Which, you know, is fair enough. People get to respond to characters however they like.

But I think what I always really valued about writing Toby was that he provided a lens through which to write about the *venerability* of dominance. I think because a lot of romance tends to take the sub's perspective for granted, this can sometimes lead to a sense that doms are these ever controlled and almost abstract beings.

I think we're invited to desire them. I think we're not as often invited to empathise with them. I'm still kind of hoping Toby offers opportunities for the latter.

2. *Paragraph begins with:* If I got to choose, I'd want to look like he does...

   Alexis: I feel we often kind of shy away from this element of queer desire: the half-competitive, half-envious side of wanting.

   But obviously Toby would just admit it openly. Because he has zero filters.

3. *Paragraph begins with:* My gaydar is genuinely defective...

   Alexis: OH GOD. You know what? I'm not even going to try and modernise this because I think it would clang awkwardly in the text. I mean, even more awkwardly than this. I am just going to have to live with being a million years old right now.

   Actually, it is fairly horrifying to realise that when I wrote this book, I made Laurie thirty-seven because it was the oldest I thought I could get away with in terms of both the age gap and what I/romance readers could conceive of as attractive.

And now I'm far, far closer to Laurie's age, writing these annotations, looking back on myself in absolute despair. Like, what did I think happened after the age of thirty-seven? We all just crawled into holes to die of decrepitude?

4. *Paragraph begins with:* He's waiting for me by the front desk, calling for a taxi.

   Alexis: OMG. A taxi. A taxi on account.

   Actually I might crawl into a hole to die of decrepitude after all.

5. *Paragraph begins with:* Next thing I know, he's dumping his full-length, silk-lined...

   Alexis: I might have a tendre for people draping their coats over each other? I think it happens a fair bit in my books.

   It's just one of those things, you know? Like tying each other's bow-ties. Nurturing and sexy and rendered a touch subversive between queer participants.

   Now I think about it, there's both coats AND bowties in this book. Push the boat out, Hall.

6. *Paragraph begins with:* And, wow, his body.

   Alexis: Alexis Hall, ensuring fictional men have body hair since...whenever I wrote this. And basically forever.

7. *Paragraph begins with:* Which is how I know it's real for him.

   Alexis: Ohemgee. A theme. The author did a theme.

8. *Paragraph begins with:* And he...well...wow...

Alexis: Honestly, I think this is more than I've ever thought or written about a dick in my entire life.

9. *Paragraph begins with:* Breathing sort of hurts...
   Alexis: Moment of looking back at past me and being like "yes."

   It's honestly pretty rare for me to like anything I've written for longer than about, hmm, five minutes? So forgive me this mild surprise and smugness.

Chapter Three

1. *Paragraph begins with:* Thirty-seven years old, and I was hiding in my own bathroom...
   Alexis: As a general rule, I try to avoid too much emphasis on sexual safety. I mean beyond what you'd get in a non-queer book. Because I think it can feel othering and potentially sort of shaming: reinforcing this idea that the only thing straight people have to worry about is pregnancy but queer folks are, you know, hideously diseased. I mean, obviously straight people can catch STIs just like anyone else, but it's not part of the rhetoric of straightness in the same way.

   And, let's be very clear, licking someone's ejaculate from your finger is extremely low risk. But then Laurie is a doctor and kinky so I imagine he's got safety routines drilled into his brain—for better or worse. I mean, he later worries about Toby being in a car crash. It's just sort of who he is.

2. *Paragraph begins with:* Against the protests of my knees, I made it to my feet and into the shower...

Alexis: Anal retentive Hall (ARH) is on the case again over the double "own" here. But I'm leaving it because I like how it emphasises how lonely and disconnected Laurie is right now. His own hand. His own pleasure.

3. *Paragraph begins with:* "Oh my God." Whatever was in his voice...

    Alexis: I'm kind of a sucker for this. Care when you don't deserve it. I mean, it's potentially quite a problematic trope. Obviously the idea of "deserving" things is messed up, but so is treating someone badly and then receiving kindness. But equally sometimes we need kindness most when we probably shouldn't get it.

4. *Paragraph begins with:* So we trooped upstairs, and I ran him a bath...

    Alexis: I was going to celebrate a reference that hasn't dated, but apparently Radox Nourish has been discontinued.

    I no longer recognise the world I live in.

5. *Paragraph begins with:* "Traditionally, baths are."

    Alexis: Speaking of settling into old age, I have to admit that while there's part of me that's thinking, "well, this is a hot, intimate scene you wrote there," there's a much more significant part of me thinking, "wow, Laurie's bathroom sounds amazing."

6. *Paragraph begins with:* "How about..." His eyes gleamed at me.

    Alexis: This is from 'Dolores' by Algernon Charles Swinburne. It's a pretty weird poem, a sort of reversal of the idea of the sacred feminine into this grim figure of cruelty and punishment. It could be very subversive. Or it could just be Swinburne indulging his kinky imagination. Which he did *a lot*.

Swinburne (a contemporary of Wilde's) was kind of an extremely messy bench, even by the standards of the messy benches around him. In his youth he kind of went out of his way to exaggerate his own depravity, which including laying claim to bestiality, atheism, sodomy, vampirism, and necrophilia. Of those, Wilde claims he did exactly none, but I have read accounts of his life that argue that he probably experienced some kind of same-sex desire. Obviously, talking about queerness in a historical context is complicated because, while ideas around queerness as identity rather than queerness as act (sodomy) were beginning to emerge, it was still far from what we'd understand by queerness today. In any case, in later life Swinburne got super homophobic, maybe because he was genuinely terrified after what happened to Wilde, but who knows?

One aspect of his personality and sexual behaviour that *is* pretty comprehensively established, however, is that he was a raging masochist.

7. *Paragraph begins with:* He blinked at me through a coal-dark fringe of water-heavy lashes...

Alexis: And yes, I did name Laurie after the hero of Mary Renault's *The Charioteer* (one of my favourite books). Read into that what you will.

I mean, okay. There's not much to read into it. I wanted to pay homage to a book that means so much to me. And while I don't think this Laurie is very *like* that Laurie, I think they both grapple with shame and repression, their carnal natures and their better natures...the white and black horses of Plato's Phaedrus, which are so significant in *The Charioteer*.

8. *Paragraph begins with:* He splashed me.
   Alexis: Of course, Toby's name carries its own literary connection. But I guess I'll get to that later.

9. *Paragraph begins with:* "They're not ugly, Toby."
   Alexis: I know romance is a place of fantasy and that's not only okay but to be celebrated.

   But I really do think there's also celebration to have in, you know, human bodies with all their flaws and challenges.

Chapter Four

1. *Paragraph begins with:* He's also the first person who's ever taken me seriously.
   Alexis: I think the gift of being taken seriously, in any context, cannot be overstated.

2. *Paragraph begins with:* I sometimes wonder what it means...
   Alexis: Avocado is the worst.

3. *Paragraph begins with:* I pad around and open all the curtains for him.
   Alexis: I reckon even now Laurie would still be the sort of person who had a paper delivered.

4. *Paragraph begins with:* And then I get performance anxiety because scrambled eggs are like this...art form.

Alexis: There might have been a touch of the author in Toby's entirely correct opinions about avocado. And there might be again here when he's talking about scrambled eggs. I will never get bored of making scrambled eggs, nor of eating them, I think. Especially with really good toast, spread with lots of butter.

5. *Paragraph begins with:* I have to laugh at the expression on his face.

   Alexis: This idea comes from 'Be Drunk' by, as Toby says, Baudelaire. I find it kind of weirdly charming that Baudelaire was stressed about the tyrannical influence of time on modern life in an industrialised, urbanised world. I mean, imagine if he knew about the internet? Or mobile phones. Anyway.

   Here's the full poem (translated in somewhat utilitarian fashion):

   You have to be always drunk. That's all there is to it—it's the
   *   only way. So as not to feel the horrible burden of time*
   that breaks your back and bends you to the earth, you have to
   *   be continually drunk.*

   But on what?
   Wine, poetry or virtue, as you wish.
   But be drunk.

   And if sometimes, on the steps of a palace
   or the green grass of a ditch,
   in the mournful solitude of your room,
   you wake again, drunkenness already diminishing or gone,

ask the wind, the wave, the star, the bird, the clock,
everything that is flying,
everything that is groaning,
everything that is rolling,
everything that is singing,
everything that is speaking...
Ask what time it is
and wind, wave, star, bird, clock will answer you:
"It is time to be drunk!

So as not to be the martyred slaves of time,
be drunk, be continually drunk!
On wine, on poetry or on virtue as you wish."

6. *Paragraph begins with:* I know so little about this man, but I know he unravels hands first.

    Alexis: This is another one of those things that I wanted Toby to recognise even without the full context of understanding. Sort of a microcosm of their kink dynamic in a way, understanding where and how Laurie is most vulnerable, even without the basic information that he's a doctor and so his hands are a significant manifestation of his identity—and self-control—within the world at large.

7. *Paragraph begins with:* Dangerous question to ask me when the answer is *everything*.

    Alexis: It's pretty much a cliché at this point for me to ramble on about particular sexual acts being associated with power/control and others not. When, as Laurie says later, as far as I'm concerned sex is less about what you do than what it means.

TL;DR It was important to me when I wrote this to present a dom, who was unequivocally a dom, who got to enjoy being penetrated. It's still important to me, to be honest.

Because if sex is about context, power is about perspective.

8. *Paragraph begins with:* "The right time to come, darling, is when you want to come."

    Alexis: Personally, I think Laurie begins to fall in love, truly fall in love, with Toby at this moment. The *darling* is a dead giveaway.

9. *Paragraph begins with: Jouissance*, is what I think.

    Alexis: I know Toby is pretty precocious for a nineteen-year-old but I kind of wanted to give him this young/old almost timeless quality. I mean, he's been raised by his granddad and his artistically ferocious mum. I think that would shape a person in certain ways. I also liked the idea of someone who sort of embodies "art" (whatever that means) just as part of who they are (like Toby is often thinking of poetry or these quite intense abstract concepts) but isn't himself artistic.

10. *Paragraph begins with:* Another of his secrets, I guess.

    Alexis: Kindness is my romance kryptonite. I return to it endlessly. I just think, of all human qualities, a capacity for kindness is probably the most attractive.

Chapter Five

1. *Paragraph begins with:* "Please...please will you..."

Alexis: I wanted to have a scene gone awry, err, scene, but I also didn't want to make it about danger or abuse, so much as emotional dishonesty. At least on Laurie's part. I think it's clear from the behaviour of his partner that the man—though he's a bit dom-by-numbers—is sincerely trying to honour what he understands Laurie's wishes and desires to be. But because Laurie is in this quite specific state of messed-upness, where he's using his body's needs to deny his emotional needs, there's no way this encounter can work for either of them.

2. *Paragraph begins with:* He stepped past me to open the door.
   Alexis: Dom the Dom sort of took life for me from this moment, even if he didn't for Laurie.

   When I wrote the scene, I was mostly focused on what I needed it to be (or rather not be) for Laurie. Something to contrast against what he has with Toby and demonstrate why he's quite so lost and cynical about his own sexual needs, while also—as I've already discussed—not crossing the line into abusive or dangerous. That led me to the broad idea of a dom-by-numbers, someone who is respectful and competent but not super creative and wrong for Laurie right now.

   Except by the time I got to the end of the scene I realised how selfish Laurie is being in this moment. He lets Dom take him home, having no intention of engaging authentically with whatever they do together. And that made me feel I was being selfish as a writer too—like I'd not created a character, but a dismissable straw man to embody approaches to sex and kink that don't speak to me personally.

Hence these moments, and later ones, where we (hopefully) get to see Dom the Dom as a whole person, someone kind and lonely and perceptive and human, not just as a paper dom or a rhetorical device to prove a point that it isn't really my point to make. Because it's kind of messed up for me to have centred a whole book on the validity of Laurie and Toby's choices, and then not extend the same courtesy to Dom here.

3. *Paragraph begins with:* For a moment, I was alarmed.

   Alexis: There's a kind of joke amongst my readers that Spires as a series is chronic for characters being extremely disorganised about exchanging basic contact information. Sort of the romance equivalent of the way nobody can get mobile phone reception in a horror movie.

   I suspect it's partly my own distaste for being contactable that's making itself manifest in my fiction. And I have tried to get better about it (although I did get a phone dropped in a river in the last Spires book I wrote, *Chasing the Light*).

4. *Paragraph begins with:* "Look." His head came up, the moonlight catching in his eyes, making them shine.

   Alexis: I know romance is traditionally preferred to be dual POV but—apparently allergic to success—I tend to want to tell stories from an aggressively single POV. I think I love the way a single POV mimics the vulnerabilities of falling in love; it makes the reader textually uncertain to match the ways the central character is romantically uncertain.

   But sometimes dual POV is the right choice, and I don't think there was any question in my mind that *For Real* was meant (insofar as anything that is consciously created is 'meant' to be anything) to include both Laurie and Toby's voices, and for those voices to be equal.

Something I did really enjoy fucking about with, though, was introducing gaps into the text—either gaps of time or, once again, gaps in perception (like this one, where Laurie doesn't know and therefore we don't know what Toby has been doing or feeling, beyond what he expresses directly now).

Basically, I deliberately wanted to avoid a situation where they just picked up the story seamlessly from each other. I wanted something a bit more...ragged-feeling? Where the edges don't quite line up but with a bit of work they fit anyway. Y'know, like the relationship itself.

5. *Paragraph begins with:* Less romantic was the groan of relief I couldn't quite suppress...

    Alexis: I think people trying to cart each other about romantically or sexily and not quite always succeeding might also be an Alexis Hall favoured microtrope.

6. *Paragraph begins with:* "You're always so smart. Are you a lawyer or something?"

    Alexis: So, err, that's nearly thirty thousand words before the protagonists exchange even the most basic details about their lives. I genuinely can't tell if I was being bold or incompetent here.

7. *Paragraph begins with:* "Tobermory?" I asked, trying not to laugh as he swung round and straddled me.

    Alexis: It takes Jasper, of course, to get this reference.

    But for context, Tobermory is the title of a short story by Hector Hugh Munro (aka Saki). The eponymous

Tobermory is a cat who is taught to talk—but, belonging to a society hostess, and being a cat (and we all know what cats are like), he immediately uses his new power over language to cause absolute havoc. The story is basically a skewering of upper-class hypocrisy in which the fantastical device of a talking cat becomes the epicentre of what is true and real in a world that otherwise comprises deceit, delusion, and pretention.

Like, for example, a nineteen-year-old dom to a man who has lost himself in a subculture that feels routine and hollow to him. In a book called, ahem, *For Real*. Look, I've never claimed to be a subtle writer.

In any case, as with most of Saki's work, Tobermory is an exquisite mixture of sharp, camp, and bitter. In other words, a perfect cocktail. It's a piece of writing I love very much and heartily recommend.

As for Saki himself, he was—like all the best people— queer AF.

8. *Paragraph begins with:* The heat of his clothed body rushed over my naked one...

   Alexis: I know I've already babbled about the complicated, perhaps even problematic, way we interact with ideas about sex and power (and it gets even worse when we bring gender into the mix). To put it in, I guess, semiotic terms, I think we often confuse the signifier with the sign: as in we assume specific demonstrations of power are, in fact, power. In this case, that the conventions of kink (whether that's who is penetrated or what commands are issued) are how control is maintained or surrendered.

Whereas, for me, mutual trust, desire, and surrender lie at the heart of power exchange. And that's sort of what I wanted to show on the page every time Toby rejects what might be more "typical" dom behaviour in favour of what feels right to him for both of them. Like every time he doesn't push or demand or assert himself. If he chooses to ask rather than command. And, here, where he offers strength when Laurie falters.

Is it the only way to be a dom/me? Of course not. Is it what every sub needs or want? Again, no. But it doesn't mean Toby is doing it wrong either.

9. *Paragraph begins with:* And he tasted deeply and simply of himself, sour-sweet, and intimate.

   Alexis: Ah romance. The genre where part of your job is thinking deeply and sincerely how to describe the taste of someone's arsehole.

10. *Paragraph begins with:* He was quiet for a long time.

    Alexis: My perspective is likely flawed on this, but I see subdrop explored in fiction a lot more than domdrop, maybe because the former is more common? But as part of being interested in writing a dom who was relatable, rather than simply desirable, I wanted to show Toby's uncertainties on the page sometimes. Taking something from fantasy to reality, even if it's something you desperately want, isn't always simple or easy. And it felt right for those emotions to catch up with him now. And, also, for Laurie to be able to offer emotional support (albeit in a slightly impatient way) without that compromising their sexual dynamic.

11. *Paragraph begins with:* "One of the few advantages of getting old..."

    Alexis: When I wrote this, I wasn't as close to Laurie's age as I am now, but I'm delighted to be able to confirm I was (and am) correct. The older I get, the fewer fucks I have to give. It feels *wonderful*.

12. *Paragraph begins with:* "You really get it, don't you?" he whispered.

    Alexis: One of the slightly complicated things for me personally in deciding to write *For Real* essentially boiled down to...how to write a kinky romance that wasn't really, or perhaps solely, about the kink? Don't get me wrong, it's fine for romances to centre on whatever they damn please. But since I tend to write in ways that are aimed at normalising aspects of identity, especially queer identity, it felt right to do the same for kink. So most of the obstacles Laurie and Toby face have nothing to do with sex. And there are repeated moments where it's made, I think, pretty clear that the most "dangerous" or at least vulnerable-making thing they do with each other is be honest about their feelings.

13. *Paragraph begins with:* "God, no. I'm not *helping* you."

    Alexis: Toby's reaction to locking up his lover's cock still kind of amuses me a little. Like, sometimes the kinkiest thing you can do is not doing the kinky thing.

14. *Paragraph begins with:* "That's your safeword, is it?"

    Alexis: This too—that Laurie and Toby would not ultimately use safewords—was a decision I wrestled with. I think it's too easy for fiction to be interpreted monolith-ically (seen as encompassing all experiences, rather than just the experiences it explores) or representationally (expressing broad ideas rather than specific ones), and I didn't necessarily want to get angry emails about how I was Spreading Unsafe Ideas About BDSM. Because, the fact is, someone insisting to you they don't believe in safewords is usually a red flag. However, I think there's also a tendency to treat safewords as sort of...magical. Like, you can't have done anything wrong if the sub didn't safeword. When the reality is, like most things, complicated. So I guess I erred on the side of letting Toby and Laurie be themselves and reflect that complicatedness.

15. *Paragraph begins with:* I carried the books into the kitchen
    Alexis: While I, too, adore people sharing what they love, I think the only thing more haunting than being stuck with a book (or books) an ex-partner left behind would be an actual haunting. And even then it would be touch and go.

Chapter Six

1. *Paragraph begins with:* Oh my God, I can't stop thinking about him.
   Alexis: This is, of course, a reference to the 'La Belle Dame sans Merci' by Keats. Obviously it's mostly just there because it's a reference poetic lil Toby would readily reach for.

   But I also liked the way it contributes to the broader themes around perspective and context. Laurie tends to see Toby sincerely as the magical one, a prince from a fairytale. Whereas Toby fears that's illusion. He is the one enchanted, transformed, to be discarded when that enchantment fades.

2. *Paragraph begins with:* The other big advantage of Joe's is that nobody really cares what I'm doing...

   Alexis: I don't know at what point in either the planning or the writing this became my kinky sex and granddad book but here we are.

3. *Paragraph begins with:* Probably a good thing she's dead.

   Alexis: I'm now closer to Laurie than Toby and I still feel this way.

4. *Paragraph begins with:* So I was a regular twinkle toes after that.

   Alexis: Same, Toby, same.

5. *Paragraph begins with:* Frogs

   Alexis: I strongly believe that fiction is fiction, not autobiography, and I'm generally careful to draw from life only in very oblique ways.

   Also the author is dead.

   But I will say that there are elements of this particular poem that may bear some resemblance to the first poem I ever wrote myself. And yet the position of poet laureate has not yet been offered me. What gives.

6. *Paragraph begins with:* The weird thing is, I do kind of get poetry.

   Alexis: I think part of the reason I gave Toby a kind of instinctive understanding of poetry was to reflect his instinctive understanding of, um, being a dom?

Like, this is the most pretentious thing I've ever allowed to exist outside my own brain, but I do feel there's a kind of correspondence between poetry—the way we respond to poetry—and the dynamics of kink. Gawd. I'm so sorry. This is awful. But I think it's that specific combination of discipline and intense emotion. As in, poetry often reaches us on deep, private, and—I seem to be using this word a lot—instinctive levels. But that doesn't happen spontaneously. It has be created and curated very carefully. And while a lot of the most, err, *interesting* poetry goes against our expectations—breaks the rules—it's only able to do so because of a full understanding of those rules and expectations.

7. *Paragraph begins with:* I ask if he wants anything, but he doesn't.
Alexis: As a writer (and, indeed, as a reader), I love dialogue, probably to the extent it's a flaw. Because I tend to write from a single POV, dialogue is one of the few ways I can give very literally the non-POV character their voice, so it's super rare that I back away from direct speech.

Usually when I do it, it's to give characters privacy at particular moments. That's mostly the case here. But I also wanted to try and capture something of the feeling of talking to someone when they're very sick. In that particular situation it's not dialogue in the way we usually think of dialogue since it's not an exchange exactly. It's more a case of seeking and affirming connection. A way of being there.

Basically, it's not what you're saying that matters. It's the act of communication. Which is a perspective that's explored in many other contexts over the course of the book.

8. *Paragraph begins with:* I nod, feeling a bit of a dork.
    Alexis: Sung by Judy Garland, of course. I'm assuming that went without saying. But just in case you were in doubt.

9. *Paragraph begins with:* I don't need to tell him what I want.
    Alexis: People usually remember lemon meringue pie from this book.

    But, honestly. I'm pretty proud of the quietly romantic felching.

10. *Paragraph begins with:* I grin at him. Touch his lips.
    Alexis: I feel if any poet was going to approve being used in this context, it would be John Donne.

11. *Paragraph begins with:* I settle myself between his legs again...
    Alexis: This is one of those lines that sneakily pleases me even now. I don't know why my brain went to Christina Rossetti at this moment, but it did. And it feels so right for Toby.

12. *Paragraph begins with:* I'm not sure what he's getting at.
    Alexis: ARH is debating because I'm concerned at having two *all*s in such close proximity. But given the state Toby is in at the moment, physically and emotionally, and the fact he's generally a passionate and excessive person, I think I'm okay with the echo. I like the idea that he's seeing Laurie constantly in these very superlative terms. All his bones ridged. All his muscles tightening.

13. *Paragraph begins with:* But it comes out of nowhere, like an awesome sneeze.

Alexis: I know it's kind of a cliché for a younger bloke to be a bit trigger happy, but I think there can be something slightly toxic about the idea that sexual prowess (and sexual domination) require absolute physical control. There's a kind of weird thing in romance novels where heroes will pop a boner at the slightest provocation (when that's the sort of thing one ideally likes to leave with puberty) but they come like wizards in Tolkien. Neither early nor late, but always exactly when they intend to.

I think there's also a lot of heteronormative and phallo-centric assumptions muddled up in the idea that the point of sex is for a dick to ejaculate and the ejaculation of the dick heralds the termination of the sex.

14. *Paragraph begins with:* Shush.

Alexis: It was very disorientating reading this moment so many years after writing it.

I will admit I've written some cringey moments. The wedding scene in *Glitterland*, for example, or the dinner between Caspian, Arden, and Nathaniel in *How to Belong with a Billionaire*.

But this one—even though I wrote it and remembered it—took me freshly by surprise.

I was like, *Laurie, how could you.*

Chapter Seven

1. *Paragraph begins with:* So I got up, showered, and went to see Grace.

Alexis: Any similarities to university traditions the author may or may not have been involved in are purely coincidental.

2. *Paragraph begins with:* "Less than you might think."

    Alexis: Laurie's kind of been a dick in the name of doing the right thing for the past, err, however many pages. I kind of hope it counts in his favour that while he lies to himself, when push comes to shove, he doesn't—he won't—lie to others. He's not Ash (from *Glitterland*) in that regard.

3. *Paragraph begins with:* She shrugged and went on in quite a different voice...

    Alexis: With this story from Grace, I kind of wanted to parallel Toby a little. Obviously their experiences are quite different and exist in differently gendered contexts, but I feel it ties into the theme of how we perceive and manifest dominance in a world that tends to view dominance very much as one thing or belonging only to certain people with access to certain privileges.

    We tend to meet doms fully formed in fiction, full of knowledge and experience, ready to fulfil our sexy fantasies. I guess—as with most things in life—I'm more interested in the journey.

4. *Paragraph begins with:* They were still smiling, but their hands plucked restlessly...

    Alexis: I really wish I was looking at this now and finding it hilariously irrelevant. I really, really wish that.

5. *Paragraph begins with:* "What did you expect me to say?"

Alexis: It kind of really bugs me that a spice harvested from orchids, served in a drink for royalty by the Aztecs, unknown in Europe until the sixteenth century, and only introduced into its common usage by the most skilled of French confectioners in the 1800s, is now a byword for boring.

6. *Paragraph begins with:* His eyes flew wide.

Alexis: So, kink and trauma, eh? What a minefield. I guess the first thing to say is that people get to deal with their trauma in whatever fashion they choose, however they like, and if that's via kinky sex then that's none of my business. I do think, however, there is a tendency, especially from the outside, to view kink as deriving from trauma. And, I mean, it should go without saying, as a default position that's...messy. So I guess I wanted to affirm here that, for Laurie and Toby specifically, it's purely and uncomplicatedly an expression of love.

7. *Paragraph begins with:* "Yeah, he's not well."

Alexis: This book is a bloody nightmare to annotate. It's either all about sex, which I'm too British to feel comfortable talking about. Or else shit that makes me deeply emotional. Which I'm, um, too British to feel comfortable talking about.

8. *Paragraph begins with:* "You could work on it."

Alexis: Having semi-recently published *Something Spectacular,* this is a strange and delightful echo to me. Apparently I've been preoccupied by the problems of this or that for a long time. Possibly all my life.

9. *Paragraph begins with:* "It's an anal hook."

   Alexis: Because of this book, readers sometimes ask me for more information about anal hooks. I tend to assume this is, you know, the equivalent of trying to embarrass teacher in class because that's the sort of thing you can easily Google. Also, what are they expecting me to say? The clue here is very much in the name.

10. *Paragraph begins with:* "That wasn't supposed to sound negative."

    Alexis: My core story, I think. Or one of them. As applied to romance, I mean.

    Obviously if you murder someone, that very much matters on its own terms.

11. *Paragraph begins with:* "Yeah. Totally. 'S'nice."

    Alexis: *Great British Menu* is a reality TV show where fairly established chefs create themed dishes for slightly more established chefs in the hope of winning the opportunity to serve that dish as part of a fancy banquet. I really enjoy it because it's basically talented people displaying their talent for the appreciation of other talented people. But it's also very British in its approach, which means everyone is a self-deprecating neurotic wreck, even when they've produced a legit culinary masterpiece. The initial judging process (with the chef, rather than an external panel) tends to be fairly discursive and collaborative, with the judging chef mostly seeking to understand the other chef's vision, asking nerve-wracking questions like "was this how you intended the potatoes to be" or "do you think the dish has enough sharpness." And in response the chef—if they're pleased with what they've done—will shuffle their feet and say something like, "well, the fish has come out the way I wanted."

This scene, for me, is a fish that's come out the way I wanted. And that's all I say.

(Though, obviously, it may not be a fish I've served to your taste.)

12. *Paragraph begins with:* "I'm sorry, Toby. But the truth is…"
Alexis: This is probably unsexy.

But honestly, I find the unglamorous bits of sex, the messy bits, kind of the sexiest of all?

13. *Paragraph begins with:* "That must be some dinner."
Alexis: I'm actually starting to feel faintly embarrassed about the number of times, both relevant and otherwise, I have title dropped in this book.

Am I going to change it though? Hell no.

14. *Paragraph begins with:* "That bull was nearly Margaret Thatcher, so don't knock it."
Alexis: This is true. There's a weird bronze bull by the station that could have been a statue of Margaret Thatcher. But in a public vote the weird bronze bull won by a landslide.

15. *Paragraph begins with:* "And that," said Toby triumphantly, "is just semantics, dude."
Alexis: While I was sweating and whining over writing these annotations, a reader, to whom I recommended Untitled Goose Game (I very much recommend Untitled Goose Game, btw), said she would give me a fiver if I found a way to include a HONK within my annotations.

Someone now owes me a fiver.

You know who you are.

16. *Paragraph begins with:* I shoved him, and his little grinning face, into Debenhams...

    Alexis: Debenhams has closed since I wrote this. It's an odd piece of pre-pandemic Oxford nostalgia that I'm kind of glad exists.

17. *Paragraph begins with:* "The Radcliffe Camera was built in 1737 by James Gibbs."

    Alexis: I don't know very much about architecture, but I've always maintained you can recognise the influence of James Gibbs if it has a big pointy bit or looks like a boob.

18. *Paragraph begins with:* "Because you're insulting me..."

    Alexis: This is, of course, a pretty direct reference to *Jane Eyre*. The scene where Jane confronts Rochester in the garden in the rain and demands her right not only to be loved by him, but her right to be his equal: "Do you think because I am poor, obscure, plain and little that I am soulless and heartless?"

    I don't think Toby is *deliberately* trying to invoke it, but I do think it's in his mind somewhat, especially because he's a character who reaches easily and instinctively for references.

    And, of course, I was sort of thinking of *Jane Eyre* myself a bit while I was writing this book. Although, to be honest, I'm always thinking about *Jane Eyre* a bit because I'm obsessed with that book. On account of just how balls-to-the-wall bananas it is.

Like, when you get right down to it, *Jane Eyre* is a pretty radical romance. Rochester is a bastion of worldly authority: he's a man, he's rich, he's educated, etc. Jane doesn't even have access to what little value women were acknowledged to have (beauty and/or family connections). And yet here she stands, powerful in soul and heart and willing to fight. I think, in a genre where we take dukes getting together with governesses for granted, it's easy to overlook just how bold, how extraordinary, this scene, and honestly the book as a whole, is.

I think in the context of *For Real*, Toby is asserting his right as a nineteen-year-old to have his needs and wants taken seriously. Obviously, as older people, we have a duty to protect those younger than ourselves. But we also owe them trust and respect and the freedom to make their own choices.

Also, I've always thought Jane Eyre is basically femdom. I know Rochester is usually seen as a template for brooding alpha heroes, but that man is, frankly, subby AF. His first textual act is to gallop out of the mist on a big black horse and immediately fall off it at Jane's feet, requiring her aid to get up again. Every time he tries to command her to do anything, he ends up modifying his own behaviour. And by the time he's trying to bigamy up with her, he's literally declared her his god. To be honest, Jane is sort of soft balling at the point she is declaring herself his equal in the rain. Both the book, and Rochester, are pretty convinced she's his superior. Because her passion, her sincerity, and her moral clarity make her so.

I wouldn't go quite that far with *For Real* because I feel

power dynamics should probably stay in the bedroom when it comes to functional relationships. But while Toby is not flawless, and has some growing up to do, it's Laurie who does most of the changing over the course of the book. To be Toby's equal he needs to learn to match him emotionally—to be as honest and as open and hopeful—not just sexually.

19. *Paragraph begins with:* College, when we finally arrived, blew Toby's tiny mind.

    Alexis: If you want to Google Magdalen College Oxford, you can see exactly where Laurie and Toby are right now. You can find a virtual tour on the website.

20. *Paragraph begins with:* Oh God. Behind the desk was Bob...

    Alexis: I still don't know if this was meant to be a homage to Oxford porters or an indictment of them. Can I say both?

21. *Paragraph begins with:* And I did, driving myself not-so-slowly mad on his fingers...

    Alexis: Yikes, I kind of assumed I'd done everything to indicate this was Magdalen without explicitly saying it was Magdalen. But no. Apparently I lacked even that mild circumspection. OH WELL.

22. *Paragraph begins with:* We lay on the desk, neither of us wanting to move despite the discomfort.

    Alexis: I don't think I'll ever tire of writing about Oxford. The colours of its skies in particular.

Chapter Eight

1. *Paragraph begins with:* Oxford, man. Fucking nuts.
   Alexis: I mean. Facts.

2. *Paragraph begins with:* "Only something sublime, darling."
   Alexis: Even reading this back, years later, I remember how much fun I had writing Jasper. It's probably not a wholly responsible portrait of an Oxford academic but...ehh?

3. *Paragraph begins with:* Laurie lets me go, steps back, and something crunches under his foot.
   Alexis: This is a reference to Oscar Wilde—who went to Magdalen (they even have a theatre named after him)—and was reputed to have said, while there, "I find it harder and harder every day to live up to my blue china." #relatable

4. *Paragraph begins with:* I'm so cross with him I say without thinking...
   Alexis: I wanted to leave Coal's art in general somewhat ambiguous (much like Marius's art in *Waiting for the Flood* & *Chasing the Light*). But the pieces referenced here were, in my head, a little nod to Courbet's *L'Origine du Monde* (if you Google that, please be aware, it's extremely NSFW).

   I also don't know quite how to express my love for this painting in a way that isn't weird because of, you know, the subject matter. But it's fascinating to me, I think because it feels brazen even now, when you'd think we'd have culturally moved past a point where we'd find a vulva, not explicitly offered to us in a context of pure titillation, shocking or transgressive. Never mind the fact that here we have a painting that bears all the usual hallmarks of an act of (presumed male) power over an objectified body (she is, after all, just a faceless body) and YET.

I wouldn't personally say it's so much an expression of explicitly empowered sexuality on the part of the subject—she's just lying there, after all, leg cocked in what looks like languor rather than seduction—but there's a...naturalism, a realism, there that makes an even more significant statement I think. This is just a body. What we bring to it is our own problem.

5. *Paragraph begins with:* "I don't want to see him."
   Alexis: I am always here for a man, or anyone really, who can do an effective forehead drape.

6. *Paragraph begins with:* For a moment, I think he's taking the piss, but then I realise he's not.
   Alexis: Sometimes I idly amuse myself by pondering Jasper's romantic future. Obviously we get a glimpse of it, as its most self-destructive, in *In Vino*. But I can't decide if he needs to work his bullshit out with Sherry or not. I think probably not? I think Sherry loves him, but will never understand him.

7. *Paragraph begins with:* When I next look up, Jasper seems to be...
   Alexis: This isn't drawn from any one occasion. But it's pieces of several. Consequently I like to think it's fairly true to life.

8.*Paragraph begins with:* My mum has parties; I know how to handle conversations like this.

Alexis: I had lots of thoughts about how Toby v. Oxford could go. I mean, I think there are all sorts of interesting choices to be made, character and relationship-wise, when it comes to introducing the love interest to the social/public aspect of the other character's life. I know I've written scenes of absolute disaster, like with Darian in *Glitterland* (although that's very much Ash's fault, not Darian's). I think with Toby, though, I wanted to kind of play on the expectations of people who happened to have read *Glitterland*. Make them fear disaster. But actually Toby is just as comfortable as Laurie—if not more so—in this setting.

I just didn't think a bunch of pretentious Oxfordians would hold much fear for Toby, having been raised as fearlessly and unconventionally as he has been. I mean, I think there are definitely limitations to Coal's approach to parenting, but she has taught him a kind of confidence—charisma even—he isn't, at the age of nineteen, capable of recognising in himself.

9. *Paragraph begins with:* "She doesn't believe in the mechanics of mass production."

Alexis: This is Walter Benjamin, from 'The Work of Art in the Age of Mechanical Reproduction.'

Much like Baudelaire, Benjamin (who was born on the cusp of the twentieth century) was living through a time of massive social and technological change. He was also Jewish and living in Germany between the first and second world wars, and wrote 'The Work of Art in the Age of Mechanical Reproduction' from France having been forced to flee his home.

Not to reduce quite a complex essay to bullet points, Benjamin is essentially grappling with the impact of the mass market nature of specifically mechanical reproduction (art has always been reproduced to some degree, after all) not only in the way art is distributed but the way it is developed. While Benjamin acknowledges that there is value in art being more accessible, he is also concerned with the loss of what he called the "aura"—the quality of a piece of art that situates it in a specific place and time, and makes it unique. The soul of the art, I suppose?

Moreover, with the rise of new art forms like film and photography emerging alongside the rise of fascism, there is, I think, a deep concern in Benjamin regarding the vulnerability of art as a product of the mass market—specifically its potential for exploitation by fascist and capitalistic forces. A concern that, in retrospect, was well-founded. I mean, even without diving into "ah, do you see, this historical thing is like the present day, ah, memes, photoshop, fake news, ah," the same year he wrote this essay, he'd see the release of Triumph of the Will, a piece of blatant Nazi propaganda that has shaped cinematic language for the best part of a century.

But to take a sharp step away from, um, fascism (nobody is ever going to let me provide annotations for my work ever again) in terms of Coal as a character, and her place in this book (y'know, the kinky sex book), I think her search for authenticity in art is there both to parallel and reflect Toby's own search for authenticity in life. Coal is grappling for herself, in her own way, with what makes art *real*. Toby (and through him the narrative) is asking the same questions about love and sex and power and his future.

10. *Paragraph begins with:* Jasper pushes away most of his crumble tart...

    Alexis: To this day, I don't know if this is because Jasper is too drunk to care about table manners, or so confident he can get away with it. Little from column A, little from column B?

11. *Paragraph begins with:* Laurie's rough with me, but in a good way...

    Alexis: I extra love that they're doing this in the cloisters. You know, in an area traditionally reserved for peace, meditation, gentle exercise, and quiet study.

    I mean, I guess they're exercising?

Chapter Nine

1. *Paragraph begins with:* "I live in abject terror of that, you know."

    Alexis: I'm kind of taking it as read that this is extremely relatable. I think there's no escaping the fact—and there should be no escaping the fact—that kinky sex comes with inherent risk (it's why, if we have to embrace acronym I find RACK more useful than SSC because what you're doing is unsafe by definition), but living with that is, like most things, complicated. Laurie's take is clearly that emotional vulnerability and kinky sex are analogously risky. My take on Robert is that he, ironically, couldn't deal with the vulnerability of reality: that he is human, flawed, capable of fucking up, and in a sexual dynamic where his fucking up was going to have physical consequences.

2. *Paragraph begins with:* "Y'know," he said softly, "that sounds like you want to be my boyfriend."
   Alexis: Reading this again after however long it's been, it strikes me that, for a book which opens with someone wanking over someone else, it's a weirdly slow burn.

3. *Paragraph begins with:* "Nobody liked my granddad except me."
   Alexis: I know this probably feels like an odd way to, err, honour the character of Toby's grandfather, but he's only on page for a single scene and I wanted to recognise him as a whole person, not just as an abstract embodiment of perfect grandfatherness. I mean in a book that is more than a little bit about time and perspective, it's kind of wild when you stop for a moment and think how much someone has lived through—how many people they've been—by the time they've got grandkids, let alone great grandkids. Like, I can't remember very clearly who I was at the age of twenty. Who am I going to be at seventy?

   In any case, I think it's important that Toby's grandfather lived a messy life and made significant mistakes, especially as regards his family. But he came through for Toby, and that matters too.

4. *Paragraph begins with:* My voice had lost something of its careful modulation...
   Alexis: I didn't want to over-focus on the dissolution of Laurie and Robert because I didn't want Laurie to be too hung up on it after, you know, six years. I think for Laurie

(and he does admit this directly at some point) the problem isn't so much that he can't get over Robert as a person, so much as he doesn't know how to find the balance of sex/kink/love/partnership he had with Robert. Although, to be fair, that could partially be down to Laurie himself not feeling able to offer emotional vulnerability along with physical submission.

In terms of Robert himself, though, I tend to shy away from making individual characters "the baddie"—or, at least, if they are the baddie, I want to ensure they have an understandable POV. And I think, to me, at least Robert's POV *is* understandable. Like Grace says, the thought of genuinely harming someone you love—of recognising how severe your mistakes have the potential to be—is terrifying. I can understand why, in that context, Robert basically shut down and ran. I think it was wrong that he did, but I do get it.

Also, I'm getting away from the point of this annotation, which was to say I was glad for an opportunity to touch on 'cheating' here in the sense that it means something to me—that is, as a sense of betrayal, which may or may not have anything to do with sex. And Robert is lying to himself here as much as he is lying to Laurie.

5. *Paragraph begins with:* I didn't want to do it, but I wanted him to make me.

   Alexis: This is super tangential and super specific even for me, but I actually find the word delta—as an image applied to human bodies—absurdly sexy because of Leonard Cohen's 'Light as the Breeze'. So I was excited to sneak it here, in a queered context, and with the power dynamics flipped.

6. *Paragraph begins with:* These were the rosary beads of my
   submission.

   Alexis: Turns out, this scene might be another fish that's
   come out how I like it.

   It's so weird coming back to the things you write so long
   after having written them, especially since I don't read my
   work once it's published. It's too easy to get neurotic about
   things you can no longer change, and consequently self-
   conscious about whatever you're doing presently.

   I think, for me, what makes the, err, particular fish of
   a sex scene work (and this is by no means intended to be
   universal—it's just about me and what I like and what I try
   to do) is when it progresses the emotional journey of the
   characters (not just in the "had sex now" check box sense
   but in the sense of telling us something about the characters that could be told no other way) and feels unique to
   them. This is obviously easier to do if there's an anal hook
   and a lemon meringue pie involved, but I do try my best to
   do it even without those elements.

7. *Paragraph begins with:* "It's fine. Freedom is being able to say
   yes *and* no."

   Alexis: I'm really glad I was able to include Grace fairly
   substantially as part of the secondary cast of this book
   (and, ideally, we'll meet her again in others). Of course,
   it's meant to be Laurie and Toby's story, not some kind
   of generalised address to the entirety of kink as a whole.
   But there's not a tonne of women dominants in romance,
   at least not in m/f. I think culturally speaking we're a lot
   more comfortable with dominant women in f/f, but m/f
   with a dominant heroine and a submissive hero runs into

a lot of the same assumptions and preoccupations about power that I basically spent *For Real* grappling with. Only you also get to add gender into the mix. Woo.

I don't want to dig into this too much because it's way out of my lane, and would take more words than I could comfortably fit into an annotation, but I think there's this persistent stereotype of submissive men as weak and unattractive, and dominant women as cold and contemptuous. And, obviously, it's fine to be any of those things, if that's what floats your boat. The problem here is that it's perceived as the default and that it revolves around a specific flavour of male pornographic fantasy, largely centred on humiliation. To put it shortly and bluntly, we essentially have a cultural concept of female domination that "belongs" to and caters to men. Which...I mean. No wonder that's discouraging to women who might otherwise be interested in getting a hot bloke on his knees for the sake of her own pleasure.

In any case, with Grace I wanted to present someone who had found a way to live authentically and happily both as a sexually dominant woman and, you know, a person, with a long-term partner and a pretty ordinary job.

8. *Paragraph begins with:* "His name's Robert," I said.

Alexis: I think one of the things it's impossible not to think about, like, *a lot* as a writer of kissing books is the 'what to do with the emotional nadir'. I can understand why readers get frustrated sometimes with what can feel like the inevitability of 'and they break up at 70 percent'. Especially because being hyperaware on a meta level that two characters are going to, at some point, get into a conflict that feels irresolvable can make the conflict, when it does appear, feel inauthentic or routine.

The thing is, though, I do stand by the work performed by the emotional nadir of a genre romance: I think it's important for the couple to have a reckoning with their own fears and insecurities, and to demonstrate the long-term viability of their relationship by continuing to choose it, and fight for it, even in the midst of crisis, betrayal, misunderstanding, whatever.

I think, to me, what makes an emotional nadir challenging to suspend my disbelief through as a reader is not when it happens, or even that it happens; it's about what has preceded it, what triggers it, and how it's resolved. While I do return to the seventy percent breakup fairly regularly as a writer (though I have written books without it—*A Lady for a Duke*, for example, has the emotional nadir about the forty percent mark and the rest of the book is the couple overcoming it), I do try to make it specific to the book and the characters involved.

With *For Real*, I think I do a fair bit of, err, edging, I guess? There are repeated moments across the course of the book that could be about to trigger disaster—like the scene in Oxford, where we're not sure if Toby is going to fit in, and then not sure how Laurie is going to deal with him fitting in too well, and this one, of course. But I think it's part of the weird slow burn of the relationship that the emotional nadir gathers about them gradually and then finally catches them when Toby, for various reasons including grief, is at his lowest.

9. *Paragraph begins with:* I gazed at Robert, mute and pleading.

Alexis: I know I've spoken a bit already about whether Robert is a baddie or not. I mean, beyond just being someone who has behaved badly.

I think here he's genuinely oblivious. Or rather still doggedly living his own lies. Which means he keeps treating Laurie as if there's nothing, good or bad, between them. That the part of their lives they shared is so over it might as well never have happened. Because that helps him keep pretending he never fucked up. Never hurt Laurie. Was never broken by that himself.

Yikes, he was never much on my radar as a central character, but I think I might want to write Robert's book now?

10. *Paragraph begins with:* He couldn't have said anything worse if he'd actively tried.

Alexis: I, err, I honestly don't think this is an unreasonable concern on Laurie's part. I think we live in a world all too keen to police the identity of others, and kink is not immune to that. You can always find someone ready to tell you that you're being a dom/me wrong or judging you for not being a dom/me in exactly the way they are. If you ask me, we'd all be a lot happier if we had enough grace to believe people when they tell us who they are. Or, if we can't manage that, at least accept it's none of our fucking business.

11. *Paragraph begins with:* "Or"—a different voice—"he could just use something better suited..."

Alexis: I brought Dom the Dom into this scene because, having decided it wasn't fair to treat him as a symbol for shit I personally don't like, I wanted to show him in a better context. One that, essentially, proves his quality for all he isn't the right partner for Laurie.

This was the moment I knew I wanted to write him a book. Challenge some of his rigidities and give him a complicated, messy, wonderful HEA with a partner who is perfectly wrong for him.

Chapter Ten

1. *Paragraph begins with:* And the way he gives that up for me...
   Alexis: This is another one of those moments where I wanted to show that Toby's inexperience wasn't an impediment to his dominance. I mean, I didn't think it was appropriate to set up a situation where he had to prove himself—that would make me no better than the crowd in this scene—but it was important to me that we get to see very clearly just how capable Toby is of looking out for Laurie not just as his partner but as his dom. That he can and will protect Laurie when Laurie might not be capable of protecting himself.

2. *Paragraph begins with:* I'm kind of bummed to learn that's still a thing that happens in your thirties.
   Alexis: ME TOO, TOBY. ME TOO.

3. *Paragraph begins with:* All because my weekend with Laurie is over...
   Alexis: I think when you're, you know, old and withered as I am these days, it's really easy to look back on your distant youth as a time of infinite glittering potential. But that elides, in the name of nostalgia, how fucking powerless being young can feel sometimes and how stuck you can get.

4. *Paragraph begins with:* In the end I go to the back of the kitchen...

   Alexis: Having worked several catering jobs, I am still haunted by the memory of the industrial tubs of mayo. I honestly think there are few things more depressing, and more horrifying, in the world. And I say this as someone who likes mayo. But once you've beheld a bucket of the stuff—wobbling and off-white and smelling of powdered egg—you will be forever changed. And not in a good way.

   Thus Toby hiding next to the heavy duty mayo and crying feels to me like an extremely vivid image of a soul in torment. Your mileage may vary depending on your exposure to industrial mayonnaise.

5. *Paragraph begins with:* The next orders come in quickly...

   Alexis: I like to feel my kinky book covers a fair bit of kinky ground. But can we please take a moment to note that competence kink has entered the building.

6. *Paragraph begins with:* "Why won't you look at me? What's wrong with you?"

   Alexis: Toby is a huge mess here, and Laurie is not...as helpful as he could be. I know we're at a 70 percent breakup moment, but I hope it feels true to where the characters are and what they're going through. I don't mean to be all "ahhh the irrationality of grief" when it comes to Toby's meltdown but, well, grief *can* be irrational and it's been building for a while. Combined with his uncertainties about his future and his uncertainties about Laurie, it's a cri de coeur cocktail.

7. *Paragraph begins with:* I stare at Laurie, who looks pale...

   Alexis: I seem to return semi-often to characters who are resistant to saying *I love you.* Whether it's about Barthes or not. I think I've even written a couple of books where the characters don't say it to each other at all. But it also feels important to me to have characters who are explicitly looking for the words—not an approximation of them, or actions that amount to them—and get them. Not because I think saying "I love you" is either necessary or magic but because loving someone is about seeing who they are and understanding what they need.

Chapter Eleven

1. *Chapter begins with:* Laurie & Toby

   Alexis: Uhhh, I'm embarrassed at myself for being so into this pretentious arty shit. But I feel slightly smug about the fact that the gaps (both in terms of chronology and perspective) between the POV sections decrease as Laurie and Toby get closer to a properly balanced and mutually fulfilling relationship. Here, despite being in conflict, they are literally on the same page which anticipates the completeness of their forthcoming reconciliation.

2. *Paragraph begins with:* In case he came to his senses sooner rather than later...

   Alexis: This is a Dorothy Parker quote. Because of course Toby would have a Dorothy Parker quote for his voice mail.

3. *Paragraph begins with:* He sits up and he's looking at me, so I kind of have to look at him back.

Alexis: Coming back to Spires after so long has involved a touch of papering over the cracks here and there. You know, fixing continuity errors and the like. Occasionally, though, I see something like Marius's pointy shoes and am genuinely a bit stunned at how well I knew these books, and these characters then, and—honestly—still know them now.

As for Marius's pointy shoes, they made a triumphant return in 2024's *Chasing the Light*.

4. *Paragraph begins with:* "Well, neither do you, so stop judging."
   Alexis: I'm sure Coal is not most people's image of an ideal parent, but she's got a point. I didn't actually want to make her a bad mother (because, ouch, what a terrible cliché to say nothing of a can of worms gender-wise), but I did want to make her a complicated person. Toby would certainly not be who he is without her; I think when he feels less insecure in general, he'll come to appreciate that.

5. *Paragraph begins with:* "Then he should stop."
   Alexis: The "Person from Porlock" was supposedly, well, a person from Porlock who interrupted Samuel Taylor Coleridge when (in the grip of opium) he was writing 'Kubla Khan.'

   Apparently the Person from Porlock detained Coleridge on trivial business for over an hour, which meant that by the time he picked up his pen again, his original vision for the poem had faded from his mind. Hence its flawed and fragmentary state.

   Orrr... Coleridge was off his head, couldn't work out how to finish his poem, and invented an unwelcome visitor by way of an excuse. Basically a Person From Porlock ate his homework.

Since Toby is such a lover of poetry, it feels apposite to mention Stevie Smith's 'Thoughts about the Person from Porlock'—where she uses the possibility of the Person from Porlock being imaginary to explore ideas of inspiration, isolation, and depression. A Google search of the name will bring this up, and it's a wonderful poem (not least because, unlike 'Kubla Khan,' it's actually complete). There's also UA Fanthorpe's 'The Person's Tale' which sadly the internet cannot produce for me. From memory, I seem to recall it's about an irate man from Porlock who had to visit Coleridge on business and found him smelly, stoned, and incoherently burbling about a pleasure dome. #JusticeForPersonFromPorlock

6. *Paragraph begins with:* She pushes the hair out of my eyes.
   Alexis: I was trying to tread carefully with Marwa here. I didn't want to make her some kind of magical, healing hospice nurse. But equally I wanted to show that she genuinely knew Toby and cared about him and wished him well. Essentially I think she has a necessary briskness to her—she deals with death and grief every day, after all—but a lot of compassion too. Which includes moving people on when they need to be moved on. Which Toby absolutely does.

7. *Paragraph begins with:* Because love is strong.
   Alexis: While Toby is not particularly religious, I think there are aspects of religious writing that stick with you and can be extraordinarily comforting at the right time.

This is, of course, an echo of the Song of Solomon 8:6 (ESV).

Set me as a seal upon thine heart,
as a seal upon thine arm,
for love is strong as death

Of course—kind of rarely for the Bible—the Song of Solomon is talking mostly about romantic love here. But I think these ideas about love (that it is powerful, that it faces obstacles, that death and love are inextricably connected) are pretty damn universal.

8. *Paragraph begins with:* Laurie rolls off my bed and stands carefully.
   Alexis: Having spoken such a lot in these annotations about the emotional nadir, I tend to try and unite characters pretty quickly—in this case, within twenty-four hours.
   Of course, I do sometimes leave characters apart for significantly longer. Sometimes it feels necessary, or circumstances demand it. But on a personal level I'm becoming increasingly resistant to "I must go away to do xyz, or prove myself abc, before we can be together" because I'm so drawn to the idea that being in love is being part of a team. And while you shouldn't drag your team- mates through all your bullshit all the time, sometimes it's easier to get through bullshit when you're not alone, and I think it's okay to acknowledge that. Yes, it's important to be strong. But sometimes we're weak too. And sometimes, through no fault of our own, there really is a lot of bullshit.

Chapter Twelve

1. *Paragraph begins with:* Or...I can try to get a different job.
   Alexis: Very proud of a fictional person I invented right now.

2. *Paragraph begins with:* He tells me how being a doctor wasn't his dream, either.
   Alexis: Sorry, Toby. That's a nope.

3. *Paragraph begins with:* "Would you... Do you think...
   Alexis: So, this scene, huh?

   I know I've spoken/written about this a lot, but something I kind of feel very personally resistant to as a writer and, err, as a person is this idea of sexual act escalation.

   Like you start with kissing and end with anal.

   Or you start with flogging and end with, um, something even kinkier.

   So basically I didn't want Laurie and Toby's sexual relationship to feel like it moved up a hierarchy of kinky to more kinky. And while I definitely did want it to become more intimate (as well it should as they get to know each other better and fall in love), I didn't want intimacy to be communicated by what they did. So much as how they did it.

   All of which is to say, that's why you're getting a flogging scene, an opening salvo for some kinky books, at the end of the story. Is it as notable as lemon meringue pie and an anal hook? Probably not. But it's an act of deep personal intimacy to Laurie and Toby.

4. *Paragraph begins with:* So I take that, the deerskin, some cuffs and snap hooks...

   Alexis: I like to think as the book progresses we see Toby (with Laurie's help) grow increasingly confident with his kinks—not just what he's into, but what he's not into. And now we've reached this moment, where he's able to dispense with the status symbol of fancy ropework for the utility of cuffs with no insecurity whatsoever.

5. *Paragraph begins with:* Then I let him go, and that's a kind of power too...

   Alexis: I think this might be a "you're on your own there, Hall" thing, but I really wanted to explore Toby's differing experiences of sexual power across the book as a whole. I think because a lot of books tend to focus on the sub's experiences relative to the dom's, there's sometimes a sense that power in this context can be quite a cold or aggressive force. And maybe some people do, in fact, feel cold and aggressive when they're beating on someone they've tied up. Obviously there are times when Toby is gleeful and sadistic and merciless, but I also wanted to show occasions when exercising his dominance makes him soft and thankful and *romantic*. Because I think sharing this kind of connection with someone is like any other connection: exhilarating, varied, and, frankly, humbling.

6. *Paragraph begins with:* Anyway, I can't find it because all his ties suck...

   Alexis: I have a real weakness as a writer and a reader for incidents like this. Like, obviously, the same tie would have offered, you know, parallelism, a callback, whatever.

But instead Toby can't find it so just moves on. Because life...sex...love...whatever doesn't have to be perfect to be *wonderful*.

7. *Paragraph begins with:* The thing that kind of shakes me a bit is not so much what I'm doing...

    Alexis: I didn't want to over-emphasise this because, well, I didn't want either Toby or anyone else to feel guilty about their sexual behaviour. But I did want to pause and give the moment weight. Because physically striking someone, even someone who has consented to it, even if it's for their pleasure, is not an easy thing or a light thing. Even if you like it. Hell, especially if you like it.

8. *Paragraph begins with:* It's crazy because even though I'm crying everywhere, I'm not sad.

    Alexis: Once again, this was me wanting to allow space for the dominant to have emotions. I honestly wish there was more space for this in general.

9. *Paragraph begins with:* And then I stand again and wait...

    Alexis: Buuut I also didn't want those emotions to feel like they existed in opposition to dominance. Like, Toby can be crying and still in control. There's no rule that says he can't be. Just toxic ideas surrounding what counts as weakness and what counts as strength.

IN VINO

"I have lost the immortal part of myself, and what remains is bestial."

William Shakespeare, "Othello"

It's the wine that's made me sentimental. Or perhaps I pity James F. Hanley, being tripped over by a child who lacks the capacity to sing and a man who lacks the capacity to count. In any case, I sing, something I haven't done for years, fallen chorister that I am. My voice—lain so long fallow—rises from my lips like a lark's. I'm honestly a little startled to discover something so pure still lingers inside me. Likely I'll rectify it soon enough, but for the moment...I still recall the thrill, guess I always will.

It must be the wine because it can't be Laurie's absurd happiness or the winsome ways of his boy. They dance on long after the song is done. I finish my cigarette, drain my glass, and leave them to each other.

Silence trails me into the cloisters. I can get another drink in the SCR. There'll be the dregs of conversation too. And Sherry, of course, the last flame amongst the ashes. But fuck him. I can't bear his perfection tonight. If he'd been born just ten years earlier, he'd be conveniently dying of AIDs right now. For symbolic reasons, you understand, representing the destruction of the beautiful and the good. Easily interpretable prime time tragedy. Unfortunately, I've never seen him suffer so much as a cold. I want to imagine him a wasted ruin, fractious and afraid, so that I can be the better man. But my mind betrays me as it always does, and I am the one who is broken. Never him. Never Sherry. He is half angel, dying as exquisitely as Saint Sebastian, barely pricked by arrows, while I weep on my knees at his bedside like Heathcliff and beg, *please don't leave me to a world without you.* He's the only person I've ever permitted to think well of me. And, let's be honest, it's touch-and-go.

As I wander without purpose, I abandon the glass on the ledge of one of the ornamental arches. Someone—a scout, a waiter, a porter, perhaps another academic—will find it in the morning and be annoyed. They'll blame a careless undergraduate, of course. I think I must be exceptionally drunk. Inebriation is like the sea—even the bed is not the bottom, and I am floating gently in some bioluminescent trench among the anglerfish and the vampire squid. But I like it down here. I've never seen well by sunlight and I prefer the company of eyeless things.

I can always tell when I'm deep deep deep because my thoughts take on the cut-glass clarity of uttered words. It's almost as if they've shaped for themselves a recipient. Not an interlocutor, for this being is always absolutely silent, barely present but for a sense of limitless receptiveness. I suppose some would call this god, but my God has no use for me nor I for him. Regardless, I am oddly comforted by the imagined existence of a listener. Someone to bear all that is ugly and unspeakable and true. And stay with me still.

Sherry might be waiting. But no. No. I can't see him

again tonight. Given my behaviour earlier, we should be in the contrition stage of our cycle, and I'm not contrite enough. I will be, though, in a day or a handful of days, when the absence of him crawls over me like gangrene. At which point I'll crawl too. I might even manage to treat him well for a little while. Oh what fuckery is this? Whoever claimed there was veritas in vino was a rank amateur. We devotees drink it for delusion and I will never be good, or good enough, for Sherry. I will never be what he deserves.

Laurie, though, has betrayed me shamefully. Our brotherhood of the unlovable. Who will be defiantly wretched with me now? He'll still visit, of course, but he'll get joy and contentment everywhere, and it won't be the same. It was bad enough when he was with Robert. So very Laurie to spend over a decade with the first man who made him beg and hurt, as if there's some kind of magic to it. I thought he'd finally moved beyond such pathetic naiveté, but apparently I was wrong. His world is not completely devoid of enchantment.

A moment of indulgence: I imagine Tobermory's fingers tightening against my throat, the wild-thing glitter of his eyes.

Surrender is as effortless as water for people like me, for people with nothing worth yielding. I gave him only a taste of it, but I could tell it tantalised him. I should have taken it further and stirred that sweet little cock of his. It's the filthiest of pleasures, picturing the betrayal in Laurie's eyes. My oldest friend, and the thought of causing him that much pain—of taking something beautiful from him—makes me instantly, powerfully hard. And to think this tender morsel of a dom believes himself a sadist.

"Dr. Leigh?" A voice from the shadows.

I'm disconcerted for a second or two that the world is not my own dark kingdom. And then I recognise one of my undergraduates. I give him the barest nod. "Mr. Baron."

We're encouraged these days to be informal. Some of my colleagues are even—God help us—matey. They call tutorials "classes" and wear blazers with jeans. Probably they aspire to host hour-long specials on the BBC, where they serve up learning like slices of pizza: The Secret Life of Shakespeare, A Century of Sodomy, Top Ten Sex Scandals of the Sixteenth Century. It makes me want to vomit. And so does pizza.

The fashion may be to ape modernity—equal access frameworks and strategic outreach and we're just like everyone else really—but I insist upon ceremony. The observances of rank. Oxford is *Brideshead Revisited* and *Jude the Obscure*. It is the city of Sidney and Wilmot and Wilde. We do not come here to be normal. We come because we are not. And we crave the brutal mastery of centuries and cold stone.

There was a girl a year or so back—from Leeds, I think—who pronounced my name as "Lay." Dr. Lay, she said, draping her flat, round vowels all over it. I didn't deign to correct her. Just let the silence seal her in grey steel. Until she fled in tears. Honestly, I thought they were supposed to breed them tough up north. To this day, I'm not sure what happened to her. Did someone tell me she dropped out? Or changed course? Or committed suicide? It's so hard to remember with undergraduates.

"Did you have a good evening?"

God save me from eighteen-year-olds attempting small talk. Not that He has ever saved me from anything before. "Very pleasant, thank you. 'Much wine had passed, with grave discourse. Of who fucks who, and who does worse.'"

A sort of giggle. "Dr. Leigh, you said fuck."

"No, I quoted poetry, with the word fuck in it. One must always be precise, Mr. Baron."

Uninvited, he falls into step beside me. He's taller than I am, with the rippling cartoon-Hercules build of a rower, broad across the shoulders, tapering to long, lean flanks. Probably rises at four a.m. every morning and races down to the river with the rest of the public-school beasts.

"Are you always going to call me Mr. Baron?"

"It's your name."

"My name is Zachary. Or my friends call me Zach."

I'm either too drunk or not drunk enough for this. In either case, I need another glass of wine. I need another bottle. "Not being of their number, I have no interest in what your friends call you."

"Okay, but it's not like we're strangers either. And, right now, aren't you off the clock?"

"Off the clock," I repeat, fuzzily appalled. "I don't work in Tescos."

"No, if you worked in a supermarket it would definitely be Waitrose."

"You're not funny, Mr. Baron."

He laughs anyway. Not the posh-boy bray I'm expecting, but something altogether...realer.

"Do you want something?" I ask, and I'm relieved to discover my tone is sharp with an edge of boredom. As it should be.

He shifts uncertainly. And I pay no attention to the pull and bunch of muscles in his upper arms. "Um, gosh. Awks. Not really. I just saw you walking and you looked sort of..."

"I looked sort of what?"

"I don't know." This unsubtle evasion is probably the only flicker of sense he has shown in the last five minutes. Possibly his entire life. "I thought I might as well say hello."

"Then, mission accomplished. Good night."

I move away as briskly as I can. The world rolls her hips and the ground lurches. The half-eaten moon swings in the sky like the hook of a pendulum. But where is the pit?

"Do you want me to walk you back to your room?" he calls after me.

Of course I don't. "If you insist."

"Cool."

I'm dimly aware of time and space. Both of them passing, drifting away from me in snail trails of starlight. It's only when we're at the foot of a staircase that I realise where we are.

"You think I live in my office?" My voice is not quite what I would have wished. Regrettably, I sound almost amused.

"Oh shit. I mean. Sorry. I... Fuck."

Actually, this is better. My rooms are full of Sherry. My sheets will smell of him. Strands of his hair will shine upon my pillows. I fumble for my keys. "Come on up."

I'm at the very top. Laurie calls it my turret. Though I have yet to experience any Tirra-Lirra-ing. I don't think I can cope with bright light, so I turn on a lamp. It's stained glass, art nouveau roses, casting pinkish dapples across the wood-paneled walls. Zachary stands uncertainly in what should be a familiar place: this site of his weekly pilgrimage to literature.

"Would you like a drink?" I ask. I'm already pouring one for me. I've got about a third of a bottle of an Australian Cabernet Sauvignon, good enough to stay drunk on.

"Maybe some water? Should I get you some as well?"

I gave him the sort of look guaranteed to reduce underprepared, over-aspirational undergraduates to tears. "Have some wine for fuck's sake."

My fingers are not as steady as they could be but I manage to pour. And then press the glass into one of his big, oar-callused hands.

"I don't really—"

"Oh, don't be virtuous, it's tedious."

He's holding his wine as if I've given him a live grenade. "It's just...my dad..."

"Drink up, Mr. Baron. 'That second bottle tells us the truth of ourselves and forces us to speak truths of others.'" I feel the laughter, grape-red upon my lips. "Though I confess I'm slightly past the second."

After a long moment, he takes a sip. "Am I supposed to be all 'deep nose and oaky finish? Base notes of berries and unicorns'?"

"Personally I've always preferred simply to drink it." I clink my glass to his. It makes the crystal sing: a sweet, clean note that hangs, then shatters in the silence.

For some reason—an instinct for cruelty turned, this time, upon myself—I glance out of the mullioned windows and down, down, all the way down into the quad. Just in time to see a knight ride by. I recognise Sherry by his shadow. By the way what little light remains glitters in his hair. Even walking away, especially walking away, he's beautiful. Long, careless strides as if loss and shame and fear have never touched him. And never could.

My palm is against the glass. But, of course, he won't look up. He has no way of knowing I'm even here. Maybe he's going to my rooms, wanting me, and I won't be there, a possibility I have no ability to process. I love the idea of disappointing him, of possessing that power. But, at the same time, every moment I am not with Sherry—and there are so many, a universe of dust—feels like a wasted one. What do you do with a man you can neither bear to be with nor bear to be without? Although, to momentarily face a second-third-fourth bottle truth: it is mostly myself I cannot bear.

There's another world, where I am different, or he is, and I push open the window. Maybe I call out to him or maybe I don't have to because he magically already knows, so I can run down the stairs and into his arms and the kiss of all kisses that I haven't quite learned how to stop waiting for. And maybe there's rain. And an ugly cat that I'm not allergic to.

In any case, it's all irrelevant because he turns the other way and disappears. There's a moment, just after, when I feel so close to weeping.

"Dr. Leigh"—a touch between my shoulder blades—"are you okay?"

I spin round. Oh yes. Zachary Baron. I'd forgotten he was here. But I invited him, didn't I?

Since there's less than usual to lose, less than nothing in other words, I let myself enjoy looking at him. He's just on the right side of brutish, powerful but refined. And the rest of him is equally appealing. Green-eyed and clean-cut, naturally patrician, the sort of face that would place him somewhere between One Direction and a minor royal. The crease of his lips is stained slightly purple.

So I kiss him.

He makes a delicious, little shocked noise. But he doesn't hesitate. His mouth parts under mine with all the clumsy fervour of half-drunk youth, and I taste the bitterness of wine upon his tongue.

He doesn't seem to know what to do with his hands.

I drop my wineglass—it's in my way—and grab a handful of his shirt, using it to drag him deeper into my kiss. But the breaking glass distracts him.

"Jesus." He pulls away, my reluctance to let him leaving a glistening trail across his chin. "Be careful."

"It's only glass."

"You could get hurt."

I laugh and try to kiss him again.

"Seriously."

"Fine." I put my hands on his shoulders and jump. He catches me and hoists me up, and I twine my legs about his waist, my gown billowing around us. "Rescue me, then."

He carries me effortlessly across the room. Then appears to have absolutely no idea what to do with me. I direct him to my chair, the fine, old wingback from which I conduct tutorials, and he sinks down into it, bringing me with him. For a moment, I'm tumbled over his lap as wantonly as a tavern wench in a pulp fantasy novel. If he knew me better, he'd pin me like this. A touch of indignity brings out the best in me. For what little that's worth.

But, of course, he doesn't. And I won't admit that I want it. I right myself, panting a little, trying to gauge how deep I am, how far I've fallen. But I'm drunk beyond landmarks and there's only dark from here.

I shove a hand between his legs. He's already hard, but I stroke him anyway. There's something strangely earnest about his cock as it jerks and strains. A puppy dog on the leash. Well, a large and vigorous puppy. A Labrador or something.

"Dr. Leigh?"

"Yes, Mr. Baron?"

"Is this... I mean. What's going on?"

"What's going on is that I'm about to fuck you. Any objections?"

"I...I don't know."

Admittedly, he's not the quickest of his year's cohort. I give him my most piercing stare over the top of my glasses. "Do you think I'm entirely ignorant of the way you look at me?"

"Oh God." He squeezes his eyes closed, a feverish flush streaking those perfectly chiselled cheekbones.

"Mr. Baron," I purr, "are you hot for teacher?"

"Yes, but—" He breaks into a strangled gasp as I squeeze him savagely.

"What did I tell you about precision?"

"You...you...said it was good."

I decide to forgive him for his inability to recognise rhetorical questions because his cock clearly requires more blood than his brain. "So you do listen."

"I listen to everything you say." He's looking at me again—surprisingly solemnly for a man getting what amounts to a hand job in Georgian armchair.

"How terribly unwise of you, my dear." I let go of his cock and run my thumb carelessly across his lips. Sadness beats inside me like a second heart. "Now, are we making this terrible mistake or not? I don't have all night."

This is, of course, a wild lie.

He kisses the pad of my thumb, which is exactly the sort of pointless tenderness I can't abide, and gives me a reckless, wine-stained smile. "Yeah, okay."

Unsteadily, I stand, turn and go to work on his belt. I have to subject him to an exasperated sigh before he realises I need him to raise his hips. He does and I yank his jeans and underwear down his thighs. Which, I must concede, are rather fine: well-defined and lightly whorled with gold-brown hair. His cock, too, is pleasantly fit for purpose, boasting both width and length, ruddily and prominently crowned. Whatever created Zachary Horatio Baron, late of Winchester College, has been liberal with its blessings. It's enough to make one positively teleological.

And it seems I'm on my knees. Old habits, as they say, die hard. *Fratres agnoscamus peccata nostra, ut api simus ad sacra mysteria celebranda.* I lean forward and drop a mocking kiss on the head of his prick. He jerks and gasps, and leaks a pearly tear, leaving me with the fleetest trace of salt upon my lips.

Back to my feet, most likely lurching slightly, grace apparently being something else I lost on the way to where I am now, I stumble out of my shoes, shed socks and trousers and boxers. The rest is way too much trouble.

Do I have a condom? In my wallet, I'm sure. Except I don't know where my wallet is. Maybe there's some still in the desk, from the time Sherry fucked me over it. He's always so fucking considerate.

Oh Sherry.

I'm right. Some ghastly American brand, of course. But beggars, etc.

Zachary has a rather dazed look as I roll the condom over his still-attentive member. Perhaps I should do this with all my (male) undergraduates. I might like them better, hard and quiet and useful.

The chair is wide enough that I can kneel over him, facing the room, my legs spread wide over his. It takes some fumbling under my gown to find his cock, but as soon as I do, I brace him and sink down.

There's lube on the condom and, in any case, I'm a whore, but that first breach is still exquisitely painful. It shocks a far too naked sound out of me. One that continues its own ragged song, and the truest I've sung tonight, as I descend. I force myself open upon on the cock of an eighteen-year-old...and feeling rushes in.

"God," says Mr. Baron. "Fuck. God."

For once, I couldn't have said it better myself. At last, my flesh meets his and he's fully inside me. Deep enough to turn my every breath into something raw and sobbing. I'm pierced, impaled, and burning like a heretic martyr. Unrepentant.

And, for a strange, teetering moment, content.

An arm makes a clumsy attempt to embrace me and that's the moment gone. I slap Zachary away and get to the business of fucking myself on his cock. My own, which has been at most academically interested in my activities, stirs and stiffens, distracting me with an itchy kind of desire that quickly becomes excruciating. Difficult to tell whether I like it or not.

My stomach muscles ache and my thighs quiver as I slip into a state of senseless arousal. I'm stifling in the robe—I must have sweated through both my shirt and jacket, and Tobermory's careful bow tie, at last, surrenders. I catch a glimpse of it out of the corner of my eye as the black silk flutters to the floor. Probably I should have thought about all this earlier. But I can't stop now. My body won't let me. I drive myself harder, faster, moaning, my hands clawing ineffectively at fabric. Basically, it's come or die trying. I'm good with either.

Reflected in the far window, where I stood however long ago, watching...letting...Sherry walk away from me, I can see our ghosts. I'm a graceless haze of black and white. The boy who pants at my shoulder barely distinguishable at all. I'm probably ruining him too. It's almost enough to send me over.

Almost, fucking almost.

My glasses slide off my nose, bounce off my leg, and go... somewhere. Now I can't see a damn thing. And I can't come either.

Not enough. Never quite enough.

I pull off with a wince and a wet squelch. Ten centuries of erudition curl their lip at me. My legs fold and I half fall onto the floor, specifically onto the lovely silk Isfahan rug, which was a gift from my mother.

Balanced on my knees and one hand, I drag my gown up

over my back. My mind very kindly provides me with a detailed rendering of the picture I must be presenting to Zachary Baron. Sprawled at his feet, flashing my haunches at him like Lady Chatterley. Of course, that almost sends me over too.

I manage to say, in my driest voice, "In your own time, Mr. Baron." And not *fuck me, please, for the love god, make me come.*

He gets down behind me. I am pleasantly surprised to discover he handles his cock with reasonable facility. Far better than he writes essays or participates in—

"Ah." Not the most elegant sound I've ever made, but he wrenches it out of me in a sublimely brutal thrust. I think what I hate most is the gratitude in it.

"Yeah? You like that?"

I have no intention of replying to so smug an inquiry but, unfortunately, he does the same thing again. And I let out another helplessly revealing cry.

He smooths his palm over the curve of my buttock. And I'm fucked in the head, as well as the arse, because the unwanted admiration in it makes me shudder.

I snarl at him. "Put your hand on the back of my neck."

That makes him falter—good, he was getting far too cocky—but, finally, he obeys.

"With conviction, Mr. Baron."

There. At last. His rowing calluses are, oh, quite something as he pushes my head to the rug. This lifts my hips enough that his next act of ingress into my person goes deep enough to knock against my heart. Or at the very least fill the cavity my heart is supposed to occupy. I wail, in terrified pleasure, and scrabble at the silk.

"How's that?"

Motherfucker. He thinks he can *tease* me.

I gather myself. Difficult when I feel split wide, as if at any moment my gasping mouth will spew forth a tide of loathly toades and papers.

"I have no intention," I said, "of providing formative feedback on your performance. Just...fuck me. Fuck me like you mean it."

What I should really say is *fuck me like you hate me*. But at this point there's very little difference.

He does, however, set about his task with both precision and conviction. Possibly even to distinction level. He keeps his hand firmly on my neck, so I couldn't get up even if I wanted to, and the other bites into my hip, most likely leaving bruises, as he hammers me into the floor. My teaching room reeks of sweat and sex and wine. And fills up with the sort of sounds it probably should never have encompassed, let alone on several hazily remembered occasions. I bite my wrist in an effort to quell some of them, especially the hitchy, little whimpers and approving oh-god-yeses that keep wanting to crawl their way up my throat and exist in the world.

I still can't reach my cock. But, as it turns out, it doesn't matter. Before I'm even quite aware of it, I'm tumbling into a smooth, grey nothing. It's something like peace, this place where my mind grants me mercy, and I'm just a body for things to happen in. I like the world rather more when it consists mainly of a cock and a hole.

And then I've come all over my mother's rug.

"Wow. Did you just..."

Reality is like getting hit by car. "Yes. Yes I did."

"You didn't even..."

I'm warm and limp and almost blissfully weak. There's some part of me that wants to lie here in my own cooling ejaculate, with my face on the floor and my legs splayed wide, letting Zachary

Baron's rather magnificent cock use me until he comes. There is, of course, no way in hell I will allow that to happen. "Yes, well," I murmur, with what little asperity I can muster, "unlike you, I'm not a sodomitical neophyte. Now would you be so kind as to remove yourself?"

"Can't I finish?"

"No, Mr. Baron, you cannot. I am not a Fleshlight."

He shifts, his still-nestled cock nudging me here and there, and dragging an unfortunate and not remotely plaintive little mewl out of me. "But what am I supposed to do?"

"Plan ahead next time? I don't know. And, frankly, I don't care."

"What, so"—there's irritation in his voice, and hurt as well, though I ignore that—"I was just supposed to get myself off and not give a damn about you?"

Since he's still showing no inclination to move, I crawl forward and do the job for him. At least, I try—my arse seems pathetically unwilling to let go. "Some of us," I explain, once I'm free, "are grown-ups and can take responsibility for our own sexual pleasure."

"I thought you were supposed to take care of each other."

I roll onto my back, tuck my hands behind my neck and cross my ankles. As if I hadn't just been playing Christmas turkey on this very—now probably damaged—rug.

Zachary Baron is kneeling a short distance away, shirt half-undone, jeans bunched around his calves, cock in his hand. As far as I can tell, given that he is mainly a blur of pink and gold, debauchery and disappointment suit him very well.

"What do you think this was?" I ask.

He gives me something I interpret as an all too sharp look. What a moment to acquire even a rudimentary clue. "Apparently it was wanking with another person."

I shrug. And wait for him to leave.

"Want to suck me?"

I imagine his cock twisting me open a second time. The vulgar breadth of it stretching my lips and the velvety weight of it—"No. I don't like the taste of latex."

"I'll wash my dick."

"If you take your penis anywhere near my sink—the area where I prepare my tea—I will unleash a fury upon you of such scope and magnitude, it will make the Plagues of Egypt look like the work of a peeved amateur."

"Right." He tries, nearly falls over his jeans, and finally makes it to his feet. He peels off the condom and drops it into the waste-paper basket.

"Don't pout, Mr. Baron."

Actually I have no idea what's doing. But his posture suggests discontent. And he's eighteen—pouting seems likely.

"Oh, I'm not." Then comes the unmistakable sound of skin on damp skin. A blur of motion at his groin.

"What the fuck are you doing?" I'm not entirely impressed by the outraged squawk that emerges in lieu of the censorious roar I was hoping for.

"You said I should take responsibility for my own pleasure."

"So you're going to masturbate over me like a horny teenager with a *Playboy* centrefold?"

He shrugs and doesn't stop.

"This is not appropriate, Mr. Baron."

"You have a really fucked-up sense of perspective, Dr. Leigh."

It's not the first time I've heard that. "I insist that you stop."

"Or you'll what? Give me bad marks? You do that already."

"Your essays merit them. Your style is pedestrian, your coherence lacking, and your arguments facile."

For some reason, my recitation of his academic failings seems to amuse him, and he laughs.

"I could report this," I suggest. Speaking of facile.

"Yeah, I can see the story of how you invited a student up to your rooms at three in the morning, plied him with drink, and made him have sex with you coming across really well."

I suddenly don't know what to do with myself. I'm drowning in my own body, in the weariness of my cock, the just-fucked soreness of my arse, the sweat drying on my neck and under my arms, the prickle of Russell cord against my bare legs. "Quickly, then."

"I'm going to take as long as I like." He lets go of his cock, and I foolishly entertain a brief hope that he's changed his mind. But he's just reaching behind to something balanced on the arm of the chair. My glasses land on my chest. "Put them on. You don't look like you without them."

I don't feel like me without them, either. People sometimes ask why I don't wear contacts, but I've never wanted to. I like my eyes armoured. I don't know how everyone else can stand to be so exposed.

"Go on."

There's a significant part of me that doesn't want to give him any satisfaction at all. But I do actually want my glasses back. So I slip them on and Zachary Baron snaps shiningly into focus. His shirt is fully open now, revealing the sculpted expanse of his torso, lightly flushed and glistening with sweat, his abs tightening and his chest heaving with his quickening breath. He's standing with his legs slightly apart, staring down at me, his cock gliding in and out of the channel of his hand. He looks like a fake Grindr profile. Or a porn site pop-up.

I close my eyes. He can do what he likes but I don't have to watch. I compose my expression into one of profound boredom. Base notes of contempt. Bouquet of superiority.

He laughs again. "You're doing your tutorial face."

Something brushes my leg—his foot, I think? My gown is prodded and pushed at. Then I feel cold air against my thighs. The hot sense of being watched.

I can't. It's too... I need to see what he's doing.

Opening my eyes again, I discover I look ridiculous. My shirt and jacket are basically intact, except for the open collar and lack of bow tie. But from the waist down, I'm naked, the length of one leg and my spent, come-smeared cock exposed through the folds of my gown. I reach down to cover myself up.

"Did I say you could move?"

I think about protesting, but I'm not sure what good it will do. Or, for that matter, if I really want to stop this. I can't deny that it has a faint...appeal. Not the act specifically but being obliged to endure it. And so I lie back with a put-upon sigh.

"Very good."

Oh no. I do not need the approval of a presumptuous undergraduate and I will not respond to it.

"You look so hot, Dr. Leigh." Zachary is stroking his cock in earnest now, long, rough strokes that remind me of being fucked. "Like a total pervert."

"You coerce me into being your wank fodder and *I'm* the one you consider a pervert?"

"You started it. I'm just being a diligent student."

I want to protest again. But I'm hampered by the fact he's right. He's done nothing I haven't told him—explicitly or otherwise. An apt pupil indeed, as monstrous as his teacher.

"Hey," he says softly. "Want me to stop?"

I shake my head.

We pass a minute or so in something like silence. If silence can encompass the sound of one man masturbating over another. I try to lie still and think of nothing.

It doesn't work. It never works.

My thoughts are everywhere. I am scuttled over by sea crabs. And nipped at. I feel filthy and objectified. And it's...thrilling.

"Holy shit, you're into this."

My cock does appear to have joined, or more accurately re-joined, the party. Rather in the fashion of Maleficent at Sleeping Beauty's christening. I subject it to my most disappointed gaze, which quells it not at all.

"So hot." Zachary appears to possess a rather limited repertoire of lewd blandishments. But points for enthusiasm.

And then, just when I am beginning to think I might get through this relatively unscathed: "Spread your legs."

"What? No. Absolutely not."

"Go on. I want to see the hole I fucked."

"No." Except for the part where I do.

"Wider."

I do not make any kind of noise. It is certainly not a whimper.

"Good." Zachary gives a deep, dark groan. "You're so slutty, Dr. Leigh."

"Your commentary is unnecessary, Mr. Baron. What have I told you about prolixity?"

He returns his attention to the business at hand. And I, once again, begin to think I'm in the all-clear. But no.

"You look really swollen. Are you okay?"

"I'm fine."

"Are you sure? Aren't you sore?"

I need, as a matter of urgency, for the discussion of my arsehole to be over. "I like it, all right? Now stop—"

"Wow, you really are a pervert." But he says it so gently that my twisted brain, normally incapable of recognising anything that could be even loosely construed as a compliment, decides to like it. "Get your hips up. I want to see properly."

"No. You've seen quite enough already."

"I'm nowhere near my limit."

"Learn to live with it."

"Always teaching." He grins down at me. "But maybe you could stand to be taught a little too."

I curl my lip. "I very much doubt it."

"How about being more considerate of other people?" He moves with unexpected agility, considering his jeans are round his knees—perhaps it's the sort of thing they train you for at public school—and grabs my ankle. "Or at the very least doing what I tell you."

"Zachary, don't—"

I flail but he catches my other foot easily and wrenches my legs up and apart. My cock jerks and spatters precome over my belly. Probably the best thing to do right now would be to close my eyes and pretend I don't exist. Or at the very least find some sort of happy place. With flowers and sunshine and...things.

"Fuck." Zachary breathes out the word. "Look at you."

Fresh heat floods me, my ridiculous prick apparently convinced that I'm already in a happy place.

"This turns you on."

I meet Zachary's eyes between the V of my legs. And discover I have absolutely nothing to say.

"You should touch yourself." He's sweating, but it looks good on him, as if he's been glazed. Or dipped in honey. "Go on. I know you want to. Stroke your slutty cock for me."

How does the saying go? When you're in a hole, stop digging?

Well, I've never understood it. Having already embarked upon a course of digging, it makes no sense to stop. You're still in a hole regardless. It would be better to say "Don't begin digging unless you are absolutely certain that you want a hole here" or possibly "Well, you've started digging, you'd better keep going or you'll starve to death alone at the bottom of a hole." Or to put it another way, this is already a staff-student-relations calamity of unimaginable proportions. I might as well come again.

I wrap my hand around my cock, which is tingling and aching with neglect, and a sort of languorous sense of sensuality rolls through me. A mortifying confession at the age of twenty-nine but I've never really been very good at masturbating. I can give myself release but little else. I get too impatient, too self-conscious. I don't think I've much cared for my own pleasure in that way. Or interest in it.

"Like this?" Oh God, that's me. Why am I asking?

He smiles. "Yeah, nice and slow, that's right."

Zachary Baron is clearly a better teacher than I am. But, then, that doesn't take much. I'm terrible at it. I am, after all, currently spread-eagle like Justine and stroking my cock to the direction of one of my students.

He runs his palms up and down my calves, along the straining muscles of my thighs. It's at once exposing, reminding me of the position he has me in, and oddly soothing. A soft sigh escapes me. This feels perilously nice, lazy spirals of bliss twisting around my cock like Mayday ribbons.

It's easy to lose myself and…I do. His hands are warm and strong and rough, the perfect combination of threatening and protective. I think at one point he kisses my ankle—there's a whisper of heat there that makes me shiver—and I don't even protest.

"You're beautiful," Zachary tells me.

Redundancy again. But all I do is moan.

"When you're not being a dick. Well, okay. Even then. Go faster now."

And I do. The increase of heat and pressure makes me writhe and arch my back. This must be sorcery. Or I have run mad. Or I'm drunker than I've ever been. Why am I doing this, and how does it feel so uncomplicatedly, untaintedly wonderful?

He drops to his knees, arranging my legs so that they curl around him. His fingers play sweetly at the crease of my groin. And dip into the tender crease of my arse. "So hot watching you like this. You're so good, Dr. Leigh."

And that's when I come. I normally rip my orgasms from my own, or someone else's, flesh. Scrabble them from the gritty scarp face of satisfaction. But this is just a soft cresting, like a spill of sunlight across my skin, that builds and gathers inside me and then I'm gasping and trembling, and my hand and stomach are wet.

"Oh," I say.

"Yeah. Fuck yeah." Zachary's free hand grips my inner thigh hard enough to hurt, most likely hard enough to mark. He's working his cock ferociously with the other, his face a mask of concentrated effort. Though evidently not the sort he applies to his Anglo-Saxon translations, which are barely average. "Close your eyes."

Clearly I'm still confused because I do.

"Going to come."

I've done many depraved things in my life. Some of them I even remember. But I'm sure nothing has felt quite like this. Perhaps nothing will again. I'm drifting quietly in my own darkness, waiting with something that is neither patience nor eagerness, and yet could be either of them, for Zachary to come on me.

Probably best I say something before I start to like it. "Thank you for the update, Mr. Baron."

"Keep your eyes closed."

Obedience makes me restless. "Perhaps I want to watch."

"Can't answer for my aim."

"You think you're going to hit me from all the way down there? Ah, the overweening arrogance of youth."

"Better...safe...than sorry. But"—he interrupts himself with one of his growliest groans—"you can keep your mouth open if you like."

"How dare you. I am not—"

He climaxes, splashing my cheeks, my throat, my lips, his come shockingly warm at the moment of impact. I'm sure I should feel degraded, and I do a little, though not particularly unusually or in a manner I would be unlikely to embrace. But there's a moment when I find it...intimate. That something from inside him is now on me. And he tastes salty sweet, like summer days, as if even his semen is wholesome.

After a moment or two, I sit up. There's come on my robe too, though some of it's mine. I use the sleeves to wipe my face. "Satisfied, Mr. Baron?"

He's slumped in the wingback chair again, knees drawn up his chin, head down. "Fuck. That was... I'm not..." He glances up, grey-tinged and clammy, his eyes wet. "I'm not feeling so great."

"If you're going to vomit"—I kick the wastepaper basket over—"do it in there."

"S-sorry." He snatches for it and droops over it but doesn't actually throw up.

He really has nothing to worry about. It would not be the first time my bin has served such a purpose. I step over the muddle of my trousers, cross to the sink, and get him a glass of water. "Here."

"Thanks." He takes it with a shaky hand. "It's probably the wine catching up with me. I don't usually drink."

I sit down on the arm of my chair, draping one leg over the other in the fashion I find most comfortable and elegant. "That's your loss, my dear."

"I don't have a very good history with it."

"What on earth has led you to believe I have any interest in your history?"

"Sorry."

"Mm, I should think so."

He sips the water, colour slowly returning to his face until he looks almost healthy again. "Did I... I mean... what we just..."

"Do you really think discussing what just happened is a remotely sensible idea, Mr. Baron?"

"I guess not." He sounds—

I don't give a fuck how he sounds. "Are you feeling better?"

"Think so. It was really... Everything was too..."

"Indeed. In which case, I'll see you at ten next Tuesday. Do try to think of something even a little bit worthwhile to say about *The Dream of the Rood.*"

He scrambles to his feet, pulling up his jeans. I'm briefly alarmed he's going to try and talk to me again, but he just shoves the empty glass at me and leaves. Probably there would have been a door slam involved if not for the green baize.

I sit for a while. The silence is sticky around me and the light that seeps through my windows is the colour of dirty water. I'm caught on the lip of dawn, the non-space between days. Even the birds, the beauty-maddened Oxford birds, who are so deceived by gold that they sing all night long, are sleeping now.

But I am desolate and sick of an old passion. I peel off my gown—I will need a new one; there's no way I can face a dryer

cleaner with this—and then my jacket, which is probably sal-
vageable, and pull on my boxers. They're the grey silk ones. A
gift from Sherry following an act of violence committed upon
another pair I claimed to be my favourites. Though, truthfully, I
much preferred their destruction.

I am faithful, Sherry. In my fashion.

The bells begin to chime a desultory hour. I could die a thousand million deaths before the sun rises.

So I open another bottle. And pour myself another glass of
wine.

ABOUT THE AUTHOR

Alexis Hall is a connoisseur of puddings. He is particularly partial to a crumble.

For more information:

Website: quicunquevult.com
Instagram: @quicunquevult

Also by Alexis Hall

London Calling
Boyfriend Material
Husband Material

Spires
Glitterland
Waiting for the Flood